VISIONS

OF

DARKNESS

MORE FROM A.L. JACKSON

Time River

Love Me Today
Don't Forget Me Tomorrow
Claim Me Forever
Hold Me Until Morning

Redemption Hills

Give Me a Reason
Say It's Forever
Never Look Back
Promise Me Always

Falling Stars

Kiss the Stars
Catch Me When I Fall
Falling into You
Beneath the Stars

Confessions of the Heart

More of You
All of Me
Pieces of Us

Fight for Me

Show Me the Way
Follow Me Back
Lead Me Home
Hold on to Hope
Hunt Me Down: A Stand-Alone Novella

Bleeding Stars

A Stone in the Sea
Drowning to Breathe
Where Lightning Strikes
Wait
Stay
Stand

Regret

Lost to You
Take This Regret
If Forever Comes

Closer to You

Come to Me Quietly
Come to Me Softly
Come to Me Recklessly

VISIONS

OF

DARKNESS

A.L. JACKSON

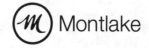

Text copyright © 2025 by A.L. Jackson Books Inc.

Published by Montlake, Seattle

www.apub.com

Amazon, the Amazon logo, and Montlake are trademarks of Amazon.com, Inc., or its affiliates.

ISBN-13 (paperback): 9781662524943
ISBN-13 (digital): 9781662524936

Cover design by Hang Le
Cover image: © Guillaume Weiler, © iMarzi, © K.-U. Haessler, © Rytis Bernotas, © KDdesign_photo_vide / Shutterstock

Printed in the United States of America

VISIONS

OF

DARKNESS

Prologue

"Gather around, children."

They stilled where they had chased each other on the lush grasses beneath the soaring tree at the edge of the meadow, and the boy with the palest gray eyes took the little girl's hand. She held on tight as he led her to where Ellis waited near the stream that wove through the sanctuary. It was the sanctuary she came to each night when she closed her eyes and fell asleep.

The head of their family, their teacher and guide, stood before them. His face was weathered and aged, though his eyes were tender as he watched over them where they came to sit at his feet.

A breeze whispered through, the perfect temperature caressing their cheeks as Ellis moved forward and tapped his fingertips over each of their foreheads. His voice was low when he spoke. "Open your ears and your hearts, little children. Remember, you are a Laven. A gift given by Valeen. The Eternal One. You have been chosen for this calling. One that you soon will learn is both a blessing and a curse."

The little girl closed her eyes as she listened to the same words Ellis instructed each night, trying to take them deep into her heart.

"As a Laven, each of you have a Nol . . . ," he drew out on a soft breath.

She couldn't help but peek to the side at the boy who was hers.

"They are the one your soul picks to stand by your side. By yourself, you are strong, but together, you are a force that can overcome the wicked ones, the Kruen who rule over Faydor."

Her stomach twisted as she thought of the Kruen she had yet to see. She was not permitted until she reached sixteen, the age of maturity for a Laven, and she sat still, her attention rapt on his words as she prepared for what was to come.

"Kruen are darkness manifested in spirit form to whisper all sins and calamities into the world, the offspring of Kreed, the malevolent, the one who betrayed our Valeen. You, my children, will one day have to bear the weight of their evils."

The boy tightened his hold on her hand the way he always did, his promise that when the time came, they would go through it together.

"Remember, you are unlike others," Ellis continued. "It will be a life of pain. One of burden and sacrifice. But take heart, young ones. You are Laven. Called to this fight for the good of man. Until then, rest here in paradise and know you are special. You are the chosen."

Chapter One

ARIA

Darkness spread over the barren wasteland. A bare glow at the edge of Faydor was the only light to guide her way as she tracked over the hard, frozen ground. Her breaths were salient as she panted around the frigid air that filled her lungs, and blood crashed through her veins as she searched through the eternal night.

Her and Pax's footsteps pounded in her ears as they ran headlong through the heavy vapor that snaked over the lifeless ground and curled around the wiry, leafless elms.

Lightning cracked across the low-hung canopy, a streak of sin and perversion.

Hisses of iniquity filled their ears, the whispers of the Kruen casting their evils into any willing mind.

She and Pax tracked one, refusing to allow its escape.

"Do not slow," Pax urged as he tugged at her hand, encouraging her to push harder as they ran over the barren terrain, through the vapors and mist that whispered of evil.

Voices intoned the unthinkable, and the sound of wickedness and atrocities cut through her spirit like blades.

Chasing the dark shadow that fled, she refused the exhaustion and drove herself into the fog that sought to suffocate. It wisped around the jagged rocks and streaked through the desolation.

She and Pax closed in on the vapid shadow that writhed and thrashed.

The Kruen started to take new shape, morphing from smoke and manifesting as whole as it reared up to stare back at them, exposing the horror of its features.

Its face was pitted and gnarled by the atrocities of its mind.

Its skin was charred and black, its body made of a thousand spindly limbs.

Red fury sped beneath its seared flesh, a visible evil that coursed through its veins.

She wanted to weep when she saw its thoughts.

She reached inside herself for the power she'd been given, harnessed it until it was a vibrating orb of intensity she could no longer contain, then projected the light outward.

Desperately trying to bind the Kruen.

To stop it.

To end it.

The energy blew from her in a barrage of white rays.

As it felt the powerful energy cut through the darkness, the Kruen split in two, and in two parts, the thick shadow slipped low to blend with the dense fog that curled and spilled out over the pitted, rocky ground. The fog shifted and roiled, boiling where the shadow wound a billowing path as it fled. It was quick to come back together as it sought sanctuary deeper in the recesses of Faydor.

The Kruen whipped around the edge of a boulder.

Pax gathered his light and stretched out his mind to bind it, and he impaled the monster on its side.

With a piercing screech, a fragment of the shadow fell, writhing before it withered.

In an instant, the remaining shadow amassed. It lashed out with its limbs, which appeared in a thousand fiery tendrils.

She and Pax broke apart to dodge it. A molten blade streaked past her arm, missing her by an inch.

Only she realized in a flash that her Nol had not been so lucky.

She screamed as Pax reeled back and clutched his side where he'd been struck by the Kruen's searing limb.

His gray eyes were wide with agony. Her Nol's pain had become her own.

Pax dropped to his knees, and she couldn't help but do the same. On all fours, she crawled to where he'd fallen. With shaking hands, she reached for him, begging, "Pax. Don't go. Stay with me. Please, don't go."

She'd all but forgotten the vicious Kruen as she turned her back and clutched Pax's shirt.

"Pax," she whispered as she reached out and touched the severe, sharp angles of his face.

But she already knew she could not keep him there.

Like a torch, his spirit surged, flickered, and then he was gone.

She had no time to rebound or stand.

Because, from behind, a strike fell deep into her flesh.

The lash of a whip that was sharp and excruciating.

And it shattered the last of the light.

I jolted upright in bed. My hands were fisted in the blanket, and my mouth was opened toward the ceiling on a silent cry that I fought to keep locked in my throat. The scream threatened to break free, and I warred against the urge to release it, knowing what would happen if I gave voice to the agony.

This was something that could not be shared.

Jagged pants heaved from my lungs as my mind spiraled through the remnants of sleep, and I blinked through the disorder as I struggled to get my bearings in the wisping darkness. To adjust to being yanked from one reality to another.

Visions continued to flash, horrors that rushed through my brain in a circuit of confusion. My heart thundered at my ribs, and I could feel the blood careening through my veins.

I finally managed to inhale a shaky, steadying breath, and I shifted to sit up on the side of the bed. Slowly, my eyes adjusted to the lapping shadows of my surroundings.

I was in my tiny room. The same one I'd awakened in for my entire life.

Safe.

It was only a bad dream.

It was only a bad dream.

I might have been able to convince myself of it if it weren't for the fiery pain that seared across my back, starting at my right shoulder and slashing at an angle to my lower left side.

And I knew somewhere in this world, someplace I could never see, Pax was suffering the same affliction. I wanted to reach out. Touch him in this realm. Find the one my heart loved with every part of me.

But I could only ever have him while I slept, and never in the way I truly wanted to.

Reaching up, I touched the top of the wound on my right shoulder, wincing at the sharp sting at the contact. It was open, as I knew it would be. Venom dripping poison into my body. When I drew my hand away, I was able to make out the dark, charred blood that coated my fingertips.

Proof of this nightmare.

My reality.

The secret I fell into every night.

Chapter Two

ARIA

It was the dead of winter in Albany, New York. Forever cold and dreary. At this time of morning, darkness still clung to the house. Heat hummed from the vents, but it was no match for the chill that seeped in from outside.

I eased downstairs slower than I normally would. My long, black hair was still wet from my shower, and the strands fell around my shoulders and dampened the fabric of the black sweater I wore.

It was baggy enough to cover the makeshift bandage I had fabricated out of an old white tee and duct tape. It wasn't like I could keep industrial-size bandages under the counter for times like these.

Mornings when I woke with a burn were always hardest. When the physical pain was so great that the only thing I wanted to do was turn around and climb back into my bed and sleep for days. The exhaustion was close to overwhelming, the toxins I could feel thudding through my veins with each beat of my heart, making it nearly impossible to face the day.

But I would.

I had no other choice than to protect this secret with every breath that I had.

To remember my purpose.

To accept it for everything it was.

The blessing and the curse Ellis had promised it would be.

I hit the first-floor landing to the clatter of activity that carried from the kitchen. Voices shouted and laughter echoed through my childhood home.

My chest tightened in a rush of affection.

These sounds? They were always a buoy to my spirit.

A spirit that could so easily be crushed if I didn't hang on to the things that mattered. If I didn't recognize the price that was paid for this peace.

No, my family could never understand it. I'd accepted that years ago. But the life of a Laven could not be understood. When I awoke each morning in my bed, I hardly understood it myself.

Hell, there were so many times that I questioned it.

When I wondered if the therapists and the doctors were right.

If my sanity had been stripped.

But I felt the truth of it pierce me like an arrow as I moved through the living room and stopped at the edge of the kitchen to take in the familiar scene.

A perfect chaos.

To the left of me, my mother stood at the stove, scrambling a giant skillet of eggs, frazzled the way she always was. She wore pajamas and her robe, and her brown hair was tossed in a haphazard knot on top of her head.

"All of you, get to the table. Breakfast is ready." She might have yelled it, but there was a tenderness to her voice. One she always possessed.

My gaze traveled the kitchen.

My sister, Brianna, was on the far side of the room, and music blared from her phone, which she had propped on the island as she practiced the routine for her dance troupe. She'd been working on it for the last four weeks, and she spent every free second trying to perfect it.

My little brothers, Mitch and Keaton, were off to the side of her, in the middle of a wrestling match, scrambling around to one-up each other. Mitch was seven and Keaton was ten, so I knew how that would turn out, even though Mitch always gave it his best.

"You didn't even pin me!" he shouted over the volume of Brie's music, kicking his legs and flailing his arms and trying to knock Keaton off from where he was straddling Mitch and sitting on his chest.

"You wish, dumbo. You're already down. I win. You gotta give me your Nerf Blaster."

"Hey," Mom chastised as she carried the skillet around the island toward the breakfast nook beneath the window that overlooked the front yard and street. "No names. Both of you, up."

"Tell him I pinned him, Mom," Keaton whined instead of listening.

"No way." Mitch shoved him, taking the opportunity to send Keaton toppling back while he was distracted. The motion knocked Keaton into Brie's path, and she stumbled to the side when he got under her feet.

A screech of annoyance left her as she bumped into the island. "Would you watch it?"

Keaton didn't even respond to her. He dove right back in for Mitch, and in a flash, they were scuffling around again.

"Mom, would you tell Keaton to stay out of my way?" Brie complained. "This has to be perfect, and they always mess me up. It's totally their fault if I get kicked off the team."

"Ugh, you guys, would you knock it off?" Mom groaned. "One morning of peace is all I ask."

Except I knew she loved every second of it, and soft laughter rolled from my mouth as I moved into the kitchen. I went straight to Brie and dropped a kiss to the top of her head. "You are not going to get kicked off the team."

"And how do you even know?" She rolled her warm brown eyes up at me. They were the exact same color as our mother's and brothers'. Anxiety played through her features, a new self-consciousness that had cropped up in her over the last year, which she tried to cover with sass.

It was rough being thirteen.

"Um, because I've seen you and you're amazing."

"You really think so? Or are you just trying to *Mom* me?"

My chest shook with a laugh, and I hugged her tighter. "*Mom* you? Never. That's just rude."

I sent Mom a playful glance, and a hint of amusement tugged at the edge of her mouth as she heaped spoonfuls of eggs onto the plates already set on the table.

Brie blew out a sigh, and I could feel her smile as she squeezed me back, her arms tight around my middle. I tried not to wince when a stab of pain shocked across my back. Ignoring the burn, I embraced her for a long moment before I released her and turned to my brothers.

"Come on, you two. Up you go. It's breakfast time, and I'm totally not walking you to school if you miss the bus. It's freezing out there." I let the tease wind into my voice as I stretched both hands toward them. Reluctantly, they each accepted one, popping to their feet as I gave them a little yank.

"I still get your blaster," Keaton mumbled.

"How about you two share it?" I offered.

Simple solutions that were never so simple when it came to these two.

Mom chuckled. "If only it was that easy." Her gaze softened as she looked at me. "Thanks for stepping in. I don't know what I'm going to do without you here."

Sadness and nostalgia whispered through her features, and it sent a wave of guilt pinching deep into my chest. I hated how much thinner and sallower her face was than it should be. The lines that were creased into her brow and at the edges of her eyes.

She was only forty-three, but she looked as if she'd aged a decade in the last two years.

All compliments of me.

Finally, things had seemed to settle around here, but only because I'd learned how careful I had to be. But that didn't mean I wasn't constantly on edge, in fear of a slipup.

Clearing the roughness from my throat, I pinned on the brightest smile I could find. "I'm still here for four months."

Until graduation. Then I would go. I knew I had to. I couldn't stay here a second longer beneath my parents' scrutinizing stares. I knew it was done out of love, but that didn't make it any easier.

My mother and father were always watching me, waiting for me to snap.

To suffer another schizophrenic break. At least, that's what the doctors had diagnosed me with the last time I'd been hospitalized.

The wound I'd sustained last night burned on my back.

If they knew what I was hiding right then? I'd immediately be back in that place. Terrified and alone. Doctors prodding into my mind like they could find a solution—a cure—for who I was.

"But you're eighteen in four days. How is my baby going to be an adult?" Affection hitched her voice.

I tried to shift the attention away from me. "Well, you'll have these three yahoos to keep you company."

"Names," Mitch peeped up from where he'd climbed onto his chair.

Laughter rolled from my throat. "Sorry. These sweethearts?"

I lifted my brow at him with the ribbing.

"'Sweet,' my ass," Brianna mumbled out of Mom's earshot as she moved by me. I gave her a gentle swat to the upper arm, and she sent a smirk my way as she took her seat.

I turned back to Mom. "What can I help with?"

"Can you grab the plate of toast?"

"Sure."

I wound around the island to the stack of toast on the counter. Mom had just had her dream kitchen put in. The cabinets were sea blue, and the countertops speckled silver and blue and white. The old laminate floors had been replaced with tile that looked like gray wood.

A sharp twinge of discomfort snagged inside me. I wanted to shun the thought that it'd been a bribe from Dad for being a jerk, but I couldn't shake it.

He'd been one a lot lately. More and more.

Protectiveness swelled from the depths of me. It was the part that hated the idea of leaving here once I graduated from high school. The part that wanted to shield my mother and my siblings.

Not that he'd become violent or was a danger to them.

He was just . . . different.

Had changed after I'd turned sixteen.

When the first wounds had shown. When I'd awakened screaming in my room the first time after I'd been burned. Unable to stop or to contain it. He'd burst through the door and had roared when he'd seen the wound slashed across my chest.

He'd demanded to know who'd done it. Ready to go on a rampage. To hunt down the monster who had dared to hurt his little girl.

But he didn't know the types of monsters that truly existed. Ones he couldn't protect me from.

I'd been in so much pain, so unprepared, so in shock that I'd told them what had happened while I was asleep, in Faydor, unable to keep the confession from tumbling free.

I'd taken them back to the dreams I'd been so foolish to share with them as a little girl. Dreams of playing in a sanctuary, in a paradise with others who had the same strange-colored eyes as mine. Ones who were like me, too young to grasp the warnings that had been hammered into my mind a million times by Ellis that I couldn't share what happened when I fell asleep.

Only what had happened that night—the first night I'd been burned—was so different. It was then they'd come to believe my imaginations as a child had changed and developed into psychotic delusions.

They'd thought I'd done it to myself.

Nerves rolled through me when I felt the air shift from behind, and I peeked toward the entryway as my father strode in. He was tall and thickly muscled beneath the suit he wore. His blond hair was wavy and had begun to gray, though he cut it short in an attempt to keep it tamed, and his eyes were a lighter shade of brown than the rest of the family's.

He sent a glance my way.

I wondered what he thought when he looked at me.

When he caught sight of my black hair and my eyes, which were the palest gray.

An unnatural gray that should never exist.

Ice cold and raging with fire.

When he contemplated the fact that I looked nothing like their other children—or like anyone else they had ever met, for that matter.

But it was more than just the strange color of my eyes. There was an energy I emitted, as if I'd brought a remnant of the supernatural with me into the human realm. Most got an unsettled sense whenever I came into the room. It was rare someone didn't shy away from it when they met me, or at least try to take a closer look to discern what was different about me.

I so often wondered how my parents couldn't see it. How they refused to believe.

I carried the toast to the table and set it in the middle.

"Thank you," Mom said.

"No problem." I glanced to my right as I took a seat. "Morning, Dad."

His gaze appraised. Speculation and distrust.

Apprehension crawled down my spine. I wasn't afraid of him, but I was afraid that he would find out. That he could see right through me to what I had hidden under my sweater.

"Aria," he grunted as he tucked himself closer to the table.

Mom took her seat next to him, though she had her attention on me. "What would you like to do to celebrate on Saturday, Aria?"

Before I had the chance to respond, her gaze coasted to Dad, her words filled with love and support and the remnants of the fear I was sure she would forever feel for me. "Can you believe it? We have a child who will be eighteen. How did that even happen?"

Air huffed from his nose as he reached out and grabbed a slice of toast. Annoyance curled through his voice. "We're celebrating her now?"

Mom winced, though she lifted her chin. "It's your daughter's birthday, Cal. And she's been doing great."

She looked at me in what could only be construed as a plea. Begging me to be *okay*.

Cured.

Or at least medicated enough that I was no longer a threat to myself.

"Whatever you want to do is fine with me," I forced out, hoping to avoid what she'd just said and what my father had implied.

All while my love for her bound my heart in a fist.

Devotion and loyalty.

But it was also riddled with the grievous knowledge that I would never be understood.

My life as a Laven would be an isolated, lonely one.

Pax's face flashed behind my eyes.

My balm. My comfort. My Nol.

Forbidden.

But I would sacrifice it all for the small pieces of him that I would forever possess.

I crawled into bed that night. Exhaustion weighed me down, no doubt thanks to the wound that would take me at least a week to fully recover from, even though the scar would forever remain on my back.

Another of the many I was covered in.

Chest and stomach. Arms and legs. A jagged one that marred my right cheek.

I curled my arms around my pillow, and my spirit shivered, angling toward the one place where I truly belonged. Where I didn't have to hide or pretend.

My eyelids fluttered, and my breaths shallowed out as I began to drift.

There was always a bare space in between. A sense of anticipation. One of joy and fear and purpose.

Weightless.

Timeless.

Light and darkness flickered at the edges of my sight.

Then my soul flashed, and I flew.

Chapter Three

ARIA

Tearsith

Aria appeared at the edge of the meadow. Peace echoed through her being, palpable and alive as she stood at the periphery of their sanctuary. Floral scents rose from the red vingas that sprouted from the fertile ground, tasting sweet on her tongue as she inhaled the comfort of this place.

Lush woods hugged the field, and light streamed through the leaves of the soaring trees surrounding Tearsith in a hedge of protection. It dappled the expansive clearing in natural warmth, in a comfort unlike anything found in another place.

The air was misty and written in a hue of silvered blue.

Here, it was a haven.

A moment's harmony before they descended into the darkest place.

On the bank of the small brook with crystalline waters that ran along the far end of the meadow, her Laven family had begun to gather at their great teacher's feet, the way they did each night. There were about two hundred of them, and through Ellis's teachings, from his own vague understanding, it was believed there were many more Laven families spread over the world. Each drawn together by Valeen's call on their lives.

They all donned the same uniform they appeared in each night, the material of the fitted pants and long-sleeved jacket brown and thick.

Aria paused as her attention sought out one thing.

She didn't have to search. She was drawn, her heart and soul pulsing out to meet with the energy that rippled back.

Pax stood at the back of the crowd, facing her, as if he had sensed her arrival.

His hair was a shock of white where it wisped around his face. A face carved into severity. The angle of his cheeks and jaw were harsh, the slash of his brow hard and fierce. His mouth was somehow plush. A soft contrast against the abrasiveness.

Gray eyes that were the same color as hers burned with white fire. So intense they made her shake. Somehow, they softened as they took her in when she stepped from the dense foliage and into the grass-covered clearing.

Sparks of energy arced between them as she began to walk toward her Nol, who moved for her at the same time. It was a connection that she had only ever experienced with him.

They met partway, and he took her hand. Warmth spread through her body.

A flame.

A balm.

She was sure she could physically feel the fury that blazed beneath his skin.

"You were burned last night." His voice came on a low, grating rasp.

They often fought through the night without being burned. But on the times when she was? She could sense the rage that scorched through his being. As if he wanted to protect her from who they were.

But he couldn't do that.

Both their fates were here, their burdens the same.

"As were you."

He blinked harshly, and he lowered his voice to shield it from any-one who might overhear. "You have to be careful, Aria. I know you were burned because of me. I cannot stand the thought . . ."

His teeth ground to stop himself from saying the things that were forbidden to be said.

"I'm fine," Aria promised. "It is part of this life. You and I know it, and we must accept it."

"The thought of you being hurt. When I wake up and know you're in pain, I . . ." His jaw clenched.

She squeezed his hand. "I know. I hate it for you as well. But you know that—"

"Good, you're finally here," a voice peeped, breaking into their huddle, and they both jerked to find Dani standing at their sides. The young woman watched them with concern, her pale eyes dimmed.

She was waif thin and so short she reminded Aria of a pixie, her eyes wide and almost too big for her delicate face. The fact that she wore her blond hair cropped with little fringes wisping out only sealed the resemblance. In her late twenties, the Laven had taken a mentor position in the two years before Aria had first descended into Faydor, doing her best to prepare Aria for what was to come.

As grateful as Aria was to her, none of them could truly be prepared for what they would face until they had experienced the depravity for themselves.

"You should come," Dani encouraged. She took Aria's hand as she glanced at Pax. He roughed his fingers through his hair, vibrating with frustration.

Even though she ached to spend one moment alone with Pax, Aria dutifully followed, allowing Dani to lead her to the gathering. Their Laven family was at Ellis's feet, and Aria and Dani joined them, sitting down on the cool grass, so thick it pillowed beneath them.

A minute later, Pax took the spot on her opposite side.

His presence was overwhelming. The only thing she could feel.

She had to force herself to turn her attention to Ellis, who spoke in front of the group.

Their eldest Laven appeared withered, his limbs spindly and thin, like the craggy curl of a great old tree. The lines carved deep in his face spoke of the evil he had witnessed, and the weight in his pale-gray eyes spoke of his unending compassion.

Respect filled Aria as she listened to him again emphasize the importance of their calling. As he gave them reason for the sacrifice they made.

"You were chosen for this, to fight the evils of Faydor, to protect humans who do not know of the war that is being waged for them. They know not of the dangers that surround them each moment. Kruen are hungry for their ruin, and you are fighting to protect them from atrocities they do not understand. Do not take that calling lightly."

Aria's stomach turned as she prepared herself for the wickedness she would face tonight.

"Remember, you are only protected here."

They could be burned in Faydor, but they could not be killed.

"When you are awake and walking on Earth, you are completely human, and you are susceptible to every vulnerability. Weaker even, as the Kruen will fight to put dangers in your path. They will destroy you if given the chance. And I know it is painful, but you must never interact with other Laven if you ever cross paths. The great book given by Valeen warns of this truth. In all of history, each time Lavens have come together in the human realm, they have been attacked. Decimated. Together, our spirits act as a beacon for the Kruen. They can easily find you, and they will use that vulnerability to their advantage and destroy you there."

Aria had never seen another like herself. But she wondered . . . God, she wondered.

Ellis paused before he spoke. "Much more than that, you must never, ever seek your Nol while awake."

Aria swore she felt Ellis's gaze brush over them, and she wondered again if it was possible that only she could feel this way in the sea of her Laven family. If the bond she shared with Pax was greater than theirs.

"Your Nol is your greatest strength here in Tearsith and in Faydor, and your greatest weakness while awake. You cannot protect them there, and it would place you both in the path of the gravest of dangers. Not only is it two Laven gathering to create a target for the Kruen, but it goes deeper than that. Your spirits cannot withstand that pressure, and the Kruen will pit you against one another, change something in your hearts the way something changed in Kreed's heart."

The traditions Ellis taught each night were found in the great book. Aria knew that Valeen and Kreed had once been bound as mates before the world had fallen. But it was Kreed who'd led the world into wickedness when he'd turned on Valeen and sought her power for himself.

Tradition said she'd been devastated when he'd betrayed her. That his heart had been turned corrupt, and because of his greed, he'd brought every cruelty into the world.

She'd warred against him ever since, the Laven her chosen ones to fight.

"Be careful, my children," Ellis continued. "Remember your calling. Your purpose. You may seek pleasure awake, a family and love and a normal life. But here? Here, you were born to fight."

At that, their family all stood, and they paired off, taking each other by the hand.

Ellis stretched out a hand toward Josephine, his Nol who had fought by his side for their entire lives. Her movements were slowed by her age as she shuffled to him.

Dani's Nol, Timothy, approached and took her hand, and she smiled softly up at him as he gave her a tight nod. A silent promise that they were in this together.

Aria's spirit sang when Pax wound his fingers with hers, and she shivered as their souls entwined.

"Are you ready?" Pax rumbled in his gravel-cut voice.

Aria looked ahead of them as the pairs stepped into the heavy woods. Their essences lit, flashing in a brilliant light before they disappeared into the bowels of Faydor.

"I'm ready."

With one last squeeze of her hand, Pax stepped forward and led them into the darkness.

Chapter Four

ARIA

I awoke to the sound of my alarm blaring in my room. It was always disorienting, being yanked from one reality to another, but mornings like these were so much easier. When we'd fought through the night and the Kruen we'd encountered had not prevailed.

It was strange that I found rest during those hours. That when I awoke, I was renewed.

Pushing up on the side of my bed, I lifted my arms high and stretched, wincing at the zinging ache that still lancinated across my back. I was just thankful it was so much better than it had been yesterday.

Flicking on my bedside lamp, I pushed to standing and moved to the dressing-table mirror. I pulled the sweatshirt I'd worn to sleep in over my head, dropped it to the floor, and angled around so I could look at the bandage I'd made.

Blood saturated the material, and I knew it would probably be leaking for at least three more days.

I had no other choice but to change it.

I started to work it free, trying not to cry out at the awful sting peeling back the duct tape elicited. Using it was probably dumb, but I didn't have a lot of options. I winced as I dragged it down, keeping my breaths even and counting silently to distract myself from the heavy-duty adhesive pulling at my flesh.

Once I had it off, I angled back around to inspect the wound in the mirror.

It was a gaping cut caused by the fiery tendril of a Kruen, the ragged edges blackened and singed and oozing in the middle.

Revulsion curled in my stomach. Could I really blame my parents for their reaction when they'd seen my first wound? Because the injuries we sustained were truly horrifying.

I wondered how long it would be until I was completely covered in them. Our wounds and scars weren't visible in Tearsith—I supposed offered as a form of reprieve—but I could only imagine what Ellis and Josephine would look like if I saw them walking in the day.

Blowing out a sigh, I climbed onto my knees so I could dig under my bed to find the small box of medical supplies I kept there, the same as I'd done yesterday morning. They were hidden behind plastic organizers filled with the remnants of the hobbies I'd had through the years. Each was something my mother had tried to get me interested in with the hope to distract me from my *imaginary* friends.

I found the shoebox tucked behind a trumpet and a box full of yarn and needles from my stint in crocheting. Sitting on the floor, I pulled off the lid and found the nearly empty bottle of hydrogen peroxide, a small pair of medical scissors, the half roll of duct tape I'd snagged from my father's supply in the garage, the scraps of a torn-up tee, and an empty container of medical tape.

God, what I would do for that right now.

Since I didn't have any gauze left, either, I opened the bottle of peroxide and poured it directly down my back.

My flesh sizzled, the pain so sharp it punched the air from my lungs.

That time, there was no keeping back the curse, and I gritted my teeth as I quietly swore beneath my breath, "God. Shit. Ugh."

I blinked through it, knowing the toxins were bubbling up like a witch's cauldron, which would be kind of hysterical if any of this was funny at all.

I nearly jumped out of my scarred skin when there was a light tapping at my door.

"Aria?" Mom's voice echoed through the wood.

"Hey, Mom. What's up?" I pushed out around the agony. I just hoped she couldn't hear the tremoring in my voice.

"I just wanted to go over something with you really quick." She jangled the knob, slowing when she realized it was locked.

"Aria?" I could hear the worry that instantly infiltrated her voice.

Crap.

One of my rules was I wasn't allowed to have my door locked. They wanted to be able to check on me at any time.

"I'm just getting dressed. Give me a quick second."

Frantic, I looked around my room, taking stock, before I quickly jumped into action. I twisted the cap back onto the peroxide before I tossed all the supplies into the shoebox and covered it with the lid. I shoved everything under my bed the best I could, then jumped to my feet.

I grabbed the soiled bandage and crammed it into my backpack, which was sitting open next to my dressing table, before ripping open a drawer and pulling out a sweatshirt. I didn't bother taking the time to put on a bra before dragging the top over my head, then ripped off my yoga pants and quickly pulled on a pair of jeans. I shoved my feet into my Chucks, then flew over to the door, unlocked it, and whipped it open.

I was sure I looked unhinged, standing there with a giant, feigned grin plastered to my face while my heart careened in my chest and bashed against my ribs.

The fear that would hold me hostage until I was able to leave this house thundered through my veins.

I hated it—hated hiding from her. Hated hiding from this woman who so clearly adored me.

She stood in the hallway, taking me in with concern and caution and care.

But what other choice did I have?

"Hey, Mom," I peeped. "Did you want to talk about something?" I widened the door in invitation.

She stepped in, and her mouth tweaked up in a smile. "I was thinking on Saturday we'd go ice-skating. We haven't done that in so long. The whole family. Then we can go to dinner at Margot's after? It used to be your favorite. Would you like that?"

Affection pulled through my spirit. "Yeah, that sounds great."

I only tensed a little as she edged deeper into my room, her gaze caressing over the drawings I had pinned all over my walls. Charcoals I'd done of my sister and brothers. Others of her and my dad. Ones of myself. Of different places in Albany and others I'd only seen pictures of that I hoped to visit one day.

The ones I'd once drawn of Tearsith and Pax had long since been taken down and destroyed.

But drawing? It had been the one hobby that had stuck. The one that truly was therapeutic. A part of me that had come to life.

"You are so talented," she murmured in awe.

"Thank you."

She peeked at me from over her shoulder. "I'm not just saying that. I hope once you graduate, you chase this, Aria. I hope you find joy in it. A purpose. That you share it with the world, because it is truly special."

My heart clutched, fisting in the hope that she had for me. I swallowed around the thickness in my throat. "I would like that."

Her mouth tipped in a small smile, and she'd started to turn when she froze.

Tension bound the air, and a stone sank to the pit of my stomach when I realized what she'd seen. Her attention locked onto my backpack where the flap had dropped open since I hadn't taken the time to zip it.

Frantic thoughts swirled. I searched for an excuse or a distraction. Anything to take back the stupid mistake I had made.

How could I have been so careless? But I'd thought it was covered, that I'd bought myself time to fully get it out of the house, where I would normally toss any evidence into a dumpster behind a restaurant on my way to school.

Her movements were wooden as she fumbled forward and slowly dipped her hand into my bag like she might be reaching for a bomb. She pulled out the fragment of white tee, which was stained a blackened, gruesome red.

She stared at it for a moment before she turned to me. A mess of tears already tracked down her cheeks. "Aria."

Grief filled my name. So gutting it nearly dropped me to my knees.

"Mom, it's not—" I rushed for her with the intention of ripping it from her hand. In those precious seconds, I tried to figure out what to say that could make this right.

Too bad I already knew there wasn't a chance.

There was already too much history.

Too much fear and pain.

She grabbed me by my sweatshirt. I gasped when she jerked it up to expose my stomach.

"Mom, no." My hands flew to the fabric, pushing it down, trying to protect the secret I couldn't give her.

"Where is it, Aria?" She gulped through the question. Around the sob hitched in her throat.

"It's not—"

Before I could stop her, she yanked down the collar of the sweatshirt. It exposed an inch of the wound where it started on my shoulder. "Aria. Please. No."

It was me who was frozen when she moved around me, and she pushed the sweatshirt up my back to expose the rest.

A mournful whimper rolled from her mouth.

She'd thought I was recovered. That I was no longer hurting myself. That it was all in the past. But I would never be *recovered*, not as long as I breathed.

"After all this time? I thought . . . I thought you were . . ." She choked over the words she couldn't fully get out.

I hadn't been burned in two months, and she hadn't discovered one in four. I should have known that my luck was running out.

Air skidded in and out of her lungs as she fought the war that suddenly broke out in her spirit.

One I could physically feel.

Her greatest fears flared to life, anguished and aggrieved in her love for me.

She finally snapped out of the shock and moved, the fixer who could not fix what was broken inside me. "Are you taking your medication?" she demanded.

"Yes—" I hadn't gotten it out before she turned to my desk in search of it. She started to rummage around on top. I grabbed her arm, needing to stop her, wanting to plead with her to turn around and *see* me.

Didn't she see it when she looked at me?

Didn't she feel it the first time she'd held me after I was born?

Didn't she know?

"Mom, please, it's not—"

"Please don't lie to me and tell me it's nothing, Aria. I love you too much for that." She ripped open the drawer on the left to find what she was looking for—the bottle of the generic antidepressant I took.

Frantic, she could barely get the lid off, her desperation clawing through her, body and soul. She finally managed it, and she dumped the pills onto the desktop. She counted them under her breath, swiping them one by one back into the container.

When she found the right number there, she whirled back around, begging, "What is wrong, Aria? Please tell me. Has someone hurt you?

Bullied you? Your friends? A boy? What is it? Please God, just tell me. Let me help you."

Her sorrow was stark.

Staggering.

Unbearable.

I wanted to wipe it away. Hold her. Protect her the way she wanted to protect me. My chest ached, my ribs clamping around my heart, which throbbed with dread.

"Mom, please, don't do this. I didn't—" On instinct, the defense fell from my tongue. One I knew better than to give.

Because it only doubled my mother's agony and amplified her fear.

"What did you say?" Tears poured from her eyes.

My throat locked, and I curled my arms over my chest like it could protect us both from this.

"What did you say? That you didn't do it?" This time, she grabbed me by the arms and shook me. "Was *he* there?" she demanded.

I couldn't swallow. Couldn't breathe.

"Was he there?" Her words escalated to a shout.

My eyes squeezed closed as visions of Pax raced through my mind.

The beautiful boy who would never be mine the way I wanted him to be.

My love.

My heart.

My soul.

"Tell me," she pleaded. "Was he there?"

"Mom," I croaked around the disordered riot that crashed through my room.

Heartbreak twisted through her expression. I could feel it. Feel it like a wound. Her hope dwindling into hopelessness. Succumbing to the belief that her daughter was insane.

This was the mother of a little girl who at four couldn't wait to go to sleep because there she would see her best friend.

Pax.

At that time, she would sit at the edge of my bed, pull my covers to my chin, and smile in soft encouragement as I told her the fantastical stories about a little boy who was four years older than me. A boy I would play with beyond the boundaries of this world.

She'd listen as I described us running through a secret paradise. Fields of flowers and high grasses, soaring trees with branches low enough to climb, dipping our toes into the stream that wove through the meadow where we'd meet.

How perfect it was there in Tearsith, a haven without pain or shame.

At seven, she'd sat at the edge of that same bed and told me I was getting too old for imaginary friends.

At ten, she'd begged me to stop, gripping my hand as she whispered that I was scaring her.

At sixteen, when I'd left the safety of Tearsith and descended to fight in Faydor, when the wounds had begun to show, I'd been forbidden to ever speak Pax's name again.

A name I was never supposed to speak anyway, but I'd never been able to keep the truth of that place contained. It'd always felt as if it was going to burst out from within me.

Her nails sank into my flesh. "Tell me!"

Pain lanced through me, this gutting, shattering hurt that blistered through every nerve.

I gulped back the tears that stung my throat and eyes.

I had to leave.

Run.

I couldn't go through it again—the doctors and the prescriptions. The psych commitments and the interrogations.

They would never believe. They would never see. They would never understand. I would only continue to hurt them, just like they unknowingly hurt me, and I couldn't stay under their scrutiny any longer.

"I love you, Mom." I choked it out around the torment that roiled through my insides, and I prayed she understood how deeply I meant it.

At my tone, confusion puckered her forehead, and before she could say anything else, I untangled myself from her hold and grabbed my backpack and jacket from the floor. I flew to the door with every intention to run, only I paused for a beat to look back, unable to just leave like that.

"I hate how much I've hurt you. I hate it. But if you know one thing, please know how much I truly do love you."

"Natalie? What's going on?" My father's voice boomed from the other side of their bedroom door. No doubt, he'd heard her shouting.

Panic lit, and I whispered, "I'm sorry."

Then I turned and ran down the hall and to the stairs. My mother's words followed me, the same as her frantic footsteps. "Aria! Aria! Do not walk out that door! Aria, stop! We need to talk about this . . . get you help."

I raced downstairs, my heart speeding out of control, sorrow pounding through the middle of it.

Because I didn't slow. I flew out the front door and into the frigid winter cold.

Chapter Five

ARIA

Tearsith
Sixteen years old

Aria emerged at the edge of Tearsith, where the lush woods were dense with foliage and peace billowed on the breeze.

She peered into the clearing where her Laven family had begun to gather, wearing their matching uniforms.

Aria's pulse skittered.

Tonight would be unlike any other she'd experienced before.

Today, she had turned sixteen.

She had reached the age of maturity for a Laven, and tonight, she would descend into the darkness of Faydor for the first time.

It was an event she had been preparing for throughout her life. Until this point, her nights had been spent here within the boundaries of Tearsith, the realm above Faydor, learning of the importance of her calling and the sacrifice that it required. Even never having stepped out of Tearsith, Aria understood that sacrifice was great.

Once she entered Faydor, she would never be the same.

She tried to keep her fear at bay, but it pulsed through her blood, and she searched, though her spirit already told her that her Nol had not yet arrived.

But Dani noticed that she had, and Aria's friend jumped to her feet and came jogging over. She took Aria by both hands as she gave her a smile of kind encouragement.

"Happy birthday, Aria."

"Thank you," Aria whispered around the anxiety.

"Are you nervous?" Dani asked, concern pinching her delicate brow.

"I feel like I should be prepared but have no idea what to expect."

Understanding passed through Dani's expression. "It won't be easy, but you were created for this."

Some days, Aria wished she had not been. She had no choice but to come here night after night. No choice but to look in the mirror each morning when she awoke and wonder if she was lost.

Insane.

Prisoner to a reality that did not exist.

It was then her spirit expanded, though, and an awareness thrummed through her veins and sparked in her soul. She shifted to peer back at the edge of Tearsith.

Pax stepped out of the woods.

So gorgeous that her heart stalled, jolting from its axis and pitching in his direction.

She had to tamp down what she knew was written on her face, the forbidden feelings that he evoked.

Not that he would ever return those feelings anyway.

She took in his face. A carved sculpture of white granite, his eyes that unfathomable gray. Everything about him was razor sharp and deadly, though every interaction she had ever shared with him had been tender and careful.

And she knew then, even if she had been given free will, she still would have chosen this.

To at least have this part of him.

No, she would never know him the way she wanted to. To be awake and run her fingertips along the angles of his face. To feel him whole and real and alive.

To exist with him, night and day.

Her heart could not believe that he would ever turn against her the way tradition taught, but what she thought wouldn't change the decree.

Dani squeezed her hand tighter as if to give her a warning that it was clear where Aria's thoughts had gone, and Aria returned her attention to Ellis.

"May your hearts forever keep the hope of your calling," the old man said. A breeze blew through, lifting the scraggly strands of the Laven's white hair in a wisping gust. In the distance, he set his compassion and favor on Aria as he said, "May you not lose faith, and may you forever persevere."

Aria tried to hide the tremble that rolled down her spine when Pax approached her from behind.

His nerves were edged in steel, the man vibrating with disquiet. His aura potent and honed into a blade.

He knew what this day meant, and she knew he wanted to protect her from it.

But there was no protecting her from who she was.

"Are we ready, my dear family?" Ellis's gaze moved over those gathered below him.

Aria's pulse sped.

Pax edged closer to her, though he'd yet to say a word.

"Yes." The agreement rumbled over the flock, and everyone began to stand, pairing off with their Nols.

Most pairs were men and women, although there were several that were two men or two women.

Timothy wound out of the mass. He came straight for Dani and took her hand. "It's time."

She nodded. "I'm ready."

Two by two, the Laven moved from the sanctuary of Tearsith to the boundary of Faydor.

She felt Pax's hesitation thrum from behind as she watched the drove of Laven stream toward the darkness that wept, whispered, and called.

"You don't have to do this." He muttered it so low she felt it like a promise.

When she turned to him, she lost her breath, felt his pain and dread as he stared down at her.

She hated that the expression on his face would never mean anything more than him being protective. He loved her, but only as his Nol. She sometimes wondered if she was the only Laven who loved their Nol for all the wrong reasons.

"You know that I do," she murmured.

"I hate it," he grated. "I hate the idea of you going there. You don't know what it's . . ."

He trailed off, as if he couldn't bring himself to describe the atrocities that were waiting for them on the other side.

Pax had been there many times. Each night since the day he'd turned sixteen four years before, while Aria had stayed in Tearsith with the other youths.

He'd walked in darkness with Dani and Timothy as his guide.

He'd been different ever since.

Harder.

Angrier.

Fiercer.

He'd fought with them until the day Aria reached maturity.

And tonight, it would be Aria who battled at his side.

"I'll be fine," she promised.

Pain flashed across his features. "I will protect you, Aria. Anything and everything it takes."

Except protecting her wasn't his call. Their pairing wasn't to be the focus of their destiny. Their fate was to fight. Most times, that felt completely wrong since, to Aria, Pax had become the meaning of this place.

"We will fight together, the way we were meant to," she said.

His thick throat bobbed when he swallowed, and strength bristled through his powerful body. He reached out his hand to take hers. "Do not let go of me. The first time will be very difficult."

Her spirit sang when she wove her fingers through his, and their souls entwined to become one.

She doubted that she could let go even if she tried.

Anxiety billowed through her consciousness as Pax led her toward the gateway, which would be invisible except for the chilling energy that lapped and coaxed, a shimmery force that drew them toward what waited beyond. To that narrow, unseen plane that hovered just above Earth's surface.

The place where darkness reigned.

She'd watched it what felt like a million times, the Laven moving toward the gateway hand in hand, the way their essence lit in a blinding light before they disappeared into the nothingness.

Tonight, Aria would learn for herself what that really meant.

Each pair disappeared until Aria and Pax were the last to stand at Tearsith's end.

Apprehension vibrated her to the bone, and Pax smoothed the pad of his thumb over the back of her hand. "I will not leave your side."

Swallowing hard, she nodded. "I'm ready."

Pax held tight as he pulled her to the gateway.

"This is it." He stepped forward and took her with him into the unseen.

A searing cold blistered through her being, and Aria realized in a flash she was not ready.

Not even close.

There was no comprehension or understanding or preparation for this.

A scream tore up her throat as they fell for what seemed forever.

Falling.

Falling.

Falling.

Darkness on all sides.

Disorienting and confusing.

Wails stung her ears, cries that called for violence and atrocities, the wickedness unlike anything she'd ever known.

Their fingers still entwined, Pax and Aria hit the bottom with a thud. The ground below them was hard and frozen.

Their Laven family raced out ahead of them and into the toiling mess of shadows and mist that screamed and howled with misery.

The Kruen that Aria had been taught of were more horrific than she could have imagined.

Pax helped her get to her feet, and she struggled to stand, to find solid ground, to see through the haze of depravity.

A heavy, black night surrounded her in a blanket of evil.

So heavy and oppressive she didn't know how to stand beneath its weight.

Voices clawed at her conscience, vile and depraved, the language of the Kruen only recognizable because, as a Laven, she recognized it in her soul.

Pax steadied her, taking her by the outside of both arms and angling in. His voice was firm, though it was cut with his own agony that she was witnessing this. "You can do this, Aria. You can. I know you can. You are strong. Listen to your heart, the way Ellis prepared you to do."

He took her hand again, and she stumbled forward over the uneven, lifeless ground. Cold pierced her like tiny darts that impaled her skin. She tried to run. To begin the hunt. Wisps of vapor and shadows raced at her feet, confounding her thoughts, their screams for violence infiltrating her heart and mind.

"Hit her, the bitch deserves it. Did you see the way she looked at you?"

"Take it. No one will notice. You deserve it more than he does, don't you?"

"Take the gun and drive to their house. How good it will feel to watch them bleed."

Aria stumbled to the right, no strength in her knees, as the cruel voices intoned into any willing soul that listened below.

"Make them pay for their insolence. You are in control. They will bow to you. Raze the rest. Set their homes ablaze, feed on the scent of their burning flesh."

She canted to the side, her feet slipping from beneath her. Pax held on to her, keeping her upright when she wanted to fall beneath the weight.

"Aria, you cannot stop now. You have to fight."

"I can't," she whimpered, the cry ripped from the anguish that writhed in her spirit.

She'd thought she was prepared. She'd thought she understood the extent of the wickedness that abounded.

But no, she hadn't come close to understanding the brutality of it.

She'd had no idea how each thought would pierce her like a knife as the Kruen whispered them into the feeble minds of humans who were oblivious to the wickedness they were being fed.

Those with vulnerabilities.

Weaknesses they didn't know they possessed.

Those who unknowingly opened themselves to evil.

Then there were those who welcomed it, and theirs were the thoughts Aria could not bear.

It was too much.

Too much.

"Take her. She belongs to you." Through the Kruen's eyes, Aria saw the vision of a little girl shivering in the corner of her room, saw the perversion of a man towering over her as he undid his belt.

Sickness spun her stomach, and she dropped to her knees, and her hand came free of Pax's. Her hands flew to her ears, and a wail of agony tore from her soul as she tried to block the voices.

To stop the visions.

To protect herself when she was supposed to be protecting those who needed her most.

Chaos whirled through her mind.

Horror and terror.

Gutting pain.

"Aria," Pax begged, taking her hand and trying to drag her to her feet.

Aria's eyes went wide when a shadow amassed from nothing and into a vicious, fiery face. Gruesome and hideous. It rose up high behind Pax, who continued to try to get Aria to stand.

She wanted to shout. To warn him.

But she was frozen, held prisoner by its eyes, which were a blackened abyss of evil. Every sin held in its depths.

A fiery arm streaked out from it. Pax was unaware in the mere flash of a second before it impaled him in the back.

Pain shocked through her Nol and roared from his mouth, his torment so intense Aria felt it cut into her soul.

He flashed and flickered.

Then he was gone.

Aria screamed.

Screamed and screamed.

Screamed as the Kruen's face lit in twisted glee and lashed out again.

She'd been told.

Warned.

But she hadn't understood.

She had no way to prepare.

The fiery tendril pierced her in the chest, and the pain was greater than anything Aria had ever felt.

Chapter Six

ARIA

"Pax!" I choked over his name as a muddled scream tore up my throat. I scrambled upright from where I'd been face down on a bench.

Gasps heaved my chest as confusion blistered through my body. The memory was so distinct I could have sworn I was right there with him.

I blinked, trying to rein my uneven breaths as I took in my foreign surroundings.

The room was cold and grimy, and dingy rust-colored tiles covered the floors. A drone of voices filled the musty atmosphere as people came and went. A voice announced over crackling speakers that a bus was arriving from New York City.

You're at the bus station.

You're fine. You're fine.

Breathing through the weight of the strain, I struggled to rid myself of the memories of the first time I'd descended into Faydor.

I rarely dreamed of the past, or even dreamed at all. Only in the moments when I didn't fully lose myself to sleep, when I hovered somewhere between consciousness and the ethereal.

Stuck in limbo.

Not awake, but also not deep enough for my spirit to have been fully carried to Tearsith.

And when I did dream, it was often of my first experience in Faydor. The night that had changed everything.

I touched the spot on my chest that would be forever scarred with that moment.

As if it were inscribed on my heart.

A moment in time when I'd met my fate.

Who I was supposed to be.

My attention traveled the area as I oriented myself.

Dreariness pressed at the windows that ran along the front of the brick building. Outside, a freezing drizzle fell from the sky, and a damp cold seeped through the walls. I hugged my backpack to my chest as if it could protect me from both the chill and the prying eyes that gauged.

Speculated.

Judged.

Those who worried I was unstable and about to snap.

I almost laughed.

If any of them had any clue about what was in my head, they would have believed that I had.

A woman in her sixties sat on a bench opposite me, clinging to her purse, not sure if she wanted to get up and move or stand to comfort me. Worry and compassion were clear in her expression.

I dropped my head to hide my eyes because I didn't want to freak her out any more than I already had, and I blew out a heavy sigh and ran my fingers through my hair to gather myself.

It was reckless—dozing off that way.

I needed to remain vigilant.

Cautious.

To watch my surroundings and protect myself, because who else was going to do it?

I was trying to flee a city I could no longer remain in.

Alone for the first time in my life.

Lost, yet seeking a new purpose.

A way to live out this life in the best way that I could, and I knew I couldn't do it here in Albany.

I couldn't continue to cause my parents pain, and I couldn't continue to succumb to the pain that they caused me.

Pulling my phone from my pocket, I checked the time. There was still an hour before my bus left. Cringing, I forced myself to ignore the missed calls and texts from my parents.

Mom had immediately known I wasn't going to school, and I'd hidden myself behind the neighbor's fence as I'd listened to her shouting my name from the front yard. Frantic, she'd run down the sidewalk before she returned home, only for the garage door to rise a minute later and her minivan to slowly drive down the street.

Searching.

It was then that my phone had started ringing incessantly.

I'd listened to her first message. She had begged me to come home.

Swore she was only trying to help me.

Was there to protect and love me.

She'd promised to get me help.

Panic had lit at that because I knew exactly what that meant, and I hadn't been able to bring myself to listen to any more of them, so I'd turned off the locator right before I'd gone to the nearest bank and emptied out my savings account.

When I got to California, I would check in with them.

I would let them know I was safe but that I wasn't coming home.

Once I was eighteen.

Once this place was far behind me.

Grief sank deep into my spirit with the thought of leaving, pain shearing through me at the truth that I would likely never see them again.

I loved them. Fiercely and wholly.

And the thought of leaving my brothers and sister behind, never getting to watch them grow and thrive and experience their joy, left a gaping hole inside me.

But I wasn't sure my parents could ever love both sides of me. They would never accept me or take me at my word—the word I'd kept hidden for years because of it.

Leaving was the only way.

I readjusted myself on the uncomfortable metal bench.

My attention jumped around at the different people sitting in the bus station lobby. Every age and every race. It was impossible not to wonder what might be in each person's mind.

Not to wonder if they were currently being attacked.

Fed lies and wickedness.

Their spirits drowned in hurt, pain, and shame.

I swore I could almost hear the voices in their minds, a low hum of ambiguity that I'd never experienced before. I tried to shake it off, worried that maybe I really was losing a piece of my sanity.

Curling in on myself, I hugged my knees to my chest, with my backpack pinned between them, while I waited. Letting my mind go there wouldn't do me any good.

I had no power here.

Awake, I was subject to every human weakness, just like Ellis had always warned. I possessed no extra insight or strength.

I was fiddling with the latch on my backpack to pass the time when I felt a sudden shift in the air.

Awareness spun, and it whipped the atmosphere into a dense, viscous dread.

My head snapped up to find my father standing just inside the sliding doors.

Staring directly at me.

In an instant, my throat closed off.

Shit.

He was here. He had found me.

His chest jutted in both anger and relief. He wasn't wearing a suit like he typically did. He was in jeans and a poofy black jacket.

My heart began to thunder, a violent pounding in my ears.

Panic grew so fast and thick it obstructed the oxygen from flowing into my lungs.

His jaw was clenched, his stare unyielding.

I should have known he would hunt for me.

Find me.

"Aria," he ground out, his voice hard and severe. He stretched out a hand in a placating fashion, as if I were a wild animal being backed into a corner. He took one step toward me. "Keep calm. I'm only here to help you."

Alarm speared through my being.

That was exactly what I felt like. A caged animal.

One to be tortured and kept.

I'd been here before.

Had witnessed what that expression on my father's face meant.

My attention darted right, then left as I searched, frantic, for an escape.

"I just want to talk to you."

Except I knew he was lying. I could clearly see his intentions. They throbbed through the space like barbs that sank into my flesh.

One word blared in my mind.

Run.

Hopping onto my feet on the bench, I jumped over the back. My soles hit the tile with a thud. I shot toward the sliding-glass doors that led out to the buses in the back, running as fast as I could through the building.

I had to get away.

I couldn't allow this to happen.

Not again.

If only I were half as fast awake as I was asleep.

"Aria!" My father's shout echoed from behind as he gave chase.

I pushed myself harder, still hugging my backpack to my chest as I made it through the sliding doors and out into the icy chill of the Albany winter.

"Stop. Don't make this harder than it has to be," he shouted, his voice curling into a growl. His footsteps pounded behind me, and people jumped out of his way as he barreled through. Shouts of disapproval and surprise rang from those who were jostled to the side.

"Get out of my way. That's my daughter. She's a runaway. Someone stop her!"

Tears burned at my eyes, but I forced myself not to focus on what he was saying. The only thing that mattered right then was getting away.

"Aria!" His anger pierced the air when he made it out the doors.

I sprinted across the paved lot, the soles of my shoes slapping through the puddles, my face impaled by the freezing droplets of rain.

I needed to make it to the next building in the hope that there would be someplace I could hide.

Harsh pants ripped from my mouth as I pushed myself faster. The muscles in my legs burned as my Chucks pounded on the ground.

Dipping between two buses, I cut through the mess of people waiting in line to board. I could only hope to distract my father. Disorient him. Make him falter or lose sense.

Only I felt him gaining, and the panic rose to a frenzy with each thud of his boots against the pavement.

Jagged breaths raked from his lungs.

"Aria! Stop this madness right now. You aren't helping anything. You're only going to make it worse."

I almost breathed out in relief when I skidded around the corner of the industrial building, only shock jutted out of me when his arms suddenly shot out to surround me.

He tackled me to the ground.

"No!" I screamed as I slammed against the cold pavement. My elbows took the brunt of the impact since I was holding my backpack to my chest, and pain splintered up my arms. "No!"

"I'm sorry it has to be this way, Aria, but you chose it." His words were shards. Animosity and disappointment.

I managed to flip around onto my back, and I started to kick and scream and squirm. I lost hold of my backpack as I smacked and hit. He grabbed me by both wrists and pinned them to my sides.

"No, let me go!" My head whipped back and forth as I tried to break free. "You can't do this to me. You can't. Leave me alone."

They couldn't do this to me.

They couldn't.

Not again.

I thrashed, but there was nothing I could do with the weight of him nailing me to the ground.

He panted through his exertion, his eyes angry, wide, and pleading. "We're only trying to help you. One day, you'll understand. You will. I promise."

"No," I cried, succumbing to sobs when I knew there was no chance I could get away.

Because he was wrong.

They were the ones who would never understand.

They were the ones who would never truly see.

Chapter Seven

ARIA

I'd never been one for Tilt-A-Whirls. The way your head spun and your thoughts came in jumbled heaves. The way your stomach rose to your throat and sickness sloshed in your ears. Adrenaline thundering in your veins as everything whirled in quick, succinct flashes.

Maybe it felt too close to falling through the darkness. The jarring of emotions as I sped through the nothingness on my way to reach Faydor below.

The feeling of weightlessness and volatility.

Like I might split apart and cease to exist.

I'd never felt it as severely as when my father ripped open the door to the adolescent mental facility. There were four chairs on either side of the narrow waiting room and a counter with a sliding-glass window on the wall directly in front of us. Doors on each side of it led deeper into the bowels of the facility.

It wasn't foreign.

I'd been here two times before.

But this?

Everything about it felt different. The way fear clotted my spirit and defiance writhed in my bones.

"You can't do this," I whimpered as he dragged me through the admissions entrance.

My mother trailed behind, her tears incessant, as endless as mine.

"I warned you I was finished the last time, Aria." His voice was low and controlled but tinged with frustration. "We've spent years doing everything for you. You're destroying your mother. You're destroying yourself. You're destroying this family. I'm not going to sit idle and watch it happen any longer."

"You don't understand."

"I understand perfectly."

Two orderlies stepped out from the door on the right side, and my throat bobbed as I swallowed and tried to rein in the chaos.

I wasn't going to win any points if I appeared to be unhinged.

"I called earlier," my father said. "I spoke with someone about my daughter, Aria Rialta."

"Yes, of course. Right this way." One swiped a card and the door buzzed. He held it open, and I was ushered into a room that was a larger waiting area than the one in front. Three small offices that served as intake rooms ran along the right wall, and there were three miniature holding rooms to the left.

I was led into the first holding room. The only thing inside were two plastic chairs, the walls bare and stark white.

"Sit, and don't make me chase you again," my father warned as if I were a small child.

He seemed completely blind.

Hardened.

And I wondered what had been fed into his mind. If he'd become cruel or if his intentions were pure.

I prayed for the latter.

Trying to keep it together, to reel in my tears, I sank onto a plastic chair. Still, I rocked as my parents were taken into one of the intake rooms and began to fill out the information with the help of a woman who sat on the opposite side of the desk.

Their hushed voices coiled through the suffocating air as she asked them questions.

Name and date of birth and a quick confirmation of past history.

But it was what my father pleaded to her that had me close to spiraling. "She turns eighteen in three days." He issued it like a secret, as if he didn't think I would hear. As if what he was implying wouldn't pierce me like a knife. "We have to do something before it's too late. We can't just let her go."

The woman reached across the desk and set her hand over his. Her mouth tipped up in a soft smile of reassurance. "Please don't worry, Mr. and Mrs. Rialta. If Aria needs the help, we are going to get it for her, no matter her age. We can get a transfer to the adult unit if necessary. Her care is our greatest concern. You can rest assured in that."

Panic split me in two.

A white-hot blade.

"No." It wheezed from between my lips. "No. You can't do this. I'm not a child. Let me go."

I didn't even realize I was on my feet and standing at the doorway. "Mom, you have to see. Look at me. Please, look at me!" Desperation bled into the words.

"Aria," she begged when she turned around. Red splotches covered her cheeks and nose, her pain so great it nearly dropped me to my knees. "This is because I do *see* you."

"No!" I raced back for the door they'd brought me through. Somewhere in the back of my mind, I knew I was only making it worse. But I couldn't ignore the voice in my head that shouted at me to fight.

Somewhere inside me, I knew this was different.

The other two times I'd been left here had been for less than a week.

This?

Their intentions rang out like a sentence.

Like permanence.

A gavel slamming down on a wooden block.

I yanked at the handle. It didn't budge.

I pulled harder, again and again. My movements were frenzied as I slapped my palms against the metal. "Please, someone let me out of here! You can't do this to me! Help!"

Footsteps pounded behind me, and a needle pierced my flesh.

"No!"

Pax.

Pax.

My brain silently shouted his name.

Willing him to come.

To help me.

To save me.

But it was useless.

Useless.

"It's okay, we have you. This will help you relax."

I could feel the detachment run through my veins, and a fuzziness began to cloud my mind.

Two orderlies took me by the arms and turned me around.

Through the haze, I met my mother's agonized stare.

"Help me," I begged, though the words were slurred.

Tears blinked from her eyes. "I'm trying to."

I slipped along the edge of consciousness. Everything felt both too heavy and too light.

My breaths were shallow, the walls of the small room where I'd been taken closing in. The space barely large enough to contain the two twin beds.

Again, I'd been told that everything would be just fine.

How I knew it wouldn't be, I wasn't sure, but I did.

Maybe that's why I couldn't fully slip into sleep, why a scream lay idle on my lips, silenced by the weight sitting on my chest.

My legs and arms felt unnaturally weak. A counterfeit, false peace that pinned me to the hard mattress.

But my insides were twisted. My gut tangled and stretched tight.

Losing it earlier was likely the most detrimental thing I could have done, but I hadn't been able to stop the onslaught of despair.

Knowing if I didn't, I would wind up here.

I guessed a deep-seated fear had been borne of this place the first time I'd been committed.

Taking in a steeling breath, I released it with a whisper of his name. "Pax, I need you. I need you so much."

Never more than right then.

I jerked up when a light tapping came from the door, and it was opened before I had a chance to reply.

"Aria?" A woman wearing wire-rimmed glasses and a docile smile on her face peeked inside, her brown hair twisted in a high bun.

"Yes?"

Pushing the rest of the way inside, she angled her head as she approached. "I'm Dr. Perry."

She had on blue tailored slacks and a floral blouse, her heels short and as smart as her brown eyes.

Fighting the exhaustion, I forced myself to sitting and leaned against the cold brick wall.

A chair screeched as it was dragged across the floor, and she settled onto it. She situated a tablet on her lap, crossing her legs as she tapped into what she was looking for.

Nerves rattled when I realized she was studying my records. She scrolled for what felt like forever, although probably mere minutes had passed.

Finally, she returned her gaze to me. "I want you to know you can tell me anything, Aria. This is a safe place, and I'm here to help you."

I could feel it radiate from her pores.

Sincerity.

Goodness.

The desire to make a difference.

I nodded, knowing petulance would get me nowhere. She would dig until she was satisfied I was telling the truth, and I knew I'd have to give her exactly what she wanted to hear.

Manipulating the system that way sucked, especially when I believed in it. Believed in the devotion of people like Dr. Perry.

They just couldn't help me—not when I'd been created to help them.

"Okay," I mumbled, my tongue still not fully cooperating.

"May I ask you a couple questions?" she asked as she glanced at her screen.

Worry blistered and blew, and I fidgeted with my fingers as I drew my knees to my chest. "Sure."

"Can you tell me your name?"

"Aria Rialta." My voice cracked, and I swallowed hard, trying to clear the residual of my breakdown from earlier.

"Date of birth?"

"February 24, 2005." I failed at keeping the resentful bite from the words.

I'd only had to make it three days.

Three days.

And here I was.

She seemed to sense where my thoughts had gone, and she sighed as she shifted forward and pulled her glasses from her face. "This isn't about taking your freedom away, Aria. This is about helping you get well so you can live a happy and productive life."

I dropped my eyes and stared at the thin blue bedspread beneath me. How was I supposed to respond to that?

"Your parents are really worried about you," she continued. "The only thing they want is to help you."

A frown came unbidden. She had no idea how much I loved my family. How badly I didn't want to hurt them. How I hated dragging them through their misconception of who I was.

"I know that."

"Yet you fight them."

Inhaling a shaky breath, I sagged against the wall.

I was so tired of it.

The fighting.

The fear.

She resituated her glasses on her nose. "Why don't we let you rest this evening since you've had a stressful day—but tomorrow I want you to participate." Standing, she stared down at me. "Deal?"

My nod was tight. "Deal."

At least then I'd have some time to figure out what to say to get free of this.

"You're going to thrive, Aria Rialta. You'll see."

Her heels clicked on the linoleum floor as she moved to the door, and she smiled back at me from the threshold. "I'll do whatever it takes to make sure that happens."

Chapter Eight

ARIA

Voices carried over the stark-white floor of the cafeteria. I pushed a heap of something unrecognizable around on my tray, knowing I should eat and keep up my strength, but it felt impossible to lift the plastic spoon to my mouth.

No way to swallow the bitterness that soured my stomach and crushed my spirit.

Exhaustion had set in, bone deep, and I found myself fighting the sleep that I had begged for earlier but hadn't come. The aftereffects of the sedative lingered in my veins, luring me toward a blissful state of unconsciousness.

Or maybe it was just the knowledge that I would soon return to Pax that pulled me in that direction. The need to be with him, to stand and fight at his side, that made me ache for the tiny bed in a foreign room that I knew would be waiting.

Closing my eyes felt like a promise that everything would be okay.

Because being a prisoner within these walls sang of torment.

A foreboding whispered from my soul.

A haunting echo of a warning.

As long as I was here, I was in danger.

I could feel it.

Perceive it like truth as I let my gaze wander over the raucous energy of the cafeteria.

I tried to figure out where it was coming from.

The threat that lingered like an omen.

Patients were scattered about, some in groups and others sitting alone like me, downcast and withdrawn, wishing to be anywhere but here. Others talked and teased, the coed situation offering the perfect conditions for flirting and crass exchanges.

The teenagers here weren't unlike the ones at my high school.

Each seeking solace in who they were, or maybe fighting against it and trying to become someone else, human nature driving them to fit in.

Others clearly revolted against the idea of conforming, claiming their individuality like a brand they wore.

I tried to guard myself against what hummed below the surface of it all.

Pain.

Grief.

Desperation.

Hopelessness.

I'd never sensed it so profoundly before while being awake. Right then, it felt as if I hovered near Faydor, not quite within its boundaries but close enough to hear the wickedness that droned within its borders.

Though here, it was distorted. Warped, misshapen moans that echoed somewhere in my soul.

I had no idea why I could feel it then, how I could almost hear the atrocities being whispered into their minds by unseen Kruen.

It was something I'd never experienced before.

Squeezing my eyes closed, I tried to guard myself against it.

One of the counselors clapped her hands and shouted over the din, "All right, everyone, finish up; dinner is almost over. Once you're done, go back to your rooms."

I didn't hesitate to stand.

The second I did, I was hit with a rush of dizziness, and I fought the weight of it as I carried my tray to the cart where we were supposed to leave them. Once I'd scraped the remnants of my dinner into the trash and set my tray on the cart, I crossed the cafeteria, keeping my head low as I followed the crowd out.

I went left, down the short hall toward my room.

Each step had become painful, the fatigue overwhelming. My wound hurt even worse tonight, the barely healing skin retorn in the scuffle I'd had with my father, reigniting the searing flame that singed my flesh.

When I got to my room, a bag my mother had packed for me was sitting on the end of my bed. The contents would have been searched. Anything deemed inappropriate would have been set aside for when I was discharged, and the rest was neatly folded inside.

Pajamas and sweatshirts and jeans. Underwear. My toothbrush and toothpaste and deodorant.

My heart clutched when I saw what was at the bottom. It was the stuffed bear I had slept with until I was seven and now kept propped on the dresser in my room, a tangible *I love you* from my mother.

Sadness swept through me, grief at what was to come and what I was going to have to do.

"Hi!"

I whirled around when the eager voice hit the air, the oxygen ripping from my aching lungs on a rasp. I gulped when I realized I was in no danger.

It was only a girl about my age standing in the doorway. I struggled to calm the frayed nerves that had me on edge.

She was short and cute, and her blond hair was in a messy twist on top of her head. She wore a sweater, sweatpants, and socks, and she popped up onto her toes and clapped her hands as if she hadn't noticed she'd just scared the crap out of me.

"I heard I got a new roommate, and I saw you in the cafeteria sitting by yourself, and I really hoped it was you. I am so excited you're here. I've been here for four days by myself, and it's so freaking boring, you have no idea. I'm Jenny." Without pause, the words flooded from her mouth.

Her loneliness rushed out with it, a palpable wave that came from out of nowhere and struck me in the chest.

"I'm Aria," I murmured.

"Oh my God, this is going to be amazing. We're going to have a blast together," she said as she scurried to her bed. After climbing on top, she crisscrossed her legs and faced me.

I moved to sit on the edge of mine.

"And you're so pretty." She said it right before she fully met the force of my eyes. Reeling back, she dropped her gaze, all of a sudden becoming very interested in a bare spot on the floor.

I hated that the sight of me caused her to have a reaction like that, the way it often did when people met my gaze.

My eyes, so pale gray they were almost completely white. Pupils close to nonexistent.

I hated for her to fear.

Only she seemed to work through it—refuse it—and she returned her attention to me, as if she'd decided she wouldn't allow my strange-colored eyes to freak her out.

I let go of a soft laugh. "So are you."

Bouncing on the mattress, she smiled, so wide. "It is seriously so cool you're here. I mean, I know it sucks and all, but at least we can go through it together, right?"

I was struck with the sudden impulse to hug her. To chase away the loneliness that was clear in her faked smile.

The urge was intense.

Powerful.

Again, it was something I'd never felt before. This strange sensation to reach out and touch.

It was so intense I had to force myself to remain sitting, to swallow it down and ignore the compulsion that crawled over me like a skitter of ants.

"So tell me what you're in for." Her voice was casual, though I could still sense the tremor.

How did I answer that? The last thing I wanted to do was ignore her need to connect with me, so I tugged down the neck of my shirt and twisted around so she could see part of the bandage that ran from the top of my shoulder and across my back.

Earlier, I'd barely been aware of them cleaning it.

When I'd been sedated and numb, they'd taken me into an exam room to get my weight, height, and vital signs. I'd squeezed my eyes closed when they undressed me and took pictures of each scar, and I'd tried to ignore their murmurs of disbelief and barely hidden disgust when they saw the new burn, which looked like a charred gash running across my back.

They had cataloged each wound as if they were cataloging my illness.

Afterward, the fresh burn had been cleaned and a bandage placed.

"You're a cutter." Jenny whispered it. Sympathy wove into her tone.

I wanted to cringe at the way she used the phrase. But I remembered from the last time I was here how patients lumped themselves together.

The cutters.

The druggies.

The psychopaths.

I had to believe it gave them a way to relate.

"You?" I asked, the question thick as I forced it up my throat.

"Oh God." She rolled her eyes and tugged at a lock of hair. Discomfort vibrated her being, though she continued to smile as if she held no pain. "My parents totally freaked out for no reason. It wasn't even that big a deal."

I waited, giving her time to continue.

A discomfited chuckle escaped her lips. "So I was dating this guy. Tyler. We got into a fight. I was super annoyed, you know, so I'd taken a couple of pills to help me sleep. That was all. It's not like my mom doesn't take them every night."

Distress underscored the lighthearted confession.

"I'm sorry if someone hurt you." I wished there was a way to take it from her. Hold it.

Sorrow flashed through her expression, so quickly I could have missed it, though I saw it like a streak of darkness.

One shoulder hiked up, as if she were trying to disregard the severity of what she felt. "He was a total asshole, Aria. Like, such an asshole."

"I hate that for you."

I could feel her warring, the way she rocked on the mattress and began to hug her knees to her chest.

"You can tell me, if you want." My spirit stretched toward hers, and I was consumed again with the need to touch her.

I'd never experienced it before.

Nothing like it.

This need that burned like a fire inside me.

Pulling me toward her like a gravity I couldn't resist.

Her mouth pinched at the side, and her words began to rush, shallower and shallower as they gushed from where she'd kept them hidden. "I didn't even want to have sex with him, but he totally begged me. He said he loved me and couldn't live without me. I believed him, Aria. I was such an idiot to believe him."

A sob hitched in her throat, and she looked away, as if she couldn't stand to let me see her pain. "He told his friends I was terrible. He even posted it on his Snapchat story with a video of me walking away from his house that night with the caption 'Who not to fuck.'"

She sucked in a breath. "The next day, everyone kept saying all these awful things to me every time they passed me in the halls. Offering to teach me since I had no idea what I was doing. That they'd be happy to pass me around since Tyler was done with me. Everyone was laughing, whispering behind my back. Even my friends."

Tears glistened in her eyes when she glanced back, and she chewed at the edge of her thumbnail while she sat there trembling. "I finally went to his house and confronted him. He laughed like I was stupid and denied ever telling me that he loved me. He said I had made it up. Told me I was pathetic. Told me that I made him sick."

Tears streaked down her cheeks. She frantically wiped at them, her tone going hoarse when she began to whisper, "I didn't want to feel that way anymore, you know? So I went into my mom's medicine cabinet, and I took a bottle of her sleeping pills. I swallowed all of them with a bottle of vodka. My mom found me on the bathroom floor. I just kept thinking that maybe it would be better if . . ."

She trailed off, leaving the thought unsaid but heard.

In an instant, I was on my knees at the side of her bed, unable to stop myself.

The impulse was too great.

Overpowering.

I took her face in my hands. The air punched from my lungs when the familiar cold streaked through my veins, though the spot where I touched her burned.

A chill raced down my spine, and darkness flashed at the edges of my sight.

A barren plane. Vapors and mist. Shadows rose and lifted and swirled through the wiry elms. The night thick, the sky low. Evil prowled across the lifeless ground.

Fear thundered my heart into mayhem, and confusion rushed through my brain.

What is happening? What is happening?

My eyes squeezed closed as I fought against the terror of the unknown, and my hands were shaking so violently I was barely able to hold on to her.

Jenny trembled beneath me just as savagely.

At the touch, an onslaught of images invaded my mind.

An insecure little girl sitting alone beneath a window in an empty room, her blond hair in pigtails, a doll clutched to her chest.

Parents who were too busy to notice.

The same loneliness I'd felt radiating from her earlier poured from her spirit, and a voice that was not her own whispered in her ear, *"You're pathetic. Worthless. You'll always be alone. No one will ever love you."*

It grew louder, more menacing.

"You little slut. Bitch. Whore. You're disgusting, begging for attention. Pathetic. How could you ever show your face again?"

Jenny's eyes were wide and confused, though she didn't try to break free of my hold.

Awareness swept through my consciousness. The instinctual call to bind the wickedness the way I did in Faydor.

Somewhere inside me, I knew it was impossible. I couldn't bind a Kruen while awake—or even hear it, for that matter.

But I did.

I heard it just as distinctly as if I were tracking it across Faydor.

I saw it then.

A shadow that took shape deep in the recesses of her mind.

A Kruen.

God, how was this happening? Panic battered against the instinct that compelled me to bind.

I shoved the panic down and fought for her, let the energy gather inside me until it was a vibrating orb, though rather than projecting it with my mind the way I did in Faydor, I pushed it out through my hands.

I fought with all of me to separate the black spirit from hers.

The Kruen reared and flailed in an attempt to deflect my attack.

I missed the first time, and energy crackled, and I focused harder, digging around inside myself to find the strength. To fight harder. I reached out with all the strength I possessed to cast out the light within me.

A light that swelled. So bright it nearly burned. It whipped out like an electric current that blazed down my arms and through my fingers.

Sparking and snapping like a strike of lightning. Agony screeched from the Kruen's disfigured, mutilated mouth when the light struck it.

In a flash of glowing darkness, it was crushed.

Eviscerated.

Dust.

Jenny's eyes went wide in shock.

Gasping, I dropped my hands like I'd been burned and backpedaled on all fours across the floor. My back slammed against the side of my bed. Pants raked from my raw throat, and my heart clattered within the confines of my chest.

"What was that?" Jenny whispered as she reached up to cover her cheeks where I'd been holding on to her.

Swallowing hard, I shook my head, barely able to speak. "I just wanted you to know you're not alone."

Uncertainty rippled across her forehead, and she slumped forward as if she'd also been drained.

"I'm so tired, Aria." It rang of confusion, and she slowly moved to drag her covers down and then slid beneath them, blowing out a bewildered sigh as she slumped onto her pillow.

Trembles continued to rock through me where I sat on the floor, propped against the bed.

Wave after brutal wave.

My shoulders heaved and my spirit screamed.

Frenetic energy scraped from my lungs.

What is that? What is that? It's impossible. Impossible.

Terror thundered through my blood, and I lifted my shaking hands to look at my palms.

My palms that had bloomed a bright, fiery red.

The door suddenly banged open.

A bolt of panic surged, and I pressed harder into the bed, my feet pushing against the floor in an attempt to get away.

Terror gripped me in a way it'd never done before.

"Oh, goodness, sweet girl, you can't be on the floor."

I peered through the fogginess of my brain at the woman who had come in. She wore pink scrubs, and her brown, curly hair was cut in a short bob. She abandoned a cart just inside, and concern radiated from her demeanor as she came to kneel in front of me.

"Let me help you."

She stretched out a hand. Warily, I accepted it, my feet unsteady as she pulled me to stand. I swayed to the side, and she looped an arm around my waist. She pulled down the covers as she guided me onto the bed.

"There we go. It's all right. I've got you."

Trembles continued to roll through me, though they began to slow.

"You're fine," she promised.

A stethoscope was suddenly pressed to my chest, and I could feel the distinct concern in her movements. "Do you have a history of panic attacks?"

"No. I think . . . I think the sedative they gave me earlier when I was admitted made me almost faint."

At least I had the fortitude to give her that. I had to be careful what I said and did, or I was never going to make it out of here.

I fought to draw air into my lungs while I lay staring at the ceiling, my mind whirring with the fear and questions that wouldn't let me go.

I'd never, ever heard of that happening while awake before.

Of a Laven binding a Kruen, or even sensing one.

Still, a comfort had begun to seep into me. A comfort that promised I wouldn't feel the same loneliness echoing from Jenny any longer.

A peace had settled into the atmosphere from her side of the room.

"That's likely it. You should feel much better in the morning." The nurse moved back for the cart she'd left by the door and pushed it over; then she pulled the long curtain that hung from the ceiling across the room to give us privacy.

"I'm Jill, the RN on duty tonight. I'm going to get you cleaned up and changed, if that's okay with you."

Her tone was soothing, riddled with compassion. Goodness spilled from her like a sieve.

"I don't mind." It was a bare mumble from my thickened tongue.

She helped me back up to sitting, and she carefully peeled my long-sleeved red T-shirt up and over my head.

"Anything you need, you . . ." Her voice faltered when the bandage covering half my back and my right shoulder came into view. Sympathy gushed from her spirit before she managed to finish her thought. "You just let me know."

I forced a nod.

"I'm going to need you to lie face down." She guided me onto my stomach so she could get to my back.

I didn't have the energy to wince when she began to peel the tape from my skin.

A soft gasp escaped her lips as she exposed the wound inch by inch, and she whispered under her breath, "Oh my God."

She'd frozen with the bandage only halfway loosened, the weight of her horror heavy as she stared at my back.

Unease twisted my stomach, the most vulnerable part of me exposed, so misunderstood.

I wanted to weep.

Finally, she gathered herself, and she swallowed deeply as she murmured quietly, "We'll get this cleaned right up. Don't worry."

She removed the rest of the bandage, then retrieved something from her tray. "This might sting a little," she warned.

It did, but again, I couldn't move. Couldn't do anything but remain motionless as she tended to me.

After she applied a new bandage, she helped me into a pair of pajamas. She shuffled me around and drew up my covers, shushing me in a motherly way.

"There you go, sweetheart. Get some rest."

She pushed back the curtain, then moved over to Jenny, her voice coated in the same compassion. "Wake up, Jenny. You need to take your meds before you go to sleep."

Jenny groaned as she stirred, exhausted as she sat up to accept two paper cups: one with water and one with pills. She tossed them back and chased them with a drink.

"Thank you," Jenny mumbled.

"Of course." Jill tossed the paper cups into the trash, then pushed her cart to the door. "You two get some rest. Let us know if you need anything."

Jenny offered an almost inaudible "'Night."

Jill slipped out, leaving the door open a couple of inches. A sliver of light streamed through the crack, barely illuminating the room enough so that I could make out Jenny's silhouette where she was tucked beneath the covers.

She rolled onto her side, facing me, her words garbled and slurred. "Do you think it's weird they make me take pills when that's the reason I'm here?"

It took every last ounce of willpower to focus on her in the dim light. I was so drained I could no longer move my limbs. "No. They just want to help you."

She nodded against her pillow. A few seconds of silence passed before she muttered, "Thank you for earlier. For letting me talk. You made me feel a lot better."

"It was nothing."

"It felt like . . ." She paused, her brow twisting in the shadows. "It felt like something."

Moments later, her breaths evened out. They were long and deep, a monotone lullaby.

Lying on my side, I closed my eyes and drifted somewhere between consciousness and sleep.

I chanted his name as lights flickered and flashed, my spirit fluttering in anxious anticipation.

Pax. Pax.

Just at the edge, I heard my name somewhere in the distance. It held me in this realm, my spirit hovering at the cusp.

I realized Jill was talking about me.

"Have you seen her back?" Her voice echoed from somewhere outside my door. Concerned frustration underscored her tone.

"What are you saying, Jill?" an unfamiliar voice asked. "Her chart clearly states there is no evidence of someone else inflicting those injuries."

"I don't know what I'm saying. It's just that I saw something similar once, back when I worked in Des Moines. Something is off . . ."

Their voices faded as they began to travel farther down the hall, becoming indistinct as I felt myself detach.

Aria floated, her spirit beaten and broken, her soul calling out to her Nol to be saved. She spun what felt never-ending until she flashed from the mortal world and the moist dirt of Tearsith was suddenly firm beneath her feet. A lush paradise welcomed her, grew up on all sides, the trees dense and their leaves thick.

He was waiting in the middle, like she knew he would be.

Stumbling, Aria took five steps out into the meadow before she crumpled to the ground.

Chapter Nine

PAX

Tearsith

"Aria!" Pax shouted.

Fear streaked down his spine as he watched his Nol stumble out from the dense forest and drop to her knees, collapsing onto the ground.

His heart raced at warp speed, and terror ripped through his consciousness as he ran to where she had collapsed just inside the boundary of Tearsith.

The entire day, he'd known she was in trouble.

Through time and space, he'd felt her turmoil. Had heard her calling his name. Louder than ever before, which he knew was something he shouldn't be able to do.

He wasn't supposed to be able to feel her while they were awake.

But he could.

He swore he'd always been able to.

The hours of the day had haunted him as he'd warred with the nearly irresistible urge to look for her.

To seek her out.

Find her in the day.

He knew better, though, didn't he? The rule that it was forbidden.

A knot formed in his gut. Somewhere inside, he knew the rules were there for a reason. Logically, he understood why. He would only put her in danger. Make him somehow turn against her, though the thought of that seemed like complete bullshit to him.

He would never hurt her.

But he also couldn't imagine putting her more at risk by going to her, either.

That didn't make any of this less unbearable, though, did it?

He dropped to his knees at her side. His stomach twisted in agony while his spirit coiled in hatred.

He had no idea what had happened to her. What had caused this or what was wrong with her. But if anyone had hurt her? They would pay.

"Aria, are you okay?" His voice scraped through the horror clotting his throat. Carefully, he turned her over where she lay in the deep grasses, and he slipped an arm under her upper back to support her, frantic as he brushed away the long locks of her black hair so he could see her face.

Her skin was always pale, but normally, it glowed with life. Tonight, it was pasty and dull.

"Aria, talk to me. I need to know you're okay."

She moaned something incoherent, and her lips barely moved as she mumbled, "Pax."

The smallest amount of relief heaved from him at that.

At least she could hear him.

"It's okay. I have you. I have you. I won't let anything happen to you. I promise you." Every word was gritted out, an oath forever carved on his spirit, one he would do anything to keep. "I have you."

Slipping his other arm under her frail body, he lifted her as he pushed to standing.

He carried her over the lush, green grasses of the meadow, his boots thudding as he treaded through the ankle-high vingas toward their Laven family, who sat along the brook that ran through the clearing.

Dani jumped to her feet when she saw them coming. "Oh my God, what happened? Is she okay?"

"I don't know. She passed out the moment she stepped into Tearsith." Fear ground out with his words.

Dani took Aria's hand, and she searched her face. "Are you okay, Aria? Can you hear me?"

A low sound rolled from Aria's throat.

Concerned awareness rippled through the mass of Laven, and in curiosity, they began to gather, their worry thick and clouding the normally tranquil peace of their sanctuary.

"Everyone back." It whipped from Pax's mouth on a command, his voice hurtling through the air with a viciousness he could not contain.

When they made room, he knelt and gingerly set Aria on the thick bed of grass.

Ellis and Josephine pushed through the crowd. Worry twisted across Ellis's face when he saw them, and he was quick to kneel at Aria's side.

"What has happened?" he asked.

"I don't know." Frustration carved Pax's response into blades.

Josephine stooped down. He could almost hear her bones creak, her long, gray hair wiry and thin. She lifted a hand and danced her fingertips over Aria's brow and across her neck.

"She is drained," she said, her voice hoarse. "Completely drained."

She moved to the stream and dipped her fingers into the cool water and returned to dribble the droplets onto Aria's lips. Aria's tongue stroked out to receive the moisture.

"There, sweet child. You must rest."

"What does it mean?" Pax could hardly force the question from his mouth.

Uncertainty furrowed Ellis's brow. "I am unsure, but it seems her energy has been zapped."

Dread pulled through Pax's being, terror at the thought of what might have caused it. Here, in Tearsith, he wouldn't be able to see if she had any physical injuries, their sanctuary shielding their bodies from any wounds they'd sustained both while awake and while in Faydor.

But he'd never seen any of their Laven family ever arrive in Tearsith in a state like this before. And his gut told him whatever had happened was bad.

Ellis suddenly stood and waved an arm at their family, the crowd roiling in the disquiet that hummed in the air. "Everyone, give us space. It is nearing time to descend on Faydor. Prepare yourselves."

Then he returned, the old man's voice held low in distress. "Could she have been in Faydor? By herself?"

Rage filled Pax at the thought.

"No. She couldn't have been. She would never descend on her own."

She wouldn't. Not without him.

"Then she must have been injured while awake." Ellis's voice was grim, covered in care and concern.

Pax's insides turned molten. He would destroy anyone who had dared touch her.

Josephine set a hand on his forearm, no doubt sensing his anger. "She needs to remain in Tearsith for the night so she can recover. Stay with her."

He held back the menacing laughter that threatened his throat. Nothing could force him to leave her side.

Still, he nodded. "I will watch over her."

"Take care of her, my son," Ellis said before he took Josephine's hand as they prepared to descend into Faydor.

A swell of protectiveness roiled in his gut as he watched them.

Pax hated the idea of Ellis and Josephine walking in darkness. Their bodies were frail, carrying the weight of a lifetime of wounds and burdens. Yet they still raced through the evils each night, and they took on the injuries that would follow them into the day.

The excruciating pain.

Pax had no love for his human family. But this? It was like watching his grandparents being beaten each night.

When he had suggested it was time they rest, Ellis had refused. He'd reminded Pax it was what they'd been created to do, and he would fight the wickedness until the day he went on to rest in eternity.

Pax remained with Aria as he watched their family file toward the invisible gateway that led to Faydor.

Each couple stepped forward, striking in a blinding flash of light before they disappeared.

Dani and her Nol, Timothy, had trailed behind. Worry churned in their gazes as they peered back.

Of any of their Laven family, Pax and Aria were closest to Timothy and Dani.

A friendship had formed. A bond of understanding. It had been forged like metal during the years when Pax had fought by their sides while Aria had remained within the safety of Tearsith.

Timothy held Pax's stare with a knowing concern written in his expression. He was in his early thirties, a tall, slender Black man, his hair cropped short.

The guy was full of life. Always willing to give and sacrifice. Compared with what Pax knew, he had lived a semi*normal* life, feeling comfortable enough to blend in and function in society. His eyes were the same pale gray as the rest of their family, and he always joked that he made good use of sunglasses to ward off the gawkers, though Pax knew that wouldn't be possible to do at all times, especially since he had become a teacher, claiming children were his calling, both in night and day.

There to teach and to protect.

It was clear tonight that Timothy warred with that calling, torn between staying and going.

Pax dipped his chin at him, promising they were fine.

Dani's wave was reluctant before they turned and stepped toward the gateway that rippled in the woods. They flashed a brilliant light before they were gone.

None would return to Tearsith tonight. They would fight until they were awakened or were burned.

Pax shifted to look down where Aria slept on the bed of grass.

Face porcelain, waves of black strewn out around her head, a halo of perfection.

His gaze tracked over her like he could see where she had been burned over the years.

It didn't matter the burn marks were hidden.

Pax knew they existed.

He could remember every fucking agonized moment of watching her go through the fate he would have given his life to protect her from.

A sigh slipped between her lips.

He wished for a way to hold her burden.

Erase it.

Carry it all.

For hours, he watched her sleep as her body regained strength and her spirit refortified its purpose.

"Pax." She finally stirred, moaning his name, though this time, her voice was clearer. He could feel her easing toward coherency.

"I'm right here."

Gray eyes so pale they were almost white blinked open. Eyes that speared through him. Eyes that were carved to the depth of his soul.

He'd known from when he was a boy that his purpose would be to protect her.

He'd also somehow known it would cost him everything.

That his life would be given.

He didn't know how, but sitting there then, he'd never felt the truth of it so distinctly.

He scooted forward so she would know she wasn't alone.

"I needed you," she whispered.

He swallowed around the lump in his throat, the words rough as he confessed, "I heard you."

He'd always been fearful to ask Ellis if he was alone in this or if others experienced it, too.

"What happened?" He had to fight to keep the fury out of his voice.

Aria blinked like she was trying to process it.

"What is it?" he demanded. "Who hurt you?"

"No one."

"Then what happened?"

Uncertainty and something that looked too much like fear passed through her features.

"What is it, Aria? You can tell me anything. You know that."

Hesitancy rolled through her as she slowly sat up. Her words shook when she forced out, "My mother saw my burn from the other night. They readmitted me to the mental facility."

Rage blazed through him, every nerve in his body frayed with the singe. "I told you that you needed to get away from them." The words snapped from his mouth. "They will never understand you, Aria."

He'd pleaded it before. He knew from his own experiences the dangers of being too close to someone who was not a Laven. He'd left his own family at fifteen—not that they'd been much of one. They'd despised him from the beginning.

Humans could sense they were different. Besides their eyes, they could just tell something was off. Could feel the undercurrent of the ethereal that ran through them.

It usually elicited fear, and people tended to hate what they feared.

But Aria had believed her family was different.

He felt bad when she flinched at his words. But God, she was setting herself up to be hurt.

Her expression twisted in uncertainty. "It's not that. I mean, I don't want to be there. I *can't* be there. But there is something else . . . something that happened there."

Dread tightened his chest. "What?"

"I . . ." She trailed off, her brow furrowing.

"Aria, I need you to tell me what's going on."

Her delicate throat wobbled when she swallowed, and she looked away for a beat before she turned back to him with the full force of her penetrating gaze. "I bound a Kruen while I was awake."

Confusion tossed his thoughts into mayhem. "What do you mean, you bound a Kruen?"

"I *bound* it, Pax. Crushed it."

His chest tightened.

It was impossible.

A shudder rocked through her body before she rushed to explain. "I kept feeling something different. All afternoon. Like I could hear the evils that echoed through the halls of that place. I thought it was just the stress. That I was tired and vulnerable. But there was this girl . . . my roommate."

Aria's tongue stroked out to wet her dried lips, and her voice was hushed. "She started telling me why she had been admitted. And I could feel *it*, Pax." She fisted both hands in the stomach of her shirt. "I could feel her turmoil. Her grief."

Her hesitation was palpable, though a newfound ferocity lined her bones. "I had an overwhelming urge to touch her. And when I did, I saw it through her mind, the Kruen who was feeding her lies. I bound it."

Words began to frantically tumble from her mouth. "I bound it. I saw it, and I bound it, and I destroyed it. It drained me. Drained me so badly that I could barely move, but I did it."

She lurched forward and grabbed him by the forearms. "What does it mean? Tell me what it means."

Pale eyes widened with the plea.

Alarm pounded through his bloodstream, and he warred with the urge to jump to his feet and rage. "I don't know what it means," he finally managed to say.

They were created to walk through the darkness of Faydor. Chosen before birth to fight for the good. To protect from the monsters that were bred to destroy.

A Laven's spirit was amplified when they slept. Permitted to cross into the plane that ran over the surface of the Earth like a wicked, infected shroud. A world where demons peered into human minds and preyed on their weaknesses.

In the day, Laven were just as vulnerable as anyone else.

Human through and through.

But if Aria possessed this power? It would set her apart. Put her in greater danger.

A tremor ripped down his spine, and he ground his teeth. "I don't know what it means, Aria, but I won't let anyone hurt you."

He would protect her till his last breath.

Aria looked into the distance, to the lush foliage that surrounded them. A haven that couldn't be touched.

But Pax knew it was all a false sense of security. In one second, she could be gone, torn from this place and taken to one where he couldn't protect her.

"Do you ever wish that we hadn't been given this?" She whispered it out into the nothingness, letting the words ride on the soft breeze that forever blew through the meadow. "That we didn't have this burden? That we were normal?"

"How could I, Aria? Not when it means I get to know you."

He knew his love for her was greater than anything else. Greater than anything he would ever experience.

It was absolute.

Born of some twisted fate that would tie her to him forever.

Her eyes both dimmed and brightened, and he could feel the swell of her nerves crash through the air. "Pax . . . I—"

Suddenly, a blinding blanket of intensity burst in front of him. A radiating light as electricity sparked in the air.

Then she was gone.

No doubt, she'd been awakened in the human realm.

On a roar of frustration, he jumped to his feet. He wanted to reach out and drag her back, all while knowing he had no power to do it.

They'd only been in Tearsith for maybe five hours, and it was far too soon for her to normally wake in the day.

He hated that she was in that place and he had no way to find out if she was okay.

A prisoner held.

He'd never forget how terrified she had been the first time she was institutionalized. How she'd wept each time she arrived in Tearsith, so misunderstood and undefined.

But *he* understood her.

He swore he was the only one who really could.

"Fuck," he spat, driving his fingers into his hair as he began to pace through the torment.

"Pax."

Shocked, Pax whirled when he heard his name, sure he'd be alone for the rest of the night.

Ellis lingered in the distance. Concern was written in the lines of his face.

"What are you doing back?" he grated, unable to keep the harshness from his voice.

"I came to check on Aria."

Pax scrubbed a palm over his face. "She was awakened."

He started to pace again, agitation burning beneath his skin as his thoughts began to spiral.

Aria was locked in a facility.

She'd bound a Kruen while awake.

She was alone and vulnerable.

He yanked at fistfuls of his hair.

"I need to go to her." It mumbled out in a desperation he'd never felt before.

Ellis was suddenly at his side, his hand on his arm. "What did you say?"

Pax looked at him. "I need to go to her. She's in danger."

He knew it.

Could sense it as strongly as he'd sensed it during the day.

"No," Ellis wheezed. Fear crawled across his features. "You must not let those thoughts enter your mind."

Pax shook his head, grinding his teeth with the anger that sprang from the depths. "What? Am I just supposed to stay here and know she's being harmed? Ignore the fact that she's in danger? When I can help her?"

"You want to protect her? If you go to her, you will only be putting her in more danger. You must remember that. You are protecting her by staying here and keeping to your Laven creed." Ellis's words were edged in urgency. "Our bond with our Nol is the greatest, most powerful connection we will ever experience. But we cannot interact with them in the human realm. We cannot. If we do, we only welcome destruction into our lives. You know what happened to Valeen."

It was something that had been pounded into his head since he was a young child. A Laven would destroy their Nol if they came together while awake.

That somehow, their souls would eat away at the other. That their love would turn to hate.

But Pax had never quite been able to accept it. Had questioned it because there wasn't one single speck inside himself that could believe he would ever hurt Aria.

"I would never turn on her."

Severity lined Ellis's voice. "The only strength the evil ones possess is when you're awake. They can't destroy you here, in this place, and not in Faydor, either. But they can in the day. Laven can be led astray in the day. You've seen it yourself. None of us are exempt from the sins that our human minds open us up to. But if two are together? Nols, nonetheless? You will be that much more noticeable to the Kruen who will seek your demise. Kreed could not resist the lure of depravity, and all the world fell because of him. And he was a god. Think of what might happen to a lesser man. How much greater their ability to tear you apart? To pit you against one another? To inflame and incite? They would bring desolation into your life. Our human minds cannot handle that sort of attack, nor can our bodies. One of you would succumb."

Death.

It was what Ellis promised.

But Pax would gladly accept death if it meant Aria was safe, because he knew, to the deepest depths of himself, that he would never cause her harm.

Ellis squeezed Pax's shoulder. "You lose sight of your purpose when you're with her. She's already overshadowed the importance of what you are."

"Fuck what I am." Pax couldn't keep the shearing bitterness from his tongue.

Ellis flinched, then pressed on as if Pax hadn't cursed his fate. "Do you think I haven't had to fight the urge to find Josephine while awake? Do you think she's not special to me in ways that no one else could ever be? That I haven't feared for her or wanted to be there for her? But it's my duty while I'm awake to protect my family. To give myself to my wife and my children. I was meant to live that life, too."

He set the full force of his gray eyes upon Pax, and his tone hardened. "Just like you must live yours."

Pax had to hold back his scoff.

As if he would ever allow anyone to get close to him there.

As if he'd ever allow himself to care.

He could never wrap his mind around the fact that Ellis was married. Had children and grandchildren.

"You don't understand, Ellis," he grated, shifting the focus of their conversation. "Something happened while Aria was awake."

"Was she hurt?" Concern flashed through their elder's expression.

Bile gathered at the base of Pax's throat, and the words were shards when he forced them out. "No, Ellis. She bound a Kruen while awake."

Ellis turned a pasty white.

"She saw into Faydor by touching a girl." Dread filled Pax's voice. "Saw into her mind. She *saw* a Kruen, and she bound it. She bound it, Ellis. How is that possible?"

The old man's skin was pallid.

"What is it? What do you know?" Pax demanded.

Pax could see the alarm rolling through Ellis, the way panic held his tongue.

Pax reached out and grabbed his forearm. "Please, tell me."

Ellis's throat trembled as he swallowed; then he lifted his chin in frankness. "I heard of it happening once."

Pax shifted, angling down so he could read what was written in Ellis's expression. His elder's dread was so thick Pax could taste it. "Who?"

"A girl. Long ago."

"What happened to her?"

Agony spiraled through the murky gray of Ellis's eyes. "I have read a vague mention of it in *The Book of Continuance*. An obscure statement that there are some of us who are given a greater gift. But I've never seen it in my lifetime. I have only heard of it once, passed down from my elder—and from his warnings, I understand that they hunted her. Hunted her until they ended her."

A blade of torment pierced through Pax's chest.

No.

He wouldn't allow it.

He would die before he let anything happen to Aria.

Seeing Pax's intentions, Ellis grasped Pax by the wrist. "Pax, you cannot—"

He was cut off when frantic shouts suddenly pelted through the air. "Pax! Pax!"

Pax spun around as Timothy burst through the edge of the dense foliage. Bending over, he rested his hands on his knees and tried to catch his breath, haggard and panting through his exertion.

Dani flashed in behind him. Tears streamed down her face.

"What is happening?" Pax yelled across their sanctuary.

"It's Aria," Timothy wheezed. "A Ghorl. I saw."

Alarm battered through his insides, and Pax flew across the meadow until he was standing in front of them.

"What did you say?"

"A Ghorl."

Pax only knew of Ghorls in Ellis's teachings. The most powerful of Kruen. Those that were so aged and mature they were nearly indestructible. He'd never come upon one himself. Had even believed them mythical.

Timothy sucked for air and grabbed on to Pax's shoulder as he stood upright. Grimness cut into his expression. "It was speaking wickedness into a man. A man who was near Aria. The Ghorl only planted the first thoughts, but they will grow. He will harm her, Pax. Snuff out her life. I tried to bind it. I fought so hard. I promise. But it was too strong. It broke apart and I lost it."

No.

Dani whimpered. "I'm so sorry, Pax. We tried."

"Where?" Pax was already running toward the boundary. To the hazy ripple in the air that would lead to depravity.

They raced to catch up.

He didn't hesitate. He jumped through the threshold.

Searing cold sliced through his being.

Holding his breath, he fell for what seemed like forever, the wails of the evil stinging his ears and sickening his stomach.

Then he collided with the darkness, landing in a crouch on the frozen ground. Light throbbed and crashed as three of his Laven family flashed in beside him.

Shadows sluiced along the ground, twisted and gnarled, seeking out the minds of their prey.

His attention darted over the dead terrain. All around, Kruen thrashed and wisped as shadows over the barren expanse.

Pax searched through the desolation and chaos, through the constant barrage of wickedness overwhelming and pressing on his spirit.

He couldn't heed his calling right then. He only had one intent in mind.

Timothy touched his shoulder. "This way!"

They tracked, each despairing as they ignored the vileness that rose up around them as they went.

"Beat it out of him. He's going to grow up rotten if you don't."

"One more drink isn't going to kill you. Get in the car, you'll be fine."

"How beautiful would her blood be, spilling out on your fingers?"

In a blur of rage, Pax sped past the calls of the depraved. He pushed himself harder. "We have to find it."

Timothy careened through the darkness, leading the way, racing in the direction where he and Dani had seen it.

It was then that a disgusting voice hit their ears, but it wasn't the one Pax was searching for.

"Take him now. His mother is distracted. You are ready for this. You need this."

Through the Kruen's mind, they could see the little boy standing on the street, a foot away from a woman who was looking at something on her phone.

Agony cut through Timothy's spirit, and he slid to a stop. Dani nearly bowled over with the weight of the voice.

Regret filled Timothy's expression when he whipped around, the voice still echoing over the desolate ground. "I'm sorry, Pax. We have to stop this."

Pax understood. "Go."

Timothy dipped his head before he and Dani changed direction and chased the Kruen into the shadows.

Pax pushed forward in the direction they'd been traveling, and Ellis ran at his side.

They tracked through the wisps and trails of shadow that swarmed and slithered, peering into each as they passed, searching for a glimmer of Aria being watched through the eyes of a man.

Ellis fought to keep up, and a pang of guilt struck Pax in the chest that he was pushing the man so hard, but he couldn't give up.

Not until he'd trampled the evil. Crushed the foulness of the Ghorl that dared to breathe her harm.

Ellis rasped through ragged breaths, exhausted, beginning to lag.

Pax drove forward.

Finally, he saw it.

A Ghorl. Twice the size of any normal Kruen. And in its mind, he caught a glimpse of the blackest hair, the sweetest soul, the grayest eyes that swam with goodness.

Aria.

She lay completely still, buried beneath a blanket.

But her breathing was too controlled, too labored, too shallow. Pax had seen enough people through the vantage of Kruens' minds, the cowering in fear and the feigning of sleep, to know intuitively that she was awake.

The Ghorl was feeding thoughts into a man's mind.

Provoking him.

Tempting him.

A man who was in her room, who Pax knew in an instant shouldn't be.

"She won't know if you touch her. She's asleep."

Images flooded Pax's vision.

The vile.

The foul.

The seed that had been planted and its ultimate progression.

Pax's knees weakened, yet he somehow became more determined.

He rushed toward it, gathering the light as he bent his mind to wrap it around the Ghorl.

It startled, detecting him before he had time to contain it.

It shattered into a million pieces, the shadow breaking apart and darting along the ground in every direction.

Hopelessness took his chest in a fist.

He would never be able to bind every fragment as it fled.

The light had to be focused on the shadow as a whole to completely extinguish it.

It would speed along the barren floor, hiding within the rolling fog, and then regather. In its regeneration, it would grow stronger.

A roar broke from his throat. "Aria!"

He couldn't let this happen.

He couldn't.

And all logic was lost.

Every warning he'd been given ceased to exist.

His purpose forgotten.

His blood pumped with fury, his mind frenzied as he searched the soiled ground for the nearest Kruen.

One he knew would lash out.

Pax rushed up behind it.

It whirled around and reared in defense, its eyes wild and vicious.

"Pax!" Ellis cried out when he realized his intention. "Do not do it!"

Pax didn't slow. He lunged forward, and he propelled himself through the air with his arm cocked back in a fist, loosing a misleading threat.

It lashed out, just as Pax knew that it would.

Satisfaction billowed through Pax when it struck him across the chest, the burn searing through him and sending his spirit toppling back to humanity.

Because if he was going to get to Aria in the day? Every second counted.

Chapter Ten

ARIA

My eyes flew open to the wispy darkness of the room. Fear pierced like talons as a nauseating sense of awareness sank into my bones.

Jenny was in her bed six feet away, her breaths rhythmic in the abyss of sleep, an even rise and fall that whispered through the air like peace.

But I felt no peace.

Forcing myself to remain completely still, I tuned my ear to the oppressive silence that hovered in the room like a wraith. My senses pushed out to try to determine what had awakened me.

Wrapped in the thin blanket, I lay on my side, keeping as still as possible.

I might have been disoriented, my mind foggy from the jolt of being torn from the sanctuary of Pax's presence, from that sphere to this one, but I was alert enough to know I needed to be afraid.

My heart galloped, and I struggled to listen over the pulse that pounded in my ears.

I heard nothing . . . yet I was sure there was *something*.

Gathering my courage, I peeked out from beneath the blanket.

Blackness cloaked the room in a murky curtain. The only light was a splinter streaming through a crack in the door that illuminated a narrow strip down the center of the room.

Somewhere in the distance, a patient wailed, but the hall beyond our room was still.

Jenny shifted and rolled to her side. For the briefest moment, the tempo of her sleep was interrupted. The pause was long enough to expose the controlled breaths that had been meant to match hers.

Shallow and regulated.

Emitted from somewhere near the foot of my bed.

Bile rose in the back of my throat, and a cold chill streaked down my spine.

It was a man, I was positive.

I could almost sense the outline of his rigid frame lurking in the dark.

Penetrating eyes burned into me as if they could see beneath my cover, leaving me vulnerable and exposed.

I hugged the blanket tighter in a vain attempt at sheltering myself.

Terror blistered through my spirit when he shuffled forward. His footsteps were light, the only sound the faint squeak of rubber-soled shoes against the linoleum floor.

Panic edged into my consciousness, and I squeezed my eyes shut as if that might be able to conceal my presence. Tears gathered and slipped free, running along the edge of my nose and dripping onto the pillow.

I fought to find the strength of sleep. Who I was when I fell through the darkness and into Faydor. To embody that power.

But I was also fully aware of the limitations of my human body.

A sob stuck in my throat when the mattress suddenly dipped at the side of my feet, and a husky, nasally breath escaped the man and slithered through my senses.

Revulsion crawled across my flesh, and my throat clogged as I gagged.

My mouth opened with the intent to scream, but no sound came. It was only a soundless plea that pitched through the air.

I couldn't let him do this. Couldn't let fear freeze me. I had to fight. Find a way.

Even though there was a piece of my consciousness that had already known my fate the second I'd seen into Jenny's mind last night.

Suddenly, brisk footfalls echoed down the corridor, and two hushed voices grew louder as they approached.

The man froze, hesitating, wavering as he leaned forward, then back again.

Somewhere close, a door banged when it was pushed open, and one of the voices carried through the wall: "Did you need something, Ainsley?"

He jolted upright at that, malevolence rippling over his body as he stood in frustration before he finally turned and silently eased back to the door.

He paused there, and I could feel his hungry gaze rove over me again when he turned to look back once more.

He pulled open the door. It cast a wedge of light across the room.

From the edge of my blanket, I peeked out to where he faced away. He poked his head out into the hall and scanned both directions.

He filled the doorway, the mass of him blocking the light, a gory silhouette.

I could see well enough to make out the blue scrubs, the squatty shape, and the buzzed, light-colored hair.

When he found the hallway clear, he slipped out, leaving the door halfway open. His footsteps echoed down the hall, then died out the farther he went.

All the muscles that had been wound so tight in my body gave, and I slumped down in a puddle in the middle of the mattress. Relief and fear trembled through me.

Tears fell hot and fast.

Quick and uncontainable, though I tried to keep the sobs buried in my pillow.

Because this relief wouldn't last for long.

I already knew.

Felt it in my soul.

The wickedness that had oozed from the man's stance, in the quivers of malicious desire that had racked through the room.

He was going to be back, and I'd already read his intent.

I could already feel his hands around my neck, squeezing the life from me.

Even though I'd only seen him from behind, I could clearly imagine the smile on his face when he did it.

When I'd told Pax about binding the Kruen while awake, I'd been foolish enough to hope he'd tell me it was normal. That it was something they'd forgotten to tell me would happen around the time when I turned eighteen.

But that hope had fizzled when I saw the fear that had flashed across his face when I'd told him. His gorgeous face that I ached to see. One I ached to reach out and touch, the same way I ached to touch his body.

Just once.

Because I would fight it—with all of me—but I was sure my fate was already stamped and sealed.

The Kruen were going to hunt me, seek me out on this sphere, and they wouldn't stop until I was dead.

I just never could have imagined they would find me so fast.

When I'd felt that dread sprout from the depths of my soul, sure that if my parents locked me away here again that I might die, I'd never anticipated how literal it'd been.

I buried my face deeper into the pillow to drown the sorrow.

A raspy scream ripped up my throat when a hand landed on my shoulder. I shot upright, reeling back until I was pressed against the wall.

Through the vapid shadows, Jenny's blue eyes went round, and she pushed her hands out in front of her in surrender.

"Shh . . . shh, it's okay, it's just me," she whispered, tossing a worried glance back at our door to make sure no one had heard and was coming to see what was going on.

Gasping, I tried to slow the way my heart ravaged at my chest. Banging through the disorder that I couldn't quell, my spirit and flesh feeling as if it were being rent apart.

"I heard you crying." Uncertainty surrounded her when she crouched down on her knees at the bed at my side. No doubt, she was wondering whether she'd made a mistake by coming to check on me.

She wrung her hands, then slowly lifted her chin to fully meet me in the eye.

Brave and kind.

Because I knew in that moment, she was truly afraid of me, and still, she took the chance.

Inhaling a steadying breath, I tried to clear the chaos from my mind.

"I don't like it here, either," Jenny whispered as she eased down onto her butt and crisscrossed her legs in front of her.

Empathy rippled from her in waves.

"I hate it, really." She gave a small shrug, hesitating for a beat before she continued, "But I'm really glad you're here. I somehow feel better just being around you."

A deep gratification burned through my chest. Even though she didn't know why she felt better, it meant something.

It meant something important.

And even if she was the only one whom I could help this way? If maybe, maybe the voices were cleared long enough for her to find healing? Purpose and hope and faith? Then it would be worth it.

I reached out and grabbed her hand. "You're going to be okay, Jenny. I know you are. You're an amazing person. I can feel it. So please don't ever let anyone tell you otherwise. I promise you they have no idea what they're talking about, because you are incredible."

Even in the darkness, I could see the blush light her cheeks. "Yeah, I think I am going to be." She squeezed my hand back. "We're both going to be."

She smiled at me, and I couldn't do anything but smile, too, connected to her in a way I hadn't been with anyone else before. "Yeah, we are."

It didn't matter if it was a lie.

Without letting go of my hand, she shifted and lay down on her side. "Is it okay if I stay here with you?"

"Of course." I lay down beside her, face-to-face. Jenny was clinging to my hand as she almost instantly fell asleep.

Brushing my fingers through her hair, I whispered, "Yeah, you're going to be okay."

No matter how exhausted I might be, I knew there was no chance I was going to fall back to sleep tonight. I wouldn't touch on that sanctuary. I wouldn't find peace.

Instead, every sense I possessed was trained outside our room, listening to each voice and footstep, every rattle and creak.

Each time someone moved down the hall, I tensed, prepared to fight.

This time, I wouldn't be taken by surprise.

Shadows passed by the door several times during the following hours, but no one paused or entered.

I didn't begin to relax until the sun finally broke through the tiny horizontal window high above our beds.

Five minutes later, a male's voice rang out as he bustled down the halls, knocking on doors as he went: "Let's go, my friends. Time to get up. Breakfast is served."

Jenny groaned and rolled over, giving me a tiny giggle when her eyes blinked open and her face was two inches from mine. "I guess that's our cue."

"Sounds like it."

I rubbed a hand over my face to chase away the grogginess as a gush of relief pressed from between my lips.

I'd made it one more day.

Chapter Eleven

ARIA

It was not fun spending your day wondering if you'd see tomorrow. If today would be cut off. If your hours were numbered.

Scanning the cafeteria from where I sat next to Jenny, I searched for anything . . . familiar.

A hint of the malignant.

An innuendo of ill intent.

My spirit remained calm, feeling no threat.

Whoever had been in my room last night must have left with the 6:00 a.m. shift change.

Counselors stood around the cafeteria, two men and one woman, casually observing us as we ate breakfast.

Again, I pushed the food around on my tray, lost in the subdued mood.

Most ate quietly, boys on one side of the room, girls on the other.

I found myself drawn to those hurting around me, and I kept having to fight the urge to reach out and touch.

To see if it happened again.

To find out if it was a fluke.

A mistake.

If I was really losing the sanity those around me thought I didn't possess.

A girl sat to my left. Her hair was chopped short and dyed jet black, and her face was drawn, the inside of her left arm crisscrossed with old scars in the shape of *x*'s. The scars were covered with fresh wounds in varying stages of healing.

Even though her expression remained flat, her thoughts swirled around me, almost palpable.

Harrowing and haunting.

Riddled with confusion and grief.

The compulsion to touch her was almost as strong as it'd been with Jenny last night. My hands tingled with the impulse, and energy rushed to my fingertips, so intense I could feel it glowing inside.

I gulped and tried to force it down.

Contain it.

Honestly, I didn't know what to do with it. How to handle this change that I didn't understand. How to harness the power. How to wield it and how to control it.

Did it really even matter if I was only going to be hunted down anyway?

After breakfast, I went into the tiny bathroom in the room I shared with Jenny. I stripped out of my clothes and peeled the bandage from my back, hissing as I did. It still burned, the lash fiery and inflamed, but it was finally beginning to heal.

I showered, then changed into a pair of jeans and a soft, fluffy black sweater my mother had packed. It felt like another hug. Another embrace. The same as the bear she'd hidden at the bottom of my bag.

I held on to the truth of her care when the anger threatened to surface.

She didn't understand.

She only cared about me.

Loved me.

Was terrified for me.

It was on me to *understand* that.

"Are you doing okay in there, Aria?" Jenny called through the door. "I mean, I love a good shower, but you know, I just wanted to check because you've been out for a minute. If you need anything, just holler! I'll be right here . . . outside the door . . . in our room."

Amused affection had me biting down on my bottom lip. It seemed I'd found a friend.

"All good," I called as I opened the door. "Just finished getting ready."

"Okay, good! I gotta hop in before they come round us up." She was already peeling her shirt over her head as she stepped inside. "We have recess in, like, five."

"Recess?"

"Uh, basically, yes. I mean, I'm not sporty, like at all, but it's way better than being stuck in this building all day. Even if it's cold as all hell out there, I'll take it," she rambled, her voice blurring when she turned on the showerhead and climbed in, though she'd left the door open so I could still make out what she said.

Right. I'd almost forgotten about them taking us outside before.

"And Dylan is going to be out there, so obvi, that's where I'm going to be," she said.

"Who's Dylan?"

"Ugh, the hottest guy here. But he just, like, leans against the wall by himself. He's clearly nothing but trouble, but oh man, he's the kind of trouble you want, if you know what I mean."

She laughed at that. "But it doesn't matter, because he doesn't talk to anyone. Like, *anyone.* I've never even heard his voice. Not once. So I just admire the view. And my poor panties, Aria, *the view.*"

She groaned after she sang it.

Warmth filled my chest.

I'd never really had friends, especially after I hit middle school, when the girls had decided I was weird and I'd realized it was dangerous to let someone inside my truths.

Not that I could ever let Jenny go there, but still . . . it felt good to have a companion.

At ten, we were ushered out back through a heavy metal door.

It was definitely a glorified recess.

There was a field of grass, a basketball court, and chairs sitting around plastic tables on a patio.

It was cold, but different from the coldness of Faydor. The air was crisp, and the sky was clear. Bright, wintery rays of sunlight slashed down from the heavens.

I tipped my face to it, relishing the warmth, terrified it might be my last chance.

A handful of patients picked up a ball and began to play a game of basketball, though most hovered around and watched. Some were detached, while others looked for a way to make connections.

A twelve-foot-high chain-link fence enclosed the entire area. On the other side of it and to the left was a parking lot, where I assumed the staff parked, and off to the right in the distance, obscured by a copse of trees, were more buildings that housed the adult facilities.

My stomach sank at the thought of being taken there. Rather than wallow in it, I studied the area, searching for any weaknesses or soft spots.

There was little chance I could make it over the fence before one of the counselors dragged me back down, though I couldn't help but wonder if it might be worth the try.

I had to fight if there was any chance I would survive.

An hour passed, and we were paraded back inside.

Everything was regimented and controlled.

Scheduled.

Not that I minded order.

I just hated that I was being *controlled* here.

I hugged my arms across my chest as I followed the rest inside, and the door locked behind us with a buzz.

Yeah, I wasn't getting through that, either.

Complaints of discontent sprouted from the group when we were led through the main room and into art therapy.

"This is so stupid," Jenny grumbled from the chair next to me. "I don't know why they make us do this. It doesn't help anything."

I shrugged. "It's okay, I guess."

More than okay. I loved it. I loved the feeling of my hand stroking over the blank paper as I scratched the charcoal pencil across it. As it grew and the lines became more defined. As the image took shape and came to life. I just sat back and let it flow.

I wasn't surprised when pale eyes stared back at me.

As he looked at me with his dark intensity.

The meadow alive around him, so real I could almost smell it.

"'*Um, it's okay, I guess,*' says *Little Miss Aria da Vinci* over here. Seriously, I'm embarrassed to even show you mine."

Pouting, Jenny glanced between the stick figures on her paper and my drawing. Mock shame hung her head.

A small chuckle escaped me, and I bit down on my bottom lip.

Her feigned offense only grew as she touched her chest.

"What, you think you're better than me?" She held up her picture, displaying the drawing that looked like a five-year-old had done it. "This is my best work, Aria. A real classic."

That time, I laughed. I couldn't help it.

Blue eyes glimmered as she grinned, and I smiled back, savoring the bond, this unlikely friendship formed in the most unlikely of places.

Smirking, she quirked her brow as she gestured at my drawing. "Bet you wish he was real. Hot damn, baby."

I glanced back down at the image.

Pax, in our sanctuary. Sitting in the high grasses.

His expression severe.

Fierce.

The same way that he always looked at me.

My chest squeezed.

She really had no idea.

Dr. Perry pulled her glasses from her face, set them on the desk, and sat back in her chair.

"Tell me how your first night was here, Aria."

Terrifying.

Gut-wrenching.

Devastating.

Beautiful and fulfilling.

Shifting on the pleather love seat where I sat, I tried not to itch beneath her appraisal. The way her eyes flitted over every movement I made.

Cataloging.

Every twitch, every gesture, every blink.

She was watching for a visceral reaction. For anything to indicate I was being disingenuous.

I drew in a deep breath to keep the shaking under control. Convincing her I was no danger to myself was the only way I was going to get out of here.

Truthfully, I'd barely made it through group therapy earlier that day.

I had no idea how to handle the new sense that had taken over me. The ability to hear the vile voices echoing from the minds of anyone who was near. It was disorienting. Crushing. Pulling me between the need to help them and the truth that I also had to protect myself.

I'd nearly been brought to my knees by the shattering pain that had splintered through my being when the female counselor had gone around the circle, asking each of us if we wanted to hurt ourselves or if we wanted to hurt someone else.

Everyone's emotions amplified.

Most had lied.

Blades of dishonesty. Shards of hopelessness and desperation.

I'd nearly ruined everything when I'd been struck with the overwhelming need to touch each of those girls as the counselor had moved around the circle.

Their pain had been almost too much to ignore, and I hated that I'd had to do it.

It felt like betraying them.

The torment and confusion that infested their thoughts.

Prisoners, when they didn't have the first clue.

By the time the counselor had made it around to me, I'd barely been able to speak, and I'd somehow managed to force out a shaky "Not today."

I was trying to play it smart.

They could only monitor us for a short time to ensure we weren't immediate threats to ourselves or others. To ensure the moment of crisis that had landed each of us here had passed.

If I could just make them believe I was okay now, I might have a fighting chance.

But I didn't have one locked within these walls.

I cleared my throat when Dr. Perry remained silent, waiting for me to answer.

"Um, it's been okay. It's weird not sleeping in my own bed, but I like my roommate."

She nodded. "Jenny is very kind."

"She is," I agreed.

Dr. Perry angled her head, her perusal soft but keen. "And how are you feeling?"

My tongue stroked out to wet my parched lips. "A bit better today," I whispered, hoping to sound sincere.

"That's what we always hope . . . that you feel a bit better with each day. But really, for that to happen, we need to help you get to the root of this, Aria. To the place that you have trouble allowing others to see, and I hope you'll trust me with that."

There was nothing cruel or evil about it.

No ill will emanating from her spirit.

But that didn't mean allowing her to go there wouldn't prove catastrophic.

When I didn't respond, she shifted her attention to the portrait I'd drawn in art therapy that now rested on her desk.

My nerves scattered as she carefully studied it, and I had to fight off the urge to snatch it back and hide it against my chest.

When I'd first entered the room, she'd asked if she could see what I'd done in art class.

Maybe I should have refused. Ripped it into a thousand pieces before she could see. If I'd been smart, I wouldn't have drawn it in the first place.

But it'd come unbidden, arising from the depths of my mind and flowing from my fingers as I let my spirit wander.

Pax had been there for a moment, the way I wished he could truly be.

In discomfort, I hugged my knees to my chest and rested my chin on top of them.

She tapped the picture, her eyes narrowed in concentration when she leveled me with an intent stare. "Can you tell me about him?"

My mouth was instantly parched.

I searched around in my brain for an adequate lie to give to a woman who was trained on how to sniff them out.

"What do you mean? It's just a drawing."

Her brows drew together. Cautious speculation. "He looks a lot like you."

She glanced between me and the drawing, as if she were categorizing each similarity.

"You have an amazing talent, really," she said, almost to herself. "It's a stunning piece of art."

"Thank you."

"And we could go on about your natural talent, but I really think we should address this man in the picture."

She rocked back in her chair, casually, as if to put me at ease. Futile, since trepidation buzzed through my being.

"Have you always felt self-conscious of the way you look, Aria? Is this perhaps an expression of your need to fit in? To find someone else who might look like you?"

Care filled her tone, and I would have found comfort in it if I didn't know her laptop sat open to my file. To the records from middle school and earlier, when I'd insisted there was a little boy who looked like me. That there were others with my eyes. Others who were just like me and met in this magical place.

I'd known I wasn't supposed to share those pieces of myself, but somehow, I'd never been able to stop myself.

"Maybe?" I shrugged, forming it as a question, looking at her with a *You tell me*. Maybe then I could nod and agree with her perception. Satisfy her concern.

Her head tipped to the side, her eyes narrowed in concentration.

"You're actually quite beautiful," she mused, though I could almost hear her rebuking herself for saying something that might be deemed inappropriate.

She cleared her throat and tapped the picture again. "So, Pax is his name?"

Unbidden, a tremor rolled through me. I bit back the panic.

"And this Pax is important to you?" she pressed.

My nerves edged in anxiety, I rushed my hand through my hair. I decided to use it to my advantage. Play the troubled teenager. I chose my words carefully. "Yes. He was always there for me when no one else understood."

Leather creaked when she shifted in her seat, and her voice grew deep. "What does he think about what you do to yourself, Aria? Does he tell you it's okay?"

She wanted to know if I heard voices.

If only she really knew the voices that I heard.

"No." I whispered it, allowing the tears to well up and fall free.

97

Appropriate for this act.

While inside, I was panicking. My spirit revolting. Telling me to get up and run. To squeeze my eyes closed and pray for sleep.

To go to Tearsith.

To find him.

Because I hated denying him.

Denying how much he really meant to me.

But there was no other way.

"I used to talk to him when I was little." The faked confession was thin and wispy. "It was just hard to let him go when I realized he wasn't real."

Frustration colored her features. "Please don't play me, Aria. I ask for your respect within these walls, the same as I will give to you. I know very well you still believe he's real. And I need to know if he's the reason you harm yourself. If he convinces you this will somehow make you feel better."

She turned her laptop around to reveal the pictures emblazoned like proof on the screen. Burns in varying degrees of healing captured in each shot.

Some old and faded.

Some puckered and inflamed.

The one they'd taken yesterday when I was admitted was still caked with dried blood.

I did my best not to flinch at the sight of them.

Sympathy might have filled her expression, but her words were enough to snuff out hope. "These are the worst injuries I've ever seen anyone inflict on themselves, Aria, and I am not going to let you go until we find a way to help you."

Chapter Twelve

ARIA

By that night, despair had settled in. Each footstep was hard to take, every moment torment as I waited for the man to return.

I'd searched for anything to use as a weapon, but considering I was in a mental facility, they were hard to come by.

The only thing I possessed was my voice . . . and my touch.

Could I use this new power? Use it against him?

I swallowed around the barbed knot of uncertainty lodged in my throat as I trudged into the cafeteria for dinner.

The evening shift change had come and gone. The night counselors were back on duty, the same as the kitchen staff, plus I saw Jill, the nurse from last night.

During the change of staff, I'd felt no deviation, no defiled lust radiating from a depraved mind, no malice hanging in the air.

Jill cleaned my wound again, smiling at the picture sitting on the nightstand next to my bed while she did. "Well, isn't he handsome," she murmured softly.

Her intonation didn't give me the impression she was trying to humor me.

I hadn't expected Dr. Perry to return it. I'd figured it'd end up in my file as further evidence of my instability. But she'd given it to me and encouraged me to keep drawing, whatever it was I felt.

"Yeah, he is," I whispered. I figured there was little I could say that could harm me. "Pax."

I left out the rest.

That he was my truth.

My soul's mate.

The love of my life.

The one I could never have.

"Seriously hot, right?" Jenny called from the other side of the drape, never wanting to be left out of the conversation. "Aria is crazy talented. I want her to draw me a boyfriend that looks half as good as him so I can fantasize about meeting him as soon as I leave this place."

A gentle chuckle rippled from Jill. "I'm sure that can be arranged, Jenny. What do you think, Aria?"

"Um, hell yeah, my new BFF will totally hook me up," Jenny answered for me.

A soft grin played at my mouth, interwoven with the anxiety that I couldn't keep at bay. "I'll do it first thing tomorrow, Jenny."

"I'm going to hold you to that. Don't forget, I like them dark and dangerous. Maybe a piercing or two in some unmentionable places."

I could almost see her waggling her brows through the fabric separating our beds.

Amusement shook Jill's head as she applied a new bandage. "How about we keep this one safe?" she suggested. "Maybe one of those super-cute gamers. A coder, maybe? You know, someone who doesn't have a bad bone in his body."

"As long as he's got black hair and a few tattoos, then it's a deal."

"And if I don't?" I couldn't help but play along.

"Then you don't get my Snack Pack."

"She runs a hard bargain," Jill teased.

"Apparently so."

Then I felt Jill sober, a sweeping of concern and curiosity. Her voice quieted, close to whispering in my ear, "It seems it would be very difficult for you to reach this area on your back."

My heart fisted in my chest, a clutching as I felt her stretch her spirit toward mine. The goodness she possessed, searching for the questions that had formed in her mind. Was there a chance that she could believe me? Would she . . . help me?

She cleared her throat like she'd immediately regretted what she'd said, and she stood up and patted me on my uninjured shoulder. "All finished."

She shoved back the drape and crossed to Jenny, watching over her as she took her pills. Then Jill moved to the door, and tenderness filled her demeanor as she said, "Let me know if either of you need anything."

Flicking off the light, she slipped out, leaving the door open a few inches.

The moment she did, terror slipped into my veins, rising up from where I'd tried to keep it contained. The horrible awareness that everything had changed howled from my soul.

Would this be my last night?

Would the monster come?

Did I have any chance if he did?

For the longest time, I fought sleep, my ears perked, my senses acute. But as the hours drifted, I could hold it off no longer.

The exhaustion.

The fatigue.

My eyes fluttered as I was dragged toward sleep.

I hovered in that bare space for a short time, trying to fight it.

But lights flickered at the edges of my sight before my spirit flashed, and I flew.

Chapter Thirteen

ARIA

Tearsith

Aria arrived at Tearsith's boundary.

The air was cool and warm, perfect where it breezed across her flesh in a bid to weave respite and relief and comfort into her soul.

But she found no solace in it tonight.

She needed only one thing.

She needed Pax.

She rushed to the meadow's edge, frantic as she stumbled into the clearing, seeking her reason. Her eyes and heart scanned the grass-covered plain.

It welcomed her like an embrace, though for the first time in years, Pax did not.

Despairing, she staggered farther out into the meadow, lifting her arms to her sides and spinning in a circle as she shouted, "Pax! Pax! Where are you?"

Her spirit wept his name.

Didn't he understand this might be their last chance?

Couldn't he hear her calling?

"Pax, please, I need you," she begged over the torment that threatened to consume.

It all became too much as the true reality of what was going to happen to her hit her full force.

She dropped to her knees.

A startled gasp tore from her throat when a hand gently curved around her shoulder from behind. She whirled around to find Ellis. The lines in his face were etched in empathy. "Oh, Aria, my sweet child, do not fear."

How could she not?

He slowly moved around her and tipped up her chin. "You are safe."

Tears clouded her eyes, which was so rare here, but she didn't know if it was possible to stop them with the onslaught of emotions.

Gusts of wind whipped around her like strands of preservation, ribbons of warmth—ties to bind her with strength.

But she'd never felt so weak.

Stretching out his hand, Ellis helped her to stand. "Did Pax tell you?" she begged.

"Yes," he answered.

He watched her with the love of a father, and she surged forward and clung to him as she begged for understanding.

"Why?" She wept against his chest. "Why me, Ellis? I don't want to die."

But she knew that was what this was, wasn't it?

A death sentence?

Ellis lost his breath in a large gush, and he wrapped her in his frail arms, which somehow remained so strong. "No, Aria. No, it doesn't have to be that way. It is not carved in stone. You have to find the strength inside yourself to fight it."

"What am I fighting?" she begged.

His expression grew grim and he spoke with caution, as if he didn't want to be the one to give her the horrible news. "Timothy and Dani witnessed a Ghorl. They believe it might have been speaking ill toward you. But you cannot let it win. Just like your life as a Laven, this special power you've been given can be both a blessing and a curse. You have to choose which it is going to be."

Oh God. A Ghorl. No.

She'd believed them to be nothing more than a mystery. Tales of terror. How could she stand against this?

"But I'm only a girl."

He rocked her, his voice hushed against the top of her head. "Yes, you are a girl. A woman who has been given a powerful gift. One few have ever known. You have always been more, sweet child. Since the moment you awoke in Tearsith, I knew there was something more in you. Something different."

He untangled her from him so he could hold her by the sides of her shoulders and peer into her eyes.

"Isn't this enough?"

The sacrifice she'd already made?

The life of a Laven was punctuated with pain and isolation.

With wounds and scars, both physical and the ones imprinted on her soul.

Fated to love a Nol that she could never have.

She understood the call. Respected it. And she was willing to give.

But this? It was too much.

An albatross.

The hands of that vile man a millstone wrapped around her neck.

"Come with me," Ellis told her, taking her hand and leading her across the meadow to the stream. He swirled his fingers through the crystalline water and murmured, "Look, Aria. Look and listen."

Through her torment, she got to her hands and knees and peered into the crystal-clear depths and turned her ear to the breeze that whispered through.

"Aria." She heard her name like a breath. A murmuring from her soul.

Confusion bound her, and she glanced at Ellis, who knelt at her side. "What's happening?"

"Valeen is alive. Present in this nature. If you listen hard enough, it is said you can hear her."

"Can you?" Her voice was cragged, her disbelief thick.

His head barely shook. "No. But you can, Aria. Maybe there is something in you that goes beyond who I am."

Nearly frantic, Aria turned back to the water, leaning forward to peer deeper. "Valeen," she begged. "Do you hear me? Do you see me? What is happening to me?"

"Aria, do not be afraid." The female voice was haunting, so quiet Aria wasn't sure she was even hearing it.

"Why me?" she asked anyway, tears still blurring down her face.

A face passed by in the ripple of the water, a vapor that twisted through like a ghost, though Aria heard her words before she was gone. "Because you are the only one who has the power to defeat this evil."

"Valeen," she pleaded, and she reached into the water, stirring it the way Ellis had done. "Valeen."

But she was gone, and Aria was no closer to understanding what was happening than when she'd come.

"Ellis." His name was ragged on her tongue.

With both of them on their knees, he pulled her into his arms. "It's going to be okay."

"How do you know?" she choked out.

"I have faith in you. And we will do everything in our own power to understand how and why. To fight it alongside you. Every one of your Laven family is to search. To listen. To protect."

He leaned closer to her ear. "And you have Valeen. I understand it now. It's what I've always felt in you."

His words were only more confounding, and she held tighter to him. "I want Pax."

She knew the admission was a clear confession of her heart. She couldn't bring herself to care or to hide it.

Ellis went rigid, his spine stiffening where he'd once been soft.

Aria jerked back. "Where is he?"

Worry passed through his features. "He has not come tonight."

"What do you know?" she pleaded, seeing the torment in his eyes.

Ellis shook his head as he edged back to hold her hands. "Each of us has our choices, Aria. I just pray you both make the right ones."

"What does that mean?"

"It means I pray that Pax will follow his duty and not do something that might put you both at a greater risk than you already are. But let's not consider that now. You need to rest. You are weary, and you need to find your strength here."

She clutched his shirt. "Ellis, please."

What she was begging him for, she didn't know.

Reaching out, he cupped her cheek. "Believe in yourself, brave girl. Do not let them steal that from you. Now, you must rest so you can fight while awake. I will seek *The Book of Continuance* and see if there is anything I can find. We will do everything we can to protect you."

And for the second night in a row, Aria found rest within the safety of Tearsith.

During that time, she ached. Ached for her Nol.

Her Nol who never showed.

Chapter Fourteen

ARIA

I awoke the next morning, blinking through the perplexity of what had happened last night. Wondering if I'd had a true interaction with Valeen or if the trauma had made me start imagining things.

One thing I knew was that I was unendingly thankful for the day.

Thankful I had another to live, even though I felt the sharp sting of devastation that Pax had never shown.

It was hard, not knowing whether he was okay. Where he was. What had happened after I'd been awakened two nights ago.

It didn't help that Ellis had been distraught when I asked for Pax.

But the only thing I could do was press on.

Today had been much like yesterday.

Structured.

Breakfast, recess, then art therapy.

The only difference was that today my mother had come to visit. She'd cried the entire time. Again and again, she'd told me she wished it didn't have to be this way.

I'd told her I wished it didn't, either.

I'd hugged her fiercely before I whispered goodbye, sorrow splitting me in two at the thought that it might be the last time I would see her.

Dr. Perry had picked around in the recesses of my mind for more information. Asking for details hidden in my drawings, as if all my secrets were concealed in the brushstrokes of my hand.

I'd cried openly when she informed me that they would be transferring me to the adult facilities tomorrow.

I would be held involuntarily, deemed a suicide risk.

I'd considered telling her of the man who'd sneaked into my room, my fear that he'd been sent to kill me, but I knew she would think it only a ploy.

A manipulation.

The only good thing to come of this was that Jenny would be discharged tomorrow.

She was happy and seemed well.

For a time, her demons were purged, and I prayed it would afford her time enough to build a new foundation. For her to fortify her spirit against the attacks, the war few knew was waged on their hearts and minds.

By evening, the hope of this morning had bled away, replaced by a suffocating despondency.

"What's up with you tonight? Are you sad I'm leaving tomorrow?" Jenny gave me one of her overaffected pouts that were completely genuine from where she sat beside me at the long table as we ate dinner. "Tell me you're going to miss me."

"I am absolutely going to miss you," I admitted. So much that the words cracked in my throat.

"What are you going to do without me?" She jostled her shoulder into mine, going for a tease as she tried to keep the emotion at bay. Torn between this friendship we'd found and her thrill that she was getting out of this place.

"Eat all your Snack Packs, I guess." I forced a giant grin.

She cracked up.

It sounded like music.

"I'll tell the kitchen they have your name on them. Deal?" She squeezed my hand.

"Deal," I returned.

She tugged on my hand a little, her voice thickening. "I really hope we can keep in touch after this."

"I do, too." My words were soggy, unable to shake the melancholy that sank into my bones.

So heavy I wanted to weep.

I forced myself to take a few bites to appease the counselors observing the room, but I was barely able to swallow around the bile that kept rising in my throat.

Sickness grew, and a foreboding filled the space.

An omen that hung in the air.

It was then that I felt it—the corruption beating against me.

In me.

Through me.

The breath wheezed from my lungs in a bout of panic, and a shiver raced across my flesh and tumbled down my spine.

Freezing cold and smothering at the same time.

As if its presence had sucked the oxygen from the room.

Jenny chattered on, as if time hadn't sped up and brought me closer to my end, immune to the obliterating wickedness that curled through the cafeteria.

Penetrating.

Bounding.

Infesting.

Gathering my courage, I turned to look over my shoulder.

Evil glared back.

It was the same man who'd been in my room two nights ago. Wearing blue scrubs, his frame squatty and thick, his dusty-blond hair sheared close to his head.

For a moment, we were locked, my gaze held prisoner by the man who was plotting my demise.

He finally jerked himself free of the bloodlust and forced himself to turn back to his work. He shook out a garbage liner and replaced it in the bin. He tied off the full trash bag he'd removed and slung it over his shoulder.

"Hello? What are you looking at?"

Jenny waved a hand in my face, and I whipped back around. "Nothing."

"Nothing? You've been in some kind of trance for, like, the last five minutes."

Her attention jumped around the cafeteria. Dawning bloomed in her features when she saw the monster who was already heading back through the swinging door that led to the kitchen.

"That guy's a creep, am I right?" She exaggerated a shiver.

I didn't need to exaggerate mine.

For a second, I considered telling her. But what was she going to do? There wasn't anything anyone could do.

Ellis's words echoed in my ear: *Believe in yourself, brave girl.*

But how could I stop this?

Not when the Ghorl controlling that man's mind had already decided for me.

"Yeah, seems like it." I shrugged like it wasn't a big deal, when it was everything.

We finished dinner, then returned to our room.

Jill came again, smiling and chatting like we were friends as she changed my bandage, thrilled to see it was continuing to heal.

"You two have a good night," Jill whispered, then hesitated at the door. "I guess I won't see either of you again, will I?"

Jenny groaned her excitement. "That's right; I'm getting out of here!"

"I wish you the absolute best, Jenny," Jill told her.

Then she looked at me in what I thought might be an apology. In an understanding that no one had ever watched me with before. Like she was on the verge of awareness. "And I wish you peace as you move on from here, Aria. Be careful, and take care of yourself."

The ball in my throat made it difficult to speak. "I'll try."

I'll try.

She flicked out the light.

Tonight, I didn't close my eyes.

I didn't snuggle down into the uncomfortable bed.

I refused the drooping of my lids, the lure of sleep whispering somewhere at the back of my mind, my soul drenched and aching for the purpose lingering on the other side.

I just waited.

The whole time, I let my spirit call out to Pax.

I whispered that I loved him. I let my spirit cover him with the hope I held for him. Basked him in the truth that the selfish side of me wished we'd met under different circumstances.

Where he wasn't only a figment of my mind.

Because what if that's all that this was?

What if I had slipped into insanity years ago?

Except I knew better.

I knew this was brutally real when, in the middle of the night, the door creaked open, and a sliver of light crested into the small room.

The same rubber soles squeaked on the linoleum floor, muted as he approached my bed.

It was so very real as I was covered by the foulness of his breath and the stench of his presence.

A wave of terror rushed through my body.

A torrent.

And I had little of that strength that Ellis had talked about.

But it was a speck.

A battle cry that erupted from the depths.

My only chance when they'd left me without defense.

I opened my mouth to scream.

Only a meaty palm flew out to cover it, cutting off the sound before it reached the air.

"Shh, don't make a sound, pretty girl," he wheezed. "There's no need to fight it. He told me you were mine."

The words dripped with wickedness.

And with it, a single tear slipped down my cheek.

Chapter Fifteen

PAX

Night hedged me in where I was hidden at the edge of the woods that grew up on the far side of the facility, concealed in the darkened shadows that hovered over me like phantoms.

I watched out the windshield of the car through the pattering rain that fell onto the pitted pavement. It gathered in soiled, polluted puddles, the droplets glinting as they hit in the diffuse light that shone from the industrial fixture above the single door that led into the side of the building.

The sign it illuminated read ADMISSIONS.

I'd been here for hours, watching the few people who came and went.

Cataloging.

Categorizing.

Plotting.

Well, I'd been plotting for two days. Ever since the night when Aria had confessed the power she held and Timothy had heard the thoughts the Ghorl had been feeding into the monster's mind.

I didn't care how many warnings Ellis had given me—there was no way I was going to sit idle and let something happen to her.

She was in danger.

I knew it.

Knew it all the way to my twisted, fucked-up soul.

My soul that recognized her across the miles and space. The connection was the only thing that had kept me from going completely mad over the years. What had kept me from becoming exactly the kind of *freak* my father had thought me to be.

Two mornings ago, after I'd found the Kruen and thrown myself on it, knowing it'd burn me so that I'd be awakened, I'd tossed necessities into a bag and left my shithole apartment in Las Vegas. I'd driven straight through because there wasn't a thing that could keep me away from her.

Yeah, I knew what city she lived in. I'd gleaned the information through the years and tucked it away. Maybe it was just the comfort in having an idea of where she lived. Knowing she wasn't that far. That her home was real.

That *she* was real.

Or maybe I'd known somewhere in the back of my mind that one day I would have to use that information.

That it would come to this.

I think I'd probably known it since the first time she was hospitalized, the day after she'd turned sixteen. She'd come crying and trembling into Tearsith that night, terrified that she'd been locked away.

She'd always been too trusting of her family, but I got that it was just her heart. She loved fully and without restraint, when in reality, she should have been skeptical of any asshole who came into her space.

Maybe I was just jaded. But I'd learned the hard way that people couldn't be trusted. Hell, I saw the proof of it in their thoughts every fucking night.

Rage held me as I sat in the car and waited for the right opportunity to make my move.

The double doors at the front of the facility had long since been locked for the night, and the only way in was the Admissions door a hundred yards in front of me.

I knew firsthand. I had slunk around the perimeter, masked by the gloom, checking windows and doors and looking for an access point, while my spirit screamed in awareness.

Howled with the knowledge that Aria was inside.

I could feel her in a way that Nols weren't supposed to be able to.

As if we shared a greater connection than any Laven before us.

I could sense her like hot, fiery tendrils that twisted through the night and wrapped me in shackles.

I wasn't exactly prone to following laws and common decency. Not when it came to the monsters who roamed this Earth and were every bit as sick and twisted as the demons we fought while asleep.

But this?

Anxiety rattled through my being.

This was an entirely different story. I was about to commit the type of crime I'd never embarked upon.

My soul thrashed in determination, leaving no question that she was worth it.

My eyes scanned the drenched lot. Freezing-cold air rose in vapors from the vents that were cut at the base of the brick walls, sending plumes of white curling into the dense, deep night.

I froze when the door opened for the first time in more than two hours. A young girl and someone who was likely her mother stepped out. The older woman popped open an umbrella and held it up to shield them as they darted to a car parked in one of the spots that ran alongside the building.

After a moment, they backed out and drove away, red taillights disappearing down the road.

The rest of the lot was dotted with random cars. I gauged that most belonged to employees, their number fewer at this time of night.

Which was why I had to strike now.

When the hour was long and the atmosphere was held in a silence that whispered of wickedness and ill-kept dreams.

A feigned solace that would not last.

Inhaling a fortifying breath, I cracked open the car door and climbed out. My leather jacket wasn't enough to stop the frigid air from sinking into my bones.

Chills rolled down my spine in a frisson of disquiet, and I crept up to a large dumpster ten feet in front of the car, checking that my gun was loaded before I peered around the metal to the entrance.

I swallowed the knot in my throat before I strode that way as if I had a different purpose than the one that pounded in my chest.

My boots thundered across the pavement, splashing through the puddles, blood careening through my veins, haphazard and wild as I hauled open the Admissions door and stepped into the blinding light of the waiting room.

Awareness impaled me.

Sharp and distinct.

She was here.

Trying to regain my bearings, I blinked, scanning the small lobby. There were three chairs on each short wall to the left and right of me, and straight ahead was a large sliding-glass reception window with a counter below it.

Metal doors flanked it on both sides.

Determination skittered across my skin, and I lifted my chin and strode across the confined space. I planted my hands on the elevated counter and peered through the closed window. To the right was a row of what looked like intake rooms. A woman was in the first one with her back to me, pulling something from a file.

Feeling the weight of my presence, she called, "Give me one moment, and I'll be right with you. You can go ahead and fill out the information on the iPad to your right—that will get you started."

Teeth grating through my frenzied nerves, I turned to the iPad and began to fill out the information requested. I prayed this would earn me access to the back. Prayed it didn't come to violence. Prayed I'd have her out of here without much incident before anyone realized she was gone.

I didn't hold on to much hope of that, though.

Not with the way grimness shivered in the air.

Ominous.

Evil cloaking the atmosphere in greed.

I could taste it.

The wickedness that emanated through the cracks in the walls.

It made me itch. Made me want to say, *Fuck the plan,* and crash through this window to get to her.

I went through the questions on the iPad, filling them out with bogus information.

A fake name and birth date and a completed mental health questionnaire.

I ran an agitated hand through my hair when the woman finally shut the file cabinet and began to weave back my way.

At least I looked the part.

Unhinged.

Disturbed.

Destruction whipping around me like a coming storm.

She stumbled a fraction when she saw me through the glass. No doubt, my appearance instantly set her on edge. I was used to it, but still, I ground my molars as she took me in like I was a monster staring back at her.

She was probably in her early sixties, her hair a salt-and-pepper gray, the mass of it in a thick bun at the back of her head.

Trepidation crawled over her spirit, though she straightened her spine, watching me with a wary gaze as she edged the rest of the way to the glass. "Are you an immediate danger to yourself or others?"

Oh, I was most definitely a danger.

"I'm just having a rough night, and think I need to talk to someone. Think my meds might be off." The words were gravel, and I yanked at a tuft of my short, white hair to add emphasis.

She exhaled a strained breath from her nose. "All right. I'll page a nurse and security so we can get you checked in."

"Thank you," I managed to say while my mind spun through every scenario.

The gun at my side burned a fucking hole in my pocket.

No question, the guard was going to pat me down.

A bolt of chaos ricocheted through me as I calculated the actions I might have to take.

I didn't hurt innocents.

But I would do whatever it took to get Aria out of here.

To my left, the door buzzed, and a woman poked her head out. She sported a short bob of brown, curly hair and a warm, concerned smile on her face.

That was, until she saw me raging where I stood.

Fear flashed through her eyes, which had gone wide.

But that fear was different from usual.

Different from the natural warning people got that I was different.

Her attention dropped to her iPad, taking in the false information I had given.

"James Aragon?" The question wheezed from her mouth, confusion in her tone, like she already knew that wasn't my real name.

Every nerve ending in my body stood on end, and flames lapped at the edges of my sight.

"That's right."

The woman's brow twisted. "Are you sure?"

"Yeah?" I said it like she was the one who was losing it.

She cleared her throat and gave her head a harsh shake, as if she were trying to shun whatever had tripped her up.

"I'm Jill, the RN on staff tonight. Come on back, and we'll get your intake questionnaire filled out." She widened the door, and I could feel her frazzled nerves as I slipped by her and into the next room.

Here, it was sectioned off. There were three small holding rooms on the left and three rooms with desks on the right.

But the only thing that mattered was the second locked door at the very back. Heavy, reinforced metal.

The door that led to Aria.

My chest tightened into a fist, and the chaos spun and banged against the walls, fighting for a way to get out.

Clawing its way to her.

I came to a stop in the middle of the room, my gaze sweeping the area, gauging my next steps.

The nurse rounded on me, her brow furrowed as she looked at my face.

Eyes roving.

Searching.

"Sir, I'm afraid you might be in the wrong place." She kept her voice a whisper. Riddled with questions. "The adult facilities are on the property behind this to the north. You can gain access on Morris Street. I can have someone escort you, if you'd like."

Her words were weighted, and an awareness was seeping in.

The way she looked at me.

Like she knew me.

But I still had to play this right. I couldn't get careless.

"Not in the wrong place." The words were gruff, scraping like dull razors at the back of my throat.

My fingers itched to grab her key card.

"I'm seventeen," I forced out.

Bullshit, yeah.

I silently begged her to accept it.

"What is your name?" she suddenly asked beneath her breath, like she was trying to keep it from the woman who currently was tapping at a computer in one of the rooms on the right.

Urgency radiated from her, and alarm gusted through my senses.

"I already filled the information out." I gestured at the iPad she held in her hand. "James Aragon. Date of birth, May 17, 2005."

Her head shook, and she suddenly reached out and grabbed me by the wrist. Emphasis underscored the words. "No. *What is your name?*"

I felt like her stare was searing into me. Burning through the rubble. Like she might have a tap into the otherworlds.

I didn't have time to answer before the door behind us buzzed and a security guard pushed through, his words rushing out ahead of him. "Sorry to keep you waiting, Jill."

He'd been fully at ease when he'd come through. The second he caught sight of me, he was instantly on guard.

His free hand moved to the Taser at his side while he stood frozen in the doorway.

Darkness spilled in from behind him and into the bright lights that shone above, the silence so acute I heard the foreboding woven in its fibers.

"Is there a problem here?" His attention swung between us, gauging the situation.

The man was tall and too thin. I'd peg him in his midfifties. He was doing his best to appear fierce. Confident. Though I didn't miss the tremors that rolled through his body.

Irritation beat a path through my senses, the lure coming from behind that door growing intense.

Severe.

Overpowering.

It was almost impossible not to listen to it and force my way through. I shifted on my feet, trying to keep the turmoil at bay.

The echo of her spirit.

The shout of her soul.

Pax. Pax. Pax.

I swore I could hear her pleading my name.

Jill turned to wave him off. "No, we just need a moment of privacy, Will. Thank you. If you'd step out for a second."

The frown he developed promised it went against protocol. "Are you sure? I'll be—"

A crash suddenly echoed from somewhere in the recess of the facility. Metal clattered against a hard floor, reverberating off the walls and traveling the hall in a flurry of desperation.

One second later, a scream pierced the air. "Help!"

Her spirit pierced and slayed, and the sparks glinting beneath my skin burst into flames.

At the commotion, the security guard whirled around.

I didn't hesitate to take the opportunity.

I acted.

Grabbing the edge of the door he had propped open with his body, I swung it open wider and shoved him out of the way.

It took him the flash of a second to realize that I was pushing around him, and a hand darted out to try to grab me by the arm. "What the hell do you think you're doing? You can't go in there."

I didn't have time for wavering.

Spinning around to face him, I cracked my elbow down on the top of his shoulder in the same motion, hoping it would incapacitate him enough to buy me some time.

It dropped him straight to his knees.

"Oh my God." Shock gasped out of the nurse, and her hands flew to her mouth. The iPad she'd been holding toppled to the ground just as there was another crash reverberating from somewhere down the hall.

My eyes met hers for one knowing beat before I swiveled and ran.

Ran toward the one person on Earth who'd ever meant anything.

My boots pounded on the hard floor, driving the mayhem higher.

A thud, thud, thud racing in time with the battering of my heart.

Aria's terror rode a sharp edge, cutting through the suffocating atmosphere like razors dragging across my flesh.

Footsteps clattered behind me.

"Hey, you can't go in there! Stop!"

Fuck.

The security guard had gotten to his feet, footfalls slamming against linoleum as he began to chase me.

Energy screamed.

Dark and alive.

Frantic, I pushed myself as hard as I could go, skidding around a corner as I hooked a left down a second hall, intuitively knowing she was in that direction.

My heart thrashed. A violent battering against my ribs. Fear and determination clotted out all other senses.

Up ahead, a man stumbled out from a door on the left.

"You bitch whore," he wheezed as he clutched his face. He was bent in half, hissing at the presence that glowed from inside the room.

In the bare light, I could see he wore blue scrubs, was short and thick, his blond hair buzzed.

Recognition slammed me.

I'd seen him before. Through Aria's eyes when I'd found her in the Ghorl's vile, nefarious mind. I had seen her huddled in fear, witnessing it through this bastard's eyes.

I didn't hesitate.

I pulled out my gun.

As much as I wanted to scatter his brains across the floor, there were a few too many witnesses for that, so I clocked him with the butt of it on the back of his head instead.

A roar of agony and rage tore from him, the bastard caught unaware, so held in his depravity he didn't have the first clue what was coming for him.

It flattened him on the floor, the piece of shit writhing where he moaned.

Orders rained from behind: "Get down! On your knees! I'm warning you, young man, if you don't get to the floor, you will suffer the consequences."

The security guard shouted it through chattering teeth.

In my periphery, I could see he had his Taser out.

I was only vaguely aware of his voice.

A voice that grew louder with the commands he kept issuing.

Because I was held.

Caught in the shattered gasp that rode on the thrumming atmosphere.

Volatile.

Flammable.

Explosive.

Because a girl stood just inside the room.

Frozen.

Eyes the same color as mine stared back.

Jet-black hair and pale-white skin, and a face forever imprinted in my dreams.

"Aria."

Chapter Sixteen

ARIA

Shock pinned me to the spot as I stared at the man who had to be an apparition.

An appearance of the impossible.

A dream that had come to life, manifested before my eyes.

Ragged breaths heaved from my lungs, my mind at war with disbelief and a crushing hope that I was terrified to put my faith in.

Time stopped as we stood there . . . just . . . looking at each other, and I had to wonder if I'd succumbed.

If this was eternity.

If the man who'd wrapped his hands around my throat with the wicked gleam in his eyes had actually snuffed out my life and my spirit was now instead convincing me of an alternate reality.

Of this.

The cognizant piece of me understood my heart still beat, and I hadn't been able to keep my hands on the vile, depraved monster long enough to bind the darkness I could feel seeping from his soul.

But I'd drawn blood. I'd known it. Had felt his hatred burn so hot as he'd stumbled back, crashing into the wall and sending a tray scattering across the floor as he spat his toxic vitriol like barbs that couldn't catch.

Now a dull hum buzzed in my ears, my feet heavy and my knees weak, as I looked at the man who seemed to be caught in the same moment as I.

One second set to "pause," where only he and I existed.

Muted light from the hall spilled over him. His hair was a shock of white. Face hewn in severe cuts and harsh angles.

But it was the pale-gray eyes I'd only dreamed of seeing in this realm that made me feel as if I were looking at my truth for the first time.

A deep, toiling sea.

Fathomless.

Boundless.

"Pax?" His name whispered from my mouth in a tumble of confusion. As soon as the sound hit the air, time sped up again, whipping back to the here and now.

Shouts echoed down the hall. A desperate intensity vibrated the atmosphere and spun it into mayhem.

"I told you, on your knees. Now. Don't make me fire this thing."

Jenny had scrambled upright on her bed, and she clutched her blanket to her chest as if it were a shield. Terror coated her being, her eyes wide in the darkness that covered the room in a cloak of shock.

"Aria, what's happening? Oh God, what's happening?" Panic wisped from her words, and she gaped at Pax, shocked to find the man from my drawing standing in our doorway.

"It's okay, Jenny. Don't be afraid," I told her—because somehow, I wasn't. "Remember that you're good and amazing and you're going to be okay."

Pax's attention whipped down the hall as the voice continued to carry: "On your knees! It's the last time I will warn you."

Then those gray eyes were back on me, and he stretched out his hand. "Aria, we have to hurry."

The sharp edge of his voice knocked me out of the stupor, and every molecule in my body snapped into action.

Running forward, I took the hand he had extended.

Energy streaked at the connection.

Staggering.

Light flashed behind my eyes and surged through my body when we touched. A shock wave that shot through me and shook me to the core.

But we didn't have time to stand there and process it.

Pax pulled me out into the hall, and his head swung in every direction as he calculated how to get us out of this.

Shouts and yells came at us from every side. A security guard stood at the head of the hall. His Taser was drawn, his stance one of protection, though I could physically feel him shaking with the horror of what was happening.

Three people were behind him, peering out from the barricade he'd created with his body. An older woman whom I didn't recognize, plus two nurses working the night shift, Jill included.

My stomach lurched when the vile man who'd sneaked into my room climbed to his knees, trying to get the rest of the way to his feet.

He swayed with the wickedness that oozed from his being, and I could almost hear the Ghorl raging in his mind, their commands for him to get up, to finish the job, to end me, as he wheezed, "You bitch. Little whore."

Pax lifted his free hand. A hand I hadn't realized was holding a gun. He brought it down hard at the base of the man's skull. A crack echoed through the air. The monster gave, his body jerking before he fell flat against the floor.

"Motherfucker," Pax spat before his attention whipped both directions, his jaw set tight as he realized the only way we could go was deeper into the facility.

"This way." He tugged at my hand, quick to step over the man. Bile burned in my throat as I hopped over him.

I struggled to keep up with Pax, who started to run, hauling me along behind him as the staff began to chase us.

My bare feet smacked against the cold, hard floor, and blood barreled through my veins. A thunder that raged and a chaos that trounced through me in a violent, hammering storm.

"I have you," Pax promised in the same rough voice I recognized all the way down to my soul.

Together, we raced down the hall with his hand firmly wrapped around mine. It was something we'd done so many times before, only this time, we were the ones being hunted and not the other way around.

"Stop!" The single word wobbled from the guard, the command ignored as Pax drove us faster.

My heart hammered.

Confusion, hope, and horror clanged with each erratic beat.

"Stop. Both of you. There is no way you're getting out of here, so don't make this harder than it has to be." The guard's voice was in the distance but growing nearer, and I could hear the clatter of multiple footsteps as the rest followed.

A crush of adrenaline and desperation hurtled down the hall and pressed at the walls.

"Aria Rialta, you must end this. You have no chance of getting out of here. You're only going to make it worse for yourself." The unfamiliar woman's voice carried, hooks that threatened to impale.

Other patients had begun to emerge from their rooms, and they stood gawking in their open doors, still half-asleep as they peered out into the commotion.

Their confusion turned into shouts, some of them cheering on the mayhem, while others shrank back into the safety of their rooms.

"Don't slow, Aria," Pax murmured quietly. Harsh with the plea.

We came up to the end of the hall, and Pax took a sharp right. We spilled into the open space of the cafeteria.

Here, it was darker, shadows filling the large area and crawling over the tables.

"This way." Pax tugged my hand as he started in the direction of the swinging door far across the room—until an orderly pushed out through it, obstructing our path.

We skidded to a stop, and the enormous man widened his stance and curled his hands into fists. His demeanor was hard, a threat ticking his muscles in aggression.

"No." Despair pitched in my chest. "Pax."

"I have you." Pax's words scraped low, and he shifted to face the direction we'd come, just as the guard came around the corner to fully box us in.

He edged forward, trembling as he cautiously encroached. The same group of three women were huddled behind him, peeking out from his sides.

"Do not move." The demand quivered from the guard's tongue. "Stay right there."

"I don't want to hurt you," Pax responded instead. His words cut through the tension like blades, a grim warning as he moved to stand in front of me. He kept the gun slack at his side, though I knew it was the one thing that kept the men from rushing for us.

Gulping, the guard inched forward. His voice cracked as he said, "Drop the gun to the ground, put up your hands, and get onto your knees. Slowly." The Taser trembled as he tried to hold it steady. "Right now. This is your last chance."

There was a sudden flurry of movement, a blur of pink before the guard's wrist was slammed into the sharp corner of the wall. He shouted in a wail of shock and pain, and the Taser toppled to the ground and slid across the floor.

Confusion bounded, and I blinked through the disorder.

Jill.

It was Jill.

Her eyes were wide with urgency as she shouted, "This way!"

She darted into the short hall to her left. The one that led to the door that opened to the fenced-in area where we had recess each morning.

Hope bloomed, and Pax didn't waver. He darted after her, and I raced to keep up.

"Jill, what are you doing? You'll lose your license for this," the older woman shouted.

The threat didn't sway Jill. She swiped her card and the door buzzed and unlatched. She tossed it open, and the three of us ran out into the frigid night.

Rain fell from the sky, icy darts that pelted my overheated skin, the cold instantly freezing my bare feet and shocking up my legs.

I refused to let it slow me.

We ran for the large metal gate that sat on the left.

Jill whirled toward us when we got to it.

Her expression toiled through a thousand emotions.

Dread.

Terror.

Conviction.

She looked to Pax as if she recognized him. "Promise me you will protect her."

"With my life." His answer was harsh.

She swiped her card and the gate buzzed open.

I could feel her sacrifice as she brushed her fingers down my cheek. She'd just ruined her own life for the sake of saving mine.

My spirit thrashed.

For the first time, someone *believed*.

"Be careful, brave girl," she murmured, her warm gaze intense.

Gratitude filled me to overflowing, and I had the urge to stop and hug her, but all I could give her was a rushed "Thank you."

Because a commotion suddenly burst behind us. My attention whipped over my shoulder to see the guard coming through the door with the orderly at his side.

"Hurry, Aria." Pax yanked at my hand, and I sent Jill a look I prayed conveyed everything I felt before we raced out into the lot.

Rain slanted from the darkened heavens. A dreary, icy gloom. Lights glinted through the mist, spilling a yellowed haze over the pavement and cutting into the murky shadows.

We raced across it, adrenaline coursing as we were chased.

Shouts clamored through the frozen air, and the older woman was screaming, "Stop them! Someone, stop them! Call the police!"

The guard fired his Taser.

I could feel the force of it cut through the air.

But he remained too far in the distance, and the barb just missed its mark of Pax's back.

We ran faster, pushing ourselves with all the strength we possessed, the same way we tracked through Faydor.

Without faltering or yielding.

Only this time, my human weaknesses followed me as we sprinted across the parking lot.

Sharp rocks cut into the soles of my bare feet, and pain lancinated up my legs with each desperate step I took.

I whimpered every time I splashed through icy puddles, the only relief that I found.

A sweet numbing effect.

Or maybe I was just completely in shock as Pax ripped open the door to an older car that was hidden at the edge of the woods that rose behind the lot.

In shock as Pax grated, "Get in and buckle your seat belt."

In shock as he ushered me into the passenger's seat and rammed his fist down on the lock on the door before he slammed it shut.

He blazed back around the front of the car, faster than when he'd been leading me, white hair striking in the glittering rays of dingy light that streamed from the lampposts.

Palms suddenly smacked on the passenger window, and I screamed as I turned to find the guard yanking at the handle and trying to rip open the door.

Pax jumped into the driver's seat. In a flash, he had the car started, and he shoved it into reverse and rammed on the accelerator.

The car shot backward, tires tearing and spinning on the wet, soft dirt. It knocked the guard to the ground, and I saw the expression on his face as he rolled, ending up on his stomach as he pushed onto his hands to stare at us through the spray of our headlights.

Disbelief and horror.

Pax shoved on the brakes at the same time as he shoved the car into Drive. It skidded and whipped around to face forward.

For a moment, it felt as if gravity had been lifted and I was floating through a weightless canopy. Not sure if I existed on this plane or another.

Then I gripped both the door handle and the dashboard when he gunned it, my body jolting forward, then crashing back to the seat. Tires squealed as we fishtailed the rest of the way across the lot.

He took a sharp right as we careened onto the wet, deserted road, then accelerated as we hit the pavement, and the tail end skidded far to the left before the car righted to the center.

And we flew.

In that same shock, I shifted to look at the man who clutched the steering wheel.

His jaw clenched.

Ferocity radiating from his skin.

And I knew there was nothing in this life that would remain the same.

Chapter Seventeen

ARIA

"Are you okay?" Pax's question sliced through the tension, eyes slanting between me and the road and the rearview mirror as we sped away from the facility.

The road blurred beneath us, and I whipped my attention over my shoulder to look behind us, too.

There was no movement beyond the rear window, and I flipped around to face forward, pressing my back into the seat and gasping for the oxygen I couldn't seem to find. "I . . . I think so."

A cloak of darkness rested over the Earth, and the heavens were heavy and low. A steady drizzle fell, and our headlights blurred through the murky fog.

Pax's fierce jaw clenched as he glanced in the rearview again before he made a quick right, the tires screeching as he peeled into a neighborhood, though he slowed his speed when he made another quick left before taking a right into a dark, empty alley.

My breaths were short and ragged, and I still clung to the door, sucking for air as I attempted to settle my heart, which rattled in my chest, to slow the furious pounding of blood that slugged through my veins.

My mind was disoriented, but my spirit was sharp.

Pax's breaths were just as harsh, and his eyes continually flicked up to the rearview mirror to ensure we weren't being followed. Tension bound the cab, lashes of energy striking through the cramped, enclosed space.

Heavy and ripe with questions I had no idea how to ask.

Unease rippled and blew.

It was as if now that the facility had disappeared behind us, neither of us knew where we stood.

Were able to process the line that had been crossed.

The rule that had been broken.

A fate that should never be.

The truth that we were here.

Alive and real and whole. No longer a figment or a fantasy.

It was surreal, being in someone's space, someone who knew you best, yet they still could be a complete stranger.

Familiar yet distant.

Unmistakable yet indiscernible.

A shiver rocked through me, my clothes drenched, and an icy chill sank down to saturate me to the bone.

Pax trembled, too, though I thought it might be from the aggression that still radiated from his flesh. The way his muscles flexed and bowed with a restrained power.

I drank him in.

He was so much the same as I knew him in Tearsith. A shock of white hair, cropped up high on the sides and longer on top. His jaw was edged in severity. Cheeks razor sharp, every angle of him so acute that I thought if I reached out and ran my fingertips over his face I might be cut.

The only things soft about him were his full, red lips, which stood out in stark contrast against his pale, pale skin.

He wore jeans and a worn leather jacket, his body long, hewn in a vicious strength that promised a different sort of wickedness than I'd ever known.

His brow was drawn, slanted with ferocity and tugging between his eyes as he made another right, carefully maneuvering us into an orchestrated maze as he wound deeper into the city.

I couldn't look away.

Here, I could see the brutalities that had marked us in Faydor.

A long scar cut through the right side of his face, starting up near his temple and extending down to his jaw. Another was puckered at the right side of his neck, hidden beneath the swirl of ink that rose out of his collar and climbed his neck.

Another was carved in at the side of his head, the hair no longer able to grow in that spot.

He looked as if he'd gone to battle a thousand times, a Viking warrior who'd run headlong into danger and had somehow made it out on the other side.

I knew firsthand that he had.

My gaze traced, moving to the only other exposed skin, his big hands that crushed the steering wheel in a viselike grip, also covered in tattoos, swirls and innuendos of the horrible atrocities we'd faced.

My stomach tilted. I could only imagine the rest that were hidden underneath.

"Are you hurt?" His gravel-cut voice curled through the silence, making me jerk, and a tiny sound escaped.

I blinked through the disquiet. "No. I don't think so."

He stole a glance in my direction. Those palest gray eyes slid over me, what should be black pupils a murky gray. He seemed to be taking stock as his attention raked over my dripping hair and soaked pajamas.

"I don't know if I can feel anything, if I'm being honest."

Or maybe I felt too much. Every sense alive but distorted by shock.

Another shiver rolled through my body.

"You're cold." He tried to turn up the heater, which still only blew cold air.

"I'll be fine."

He rolled his bottom lip between his teeth, his stare long, before he ripped his attention away and took a sudden sharp left.

He cut across the road and veered into a parking lot behind an apartment building, then whipped into a spot and shut off the engine.

He'd turned and had my face in his hands before I could process the movement. My frozen skin felt singed by the heat blazing from his palms. His pale eyes were wild, raving with hate. "Did he hurt you? Did that motherfucker get to you?"

My tongue stroked out over my dried, trembling lips, and I could barely speak around the thickness in my throat. "No . . . He tried. But I fought him off. Right before you came."

"God, I want to go back. End him."

"You can't," I choked out.

He blinked, his hands burning my face, the pad of his thumb brushing under the hollow of my eye. "I can't believe it's you."

Pax warred, his body a reel of uncertainty and indecision, before he jerked away and tossed open his door. "We have to go."

He was already around to my side of the car by the time I'd gotten unbuckled, and he ripped open the door and extended his hand.

My head spun, trying to keep up with the change in his demeanor. To catch up to this. To the threat that lurked all around.

Without saying anything, he began to guide me through the shadows, keeping low as we slunk between the cars.

"What are we doing?" I whispered, my thoughts jumbled, feeling as if I were being pulled in every direction.

"Changing cars."

My brow drew tight, and, as if he could feel the silent questions whirring through my mind, he murmured low, "This morning, I bought the car I came to get you in. Paid cash for it at a junk lot. I didn't want to take mine to the facility. We can't have them able to track us that way."

Air heaved from my lungs as reality began to sink in. We were in very real trouble. Pax was going to be seen as the criminal, when he'd been the one to come rescue me.

To save me from a man who'd been compelled to hurt me.

New fears dumped into my brain, tumbling and twisting as Pax hurried us across the lot.

As we approached a white two-door Infiniti, he let go of my hand, reached into his pocket, and pulled out a set of keys. He pushed the fob, and the car lights flashed as the locks disengaged.

He opened the passenger door, his attention raking over the area to make sure we were in the clear. "Get in."

I fumbled into the car and buckled, my entire being trembling as he climbed in on his side and started the engine. He turned the heat to high and reached over and turned on my seat heater.

A chill swept through me when the heat began to thaw my frozen flesh.

He pulled out of the lot and onto the road, keeping his pace controlled as he took a few turns before he got onto the freeway that would take us out of Albany, never letting his guard down as we traveled through the city where I'd grown up.

The place where my family lived.

The place I was leaving behind because I knew there would never be any way I could return to it.

It wasn't until the lights of Albany faded behind us that I finally braved the single question that had been plaguing my mind.

"How did you know?" It scraped through the friction that sparked and shimmered in the air.

For a moment, he didn't say anything before he blew out a rough sigh, a tattooed hand slanting through his hair in frustration. "You think I didn't know you were in trouble, Aria? That I didn't feel it?"

My chest squeezed. He'd heard me. Through time and space, he'd heard me. When no one else ever had, not even those surrounding me in the day.

Hesitation radiated from him, a quiet fury that bristled beneath his clothing. It made the leather appear to writhe over his body. His teeth gnashed before he spat, "Timothy saw the Ghorl. He saw its thoughts, Aria. He saw the truth of what that monster was sent to do. And I knew I had to come for you."

"It's forbidden for you to intervene." It was a whisper, my gaze out the windshield as the world sped by in a slurry of the woods' blackened greens that pressed close to the highway.

All the warnings we'd ever been given writhed in the space between us.

We would only bring ourselves danger.

Be more noticeable to the Ghorl and become targets.

Become vulnerable to their destructive thoughts.

Turn against one another.

A hand suddenly darted out to grab me by the side of the face. A gasp rocked up my throat, and I couldn't do anything but turn to him, to the force of his hold and the weight of his eyes. "Make no mistake, I would break every fucking rule in this world *and* in that one to keep you safe."

For a beat, we were locked on each other, the way we were in Tearsith.

Understanding passed through the connection.

A second later, Pax pried himself away and returned his attention to the road that blurred beneath us, the white lines whipping by as tension wound with his promise that continued to whisper in the cab.

My stomach twisted as I watched him.

The hard, harsh shape of him that was cut all the way down to his middle. To the darkest recesses where I could almost see his own demons play.

Trapped in a mystery of who we were and who we were supposed to be.

I fiddled with my fingers, then asked, "Where are we going?"

In pure agitation, he roughed a hand over his head again. "Away. Where I can keep you safe."

No question, we both were wondering if that was even possible.

I lifted my gaze to him. "I hate what I've gotten you into."

His head barely shook, and the tattoos on his throat rolled when he swallowed. "Don't you dare apologize, Aria. I was already there."

A sticky awareness climbed through my ribs and compressed my heart. "They're going to call the cops, and they're going to come for us."

It wasn't a question.

Pax's nod was clipped. "Yeah, they're going to come for us."

"Thank you." It was out, hanging in the turbulence that rippled between us.

He didn't respond to it; instead, he reached and squeezed my hand, something close to pain in his voice. "You should try to get some rest."

I wavered, and his hold tightened. "Everyone will already be in Faydor, so you won't have to explain anything to our family. Go. Rest. I'll be here when you wake."

I ran my hand up my arm, trying to chase away the thick dread that had settled into my marrow.

The consequence of what we'd done. While the other part of me rejoiced.

Unable to process that he'd come.

That he was there.

For the first time, I was next to the man whom I'd only imagined I could be with this way.

Real and alive and awake.

But that joy was short-lived. Because somewhere deep inside, I knew what it was going to cost.

Chapter Eighteen

ARIA

I jostled awake when the car shook over a new terrain, to the wisping shadows that came with the earliest hour of the day. The horizon hinting the barest gray.

I blinked to try to orient myself. To catch up to where I was and what had happened, although the events of last night would be impossible to forget.

The tires ground over the dirt lot of an old motel, and Pax quickly pulled his car around in front of a single glass door stamped with the words MOTEL REGISTRATION. He came to a stop, the engine still purring while the jagged beats of his heart filled the cab.

A silent thunder that reverberated the space and pounded through my bloodstream.

"Where are we?" I mumbled as I sat forward, fighting for full coherency.

"We just passed the Pennsylvania state line. We're in some blip of a town. Hoping no one will recognize us here."

I looked out the window at the motel. It was as if it hailed from another time. It was a single-story building, painted blue, with a sign out front flashing VACANCY in a jaundiced light.

His hard gaze scanned, searching the area before he put the car into park but left it idling. "Stay here and lock the doors. Don't open them until I come back."

I nodded. "Okay."

He hopped out, attention roving again, searching the shadows before he dipped through the entrance.

Unbuckling, I sat on the edge of the seat so I could better watch my surroundings.

Vigilance was the only thing that was going to save us, if that was even possible at all.

Five minutes passed before Pax came back out. He strode toward the car. There was no tearing my eyes from him as he wound around the front.

My heart panged with the forbidden love I'd always had for him, and my stomach twisted in the tiniest quiver of fear.

He was different here.

Of course he was. No doubt, I was different to him, too.

There was an unease that pulled between us, strangers drifting in that familiarity that would bind us for all our lives. A familiarity we were never meant to experience here.

He opened the door and slid back into the driver's seat.

His movements were stealthy and smooth.

The man was tall, his body lean, though I could almost feel the sinewy muscle bristle with strength beneath his clothes. Could sense the darkness that edged him in sharp severity.

Another shiver rolled down my spine.

There was something about him that was almost menacing.

Predatory.

Again, I was struck by how I felt like I recognized him all the way down to his soul but knew so little about him here. The glimpses into our everyday lives were shallow. Scraps we'd thrown together to form a patchwork picture of who we were while awake. Which I knew was how he'd found me, likely from when we were young, when we'd spent time in the safety of Tearsith. Playing and talking before everything had changed the night Pax had first descended into Faydor.

He put the car in Drive and wound around the side of the building. There was a long row of doors, the entire length fronted by angled parking spots. He slipped into the one in front of Room 12.

He shut off the engine.

"Wait right there."

He was out and around to my side in a blink, and he helped me out into the freezing cold. Dampness still saturated my clothes, my feet bare, and I felt him wince as he quickly ushered me to the door.

Metal scraped as he slid the old-style key into the lock, and once it gave, he reached in to flip on the light. He slunk inside, and I realized he had the gun drawn as he wove through the room, hugging the walls, checking every corner and niche.

I gulped.

Terrified it might be possible that the fiends had already found us here.

"It's clear," he rumbled.

I eased in.

The room was dank and stale. Two full beds covered in brown bedspreads sat against the left wall, and a television that should have been obsolete sat on a dresser across from them. A round table with two chairs was situated under the window, and the door to the bathroom was on the far back wall.

"I'll be right back," he told me as he slipped back out into a morning that broke at the cracks.

I nodded through the thickness, hating that I felt ill at ease, hating the tension that strained between us.

But I guess that was what happened when worlds collided.

There were fractures.

Pieces that didn't fit.

I wandered deeper into the room, trying not to cringe at the sharp sting elicited by the cuts I'd sustained on my feet. I was sure they were torn to shreds.

Pax returned with a duffel bag, which he tossed onto the bed closest to the window. He locked and bolted the door before he turned around and stared at me from across the space.

Energy pulsed.

Whipping through the small room as he watched me with those pale, pale eyes.

Awareness rippled across my flesh and lifted goose bumps on the nape of my neck.

Pax scrubbed a palm over his face. "You need to get out of those wet clothes and into a hot shower. You're shaking."

I was, but I didn't know if the cold had anything to do with it.

"A shower would be good," I agreed.

I finally tore myself from the grip of his gaze and waded through the discomfort and into the bathroom.

I stripped myself of the still-damp clothes and turned on the shower. It took a minute before steam filled the room, and the heated spray felt like tiny pinpricks of fire against my frozen skin when I stepped into it.

It took only a moment to get acclimated, and my entire body shuddered as I gave myself over to the warmth.

I let the water pound into my knotted shoulders, let it seep and soothe and wash away the terror of what I'd felt during the night.

Because I might not know the future or where we would go from here.

But for now?

For now, we were safe.

Turning off the shower, I stepped out, grabbed a thin white towel, and wrapped it around my body. I used another to dry my thick mass of hair the best I could.

I glanced at the pile of wet pajamas on the floor. The idea of putting them back on was less than appealing.

Blowing out a sigh, I dug my underwear out of the pile, found an old blow-dryer under the sink, and dried them enough that I could put them on.

Then I rewrapped myself in the towel and unlocked the bathroom door, inhaling a shaky breath as I thought of what was waiting for me on the other side.

But I couldn't tiptoe. Couldn't give in to the human side of me that swarmed with the flutter of butterflies in my belly. Couldn't give consideration to the millions of times I'd thought of us like this.

We had enough to worry about without me treading through awkwardness.

Enough trouble without my heart clutching in anticipation at seeing him again.

Only I froze when those pale eyes snapped up as I stepped out. I clutched the thin towel to my chest, feeling more exposed than I ever had in my entire life as his gaze raked over me from where he sat on the bed, digging through the duffel bag he'd brought in.

It was like it was the first time he'd given himself permission to look at me.

Like he was cataloging.

Categorizing.

Locking it away to memory.

The scars that were exposed and the tangle of my wet hair and the droplets of water that snaked over my shoulder and rolled down my arm.

He'd done it all in the flash of a second before he dropped his attention back to the bag, though he gestured with that sharp chin to the bed opposite him. "Sit."

I shuffled forward, trying not to wince with every painful step, still clinging to the towel as if it could shield me from the questions that whirled. As I fought with the urge to go to him, to touch the harsh angles of his face, to know him here the way I knew him in Tearsith.

But there was a barrier between us here.

An invisible chasm that gaped.

Still, I couldn't look at this man and ever believe that he could be a threat to me. That he could ever turn on me the way we'd been warned. That he could betray me the way Valeen had been scorned.

I came to the end of the bed, wavering where I stood.

His teeth gritted as he glanced up at me where I was a foot away. "How are you feeling?"

Uncertainty pinched my face. "I honestly don't know. This feels impossible. Like it isn't real. I keep thinking I've fallen into some strange dream."

He scoffed. "As if what we fall into each night isn't strange?"

My teeth gnawed at my bottom lip. "I know. The number of times I wondered if I really was crazy. If I'd made it all up. If you were real."

Tension bound his shoulders, and he didn't look at me as he continued pulling things from the bag.

"Do you regret coming for me?" I whispered. Trying to break through. God, how was I supposed to handle this? I'd ached to see him for so long, but I never could have imagined that it would feel like this.

"Why would you say that?" The question grated into the dense air.

"You seem angry."

He shocked me by whirling to face me. "Of course I'm angry, Aria. They locked you away in that place. Left you vulnerable. Some monster almost got to you. And now—"

His teeth snapped as he stopped himself from saying whatever had been on his tongue, and he turned back to the supplies he had laid out on the bed.

A tremor rolled beneath the surface of my skin.

As if he'd felt it, he sighed in regret. "Please sit, Aria."

My nod was slow as I sank onto the edge of the bed. "I'm going to be running for the rest of my life, aren't I?"

As short as that was likely to be.

Because we both knew my time would run out.

Pax roughed his right hand, which was tattooed with the gruesome face of a Kruen, over his head. The action was something I'd seen him do in Tearsith when he was upset, and it clearly carried over to here. "We don't know that."

"Don't we, though? I knew the second I bound that Kruen while awake that it set me apart. That the Kruen would take note and come after me. I'd never fathomed it could be a Ghorl. That they even really existed." I looked at him, unashamed to offer him the truth. "I'm scared, Pax."

I didn't want to be.

I wanted to be brave. I wanted to find the courage that I had in Faydor.

To fight.

But what had already happened had been terrifying, and I wasn't foolish enough not to know it was just the beginning.

Pax angled toward me, his raspy voice a murmur. "I know, Aria. It fucking scares me, too. But I'm here, and I'm not leaving you until I know you're completely safe."

"Ellis is going to—"

"You can't worry about what Ellis says or thinks right now." His words were shards of aggression, cutting me off. "Right now, the only thing that matters is getting you away from the dangers in Albany. We'll figure the rest out later."

Warily, I nodded, and he stood from the bed.

Towering.

Obliterating.

Stealing oxygen and reason.

My nerves scattered at his proximity, a frisson whipping through the room as he took the one step required to stand over me. White flames licked in the depths of his gray eyes as he looked down at me. I didn't realize he was holding a T-shirt until he muttered, "Here. Put this on."

Rather than handing it to me, he unfolded it and carefully worked it over my head.

I wound my arms into the armholes before he pulled it the rest of the way down.

The material swallowed me, and in an instant, I was surrounded by his scent.

Leather and soap and something deeper that whispered of masculinity.

As if his magic had been woven into the threads.

Or maybe it was just *him*.

His aura and his potency.

The one I'd found only in my dreams, who now was right there.

Alive and vibrating with an energy that was more powerful than anything I'd ever known.

I pulled the towel out from under the shirt and tossed it to the floor; then I tipped my face up to him, barely able to get the words off my thickened tongue. "Thank you."

Reaching out, Pax swiped the calloused pad of his thumb over the small scar at the edge of my mouth. "I was created to take care of you, Aria, and I would never turn on you."

A shiver rocked down my spine.

Before I could say anything, he'd torn himself away, turning his back as he pulled something from the duffel bag.

A second later, he was kneeling in front of me with a first aid kit. A flash of heat rolled through me when his hand curled around my ankle. He lifted my leg enough that he could inspect the bottom of my foot.

"You're hurt." It was close to a growl.

My laugh was ironic. "I've suffered much worse."

Gray eyes jumped to my face. Fury blazed in the roiling pools. "You shouldn't have to."

The air grew thick, so dense it was close to suffocating, and I struggled to breathe. "There have been so many times that I prayed for it to go away. That I'd be saved from the misery. And when I bound the Kruen awake . . . ?"

A tremble rolled.

Pax's or mine, I didn't know.

Softly, I continued to speak. "I'd thought . . . I'd thought it wasn't fair. That it was too much. That I couldn't bear it, and I begged Ellis for an answer. For a way to take it away." My tongue stroked across my dried lips. "But I know it's my purpose, Pax. I could never change that. And in the end, I wouldn't want to."

For a moment, he looked like he wanted to argue. Refute my claim.

Instead, he sat higher on his knees, his beautiful, furious face an inch from mine. "I won't let anyone hurt you."

It was an oath. Shards of broken glass.

I didn't know if I was brave or foolish for reaching out. But I trembled my fingertips over the scar that ran along the right side of his face.

His eyes squeezed closed, and his jaw clenched as if my touch caused him physical pain.

He remained there for a moment.

As if he were allowing himself to relish the connection before his powerful gaze opened to me. "My purpose is to take care of you, Aria. To protect you until we figure out how to keep you safe."

There was a warning behind it.

A rejection I understood, but one that still slayed.

We couldn't be together. Not the way I wanted us to be. This was temporary. And I had no idea about his life here.

Who he loved and who he held.

Here? He was all but a stranger to me.

Pain clutched my chest, this love I'd kept secreted away, throbbing from within and seeking a way out.

He began to tend to my feet, swiping an alcohol pad over the cuts before he applied an ointment.

"That should help," he murmured as he pushed to standing, though he remained right there, an inch away, his presence rippling over me in waves.

"Thank you." I could barely force it out.

His nod was slow. "You need to sleep. Rest so you can heal."

"And what about you?"

"I'm going to keep watch. Once you wake up, I'll sleep for a couple hours."

"Are you—"

"Don't worry about me, Aria," he said as he turned away.

Did he think that was possible? That he didn't count? That he didn't matter to me?

But I couldn't argue with him or make him see right then.

Exhaustion was setting in.

The lack of sleep and the weight of the fear catching up.

The adrenaline from earlier had drained, and it'd left my limbs heavy, my mind muddled with too many things.

Four days ago, I'd been a senior in high school, contemplating how I was going to leave my family once I graduated.

Heartbroken over leaving them behind but knowing it was the only way I might be able to live in any semblance of peace.

Now everything had changed.

The shaky facade of my normalcy rocked.

My foundation cracked.

Now on the run with a man I was never supposed to meet.

I shifted to pull the scratchy covers down and slid under them, facing away as I pressed my eyes closed.

I hovered there in the nothingness.

In that shimmery space between awake and asleep.

And the moment before my spirit detached, I heard Pax's whisper somewhere in the distance. "Happy birthday, Aria."

Chapter Nineteen

PAX

Light streamed through the cracks in the drapes, rays spearing into the dim light and covering her in glittering gold.

Her breaths were deep and long as she slept. As she found the peace that I so desperately wanted her to possess.

Rage threatened to close off my throat when I thought about not knowing how long that would last.

I scrubbed an agitated hand over my face. How the fuck would I ever be able to give that peace to her?

For hours, I'd watched her sleep, sitting on the side of the shitty twin bed, my stomach in knots as I contemplated what all this meant.

Finally, I'd started to pace the small room because I couldn't remain sitting still. Thinking if I kept moving, I could find some clarity. An answer. A solution to get her out of this.

Anxiety tripped through my bloodstream.

I'd had one singular goal in mind when I'd left Las Vegas three days ago.

Get to Aria and get her out.

But there hadn't been a whole lot of time to contemplate what we would do after.

Running seemed the only prudent answer.

The problem with that was, whatever you were running from always had a way of catching up to you. And no matter where we went, evil would lurk in every corner.

Wickedness covered this Earth in a shroud that humans were blind to.

But I saw it clearly.

Every night and every day.

I knew the sickness. Knew the depravity.

I didn't only hunt it in Faydor. I hunted it while I was awake.

It'd been my sole purpose since I'd understood what this calling meant.

Now my gaze slanted to Aria. To the purpose I should have known would be mine all along.

The tiniest moan murmured from between her lips as she shifted from her back and rolled onto her side, leaving her face fully turned toward me.

I guessed what I'd been most unprepared for was what had slammed into me the moment I saw her.

The way the protectiveness had pulsed, a blast hitting me so hard that it'd shattered the boundaries of the way I'd seen her before. It had been my own thoughts that veered in a direction I couldn't let them go when I first saw her in the flesh.

My gut had tangled in a need I should not feel.

Hungry for something that I knew better than to ever take.

It wasn't like I hadn't known she would be a beautiful woman. But I'd convinced myself that I could never see her that way, even though it'd grown harder to keep my thoughts from drifting that way over the last year.

It'd become impossible when she'd been standing in front of me.

Whole and in the flesh.

Knocking the fucking breath from my lungs. And when she'd reached out and touched me with those tender fingers? I'd nearly come undone.

I gave a harsh shake of my head to stop the thoughts from spiraling. From devolving into indecency.

I knew the warnings. The tales that had been given. How Valeen had loved Kreed, only he'd desired her power more. His greed to rise above her had cut them in two, and that sundering had created Faydor, the Kruen his offspring.

We'd been told that as Valeen's children, we would suffer the same consequence. That our duty to our Nol was only to fight the evils of Kreed, and anything beyond that would lead only to destruction.

Even though there was no part inside me that could ever imagine turning on her, I couldn't take that chance. Couldn't allow my thoughts to go that direction.

My responsibility was protecting her.

That was it.

I paced back to the window, and I used the barrel of my gun to nudge back the drape an inch so I could peer out.

I'd already done it a hundred times.

Ensuring it was clear.

My nerves edged into a frenzied chaos that I knew better than to try to shake.

I squinted against the blinding light, the winter sky clear and crisp.

I scanned our surroundings.

There'd been little movement since we'd gotten here, the motel mostly quiet. There were only three other vehicles in the spaces in front of the motel rooms.

On the opposite side of the lot was a diner. It was busier there, and a handful of cars and pickups were parked in front.

Two semitrucks sat in an open field in between, and I'd seen one of the drivers amble into the diner an hour before.

The other I had yet to see.

Another of those soft moans echoed from behind me. I swore I could feel the air stir as she shifted. Could feel her presence caress over my flesh like the greedy brush of fingertips.

My teeth ground as I turned to look at her.

Aria sat up, and the covers slipped down around her waist. My gray tee draped over her tall, slender frame.

Her long, black hair rained around her, though it was a matted, tangled mess. The midnight locks only made her pale skin seem paler, only it glowed, vibrant in the bare rays that flooded the room.

Glinting sparks that grazed the defined angles of her face.

She was a clash of severe and soft.

Her cheekbones high and her nose straight.

Her plush mouth contrasted her acute edges, a pink bow of temptation, her chin kissed with a dimple.

But it was those eyes that matched mine that nearly did me in.

The way they watched me like they could see through to the deepest places inside me.

Into places I didn't allow people to go.

But this was Aria we were talking about, and I didn't know how to stand in the weight of who she was and who she could never be.

"Hey," I managed to grumble.

"Hi," she whispered. Uncertainty bound her brow, and there was no missing the unease cut into her consciousness.

"How do you feel?" I asked.

Her head barely shook, and she blinked at me, gaze so intent I thought she was trying to see right through me. "Like I woke up in a world that isn't supposed to exist."

"It's your world now, Aria."

Swallowing, she dipped her chin. "I know."

"Was any of our family in Tearsith?"

Her head shook. "No. I was alone."

"Good. I wanted you to rest."

"I did."

We wavered in that apprehension for a few seconds before she looked up at me. "You should do the same now."

"No point in it. I won't be able to sleep. We need to get you something to wear and something to eat; then I think we'd better be on our way." Sitting idle would only make us easier targets. We needed to keep moving.

Concern edged into her expression. "But you're exhausted."

"I told you before that you don't need to worry about me."

Soft disbelief filled her features. "Don't ask me not to worry about you, Pax. You know that's not possible."

I swallowed around the lump in my throat, unable to give her an answer, to open my mouth and give voice to this thing that swelled around us, a current so fucking strong it held the power to drag me to the depths of the darkest sea.

I glanced back out the window to the calm that still remained on the other side. "There's a store across the street. I'm going to see if I can find anything for you to wear. Don't open this door for anyone, okay?"

She nodded again. "I won't."

Her words were thin—and shit, I hated the pressure that strained between us, but falling into comfort wasn't going to do either of us any good.

"I'll be back as quickly as I can." I tucked my gun into the waist of my jeans, hiding it under my tee before I pulled on a coat and slipped out the door. My stomach was in knots at the thought of leaving her for even a second.

I rattled the handle, making sure it was secure, before I jogged across the dirt lot, figuring it'd be faster to go by foot.

There was no shaking the sticky sense that crawled over me.

The urge to return to her.

To stand by her.

A lure that called for me to return to her side.

It was going to be a fucking problem.

With a break in the traffic on the two-lane road that cut through the desolate town, I ran across it toward the small discount store situated in a rundown strip mall on the other side.

A bell jangled overhead when I tore open the door. The eyes of the woman behind the counter went wide when she saw me. Alarm blanching her skin white at the sight of me.

I ignored her.

I was used to it.

The way people shifted on the disquiet that infiltrated the air because they knew there was something about me that was off.

Wrong.

Inhuman.

Most dropped their gazes. Unable to look me in the eyes. Turned away. Crossed the street when they saw me coming.

Others seemed drawn to it, feeding off the morbid curiosity and the fear that spiked their blood with a heady rush of adrenaline when I got into their space.

No matter their reaction, they all knew I was dangerous, but none of them had a clue what the fuck that really meant.

I scanned the store. It basically stocked a little bit of everything. Housewares and toiletries, cleaning supplies, some packaged food. Clothing and shoes ran along the far side.

I moved quickly down the aisles. There wasn't much of a selection, but I grabbed whatever I could. Based on the way Aria swam in my shirt, on the way I knew her, the way she was so much the same and so goddamn different than she was in Tearsith, I surmised she wore a small.

She was close to being too skinny.

Like this reality had worn her thin.

Even though every part of her radiated with a bridled strength. Like here, her ferocity had remained untapped, but it might come ripping out at any moment.

I found some leggings and tees, underwear, some copycat Vans, and a package of fuzzy socks. Two sweatshirts. Then I headed to the toiletries section and piled whatever shit I could get into my arms, and on my way to the register, I snagged a green duffel printed with You've got a friend in Pennsylvania from an endcap.

Doubtful.

I could feel the stare of the cashier tracking me the whole time, and she eased back from the counter as I strode her way. I dumped the pile onto the counter. The whole time, I kept looking over my shoulder, out the panes of glass to the motel across the street, ready to go flying in that direction if the energy shifted even a fraction.

"Will that be everything?" The woman's voice shook as she eyed the items.

"Yeah."

She kept fumbling and trembling as she scanned everything while I stood there itching like a beast, the urge to get back to Aria close to overwhelming.

"Your total is $173.57." She basically issued it to her feet, the discomfort seeping from her so thick that I felt sorry for her.

But what the fuck was I going to say?

Spit out that I wasn't going to hurt her?

That it was my job to protect her?

Digging into my back pocket, I pulled out my wallet and counted out $200 worth of twenties. I tossed them on the counter before I grabbed the plastic bags she'd filled and strode for the door.

Surprise echoed from behind me, and finally she called when I got to the door, "Don't you want your change?"

"Keep it," I threw out, voice rough, pushing out and heading for the motel. Needing to get to Aria.

The dull hum I'd always felt somewhere at the back of my brain screamed.

It was the same one that had led me to her in Albany.

A compass that existed somewhere in my spirit.

One that promised there wasn't a place she could go that I wouldn't find her.

I'd always thought that it'd been another messed-up consequence of being who I was. Human but . . . not. The constant noise in my head that so often had made me feel like I was losing it.

Now I got that it was Aria.

She was the sound.

The drum.

The chaotic, frenzied song that beat inside me.

I ran across the street and went directly to the door. Relief heaved from me on the breath that I'd been holding when I found her sitting on the side of the bed, raking her fingers through the matted locks of her black hair.

I tossed the bags onto the end of the bed. "You won't be winning any fashion awards, but I found a few things."

She choked out a small surprised laugh as she peeked into the bags before she peered up at me with the tiniest smile hinting on her mouth. "I'll have you know I only wear name brands."

Air huffed from my nose, and something in the hardened cavity of my chest cracked. Surprised that she found any lightness or ease in the middle of this mess.

"Is that so?" I played along.

"That's right. These are not going to do." She pulled out the white canvas shoes and waved them like proof.

"Always knew you'd be a princess." My haggard voice had somehow pitched into a tease.

Her eyes widened in a razzing challenge. "A princess? Are you trying to offend me? Tell me that's not what you imagined when you woke up every day and thought of me."

Every molecule in my being softened as I stared at her. This woman who was barely more than a girl, but the things she'd faced in this twisted life shackling her with more horrible experiences than any one person had ever suffered before her.

"Maybe that's what I hoped. That you were a princess living in a castle. Safe and protected."

Any playfulness that had been in her expression drained. "But it's not been that way for either of us, has it? And I can't help but wonder what that looked like for you."

Sincerity wove into her words, this care that slipped through me in a way that I couldn't let it.

Aria understood more than she should, like she recognized what had been carved inside me.

This loneliness.

The solitude.

I'd learned to find comfort in it. Knew it was for the best. Getting close to someone only hurt you in the end, and I could afford no attachments.

Could trust no one.

Aria's teeth plucked at her bottom lip, so fucking pretty, so fucking real.

The hollowed-out hole inside me throbbed.

I should have looked down, turned away, except her expression shifted, and I was trapped when it twisted into awe.

"Thank you, Pax. For this." She hugged the shoes to her chest, and she swallowed hard. "For coming for me. For fighting for me. For putting yourself on the line for me."

With a gentle shake of her head, she blinked. "I know what this sacrifice means. How great it is. That it is *too* much." She clutched the shoes tighter. Emphasis poured from those plush, pink lips. "And to know that you heard me? That you heard me in my torment? That you heard me calling for you? I don't—"

She clipped off, her brow pinching before she was whispering in reverence, "I didn't think it was possible. I never hoped to think it was possible that you'd know. That you could find me. That you could feel me."

A tremble rolled through her body. "You saved me. I don't know what would have happened had you not come."

My hands curled into fists.

I had to remind myself that this was temporary.

Still, I moved forward, took her by the chin, and stared down at the one face that had ever meant anything in my life, the one that had been marked in my mind and imprinted in my soul, and made a promise that I was forbidden to make. "I will always come for you."

Chapter Twenty

ARIA

The diner wasn't busy, Pax and I the only patrons in the restaurant other than two booths that were occupied and the solitary man who sat at the bar, sipping from an endless cup of coffee.

I shifted on the red pleather upholstery, the stiff material creaking beneath my weight, and I fiddled with the handle of my coffee mug as I stared at the man across from me as if I could sort him out.

Dig through the hard layer that lined his being.

Morning light poured in through the window, casting a spotlight on the harsh angles of his face as he studied me. He was somehow slung back in the seat, though he had both hands wrapped around a mug that sat on the table.

Just looking at him made my heart skitter, pitching with errant, extra beats.

Everything about him was menacing. A warning to keep your distance.

But God, I wanted to be closer.

He'd removed his coat, and tattoos covered every inch of his exposed flesh, each painted in horrors, some in color and others in all black. It was as if he'd used his body as a diary, a place to record his darkest secrets.

The scar that cut through the right side of his face only made him appear more terrifying. Proof that those secrets were dark and gruesome.

But I knew it was those keen, tormented eyes that set him apart from anyone else.

Labeled him as something to be feared.

"What are you thinking right now?" I suddenly whispered, pushing closer to the table that separated us.

Pax let go of a disbelieving chuckle. "That I can't believe you're sitting across from me."

Heat flooded my cheeks as a rush of warmth skidded through my veins. "I can't believe it, either."

"Looking at you sitting there is like I got an answer for every single question I've ever had," he admitted.

I diverted my gaze, and I fiddled with the fork that sat on my napkin. "I know. It's like . . . the fear that I'd forever harbored that I was wrong in some way? That my makeup was distorted? It's gone."

Disquiet gusted across Pax's face, and his fingers, which were inked with an innuendo of the vapor in Faydor, twitched around his mug. "But this new fear is bigger."

Air puffed from my nose as I lifted my attention back to him. "And it's met with just as many questions. But I . . ." I paused, unsure if I should say it, if I should admit the way he made me feel. "But it doesn't feel so lonely anymore."

Regret tightened his expression, the truth that this was fleeting.

We both jumped when our server was suddenly standing at the side of our table. She glanced between us in an apology for interrupting as she topped off our coffees. "Your food is almost up. Is there anything I can get you in the meantime?"

"No, I think we're fine, thank you," I told her, keeping my gaze low as I barely glanced at her, trying to remain as inconspicuous as I could, even though I got the sense it was an impossibility.

I doubted there was a single person in there who hadn't noticed us.

She dipped her head and scurried away.

"Have to give her credit . . ." Pax's deep voice cut through the air. "She barely flinched when we first sat down."

"What do you think goes through their minds when they see us?" I whispered it. A secret only we could share.

He shrugged a shoulder, though it didn't come close to being blasé. "People always fear the unfamiliar. What doesn't make sense to them."

I had so many things I wanted to ask him. What his life was like. Where he came from. Who he was. But he scanned out the windows again toward the road, tensing when a Highway Patrol rolled by.

Worry thickened my throat. "Are they looking for us?"

Agitation twitched at the edge of his jaw, and he seemed to war before he spoke. "While you were getting changed, I searched for news articles. It's all over the place in Albany. Mostly pictures of you. When you were younger and a few more recent. A statement from your parents asking for help to find their mentally unstable daughter."

Sorrow bound my being. The swelling kind that made me feel as if I might drown in it. I could almost feel the distinction of my mother's pain. Her worry and her grief calling out to me from across the miles that separated us.

God, how could I turn my back on her? Make her worry this way?

Pax continued, "Cameras got a shot of my profile. They're looking for the car we ditched. First reports had it labeled a kidnapping."

I winced. How were we going to survive when threats were coming at us from every direction?

He scraped a palm down his face. "That nurse, though? The one who helped us?"

"Jill."

Gratitude swelled.

His nod was clipped. "She made a statement that you'd been unsafe there, that a janitor had developed an obsession with you, and you'd run away with a trusted friend."

Another rush of gratitude filled me, this virtual stranger who had put herself on the line for me.

Believed in me.

"That doesn't mean we're not wanted, though, and the way I went in isn't going to help things."

"It was the only thing you could do."

"Not saying I regret it. It's just something that isn't going to stack in my favor."

My lips tugged down at the sides. "You're the bad guy in this situation."

Incredulous laughter rolled through him, low and dark. "I am the bad guy in many situations, Aria."

He kept alluding to it. The truth that I didn't know him here. That he was as dangerous as he looked.

I'd forced myself to sit back from the lure of it when the server approached, carrying our order.

It did nothing to shatter the connection that strummed between us, a constant hum in my veins and a prodding from somewhere in the recesses of my soul. I was sure that I did know him, in every way that mattered.

"Here we go. Three eggs over medium with sausage and white toast." She set a large plate in front of Pax. "And a Belgian waffle with strawberries and whipped cream for you."

My stomach rumbled and my mouth watered as she placed the towering goodness onto the table. It wasn't until then that I realized I really hadn't eaten in days. Not since before I'd been admitted to the facility.

It felt like an eternity from then.

"Thank you," I told her.

"My pleasure. Anything else I can get for you?"

"I think we're good."

"Just let me know if you need anything else."

I watched her walk away, and when I looked back at Pax, I found him staring at me. The slightest smirk hitched at the edge of his mouth.

"What?" I asked him.

"Are you eating dessert for breakfast?" The tease played across his features.

I liked it too much. Him looking at me that way.

"It's my eighteenth birthday. I think I'm allowed."

And that impenetrable stone that normally hardened his expression had gone gentle. "I think you're more than allowed, Aria. You deserve so much more than this."

"I guess if there's anyone I could share my eighteenth birthday with, it would be you."

My mother's face flashed behind my eyes. My sister. My brothers. What were they doing now? Was my mother pacing? Was she driving her minivan around the city? Was she on her knees?

My eyes squeezed closed with the weight of it.

"My mom wanted to take me to my favorite restaurant and for us to go ice-skating this weekend." I admitted it quietly.

It felt like I was letting go of a dream. But I'd already known I had to leave. That I couldn't stay under their watch, causing them pain.

Affliction carved through Pax's features, and he sat forward a fraction. "I'm sorry."

A single tear got free, and I swatted at it. "I just . . . can't stand the thought of her worried about me. Can't stand her thinking that I'm . . ."

I trailed off, choking over the torment.

Pax stretched his hand over the table and set it over mine.

"Wish it was different," he said.

"I know. I do, too." But I doubted he knew how much different I wished it could be. "So what do we do now?" I asked.

"First and foremost, we have to keep you safe. Keep moving. Stay one step ahead of both the authorities and any Kruen or Ghorl who might seek to do you harm. Beyond that, I think we need to find out why this is happening to you. How you're healing people in the day. If there's anyone else like you."

My brow furrowed. "How do we do that?"

Pax blinked through this frustration. "I can't believe that these bare specks of information about how we've come to be is it. I mean, fuck, we go to sleep and end up somewhere else to fight against all evils in the world? And we're just supposed to believe we were randomly chosen to do it? I have never been able to wrap my mind around it."

"Yeah, I've thought about it many times, too. It's always felt like a bad dream—all except for the scars I wake up with."

His nod was measured, and he took a bite of his eggs, chewing slowly before he wiped his mouth with a napkin. "Don't you find it strange that there's never any mention of us in society? That there's no history here? That no one has noticed and talked about us? Written about us? Even if it was chalked up to mythology?"

We knew from teachings that we weren't completely rare. There were many other Laven families like ours. Each drawn together to their own sanctuaries and descending into Faydor in their given times.

Awareness sat heavy on my chest. "It's because we've been sworn to secrecy. Told to never speak of it to humans."

Except I'd done it. Many times over. Unable to keep the truth of who I was from bursting out of me.

"I have a hard time believing no Laven in all of history didn't break that law," Pax challenged.

"Like I did . . . with my parents."

"Yeah," he said.

"There has to be something out there. Something that could help us," he added.

I realized I hadn't told him my experience when Ellis had led me to the stream. "Ellis took me to the stream to seek Valeen."

Surprise flashed through his expression. "Did you hear her? See her?"

None of our family ever had. It had always been believed that she spoke to us through *The Book of Continuance*. That everything we needed, we would find there.

Somehow, Ellis had considered that I might be able to do it.

"I'm not sure. I heard a vague, indistinct whisper."

"What did she say?"

"That only I had the strength to defeat this evil."

"What evil?"

Uncertainty billowed through my spirit. "I'm not sure. The Ghorl, I guess."

He sighed in frustration. "There has to be something. Something more than the little information we've been given."

I took a bite of my waffle, contemplating before I asked, "What are you hoping to find?"

His left shoulder hiked toward his ear. "I don't know. A clue. Something that could give us any insight into you. How it's possible that you bound a Kruen while awake. You're unlike anything we know."

Pax hesitated, regret glittering in the white flames of his eyes.

My head tipped to the side as I frowned. "What is it?"

He warred, then said, "Ellis said he'd read in the book a mention of there being Laven who had greater powers than others, and there was . . ." He hesitated before he added, "There was a legend passed down from his elder of there being someone like you long ago."

My stomach lurched. "Why would he never have spoken of it before? In all our teachings?"

"I'm guessing because there were no others like us. That it seemed an anomaly, and he didn't want to add a new burden to those we already carried."

A new burden.

I felt the weight of it then.

The dread that dimmed Pax's expression. The aggression that lined his jaw.

"Tell me," I demanded. The last thing I could handle was him keeping things from me.

He inhaled a deep breath before he leaned forward. "He said she was hunted because of her powers. Because she became such a threat to the Kruen."

He left out what was abundantly clear.

They had ended her.

His hand was suddenly squeezing mine from over the top of the table. "But I promise you, I won't let that happen to you. I will find a way to stop this. Once we put more distance between us and Albany, we'll find someplace to research. See if we can uncover anything that might help us. Whatever it takes, I'm going to make sure nothing happens to you."

I turned my hand so I was holding his, hanging on because I didn't know how to process all this.

I'd known deep inside that I would be hunted because of these powers. Powers that I had no idea where they'd come from. But there was something else altogether about getting the confirmation this way.

My spirit wept for the Laven who'd had to suffer it, wept for the loss I would soon sustain.

My mother's face flashed through my mind again.

She would be devastated, destroyed when I was found. And she would never understand.

Regret churned through me, the pain of leaving her tormented this way.

"I promise," he reiterated before he unclasped his hand and turned back to picking at his food.

He and I fell into a strange, disoriented comfort after that, slowly eating, processing, trying to come to terms with the place we'd found ourselves in.

Once we finished, our server left our bill. Pax pulled out a wallet that was stuffed with cash and placed two twenties onto the slip.

I eyed it. I had nothing. I was completely dependent on him.

"Do you have a job you're supposed to be at?"

A dark chuckle rolled out of him as he slid from the booth. "No, Aria, I don't have a job that I need to be at. Come on. We should get out of here."

I wavered in the questions that rushed at me.

Insecurities and uncertainty had me shoving them down, and I pushed from the booth.

I tried not to shiver when he placed his hand on the small of my back.

It didn't work.

Not when every time he touched me it felt as if I were being zapped. Charged with the impossible. This need I'd never experienced before, whipping like a storm inside my belly.

I was a fool for even allowing the thoughts. We had so much more riding on this than whatever attraction I felt.

But this was Pax.

Pax.

The one. The one who had forever possessed me.

He guided me through the restaurant. Tension radiated from his body, his attention continually scanning, calculating everything as we passed.

I did, too, furtively peeking at each person. The thoughts that swarmed them grew louder the closer I got to them.

The struggles.

The grief.

The hopelessness.

I wanted to reach out but knew I couldn't do it, that we couldn't afford to draw any more attention to ourselves than we already had.

We moved along the bar, and my regard traced over the old man who was sitting there. Loneliness radiated from him, a constant vat that dragged him to the depths. We kept moving, and I made eye contact with another man who'd just slipped onto a stool.

Short, blond hair with brown eyes, maybe in his midforties. He gave me a curious smile, one I didn't return, and Pax hurried us out the door and into the frigid day.

The blue sky glowed white overhead. Painted in a cold winter clear. I shivered in the break of it, and Pax urged me forward, guiding me around the side of the building to head back toward the motel room.

Only I stalled out, gulping around the sorrow that possessed me again. Unable to take another step until I addressed it.

His powerful presence covered me from behind.

Almost oppressive in its watch.

I turned to him, trying not to allow the sight of him to punch me in the gut again, trying to rein in everything that I'd felt for him for so long.

But looking at the one who burned like a beacon in your soul and facing them in an entirely different reality was hard to do.

"I have to somehow get in touch with my parents," I told him, my decision firm. "Let them know I'm safe."

"Safe, Aria?" Disbelief pinched Pax's eyes, his coarse voice scraping my flesh.

The energy he emitted crackled as he slowly took a step forward.

A semitruck rumbled by on the road, sending dust billowing through the air. Pax spoke through the scatter of debris. "You're not safe. None of this is safe. And the only thing calling them will do is make the situation worse."

He was right. I knew it. But knowing it didn't matter.

I couldn't leave my mother in torment.

"I can't go on, knowing my mom is terrified for me, Pax. I can't pretend like I don't know that she can't function because the only thing she can think about is me. I can't pretend my brothers and sister aren't being affected. I can't."

Pax edged even closer, speaking around gritted teeth. "You're running because of them. Because they locked you away because they don't understand you. They don't understand you and they never will. You have to let them go."

His words were harsh. Almost cruel in their delivery. As if it were the only way he could get through to me. But he didn't understand these pieces of me, either.

"I love them."

It was simple, and the way his jaw clenched made me sure he didn't understand.

He'd never experienced it here.

And that nearly killed me, too.

"I can't just forget them, and you can't ask me to."

For the longest time, he stared at me like he wanted to argue.

Finally, he looked to the ground. "Goddamn it, Aria."

He inhaled through his nose, agitation lighting him up before he pulled the oldest phone I'd ever seen from his coat pocket.

It was bulky and as obsolete as the television in the motel room. "Here."

I stared at it like he'd handed me a bomb. I guessed he had.

"Make it fast."

My hands shook as I dialed my mother's number, and all the breath left me when she answered on the first ring.

"Hello?"

Grief hitched in my throat with the desperate cry that infiltrated the single word: "Mom." I choked it out. Eighteen years of pain and misunderstanding bled out with it.

"Aria, oh my God, Aria." She gasped it around sobs.

Tears slipped free of my eyes.

"Oh my God, Aria. Where are you?" she begged. I could tell she was pacing, the phone clutched to her ear.

"I'm safe."

"Please tell me where you are. I'll come for you. Whatever trouble you're in, it's okay. We can talk and make this right. I promise—"

"I'm not coming home."

Despair seeped into her voice. "Please, don't say that. Don't ever say that."

Agony burned in my chest. "I just wanted to let you know I'm safe. I'm safe. I promise I'm safe. And I want you to know how much I love you. That I understand why you've done the things you have, but

169

I also need you to understand that I can't live under the weight of that any longer."

"Aria," she cried.

A commotion clattered through the connection, a crash and the shattering of glass before my father's voice suddenly came through the line. "Where the hell are you, Aria? Do you understand the kind of trouble you're in? Whoever you're with is going to pay the—"

I yelped when the phone was suddenly yanked out of my hand. Pax threw it to the ground and stomped on it with the heel of his boot, crushing it in one swift blow.

My hands flew to my mouth to cover the sob. There was a huge part of me that wanted to gather up the broken pieces and put them back together so I could hear her voice again. The part that wanted to succumb.

Give in.

Because I ached.

I ached for the woman who I knew was on her knees on the floor right then. Weeping for me.

"We have to go." A dark urgency filled Pax's tone.

But I couldn't move. I gaped at the mangled mess that was left of the phone, a cold realization gliding through my veins.

I couldn't go back.

I could never return.

I would never see her again.

Pax's mouth was suddenly so close to my ear, his hold soft where he curled his hand around my elbow. "I know. I know. But it's too risky. We can't take this kind of chance again. I can't take that kind of chance with you. It's not tied to my name, but that doesn't mean someone can't tap in and track it."

Numbly, I nodded.

"Let's go." Pax led me quickly across the lot. I fumbled along at his side, his strides so long and fast I had to almost jog to keep up with him.

I felt a disorder in it. A chaos that clouded. Particles from the piece of me that had been ripped from my soul.

As crushed as the phone had been at my feet.

My thoughts drifted to the past. When my mother had watched me with adoration rather than fear.

"That imagination is something else. I bet you will write a book one day. Promise me one thing?"

Aria gazed up at her mommy, eager to hear whatever she would say.

"Never give that imagination up. Never stop dreaming. It shines so bright inside you."

Aria giggled and snuggled down deeper in her covers. "I won't, Mommy. I promise."

She tapped Aria's nose. "I love you more than anything in this world. Now, sweet, sweet dreams."

They'd been sweet, sweet dreams that had turned into our nightmares.

I choked around another sob, and that chaos spun. Into the air, where it whipped like a coming storm.

Dark clouds gathering in the distance.

It covered me in a slick of cold dread that lifted the hairs at the back of my neck.

I stumbled, unable to move my feet as Pax tried to drag me across the dirt lot to where his car was parked in front of the motel.

But I couldn't do anything but look, my eyes wide as I lifted them to find a man who stood at the door to his semitruck.

I felt it crawl over me.

Evil.

I breathed it in through my nostrils, and it gushed through my veins in a streak of malignance.

Nausea boiled in my stomach and clawed up my throat.

Pax tightened his hold around my elbow, and he pressed his mouth to the side of my head. "Keep moving, Aria. Keep moving. Do not stop. Do not stop."

He increased our pace, and he hurried me to the passenger side of his car, where he urged me into the seat.

Our bags were already stowed in the back.

He rose, straightening to his full, intimidating height, and I felt the crash of aggression blister through the cold as he glared over the top of the car at the man who remained in the same spot halfway across the lot.

Then Pax slammed my door shut. One second later, he was in his seat, starting the car, and whipping out of the dirt lot.

While my fingertips dug into the door as I watched out the passenger window with wide eyes as we flew by the malevolence that oozed back.

Chapter Twenty-One

ARIA

We'd been traveling for almost five hours when we hit the outskirts of Pittsburgh, Pennsylvania.

"Think it'd be worthwhile to hit a library here, yeah? See if we can dig anything up?" Pax asked. "Why don't you see if there's one right off the freeway?"

He had another phone, one that was much more modern than the brick he'd given me earlier, this one also unassociated with his name.

I gave him a nod as I took his phone and made the search. "In three exits, there's one that's about five minutes away."

Pax's nod was sharp, his attention keen, never letting down his guard. He took the third exit and wound through the city, following the directions.

Pax pulled into the small parking lot of the library, located on the side of the two-story redbrick building, and I looked up at it, too afraid to hope that we might find any answers inside.

"We're going to discover something in there. I can feel it," he said as he pushed the button to kill the engine. "Let's get in there and see what we can find."

Doubt swarmed in my consciousness. "Have you ever searched before?"

Pax sighed. "Once or twice, but I didn't go deep. Just some stupid searches that never produced anything. You?"

My head shook. "No. I was always too concerned with trying to convince my parents that I wasn't crazy to take the chance."

The fierce lines of his expression softened. "You're not. This is real. You're real. Don't ever fucking be ashamed of it."

As soon as he said it, he quickly clicked his door open, and he was around the car and at my side by the time I was opening mine. He kept a protective hand at the small of my back as he led me around the front of the building, forever on guard as we moved.

A bell jingled overhead as Pax swept open the door, and he stood aside for me to enter ahead of him.

Inside, it felt more like a used bookstore than a library. Racks of shelves stretched out from every wall, signs tacked to their ends indicating genres. Books bound in every color lined the shelves—old, cloth-covered hardbacks and worn, dingy paperbacks. There were random couches and seating areas scattered about, and a woman was working the checkout desk in front.

I guessed she was probably in her sixties, and she wore her black hair streaked with gray cropped close to her head.

She recoiled when she lifted her attention from the person she was checking out, so startled she took two steps back and banged into the shelf behind her. I wondered if those reactions would ever cease to sting.

Pax tugged at my elbow, urging me to move. "This way."

We followed the signs that guided us through the library to the stairs at the far back. They led to a large open loft that overlooked the main floor below. We ascended, and there, the walls were lined with shelves. But in the middle was a bunch of long tables, and against the far wall was a group of four dated computers.

As far as I could tell, there wasn't anyone else up there. A slow quiet clung to the air, the only sound the distant shuffle and the murmured voices below.

Pax went directly for the back wall. He pulled up an extra chair in front of a computer, and we both sat.

"Do you think these things still actually work?" He seemed more than skeptical when he poked at a key. The screen bloomed to life, though, and he didn't hesitate to click onto the internet.

One second later, we were looking at a search bar.

We both just stared as uncertainty bristled around us.

"I don't even know where to start. How to put it into words," I whispered. How did you give voice to the inconceivable?

"Think the only thing we can do is just go for it," he responded.

Pax leaned forward and typed in the one word that I'd never had the courage to even speak.

Faydor.

Chapter Twenty-Two

PAX

Disappointment sank like stones to the pit of my stomach.

It was a bunch of fucking gibberish.

Misspellings.

A couple of people with the name.

"Damn it," I grumbled, and Aria peeked over at me before she reached out and typed *Laven*.

A bunch of names populated that time. Lots of last names bearing the same title.

My spirit twisted in a bid of hopelessness because, God, I was trying so hard, but I had the sinking sense that we might be grasping for something that wasn't there.

Determined to find a solution in the middle of obscurity. We'd been sworn to never speak of our time while asleep, but still, we were humans during the day, and I wasn't sure how, in all of time, those oaths had been kept.

Couldn't believe that one person hadn't dished, even though they'd likely have been labeled the same way as Aria had been.

Unstable.

Still, there had to be something.

An answer.

I had to find one.

Aria's survival was riding on it.

Frustration heaved from her on a weighted exhalation before she deliberated, then leaned in again and let her delicate fingers move over the keys.

Tearsith.

We both were holding our breath as the screen switched, and our eyes quickly scanned the results.

More misspellings leading to other entries. Some board game. A couple of random people.

Not much.

Except there was one tiny image that populated at the bottom of the page. One that stopped both of us in our tracks. The oxygen hitched in our throats, and our hearts picked up a reckless rhythm of disbelief.

Aria glanced at me in a second of stunned wariness before she maneuvered the mouse and clicked on it.

"Oh my God." A whispered gasp rushed from her, and the air was punching from my lungs.

It was a painting.

A painting of the place we knew. Our sanctuary. A meadow with a stream running through.

People were there, sitting on the green bank among the vingas, wearing the same brown clothing as us when we showed up in Tearsith every night, though it was obvious from their hairstyles the image was dated.

"I can't believe it." Aria stretched out a trembling hand and brushed her fingertips across the screen as if she could reach it.

Our truth.

And, for the first time, we had confirmation that it was someone else's truth, too.

And fuck, I wasn't sure that this life had ever felt more real than right then. Sitting beside my Nol and seeing this.

I glanced over my shoulder to make sure we were still alone.

"Who's the artist?" I asked when I turned back, my voice craggy with urgency.

Aria scrolled through the painting's description.

"*Tearsith* is a nineteenth-century painting by Abigail Watkins."

The name was hyperlinked, and Aria clicked on it.

Abigail Watkins was an American painter.

Born: February 16, 1871, in Pendleton, South Carolina

Died: March 4, 1902, in Charlotte, South Carolina

Known for: Painting

Spouse: Ambrose Watkins

Parents: Robert Ray Smith, Beatrice Louise Remington

Abigail Watkins was known for painting. While the peers of her time had moved on to realism and impressionism, Abigail's works were notable for their mystical elements and her flair for the demonic, her style lending itself to the romantic period preceding her era. Abigail Watkins's works were virtually undiscovered until after her unfortunate death at thirty-one years old. While it's believed most of

her works were destroyed in the house fire she succumbed to, five paintings were recovered and are
now on display at the Art Institute of Chicago.

We both were fucking shaking as we clicked through the five images lined up beneath her name.

The first was the original we'd seen, the one labeled *Tearsith* at the edge where she'd swiped the letters across the bottom. The others were unnamed, but that didn't mean we didn't recognize them.

Two were depictions of the bowels of Faydor, the barren plane we knew so well. One was a landscape, as if she had perfectly defined the hell where we found ourselves each night. In another, a Kruen had risen high, amassing from shadow to its macabre form. Its face was a void, with innuendos of shape and holes for its eyes that led to eternal nothingness. A pit of darkness and despair. This Kruen had six spindly, branch-like limbs that flamed with fiery tendrils as it prepared to lash out in defense.

The other two were varying portrayals of Kruens peering down from that unseen plane, devouring the innocent below. These were grisly. Gore-strewn. A clear parable of how she interpreted the devastation they wreaked.

"We aren't alone, are we?" My words were hushed. The search might not have given us the answers we'd been looking for, but I thought there was something comforting about it. Seeing it beyond the borders of our minds.

Aria shifted her attention to me. "No. We aren't. It's strange to have felt alone for so long, and this somehow feels . . . like an affirmation."

"It's a piece. A start." With it, I had to believe there was more.

Aria turned back to the screen. "I just wonder who she was. What she was like. She died so young. In a house fire. How awful."

A bit of that hopelessness bottomed out my stomach. It was so long ago, so I doubted we would find any connections. As cool as it was to have this piece of who we were, we needed a ton more information if it was going to make a difference for Aria. We needed something solid. An answer for who she was.

If we could find out who the Laven was who'd held the same powers as Aria? Find any history on her? Find out exactly how the Kruens or a Ghorl had tracked her down and destroyed her?

Maybe then we could find a way to truly protect Aria forever. Help her tap deeper into who she was.

Maybe I was grasping at straws. Any sort of solution.

But we had to try to find something.

"It says she was married." Aria reached forward to click on Abigail's spouse's name, but we both froze when we felt a presence cloud over us from behind. We'd been so engrossed in what we'd found that neither of us had heard footsteps.

Violence pulled tight across my chest. It was so goddamn reckless to have let my guard down like that.

In a rush of protectiveness, I shifted in the chair, and I glared over my shoulder. Every muscle in my body was bunched and prepared to strike.

It was a man, maybe in his late thirties or forties, and he'd gone to the Healthy Lifestyle section, which was against the far wall. He kept peering our way, trying to keep it covert, like I couldn't feel his curiosity spearing into us.

"We need to go," I mumbled under my breath, frustrated as hell that we hadn't even gotten the chance to check news articles.

Aria looked back at the screen, wishing to push further, to dig deeper.

"We'll stop again. At another place," I promised.

We just couldn't sit idle like this when we'd captured someone's interest.

I didn't feel a whole lot of evil radiating from the guy, but right then, with the sense I'd gotten from the trucker, we couldn't take that chance.

Nodding, Aria stood, and I ushered her back across the loft and to the stairs. I could feel the weight of the man's attention follow us the entire way.

And I wondered how strong the Ghorl was who had been feeding evils into the janitor's mind. How fucking in tune it was. How far it could reach. I wondered if the monster could feel the man's interest, would take advantage of it and manipulate him in a single beat.

Could he take him from mild intrigue to bloodthirsty?

The only thing I knew for sure was that I didn't fucking like it, and when he turned and started back in our direction, I hurried Aria down the stairs. By the time we hit the bottom landing, we were close to a jog, me at her side and rushing her toward the front door. "Keep moving, Aria. Don't look back."

We were almost through the door when from out of nowhere a hand reached out and gripped Aria's arm.

Aria'd had her head down, and a yelp of surprise left her at the contact. I whirled, getting between the person and Aria, backing her out of the threshold while I prepared to fight.

"Stay the fuck away," I growled before I could even process who was there.

My tension minimally eased when I realized it was the older Black woman who'd been working the checkout.

Fear over the way I'd responded to her was clear in her expression, though it was mottled with something I couldn't quite pinpoint. Still, I kept moving backward, edging Aria through the door while I made myself a barricade of protection in front of her.

The woman stepped forward, and she reached out like she was trying to grab on to a ghost. "I know what you are."

She whispered it in reverence.

In grief.

Shock blew my eyes wide. What the hell? Did she just imply what I thought she did?

"I don't know what you're talking about," I gritted out.

We couldn't trust anyone.

I could feel Aria trying to peer out from around me. Shock rippled across her flesh, and her heart beat manically against my back.

"You do. You know," the woman pressed.

She reached again, though this time, I noticed she had her hand balled around something she held in her palm. I stalled out, my gaze sweeping from her to the man who was now downstairs.

She swung her attention his way before she turned back to me and urged, "Take it."

I resisted for only one moment before I accepted the crumpled piece of paper from her hand. The second I did, she turned and called, "What can I help you find?"

It was a clear distraction.

I swung around before I could watch anything else play out, and I took Aria by the elbow as we darted back onto the sidewalk. We rushed, our feet pounding on the concrete as I led her back to the car. I jerked open her door and she jumped in, and I rounded the front and slipped into my seat. I peeled out from the lot, heading back in the direction of the freeway.

Aria blew out the strain, her fingers driving through the long locks of her black hair before I felt her gaze washing over me. Confusion and hope bound her spirit. "The woman. She knew what we were."

My stomach clutched, and I exhaled as I passed over the piece of paper that I still had crumpled in my hand. "Think so. What does it say?"

Cloaked in anxiety, Aria unwrapped it. "It's her name and a phone number. Maria Lewis. And there's another name: Charles Lewis. She wrote that one in all caps, like she wanted to emphasize it."

"She wants us to look him up," I surmised.

"I think so."

"The next place we stop, we'll find somewhere to do it."

Aria sank back in her seat, taking in a bunch of breaths before she whispered, "I feel it, Pax. It feels like maybe the answers are right there, hovering all around us, and we just can't see them yet. But I also can feel the devastation coming, too."

Fear clamped around my heart, and my teeth ground as I uttered, "Then that means we have to head it off."

Chapter Twenty-Three

ARIA

It was strange not having a real destination. We were simply driving, although it was clear Pax wanted to put as much distance between New York and ourselves as possible, so I assumed we were going to end up somewhere on the West Coast.

We'd driven all day and well into the dark, and it was past ten when we pulled into another crummy motel about fifty miles on the other side of Saint Louis, Missouri. This one was two stories, the doors also accessed directly from the outside.

Pax said it was safer that way; it was best if we weren't trapped inside a building if we needed to make a quick escape.

We climbed the exterior steps to our room on the second level, each of us loaded down with bags, plus I carried a large brown sack from a local burger place where we'd gone through the drive-through.

Pax slid the key into the lock, and he again went inside and searched the room before he gave me the all clear and I shuffled in.

It was much the same as the last one, though here the interior was a dingy, dust-tainted blue.

Two beds on the left. A table directly to the right.

I dumped my bag onto the farthest bed before I placed the paper sack on the small table.

Grease saturated the bottom, and the heavy scent of french fries floated into the air.

My stomach grumbled.

"You'd think I hadn't fed you all day." That low voice slipped over me from behind. So close that it sent a rash of chills skating over my flesh. I did my best to shake it off. To pretend I wasn't affected. To act like my body didn't shiver and my spirit didn't ache.

I wondered if he could feel it.

If he ever had.

If every time I entered Tearsith, he could see the wash of what radiated from me.

This love that felt trapped inside, a secret shrouded in our mystery.

"I guess I'm making up for when I was in the facility," I told him, lifting a shoulder to my ear as I tried to play off the reaction I had to him.

That reaction had only grown in the distance we'd traveled today.

Today I'd had time to just . . . study him.

Watch him as he'd driven for countless miles, the man hedged in a cloak of armor so hard he might as well have been covered in jagged, unpolished steel. His attention rapt and never failing.

But there were moments when that ferocity would slip.

For the barest moment when he'd glance at me. As if he found some kind of solace that I was there. Real and whole and safe.

During that time, I'd tried to process the events that had happened over the last twenty hours. To catch up to the change and to prepare myself for what was to come.

"Good. You need to keep up your strength."

"I know."

Pax moved around me and pulled out the contents of the bag. Two cheeseburgers and two orders of fries. "Sit."

I complied, pulling out the chair and sitting across from him. He didn't hesitate to dig in, wrapping his mouth around the burger before he began to chew. The muscles in his jaw flexed as he ate, red lips almost hypnotizing as I stared.

A tiny scowl pinched between his brow since I was just sitting there, and I dove in, groaning a little when I bit into my burger.

"I always wondered what it would be like if I met you," I finally chanced once I'd eaten half. I took a fry and dipped it in ketchup, watching him from over the table as I placed it into my mouth.

"Don't quite add up to what you'd imagined, do I?"

In contemplation, my teeth raked my bottom lip. He tracked the movement with that searing gaze.

"I think you're exactly what I imagined. Fierce and brave and wearing the kind of chip on your shoulder that only someone like us could earn. Walking around with an edge of aggression. Suspicious. Never trusting a soul you meet."

"That's because people can't be trusted."

I popped another fry into my mouth to buy myself time before I tilted my head as I looked at him. "You believe that of everyone? That they're fundamentally bad?"

He grunted as he took another bite of his burger.

I wondered if it made me a freak that I wanted to reach out and run my fingers through that rough sound.

It wasn't as if I had any experience in that or had anything to compare this feeling to, but I knew well enough that I could never feel this way with anyone else.

"I think people are easily swayed," he answered. "Deluded into what they want to believe. Opening themselves to wickedness anytime they want something badly enough. Excuses conjured in their feeble minds as vindication for their actions."

Air wisped from my nose.

Pax arched a severe brow. "You don't agree?"

"I think humanity is more complex than that, and our survival instinct often presents itself as greed. I felt it distinctly when I was in the facility. When I could feel the emotions radiating from everyone around me. The desperation to survive, while the hopelessness to do it was all consuming."

I paused before I asked, "What about this woman, Maria? Are we going to trust her? Contact her?"

The piece of paper with her number on it burned in my pocket.

Uncertainty crested in his spirit. "Not sure that we can trust her, but I think we need to at least try to figure out what she was trying to tell us."

"It feels insane that someone recognized us."

Pax chewed on a fry. "I know."

He wavered before he continued, "You felt it, didn't you? Earlier? The Ghorl who was feeding thoughts into that trucker's mind?" The question grated, Pax finally giving voice to what we'd both known when we fled from the motel earlier this morning.

I was being tracked.

Hunted.

"Yes."

"How?"

My head shook with uncertainty, with the vestiges of what had swelled in the frigid air that had gusted across the lot.

Palpable.

A darkness that had enclosed and covered me in a slick of corrosion.

I swallowed around the clot of dread that threatened to close off my throat. "It's like a . . . new sense. Like it's pulling at my flesh and digging at my spirit. A shout of silence. An intonation of depravity. If I'd have gotten closer to him? I would have heard what he was thinking. And I know if I would have touched him, I would have seen exactly what had been in that man's mind. I'd have seen the Ghorl telling him exactly how to hurt me."

A low growl reverberated in his throat. "I won't let anyone get near you."

"How did you know?" I asked, attempting to distract him from the rage that gathered like storm clouds in his pale eyes.

It took him a moment to answer. "You chase evil long enough and it becomes easy to recognize."

With the way he seemed to calculate what to say, I could tell he was leaving something out. That there was something more to him than he was letting on.

Pax suddenly pushed up from his chair and leaned over the table in my direction before I had the chance to delve deeper. A white, shadowy flame.

A dusky luminosity.

He hovered over me, the oath grinding from his mouth. "Until we figure out how to keep you safe? Permanently? As far as I'm concerned, I'll be treating every person we cross as a threat."

We remained there, held by a tether that blazed, a string tugging so hard at my chest that I couldn't breathe.

Pax finally blinked and stepped back, as if he was berating himself for getting so close to me. "I should take a shower," he said toward the floor, roughing a palm over the top of his head.

"I'll be right here." It was my own promise. Trying to assuage the fear that radiated from him. The fear of letting me out of his sight.

With a tight nod, Pax strode across the floor and into the bathroom, and he clicked the door shut behind him.

A second later, the pipes squealed as the shower was turned on. The walls were so thin that I could hear the rustling on the other side, the pounding of the water onto porcelain, the swoosh of fabric, the jangle of a belt.

I squeezed my eyes against the visions that assaulted my mind.

Because I couldn't picture him that way. Naked as he stepped beneath the spray.

I couldn't keep from wondering what it might be like if he saw me the way I saw him.

From wondering if he felt it.

I knew I was being foolish, lost to a child's crush, to a bond that resounded with so much strength that it could easily be distorted and confused. But I wasn't a child anymore.

I could only imagine the way he'd spent his human life. There was no way he hadn't . . .

Jumping from the chair, I clipped off the thoughts because that was something I refused to think about.

Devolving into it would only hurt.

It wasn't his fault that I'd always thought of him as mine, but I had no claim on him here.

I stuffed our burger wrappers into the paper sack and shoved it into the garbage; then I climbed onto the small twin bed and leaned against the headboard, trying to slow my breaths. To calm the ravaging beat in my chest. But the harder I tried to clear it, the more I seemed to focus on the sounds coming from the bathroom. The shower when it turned off and the squawk of the metal curtain hooks being dragged against the rod.

I'd worked myself into some kind of anxious frenzy by the time the door finally snapped open, and there was no stopping the gasp that slipped from between my lips when he stepped out, wearing a fresh pair of jeans and rubbing a towel over his wet hair.

He was shirtless, chest and shoulders and abdomen bare, and in the dull light, my eyes raced to take him in, hungry as I searched for every scar beneath the designs that covered his skin. The dark images swirled and played over his flesh like sentient entities.

Muscle bristled beneath, packed and hard and rippling with that sleek strength he emitted.

He stopped right outside the door.

We both froze.

Locked.

Ensnared.

"You can't look at me like that, Aria." The gnarled warning cut into the severity that writhed between us.

My attention snapped from the barren wasteland tattooed on his abdomen and chest to meet the white fire in his gaze.

"I don't think I could stop looking at you." The admission flooded from me on a needy breath. "How could I when you're like looking at my truth? For the last ten years of my life, I've been told you were a figment of my mind. A piece of my warped imagination. That I was delusional. And here you are with blood pounding through your veins."

"Aria." His molars ground so hard I felt the force of it crack in the room.

"You are so beautiful." It scraped out without permission. "Your body that has kept your scars, those eyes that hold your secrets. And I know your heart is, too."

The air in the small room grew dense, every molecule enclosed. Trembles rocked through it. An awareness that thrashed and begged in the space between us.

"I'm the last person you should see that way."

"You're the only person I could see that way." I figured I didn't have time to be shy or modest. Not when this might be my only chance at confessing this.

My only chance at confessing what burned inside me.

I didn't know how many tomorrows I had left.

The words were a whisper of desperation from my lips: "How do you see me?"

A groan curled up his thick throat, and he tossed the towel he was using to dry his hair to the floor before he took two steps to bring himself to the end of my bed.

His movements were slow. Filled with caution. With a reservation that rattled him to the bone.

"I see the one person who has ever meant anything to me. I see the one I've been sent to protect. I'm looking at my purpose, Aria. But it has to end at that."

"Why?"

He choked over a pained, disbelieving sound. "You know why."

"And maybe I don't care. Maybe I want to take one thing for myself. Just once. I'm eighteen and I've never been kissed, and I might die tomorrow."

I couldn't believe I was telling him any of this. That I'd laid all my insecurities and inexperience at his feet. But it all left me in a bid of gravity.

"Don't fucking say that," he spat as he surged forward. He dropped to his knees at the side of my bed.

I moved, drawn, sitting up and draping my legs over the side, because the only thing I wanted to do was erase that space.

Heat blasted from him.

The man was a furnace.

"Don't fucking say that." It was a whispered plea this time. "I'm not going to let anything happen to you."

"And what if it would kill me if something happened to *you* trying to protect me?"

He took my hand between both of his. "You're worth any cost. I've known it my entire life."

Tears blurred my eyes, and he reached up and wiped away the one that slid down my cheek.

"I would never ask that of you." Except I had, hadn't I? My spirit had beckoned him through the darkness. Shouting to be rescued when I'd been trapped.

"You don't have to ask for what has already been committed." Fingertips trailed down my cheek, gathering more moisture before barely brushing over my trembling lips.

Shivers rolled, a flash fire that made me shake, and the love I'd forever feel for him flailed from within, begging to be acknowledged.

The brittle ice of his eyes had gone soft, a lapping sea as he stared, though his muscles were taut with restraint as he kept brushing his fingertips over my lips. "How is it possible no one has ever kissed you?"

"Who would want to get close to someone like me?" It quivered out.

The loneliness of the life we lived.

Solitary confinement.

Not that anyone could have gotten close to me anyway.

Not when my soul only wanted him.

"Any man would be lucky to get close to you, and I would give anything for that, but you know I can't. I'd be a bastard for touching you. I won't taint you. Won't take that risk. You have your whole life ahead of you."

My throat tightened. My heart a riot that bashed against my chest. My mind a spiral of the things he'd given me.

I would give anything for that.

I won't taint you.

God. Did he somehow think he wasn't worthy of me? That this man who'd risked everything—his freedom and his life—wasn't good enough?

I wanted to argue, but I couldn't make any sounds come from my thickened tongue, and Pax slowly stood, his gorgeous body towering over me, a fortress.

He reached out and cupped my cheek.

"We have to go back."

Each time I'd slept, I'd done it out of sync with our Laven family, and I had hidden in the sanctuary of Tearsith while they fought.

My nod was weak, but he was right.

Faydor was calling.

And we couldn't resist it any longer.

Chapter Twenty-Four

PAX

Tearsith

Pax closed his eyes, and he hovered in the nothingness.

Weightless.

Boneless.

He floated higher, where lights flashed and flickered before he emerged at the boundary of Tearsith. A lush paradise that surrounded them.

Aria was already there, standing at the edge and peering out into the meadow like she no longer knew where she belonged.

He eased up behind her.

She shivered. The way she had at the hotel when he'd been a fool and had gotten too close to her.

How fucking gorgeous she'd looked, sitting on that bed. How he'd wanted to crawl over her and press her into the mattress. Unwrap her. Trace his fingers over every scar on her body.

It'd only made it worse when he'd gotten on his knees at her bedside and run his fingertips over her lips. He had nearly broken when she'd confessed what she wanted aloud.

But he couldn't go there.

It would only make their situation worse.

Distort their purpose.

But he already felt a hazy film clouding his sight and mind. The way his stomach twisted when he looked at her and how he kept getting hit with a bolt of need whenever their skin brushed.

He had to wonder if maybe that was the true reason they were forbidden to find their Nol during the day. If their connection became too powerful and the objective was skewed.

Maybe it made him a piece of shit to question Valeen. But to him, Valeen was little more than a mystery. Removed. Never a tangible piece of them. Her words only spoken through Ellis, where he found her teachings in the great book.

If Pax were being honest, he'd always questioned everything.

He eased up to Aria's side and looked out to see that most of their Laven family had already arrived and were gathered at Ellis's feet.

"I don't know how to face them," she quietly admitted.

"You haven't done anything wrong. I was the one who came for you. I'm the one who broke the decree, and I'm standing beside you without one regret."

She let go of a shattered breath.

"We're in this together," he promised, his voice urgent, and she nodded as she stepped out from the fringe and edged across the soft grasses. He followed a foot behind. A shield that covered, ready to step in.

He knew when they felt them coming. The way Ellis's words trailed off and a ripple of apprehension traveled through the crowd as everyone shifted to watch their approach.

Aria stumbled a step, and Pax placed a hand at the small of her back.

A soft encouragement that burned through him like a wildfire.

Singeing every nerve ending in his being.

"It's nearing time to descend," Ellis said, though his attention remained on them. "Everyone, prepare yourselves."

Their Laven family stood, unsure, though they began to pair off.

For a moment, Ellis hesitated, in what appeared to be both dread and relief, before he started their way.

He met them midway in the field. Torment twisted through his expression. "We've been worried."

He glanced between the two of them. Clearly Ellis already knew that Pax had gone for Aria. The measures he'd taken to protect his Nol.

Aria trembled. "They have already begun to hunt me."

Ellis's nod was knowing, tremoring with his age, his pale eyes dulled yet filled with compassion and fear. "Sweet child."

Agony sliced through Aria.

Palpable.

Though she lifted her chin as if she'd already accepted her fate. "I will fight until the day I die."

Pax couldn't contain his growl. Couldn't stop the hostility that rose from the depths of his soul.

Ellis felt the resonance, Pax was sure, the way apprehension filled his features.

The two stared at each other, though Pax stepped back when Dani cautiously approached the three of them. Her love for Aria was patent, her hands shaking when she reached out and pulled Aria into her arms. "Oh God, Aria, I've been so worried about you."

Aria fell into her and allowed her to hold her up. "I'm okay. I'm okay."

It sounded as if Aria was trying to convince herself.

"I need to speak with you." Ellis's voice was low and dire, and Pax glanced to Aria, not wanting to leave her side but also knowing this was inevitable.

He knew the choice he'd made would be met with condemnation.

Pax followed Ellis across the meadow until they stood beneath a massive, winding tree, its entwined, low-slung branches covered in moss and white flowers. Its canopy stretched over them like a sentry.

"You've gone to her." Ellis said it the moment he turned around, the words craggy and grave.

Pax looked back to where Aria was surrounded by Dani, Josephine, and a handful of other Laven whom Aria had grown close to.

His jaw clenched. "Yes."

Ellis emitted a sound of reproach, though it was pained and woven with alarm. "You've broken our greatest rule. The one I warned you of time and again."

Pax's attention snapped back to his guide. His teacher. A man he held in the highest regard. It was a regard he couldn't heed. "And I'd break it a million times over if it gave her even one more day."

"You put her in danger. Put yourself in danger."

An incredulous laugh ripped from Pax. "I put her in danger? She would have died in that facility if I hadn't gotten her out. The one Timothy had seen had already gotten to her. He was in her room when I arrived."

Ellis's pale face blanched. Stark white. Still, he said, "Your purpose is here. To fight here . . . in Faydor. You've lost sight of your meaning. Of who you are supposed to be."

Pax angled his head in his elder's direction, his words jagged. "My purpose is to protect her." He'd known it his entire life; he'd just finally figured out what that really meant. "Saving her *is* my meaning."

"Have you forgotten the lessons of Valeen and Kreed?"

"And what exactly do you expect me to do? Turn my back on her? Leave her alone on the street? Take her back to her parents, who don't understand her? The ones who put her in harm's way to begin with? I won't." The promise grated from Pax's tongue.

"Pax . . . you must—"

Their argument was cut off by Timothy, who was suddenly at their side. He roughed a hand through his shaggy brown hair, caution and care in his expression.

"Forgive me for interrupting," he told Ellis, though his eyes were on Pax. "Dani and I . . . We have been searching."

Rage and hope stirred inside him.

"What have you found?" Pax demanded.

"We found the Ghorl. It is fast, and it is strong and terrifying. More powerful than anything I've ever witnessed. But I saw it, Pax. It has one single thought. One single goal. And that goal is Aria."

Pax had already assumed that, but the confirmation pierced him like an arrow.

He swore, and Timothy's nod was grim. "We couldn't even get close enough to it to try to bind it. I'm sorry."

"It must be stopped here." Wisdom was carved into Ellis's edict. "If it's only this one . . . then perhaps we can stop this."

He didn't say it, but Pax knew what he'd implied.

Stop the hunt for Aria.

Only you have the strength to destroy this evil. What Aria had told him about what she'd thought Valeen had conveyed to her spun through his mind. If it were true? If Valeen had actually shown herself to Aria? Then Aria might be the only one who could do it.

Pax grabbed on to the hope, and he silently promised she wouldn't have to do it alone.

"I will speak with our family before we descend," Ellis said.

"Thank you." Pax's words were thick as he spoke to Timothy.

"You know I would do anything for her. For both of you," Timothy promised before he turned and headed back toward Dani, who still stood talking with Aria.

Pax started to turn, to go to Aria so they could descend. So they could fight this beast, crush it, pray it would be her threat's end.

Only Ellis took him by the forearm before he had the chance to move. His instruction was hushed, though cut in emphasis. "I understand, Pax. I do. So protect her while awake. Stand at her side until we see this through. We will find it and destroy it here."

Pax gulped as Ellis tightened his hold.

"But you must leave her then. Once this is finished. And you must never give in to what I see in your eyes. You cannot risk the aftermath of giving your heart that way. You might think you're strong enough to resist it, but you will turn on her."

Pax wanted to argue. To swear it could never happen. Not when she was everything. He restrained himself and gave Ellis the promise he knew he was duty bound to uphold. "I will."

"Good. Then I say we go destroy this monster." Ellis wound around Pax, walking toward the sea of Laven. "Family, gather around."

Pax followed, moving to Aria's side.

She glanced at him with those questioning, fathomless eyes. He took her hand as the voices trailed off and everyone gathered around Ellis, whose expression was both direct and grim.

Their elder turned to speak to the crowd. "As Laven, we each face special obstacles while awake. We are attacked in every direction, Kruen tossing thoughts in those who cross our paths. I know you understand this firsthand. You know the complexities of this life, even though they are difficult to understand. And Aria's . . ."

Everyone's attention slanted to her as he continued to speak. "Aria's situation appears to be even more complex than any of us here have ever known. She has . . . bound a Kruen while awake."

Shock rippled through the mass, rumbles of perplexity, the impossibility of who she was and what she had done, and Pax clutched her hand tighter when she trembled as a flock of pale eyes swept over her.

In sympathy.

In support.

In confusion.

None of them could comprehend what was being said. None of them had an answer.

Pax was hell-bent on finding it.

"And as such," Ellis continued, "it seems she has become the target of a single Ghorl."

Gasps went up all around.

"Timothy and Dani have witnessed its thoughts, and those thoughts have one purpose: seeking Aria's demise. We must stop it. For our sister. Listen as you hunt for the one who seeks her. Together, we must find it and snuff it out."

Agreement rolled through the crush, and their family began to descend, two by two, edging up to the invisible gateway, to the force that drew them toward darkness.

Each flashed in a brilliant light before they disappeared.

Pax and Aria waited at the back, and he squeezed her hand even tighter. "However many nights we have to spend searching, we will find it and we will destroy it. Do not forget what Valeen told you. You have the power, Aria. It's you."

Surprise gusted through her before she gave him a small nod. "I will give everything to try to find it within myself."

They stepped forward together.

A searing cold blistered across his flesh, and he clung to her hand as they fell for what seemed an eternity.

Darkness reigned on all sides, disorienting and confusing as they tumbled and spun and hurtled through the desolation.

Violence filled their ears, the call for wickedness, the beckoning for desolation.

He never let go of her hand.

They hit the frozen ground, and the barren expanse of Faydor opened in front of them.

Their Laven family raced headlong into the roiling chaos. Into the mist and shadows that howled with depravity.

The instinct was to fight. To engage. To chase down the foul and end it.

It felt nearly impossible to keep moving, to ignore the innate reflex to battle the disgusting thoughts as they passed.

But they couldn't stop.

They couldn't slow.

Aria was at his side as they tracked over the rough, barren terrain, through the heavy vapor that concealed and camouflaged. The barest light glowed at the edge of Faydor, the darkness so thick it was noxious.

Ice-cold poison that they inhaled into their lungs.

Aria kept stumbling at the wickedness that was intoned. Her need to intervene was almost too powerful for her to ignore. The pain she emitted was overwhelming.

Unbearable.

Pax gritted his teeth. "We have to find it, Aria. Right now, our only job is saving you. You can't protect the blameless if you're not here to do it."

The words raked up his throat, low and desperate, and Aria pushed herself harder. They increased their pace, racing through stricken darkness, twisting around the boulders and lifeless elms.

They inclined their ears, listening in on the screams and taunts, the wickedness that oozed, the evils that possessed.

They ran for hours.

Hunting.

Searching.

Lost in the bowels of nothingness. A wasteland of greed.

He'd begun to lose hope when he got the barest inclination. When he picked up on a sound. A tone that reverberated through the frigid air and flamed at his soul.

The Ghorl.

"Climb the stairs. Break the lock. She's waiting. You get to fuck her if you do. She's never been touched. She's yours. Then let her blood spill over your fingers."

Catching a glimpse of the Ghorl's mind, Pax saw his car parked in the lot, two spaces down from the set of stairs that led to the upper level of the hotel where they were staying.

Where they were asleep inside.

Aria saw it at the same time, and she gasped. Her knees went weak, her feet close to failing as she stumbled over the rocky, rutted ground.

Pax tightened his hold on her hand.

"I won't let him touch you. I promise you. We have to remain strong. Fight."

Resolve rushed through her on a palpable wave. Bottled strength that rose from the depths, where it had been dormant and hidden away.

Pax was sure Aria didn't have the first clue of how powerful she really was.

What remained untapped.

But he knew exactly why she was such a threat.

They drove themselves toward the voice, hurtling across the ground.

"Do it. Go up the stairs. Move. You have nothing to lose. Everything you want is on the other side of that door."

Running through vapor and mist, they rounded a boulder, and the Ghorl came into sight. It writhed in a bubbling, black mess on the pitted, desolate ground.

Both liquid and shadow.

Different from a normal Kruen. It throbbed with untapped power.

With a wickedness so great it bleared their eyes and distorted their senses.

Together, Pax and Aria found the light within themselves, the power to crush the iniquity, and they projected it toward the Ghorl. They needed to surround it before it could realize they were there.

Only it sensed their approach, and it flailed, gathering to take new shape as it reared up to stare back at them.

Its flesh was pitch-blackened char, though you could see the evil pump through its veins. Its face a gnarled mesh of depravity, its mouth deformed and twisted as it bared its jagged teeth. A flash of a second later, it had transformed into shadow, and it broke into two fragments as it raced away.

Curling and twisting in a bid to disorient them.

"Follow the largest fragment." Aria rushed, her breaths ragged as they chased. They struggled not to lose it, trying to track it to the place where it would come back together so they could bind it as one.

Their only hope was to eradicate it when it was whole.

Only the thoughts the Ghorl had been feeding into the man had already been seeded.

Had already taken hold.

Pax suddenly lurched, and his hand slipped from Aria's as he was shocked awake.

Chapter Twenty-Five

PAX

I bolted upright, jarred as I was tossed between two worlds.

Disoriented as I was swamped by the darkness of the room.

But my heart pounded at a million miles a minute. Each harsh beat battered at my ribs.

Awareness crawled over my flesh, and the sweat that drenched me was thick and sticky.

Evil coated the room.

There was no missing the stench of it.

Squinting, I tried to adjust to the dim light as I listened for what had pulled me from sleep.

Aria's breaths were long and shallow as she continued to race through Faydor. Her body vibrating and ticking beneath the covers on her bed.

But the rest of the room was too still.

Too quiet.

It was then that I saw the shape move out from where it was hidden in the shadows against the wall.

Rage clouded my vision, and I could barely breathe with the adrenaline that dumped into my system. With the rage that careened through me.

The man was tall and thin, his light hair shaggy and unkempt. His hands were in fists at his sides, and all his attention was trained on where Aria slept.

It was the trucker from earlier today. The one we'd seen outside the diner. The one who'd sent a cold dread skidding down my spine.

Bloodlust seeped from his pores and infected the oxygen.

Deranged.

Half-mad.

In that moment, I realized the man didn't possess half his senses.

He didn't even notice I was there.

Brainwashed, his spirit sold on destruction.

His entire intention was on Aria.

He took another step forward.

Nausea churned in my gut and fury blistered just under my skin, but I forced myself to remain still.

To calculate.

To use his oblivion for my benefit.

Keeping as quiet as I could, I slowly shifted, and I climbed to a crouch in the middle of the bed. I cringed when the springs creaked, but he didn't flinch.

Didn't turn or observe.

No self-preservation.

No survival instinct.

Because the Ghorl had convinced his feeble, wicked mind this was the only thing that mattered.

His sole purpose was Aria.

The hammering in my heart intensified and became a thundering in my ears, and I swore silently when I realized I'd been stupid enough to leave my gun in the duffel bag tucked on the floor at the foot of my bed.

Sweat slicked my skin as each second stretched on.

A bated eternity.

Waiting for the perfect moment.

Ensuring the monster was completely distracted and unprepared before I struck.

He edged forward again, and the soles of his boots scuffed on the thin carpet as he tried to keep himself secreted as he came to the side of her bed.

The sick motherfucker stared down at her, but he had fully turned his back to me.

A mistake he was going to regret.

The second he reached out with his grimy hand to touch her face, I attacked.

Springing forward, I jumped onto his back, and I wrapped my arm around his throat and squeezed.

That was all it took to snap him out of the trance he'd been under, and he roared, clawing like a beast as he raged and grappled to take hold of my arm, the asshole spinning around in an attempt to knock me off his back.

Chaotic energy spiraled through the room.

A cloud of frantic desperation.

"She's mine." His voice was dark. Cloaked in wickedness.

I only squeezed tighter, cinching down, refusing to let go. "You disgusting piece of shit. I will end you."

The words hissed out of my mouth and into his ear.

A scream pierced the air.

Aria.

She scrambled onto all fours as the commotion jarred her awake. Her pale eyes were wide, close to glowing in the night as she struggled to process where she was and what was happening.

A lecherous groan rolled up the bastard's chest.

"Yes," he grunted. "You're mine. He gave you to me."

Shocked horror blanketed her expression.

Disgust.

Revulsion.

Fear.

"Get to the car, Aria!" I shouted as I fought the fiend who reared, bucking like a bull. "Hurry!" I gritted, hanging on, knowing I couldn't give a fraction.

The fucker was strong, and the bloodlust made him stronger. Delirious with the thirst to hunt and destroy.

She gasped, croaking as she slid off the side of the bed and onto her bare feet. "Pax."

Her voice acted as a lure, and he stopped spinning and fighting me and instead fumbled in her direction.

Only three feet of space separated the beds, and it boxed her in where she stood in front of the single nightstand. Panic roiled through her being, and she backed farther against the wood while I yanked my arm tighter around his neck.

I wanted to end him. To reach through his black soul and find the Ghorl on the other side and squeeze until neither of them existed.

"Aria, go. Get to the car. You have to get out of here. Hurry!" It wheezed from my lungs, and I drew up a fist and started pummeling the bastard on the side of the head, crack after crack landing at his temple while I held on tight with the other, trying to buy seconds so Aria could get around us.

"Go!" I shouted between the barrages of my fist. "Take the keys and go."

The asshole flung and flailed, trying to knock me free, grunting, "She's mine. She's mine. You can't have her."

"Aria, go!" It boomed against the walls.

Only he stumbled forward another step, so close that she was pinned to the nightstand as he reached his dirty hands in her direction.

Fury whipped and blew, and I fought with everything I had. I refused to give or let go.

I'd promised her I wouldn't let anyone touch her.

I meant it.

I meant it.

She was my purpose.

My reason.

My reason, who turned so fast she became a blur, and I thought she was going to jump onto the bed and scramble around us, but she was whipping back around with the lamp from the nightstand in her hands.

Glass shattered as she cracked it across his face.

The monster flailed backward, palms going to his face as he howled in agony. "You fucking bitch. I'm going to make this hurt. Gonna cut you up so good."

My muscles burned as I squeezed tighter, and I used my other hand to pull my forearm harder against his throat.

He staggered back, floundering on his feet until we crashed into the wall. My back slammed against it, and air gushed out of my lungs at the impact. But it didn't matter. I was used to the pain.

He raked his nails at my arm, trying to break free.

Gurgling sounds started to claw up his throat, the air wheezing thin as it evaporated from his lungs.

"Go, Aria!" I shouted. "Get in the car. If I don't come out in three minutes, you have to go. You have to protect yourself."

Hesitation flashed through her eyes before she darted across the room and grabbed the keys where I'd left them on the table. A whimpered cry jutted from between her lips as she blew past us, then ripped open the door.

A blast of freezing cold surged into the room, and Aria raced out, wearing only pajamas and socks, long, black hair flying behind her.

The fucker wailed in agony, like an intrinsic organ was being cut from his body.

How badly I wanted that. To cut him to pieces the way he threatened to do to Aria. He deserved no mercy or grace. I knew he was wicked. To his core. He'd opened himself to the Ghorl.

Welcomed it.

Begged for it.

I could feel it emanating from him. Just the same as I could feel it emanating from the monsters I hunted in the day. The way I knew who to track. Who to end.

He finally dropped to his knees, but still he clawed at my arm, his last-ditch effort at breaking free before he finally went limp and slumped face-first onto the ground. I squeezed tight for a few seconds more, ensuring he was permanently down, before I staggered to my feet.

Harsh breaths rasping from my mouth, I grabbed our bags, which were already packed and waiting, and ran out the door.

Frigid ice pricked against my heated flesh, and my attention scanned the area, looking for anyone who might have heard the commotion and come out to see what the disturbance was about.

Thank fuck the motel was empty enough that no one had heard.

I hurtled down the walkway, bags bouncing at my sides as I ran. Desperate to get to Aria, who waited below in the driver's seat with the car running.

Plumes of frozen air billowed out from the tailpipes, and I rushed for the stairs.

Only I felt the evil suddenly crash into me from behind, the heavy footsteps that pounded in a flurry of madness.

I whirled around, dropping the bags as I went. His fist was already there, cracking into my left jaw.

Pain splintered up that side of my face. It only incited my fury. The rage that crackled through me in a storm of aggression.

Blinding.

I went for him, throwing blow after blow.

He battled back.

Grunts and slurs and groans flew as our fists landed again and again.

Blood poured from the wounds that busted open on our flesh.

But it was my savagery that reigned.

I threw another punch, landing it with all the strength I possessed.

It was enough to send him reeling. So far that he hit the railing at the base of his back. His arms windmilled, his balance lost, before he tipped over the top.

Falling backward.

One second later, I heard the sickening crunch on the pavement below.

A muffled scream reverberated from within the car where Aria waited. Horror streaking far and wide. I rushed up to the railing, and Aria was twisted in the driver's seat, terror cloaking her as she looked through the window at the mangled body that had landed six feet to the left of the car.

Blood poured from the crack in his skull and pooled around his lifeless form.

But there was no time to process what had just gone down. I grabbed the bags, bounded downstairs, and tossed our things into the back before I jumped into the passenger seat and shouted, "Go!"

Chapter Twenty-Six

ARIA

Eyes wide, I gunned it in reverse. The tires spun on the loose gravel as we flew backward.

My hands and spirit were shaking so badly that I could hardly hang on to the steering wheel.

Consumed by the fear and a sickness that had sunk so deep into the middle of me I wasn't sure how I continued to see—though I couldn't tear my attention from the creep who lay in a broken pile in the middle of the pavement, either.

Lit up like the remnants of a massacre in the headlights.

I would have chalked it up to a nightmare if I didn't know the true brutality that waited for us in sleep. If I didn't understand what had sent this disgusting man after me.

When I was out far enough, I rammed on the brakes, shoved the transmission into Drive, then floored the accelerator. The engine roared as we careened across the deserted lot lit in the dingy blur of lights that glowed from the building.

Both horror and relief thundered through my being, all mixed with a solid dose of shock. My breaths were jagged, harsh, and discordant as they wheezed into the air, and my heart refused to slow as adrenaline barreled through my bloodstream.

I'd seen so many terrible things in my short life, witnessing them through the vantage of a Kruen's mind. Atrocities that scarred and flayed, weaving their way into my consciousness to become part of my psyche.

Twisting my hopes and beliefs into chaos and uncertainty.

Into grief and despondency.

But I'd never, ever seen it this way.

Up close.

Playing out in real time.

I'd never had to witness the true consequence of a Kruen's most wicked thoughts.

The tires squealed as the car skidded onto the street. My insides were trembling so hard that I wasn't sure I could stay on the road.

I was rattled to the bone.

To my core.

Palms sweaty, I squeezed the steering wheel tightly, my knuckles blanching as I struggled to focus.

To squelch the panic that lifted in my throat and the tears that burned at the backs of my eyes.

I just had to drive.

We just have to get away.

It is going to be fine.

It is going to be fine.

It has to be.

I jumped when fingers barely brushed over my upper arm.

Fire and heat.

"Are you okay?" Pax's words were shards. Sharp enough to cut.

Gulping, I could barely nod. "Yes. Are you?"

I finally allowed myself to glance at him. The horror I'd been feeling left me on a rasp. "Oh my God, Pax."

I hadn't been able to look at him once he'd come downstairs. My attention had been chained to the man who'd fallen to the ground six feet from the car. Unable to believe that it had happened.

He was dead.

Maybe most of all was knowing one misstep and it could have turned out completely differently. He could have gotten to me, or he could have gotten to Pax.

My sight blurred with the truth that it could have been my Nol who'd fallen over the railing.

It could have been him.

And maybe that was why I hadn't been able to look—because I was terrified for Pax. The fight he was embroiled in to protect me. What he was sacrificing. The disaster he was getting himself into. The danger he was facing.

For me.

For me.

He was doing it for me.

And the reality of that came crashing down as I finally took him in.

Blood ran in a web of rivulets down his face, and there was a giant smear on his forehead.

It streaked from somewhere near his temple, and there was a gash that continued to pour blood from his right upper cheek. Another was busted open at the edge of his lip.

Through it, gray eyes stared back, wild and untamed. An inferno of white flames. "It's not me I'm concerned about, Aria."

"You're hurt," I choked out.

"I'm fine." His teeth ground, and he glanced over his shoulder to peer into the night that gathered behind us. Trees enclosed the road on both sides, standing tall like patrols as the small town where we'd stopped disappeared into the nothingness, the murky moonlight above us a cold winter glow.

He heaved a sigh when he flipped back around to face forward in his seat, and he lifted the hem of his shirt and rubbed it over his face like it might stand the chance of wiping away the evidence of what had happened.

"Fuck," he breathed once he let his shirt go.

"He's dead." I didn't even phrase it as a question. I was already sure. Still, it poured out of me like the toppling of a vat filled with disbelief.

Pax ran the back of his hand over his mouth as if he could wipe away the bad taste. "Yeah, Aria. He's dead."

A tremor rocked me. An earthquake that shattered through the shaky foundation I'd been standing on. Bile clogged my throat.

A single tear got free and slipped down my cheek.

"He deserved it," Pax growled as if he'd felt the ground shift. The piece of me that cracked away and couldn't be reclaimed.

"Because of me," I whispered.

"No. He's dead because he's evil. Because he welcomed it. He wasn't innocent in this, and you hold none of the blame."

I knew it. I knew it the second I'd thought to reach out to touch him.

To try to bind the wickedness through his mind.

Only, rather than the overpowering urge to place my hands on him the way I'd experienced in the facility—with Jenny, with the others—I'd been repulsed. My soul had persuaded me there had been no way to reach him. No way to pull him from the vile depths where his spirit had descended.

It didn't make any of this any easier, though. It didn't erase the vision of him falling over the railing and smashing into the ground.

And it did absolutely nothing to eradicate the mess we were in.

Fear trembled through me. Stark and devastating.

"You're worth any sacrifice." Pax said it as if he'd read my thoughts. As if he had direct access to them. As if he could feel every beat of my heart.

I squeezed my eyes closed for a flash of a second. "I just want us to be free, Pax."

"The only thing that matters is that you're safe."

"And what if I want you safe?"

"I've already accepted my fate in this." His voice rang with finality.
That was a fate I refused to entertain. "Well, I don't accept it."

"There's no price I wouldn't pay for you, Aria." His voice was a
blade, cutting through the energy that screamed between us.

His penetrating gaze burned into the side of my face.

The words carved directly on my soul.

"This life never made any sense to me," he said slowly, his words a
low rasp. "I couldn't understand *why*. How we could be given such a
burden. If it was even real. If I even existed. I didn't get any of it. Not
until two nights ago when I first saw you."

Longing wound through the pain, and I glanced his way to find
those glacial eyes staring back. I returned my attention to the road as I
whispered, "A piece of me came alive that moment, too."

"But it's a piece of us we can't keep."

"Does it have to be?" The question slipped free without me giving
it permission.

Sighing, Pax scrubbed a palm over his brutalized face. "You know
that it does."

I knew that he was right. Or at least that he was speaking the truth
of what we had been taught. But there was nothing that could allow me
to believe that this man would ever turn on me.

Hurt me.

Not when he was so willing to sacrifice anything.

We fell into a knowing silence that whispered and moaned as I
drove through the night.

An uproar still beating in our spirits, the terror still stark, like
hounds chasing us down the road. Demons we could never escape.

Neither of us spoke until I saw a sign for a rest stop about an hour
and a half outside the town we'd fled.

"We need to get you cleaned up," I murmured into the tacky
stillness.

Pax hesitated for only a second before he gave a tight nod of
agreement.

I took the exit, the car passing beneath the double rows of streetlamps that ran on either side of the road. Blips of light pressed in through the windows and flashed over Pax's wounds like a strobe.

He scanned the area as we pulled into the rest stop's clearing. It was close to four in the morning, and there were three semitrucks parked side by side in the long spaces reserved for them. Their lights were cut, but their engines still ran through the night.

There was no stopping the flare of panic.

The fear that any one of them might have been sent for me.

And I hated that I might not look at anyone the same ever again. That I might be terrified of any person I encountered for the rest of my life, however short it was going to be.

Pax gritted his teeth, his voice hard but hushed in its encouragement. "They likely pulled in to sleep for the night. There's little chance we'll run into them."

Nodding, I swallowed around the knot in my throat and kept to the right at the fork that led to the parking lot that was reserved for regular vehicles on the far side of the buildings. Relief left me on a breath when I saw there were no other cars parked on that side. I slipped into an angled spot and turned off the engine.

Pax shifted in his seat to rummage around in our bags, his big body filling up the space with that energy only he possessed.

He passed me the shoes he'd bought me yesterday. "Put these on."

I somehow managed to do it while in the driver's seat, and he shoved his feet into his boots without lacing them.

He again glanced around the area before he slowly unlocked the door and climbed out, then reached behind his seat to pull out our bags.

I hurried to get out, trying to ignore the frozen wind that howled through the soaring pines that towered over the area, my thin pajamas no match for the chill.

Pax had already rounded the front of the car by the time I'd stood, and he took my hand. A rash of shivers streaked through my body. A clash of cold and overpowering heat.

His jaw clenched, and he forced out, "Let's go."

We rushed toward the buildings that housed the restrooms, keeping low and vigilant. He pressed us up to the exterior wall, and he peered around the corner before he gave my hand a tug when he found the other side empty, making sure that no one saw him in this state, not when we'd left a man dead a hundred miles behind us.

We slunk across the small courtyard toward the restroom. Pax again pressed us to the wall, peering around the corner and through the gaping door before he eased us inside.

It was only a fraction warmer within the white block walls, the only relief the protection from the wind. Two bright lights shone overhead, one over the two stalls and another over the sinks.

There were no mirrors or windows, and I gagged a little at the putrid stench as I tiptoed over the grungy brown tiles.

Pax grunted. "Not exactly the lap of luxury."

"I think this is an opportune time to remember I'm not the princess you were hoping I was going to be," I attempted to joke. To add some lightness to a disaster that weighed so heavy I thought I might suffocate beneath it.

Only a small cry got free when Pax finally turned around and faced me.

In the glaring light, his injuries were more distinct.

The cuts were deep, and bruises were starting to show where his skin had begun to swell.

"I'm so sorry," I wheezed.

"You and I have both been through far worse, Aria."

My teeth clamped down on my bottom lip as he brought voice to the pain we endured in Faydor.

"I still hate that it happened," I murmured, edging closer while he propped our bags on a sink to keep them off the floor. He dug into his duffel, pulled out a large first aid kit, and balanced it on top; then he rummaged around inside it, eventually producing a bottle of peroxide, bandages, and clean cloths.

He turned on the faucet and leaned over the sink. Over and over, he splashed cold water onto his face to wash away the blood, which had begun to dry and cake, before he doused a cloth in peroxide.

He hissed as he began to scrub it over his wounds.

"Let me." It was issued like a plea to his back. Wanting to do something. To change it. To somehow make it better.

"You don't have to take care of me." With the way he grated it toward the brick wall, I wondered if anyone ever had.

"No, I don't, Pax—just like you didn't have to come for me, but you did it anyway."

Air heaved from his nose, and he planted his hands on the sides of the sink and dropped his head between his shoulders. "I'm not sure that's true. I don't think I could have ignored your call. Don't think I could have ignored the lure of you."

Trembles raced through me, and I doubted it had a thing to do with the cold. Because I felt hot. Itchy with the need to act. With the need to touch. It was close to consuming when he finally turned to face me.

Everything about him was overwhelming.

Potent and extreme.

The sharply hewn edge of his cheeks and the inflexibility of his stony jaw.

The slash of his powerful brows and the plush of his lips.

But it was the icy flames of his eyes that were completely captivating. That would swallow me down and take me under. The promise that haunted me in my dreams.

I took a step forward.

Energy thrashed.

His breaths turned hard and shallow, panted in the bare space that separated us. He watched me as if I might not be real, either. Like he was terrified I might disappear. Like he wanted to hang on but had already made an oath to himself that he had to let me go.

Unable to look away from his face, I took the cloth from his hand, and I began to gently dab it on his wounds.

Carefully.

Tenderly.

Needing him to understand through my touch what he meant to me. What he always had. Only that feeling had changed and shifted and taken new shape once he'd come to me in the flesh.

Because he was here.

Whole and real.

Flesh and blood and spirit.

The one person I'd ever truly wanted.

The one I'd needed.

The air thickened, and I thought I could hear the hands of time slow as the connection that had forever bound us crackled in the room.

A foreign blaze ignited.

One that warmed my insides. One that was stoked with every rough caress of his eyes.

I hoped in it he could feel my appreciation for what he had done.

That he could feel that piece of me that had come alive.

The piece I wanted him to keep.

My lungs constricted as I stepped even closer so I could apply the bandages: one to a small cut above his eye and a butterfly stitch, which I used on a deeper gash on his cheek.

The entire time, Pax remained silent, though the thoughts that swirled in his mind were so thick and loud I was sure I could hear them.

Like whispers he uttered directly into my soul.

His need and his terror. His desire and his fear.

And I thought maybe . . . maybe he felt the same. Maybe he ached for me the way I ached for him.

The fluttery buzz that whipped through my belly and the tension that strained and pulled and possessed.

"Here," I muttered, my fingers shaking as they went to the hem of his soiled shirt. I began to nudge it upward, and Pax emitted a low groan as I continued pushing it higher.

Inch by inch, it revealed the peaks and valleys of his muscled abdomen.

Slowly exposing the scars that had been carved into his flesh and the colors and shapes that had been woven over them.

The designs veils of our truth.

Reaching up, Pax tugged the fabric the rest of the way over his head, and he vibrated when I got brave enough to softly trace my fingertips over a scar on his side.

A live wire that had been possessed by the energy that howled.

A power that was ethereal.

Otherworldly.

I felt it battering the exterior walls of the cold, barren restroom when I touched him, felt it penetrate my soul as he stared down at me with a potency that stole through my insides.

"Aria," he murmured.

I shook as I returned the whisper of his name. "Pax."

He let the pad of his thumb trace the scar that ran along my right cheek.

I leaned in to his touch.

"You're wrong, Aria. You are a princess. One I'd be a bastard to touch."

We remained there for a long moment.

Held.

Bound.

A piece of us anchored while the rest was lost to treacherous, violent seas.

Pax suddenly cleared his throat, and he ducked away and turned his back to me.

He'd only moved a foot, but it felt like a cavern had split open between us.

He dug out a clean shirt from his duffel, pulled it over his head, then tossed everything back into the kit before he stuffed that into the duffel and zipped it.

"We need to keep moving." A new hardness underscored the words, and he kept his gaze averted as he extended his hand for me to take.

He flinched when I did, the contact a searing burn that flamed, a burst of light flashing behind my eyes.

He led us back out, moving cautiously the way he always did, though now that he was cleaned up and had erased the evidence of the altercation, he didn't pause to look around the corners. He just hurried us toward his car.

I still had the keys, so I clicked the lock, and he led me directly to the passenger side. He tossed our bags into the back. Once I was inside, he shut my door, then rushed to climb into the driver's seat.

Headlights suddenly speared across the lot as a car approached.

He started the car and was getting ready to back out, only he had to wait when the car slowly continued behind us and pulled into a parking spot three down from my side.

Pax quickly pulled out just as the driver's door opened, illuminating the interior of the small SUV. But it wasn't so fast that I didn't catch sight of a little girl who had her face pressed to the back driver's-side window.

An unfamiliar face.

One I'd never seen before.

Still, my heart stalled out.

Because pale, pale gray eyes were staring back at me.

Pax shifted into gear and gunned it back onto the freeway while I tried to breathe around the clatter in my chest.

"Did you see her?" I finally managed to wheeze.

Pax hesitated for a prolonged beat before he reluctantly answered, "Yes."

Chapter Twenty-Seven

PAX

I drove southwest today. No real destination other than away. As far away as we could get. Like we could actually outrun any of this bullshit when it would only be waiting for us up ahead.

Every direction was fraught with peril.

Every road leading to our downfall.

I glanced to where she was curled up in the passenger seat.

Asleep.

For a moment, that beautiful face angled toward me was serene.

Lost to the smallest amount of that *peace* that I wasn't sure she could ever find when she rested within Tearsith's sanctuary. Her eyes had finally drifted closed just as the sun had breached the horizon and splintered the darkness with glittering white rays that had glinted over the expanse of snow that covered the Earth as we traveled.

She'd fought it, wanting to stay with me, before she finally let go when I'd whispered, "Sleep."

The rest of our Laven family would have long since disappeared. Most awakened by now to walk through the day or still fighting in Faydor. She'd be alone, where she could find true respite from the darkness that hunted us.

Where, for a few hours, she could be removed from it.

Elevated from it.

Which was where I wanted to keep her.

All except for the twisted part of me that wanted to drag her into the depths of my own depravity. The part that wanted to give in to the way she'd looked at me while she tended to my wounds.

Like I could be everything to her if I'd just give in.

The woman was my ultimate temptation.

And fuck, that temptation was getting harder and harder to ignore. The way her fingers had felt when she gently traced them over one of the scars that littered my body. The way she'd whispered her care for me, a direct buoy to my disfigured soul. The part that wanted to turn myself over to the need that thundered through my blood whenever she was near.

It was the sick part of me that wanted to tear apart her innocence. Write myself all over it. Claim what was forbidden. This inkling at the back of my brain enticing me into believing she'd always been meant for me.

A tiny moan filtered from between her lips, and I clenched my jaw to fight the rush of lust that slammed into me at the slight sound, but there was no way to stop the way my stomach tightened into a fist of want.

You can't have her.

I silently chanted it, driving it home and praying it would take root.

Aria was innocent.

Pure.

And I wasn't fucking close to that.

I scrubbed a hand over my beat-to-shit face to break myself from the dangerous spiral of thoughts. I mean, fuck, she'd never even been kissed.

But that danger went so much deeper than marking her with the physical. Deeper than her innocence. Deeper than the life I'd led while awake.

It was this bond.

This bond that was so fierce and unrelenting that once our time together in the waking world was severed, I wasn't sure how either of us would continue to stand. Experiencing the connection this way and then having it ripped from us.

I wasn't sure how the fuck I would ever walk away from her.

Taking it further past the boundary I'd already overstepped would only make it a million times worse once the time to leave came.

A cut so deep and unbearable that it would leave a scar far worse than either of us had ever sustained.

Knowing it didn't take away this feeling, though. The surge of possession I felt when she shifted in her seat, moaning again before she blinked open the palest gray eyes.

Face so pretty it pierced me in the chest. Mouth soft and plump and pink.

Everything about her was so familiar and warm and right that I had to force myself not to reach out and trace my fingertips down her cheek. Not to dip them in and take.

She stared for a moment before she turned her gaze away as heat rose to kiss her pale skin, like she'd borne witness to every salacious thought that had churned through my mind, and she sat up and stretched as she peered out the windshield.

"Where are we?"

The terrain had become flat, grasslands interspersed with small towns. The trees here were less dense, their branches spindly and barren in the winter cold.

"We're getting close to Oklahoma City. I figured that's where we'll stop for the day. We need to rest. Shower and eat. Pick up supplies and get better clothes for you to wear. Maybe find another library to dig deeper into what we found yesterday."

She looked down at the white tee she had on, which was smudged with my blood.

A reminder of what had happened last night.

Only it wasn't the man who'd come for her that she immediately mentioned.

"I can't get that little girl off my mind," she whispered instead. "I almost thought when I closed my eyes and stepped into Tearsith, she would be there."

Unease rattled through my consciousness. Still, I tried to play it off as inconsequential. "She's not a part of our Laven family, Aria. Seeing her was just a coincidence."

I didn't know why it felt like a lie when it should be the truth. When it shouldn't matter. But there was something about it that wouldn't let me shake the disquiet, either.

"A coincidence? When I haven't run into one single person like us in my entire life? Paired with the fact we met a human who recognized us as Laven yesterday?" Questions filled Aria's voice, and I felt the weight of her peering over at me.

I couldn't respond.

"Have you ever met one of us?" she pressed. "Someone from another Laven family? Or even seen one?"

My head shook. "No."

Contemplating, she sat back, her teeth clamping on that full bottom lip. "There's something about her that makes me believe she's important."

"There's little chance you'll ever see her again. She's hundreds of miles away from us by now."

Aria's head barely shook, and I felt a rush of her hidden power flare. "I think I could . . . feel her. Like she needed me."

I couldn't do anything but reach out and curl my hand over hers, which she had fisted on her lap. That fucking fire that wouldn't dim burned up my arm at the connection. I gritted my teeth against the force of it while Aria vibrated beneath my touch.

"You can't think about that right now. Right now, we're fighting for you. We have to keep you safe so you can be there for those who *do* need you. God knows, those numbers are greater than either of us could ever comprehend. I need you focused on *you* right now."

Her stare seared into the side of my face. "But that's the thing, Pax. You and I both know this has never been about me."

I heard her silent words come in behind them. The same as the ones I'd confessed to her last night. She'd already accepted her fate in all this.

"This world needs you." My voice rasped with emphasis. "It needs you, and you have to remember that. There's not going to be any surrendering or succumbing. You have to fight, and you have to fight with everything you have. You have to fight for *you*."

Unease quivered through her body, and when she didn't say anything, I tightened my hand on hers, words close to a growl. "Do you understand me?"

She finally squeezed back and whispered, "Yes."

And I think we both knew it was going to be a fight to the death.

About an hour later, we got into the city. Weird, but I found some kind of twisted relief in it. Found my heart slowing as we eased into the maze of cars and people. It felt as though we might be able to disappear into the fray and get lost in the shuffle.

It was what I'd always done, because it seemed easier to blend in with the throng. I'd put my head down to keep myself hidden in the mix, though I wasn't sure that was going to remain true with Aria and me together. And certainly not when it felt like every single person we crossed paths with might be a threat.

Still, I followed the directions on my phone, heading toward a Target located in the middle of the city.

I made a couple of turns until I was pulling into the store's parking lot. Thankfully, the lot wasn't that full.

I found an open spot, and Aria dragged a sweatshirt over her head, then ran her fingers through the matted pieces of her hair.

Disheveled with dark bags under her eyes, but she was still the most beautiful thing I'd ever seen. I didn't realize I was staring at her until her teeth clamped down on her bottom lip and more of that redness splashed her cheeks.

"What?" she asked on an unsettled breath. "I'm a disaster, right? So much for blending in."

She went to pull down the mirror. On instinct, I reached out and took her by the wrist. "No, Aria. You're perfect."

She froze.

We both did.

Caught in something that kept trying to sweep me under. Energy blazed through our touch. A fire that wrapped my arm in tendrils of flames.

Searing.

Scoring.

Magnified by the magic or whatever fucking power it was that hauled us away each night.

I finally released her because I couldn't keep touching her without spurning my purpose.

I scanned through the windshield to make sure a threat hadn't already met us here. When I found it clear, I cracked open my door. "Come on, Princess. Let's find you something decent to wear."

She let go of a surprised laugh, and fuck, I liked it, making her feel even a second of lightness in the middle of the turmoil.

When I stepped out, the air was crisp, but it was a whole ton warmer than it'd been on our previous stops. Aria lifted her face toward the warmth of the sun as she climbed out, inhaling deep, taking a minute to let it seep in and infiltrate.

I was at her side when she finally opened her eyes. "I think I love it here," she breathed.

A smirk threatened as we started across the lot. I kept close to her side as we walked, never complacent in my watch, though I was playing it as easy as possible. "In Oklahoma City?"

A tiny smile flitted across her lips. "It feels easier to breathe. Like the world has opened up. Like I can see forever and the sky has no end."

I think I got what she was getting at. The dense woods and soaring trees in New York had been beautiful but suffocating. Rising up and closing in. Gorgeous but disorienting cages you couldn't see through.

I thought it was the way Aria always had to have been.

Caged.

Closed in because her parents had been terrified of her getting out.

"And that's exactly what we're going to find for you—a world without end. One with possibility."

When I said it, she peeked over at me with affection on her face.

At her expression, little bolts of lightning ignited inside me in a firestorm of greed.

Fuck, it was painful not to reach out and touch her, but I kept it under lock and key, putting one foot in front of the other.

The doors swept open as we approached, and I grabbed a cart. We went directly to the toiletries. "Get whatever you need."

Aria hesitated, reservations flying through her as she chewed at that decadent bottom lip. I didn't think she had the first idea of what she was doing to me.

Finally, she asked, "How do you keep paying for everything?"

I'd never missed the way her eyes had creased in speculation every time I'd pulled out a wad of cash to pay for a motel room or food.

"Money is not an issue." I couldn't help but bite it out.

Confused concern twisted across her brow. Aria felt it. Sensed it. The undercut of what I'd said. I wasn't ashamed of taking from the corrupt. Wasn't ashamed of putting a permanent stop to their misdeeds so they didn't have a chance to hurt anyone again. But I wasn't sure that Aria could stomach the details of it, either. Or maybe I was only protecting myself. Because I didn't want her to see who I really was. What came so easily for me.

"How is that?" she pressed.

Uncertainty gripped my chest, but I took one step closer to her, my words held in a whispered secret. A shallow piece I was offering because there were some things that I just couldn't keep from her. Had a hunch that she had a direct view to them swirling like decay deep inside me, anyway.

"I take from those who only cause harm. Those who have no good left. Those I've stripped of their power because they use that power to inflict pain. Their greed is their ultimate demise."

I knew it was cut with a warning, and I'd fully expected her to flinch. To back away. Instead, she blinked with a soft nod.

Like she fully got it. Understood it. Like maybe she approved of it.

We stayed that way. Too close. Breathing the other in.

Before I did something stupid, I cleared my throat and took a step back.

"You should probably grab the things you need."

She stared at me for a beat longer before she gave a tight nod, and she began to load the cart with a bunch of girlie shit.

Scented soaps and lotions. Shampoo and conditioner. All of it coconut.

There was no stopping the amusement that tugged at my chest.

"Are you trying to smell like a tropical island?" My hands were fisted around the side of the cart as I stared over at her.

Black hair cascaded around her unforgettable face. Those striking eyes. My fingers tingled with the urge to reach out and trace over the scar by her chin when her smile tweaked at that side. Like the action had now become natural.

Her eyes swam, a toiling ocean of gray. "Don't you ever want to run away, Pax? Run away and wake up in a different place?"

"Isn't that what we're doing?"

"But are we really going anywhere? I used to think when I was little that maybe if I went somewhere else, I wouldn't end up in Tearsith." Her attention dropped to her feet for a beat; then her voice filled with self-deprecation as she continued, "We went to Disney World once . . .

when I was seven. I cried the whole way because I didn't want to go. Because I was afraid that when I went to sleep, you might not be there."

She chewed at her bottom lip and peeked at me when she said it.

Memories of that time slammed into me. When we were young. When we were innocent. When I couldn't wait to meet with her because she was my safe place. The place I'd go to escape the brutality of my childhood.

When I hadn't understood anything except for understanding her.

The horrors of fighting in Faydor had almost erased that.

The innocence.

But Aria had never lost hers.

The girl was so fucking good.

"I remember," I said, the vague memory fluttering at the back of my mind. Close to forgotten, where that time had been stored away. "I remember how you'd run out to hug me the second you saw me and said you were worried you'd never see me again. Only you would think going to Disney World was a punishment." My voice went soft with the ribbing. A gentle tease. The affection growing far thicker than I ever should let it.

A pink blush kissed her cheeks, and she dipped her gaze before she turned it back on me, the softest smile playing on those lips.

So red they could drive a man to distraction.

"It would have been, had I never seen you again. But now . . ." She trailed off as she turned to select a razor before she tossed it into the cart. "Right now, I almost wish that I could. After what happened last night? I wish I could go someplace, go to sleep, and I'd be normal like everyone else. Even if it was only for one night."

Shame filled her admission, like she should feel an ounce of guilt for wishing it didn't have to be like this.

"And this is where you'd go . . . to a tropical island?" I wanted to ignite the dream. Her fantasy. Because this moment might be the only escape she could get.

"It seems like a good place. The warmth. The sun. The ocean breeze."

"You're going to need a bathing suit."

I did my damned best not to imagine her in it.

She grinned at that. "I guess you're going to need one, too."

"Ah, you'd be taking me to this deserted island?" Playfulness ridged the question.

"Why would I want to go anywhere you're not?" Her voice became a wisp. Severity curled through the connection and grappled to take hold.

I scraped a hand through my stark-white hair to break it up, and I glanced to the side, only to find a woman watching us from the corner of her eye. I didn't feel any cruelness coming from her. No ill intent. No recognition like she was wondering where she'd seen us before, either.

It was just that uneasy awareness that we were different.

"We should move on," I mumbled, and Aria peeked in that direction, sensing the woman, too.

But Aria seemed to do that with everyone we passed. Pausing for an undefinable moment. Held in their aura for a flash. Her spirit tangling with theirs for a beat. That power flowing and surging as she was subject to the voices in their heads.

She dipped her head in agreement.

We went to the pharmacy area, where we restocked on bandages and tape and medical supplies before going to the food section to toss in waters and snacks. We rounded up with the backside of the store to hit the clothing.

I was quick to grab a few things for myself before we headed into the women's section.

"Is it warm where we're going?" she asked.

"It's no tropical island, Princess." I sent her a smirk. She laughed under her breath. Low and throaty and so goddamn sweet.

"Dang, and here I had my hopes up," she said as she started to hunt through the displays. She grabbed a few tees and bulky sweaters, three pairs of jeans, a pair of tennis shoes and socks, underwear and two bras.

I had to restrain the words from letting loose, tongue watering with the need to offer her my opinion on her selections. Because I was pretty sure black would look so damn good against her pale, milky skin, and I had to beat back my thoughts from spiraling that direction.

"You should get a jacket, too," I told her.

I honestly didn't know where we'd land or if we'd ever end up any-where. How long this was going to last. The one thing I did know was sitting in one place for too long seemed like welcoming tragedy.

Pushing the cart, I followed her to the jackets and coats, and Aria peeled off her sweatshirt so she could try one on. She pushed her arms into it, pulling out her hair from the back as she turned to me.

"What do you think?"

It was black vegan leather and cropped, and she was just so perfect and right, her gaze open and unforgiving.

Vulnerable and unguarded.

Shy but wanting to be seen.

Because that cage had kept her from experiencing any of that.

Dating. Boyfriends. Kisses.

Pleasure, when we got so fucking little of it.

All while it made me fucking irate to think of someone else touch-ing her.

There was no resisting rounding the cart, from taking each side of the jacket, bunching them in my hands and drawing them together at the chest. I tugged her toward me at the same second.

Our noses were close to touching, and the gasp she released was mine.

"What do I think, Aria?" My voice turned jagged. "I think you're beautiful. And if I dreamed, I would dream of you."

She exhaled a shattered breath, and I forced myself to step back. To let go. Knowing I was letting things fall from my mouth when I shouldn't.

But how could I keep them from her?

"We should get out of here," I said, returning to the cart. I started to wind it through the racks.

It took Aria a second to move, and she was peeling off the jacket and putting it into the cart when she caught up, her voice soft when she whispered, "I dream sometimes, Pax—and it's always of you."

Chapter Twenty-Eight

ARIA

Pax scanned our items in the self-checkout lane.

Quick.

Efficient.

Gaze always, always scouring the area as the scanner continually beeped, never ceasing in his oath to defend. I knew that he would. He'd more than proved it last night.

But it was the promise of his words from a moment ago that had left me staggered. Shaken me so badly that I kept peeking up at him as I loaded our purchases into bags. What filled me with the urge to trace my fingertips over the spot where he clenched his fierce, defined jaw, to drag my nails through the stubble and return to whatever it was that we'd shared last night.

Push into it.

Into the place where I could fall. Just for a little while. Into his warmth and his safety and his touch.

I wanted it, even if it was only once.

That need got tangled with the constant impulse to reach out and touch the people who jostled around me.

To listen.

To heal.

To slay.

To free them of the chains. To loose them of the voices that haunted and howled, so loud that I could almost hear the snare of it beating through me.

It'd been bearable when we were in the middle of the store since we kept our distance from others as much as we could. Dim enough that I'd managed to resist the call, even though it made me feel sick to walk away when every fiber in my being told me it was my purpose.

The reason I was here.

It was harder here, where people crowded together around the registers.

Blurred intonations hummed around me.

A low drone that fizzled and curled through the air.

"Take it, no one will notice."

"Kick the little brat's ass when you get home. He's so spoiled. Rotten to the core."

"Wouldn't it feel nice to drag that razor across your flesh? To see the blood flow? Don't you miss it?"

"Look at her. She wants you. Get her number. Your wife will never know. How long has it been since she's let you touch her? It's her fault, anyway. She drove you to this."

It was the first time I'd been around so many people since I'd been admitted to the mental hospital. Since I'd first touched Jenny and found a new way into the darkness.

Voices penetrated now.

Growing louder.

I squeezed my eyes like I could shield myself from them.

"Are you okay?" Pax's rough words cut into the disorder.

"Yeah, I'm fine."

Only it became too much when a wave of wickedness suddenly rolled over me. A dark, suffocating cloud. Black smoke that filled the atmosphere.

Consuming.

Overwhelming.

An infant wailed. Inconsolable.

Hopelessness coiled in the darkened mist.

I tried to squeeze my eyes against the assault.

"Why would you bring him into this world? Why would you put him through this? Think of all the pain that is to come in this life. Why do you think he won't stop crying? He already knows. Do it when you give him a bath. Put him out of his misery. It will be painless."

I gasped as my eyes flashed open. Drawn, they landed on a woman who pushed a cart into the store with an infant seat set in the basket.

She swiped at the tears on her face, and she reached out and rubbed the baby's belly. I couldn't hear it, but I saw what she said: "Please stop crying. My sweet boy, please stop crying."

"He won't. You know what you have to do."

Grief filled her.

Harrowing. Devastating.

"It's okay. No one will blame you when they find you bleeding out. They'll know you can't live without him."

The compulsion to touch her was the strongest I'd ever felt.

With my hands tingling and my heart racing, my spirit was already there. Energy rushed to my fingertips, a bright, blinding light that lit the way.

We were only halfway through checking out, and I gulped around the disorder, barely able to choke out to Pax, "I need to use the restroom."

A question marred his harsh brow, only a heartbeat needed to fully take me in. Concern immediately slipped into his features. "Let me finish, and I'll come with you."

"You don't need to come with me to the restroom, Pax."

It wasn't that he wouldn't understand. It wasn't as if he hadn't been subject to the same vile atrocities we witnessed each night.

It was that his purpose was different from mine.

His purpose was protecting me, and I couldn't take the chance of him getting in the way of what I needed to do. I knew he would always put me first, whatever the circumstance.

"The fuck I don't," he spat, low.

Another swell of depravity inundated me.

Dark.

Disorienting.

Blinding.

My lungs squeezed with it, my body vibrating with the need to go to her.

I set my hand on his chest. "Don't box me in, too. I'm not helpless or weak."

He looked like I'd struck him, the man torn. Worry pinched at the corners of his eyes while understanding lapped through the chaotic gray. He both wanted to argue and also knew that I was right.

"I'll meet you at the car. I'll hurry," I promised.

Dread curled through his expression. "Don't trust anyone, Aria."

I gave him a tight nod, then hurried away. I could feel the weight of his gaze burning into my back as I rushed toward the hall that led to the restrooms just inside the entrance. My entire body buzzed with the energy that skimmed over my skin.

I knew the second Pax looked away, could feel it just as I reached the hall, and I turned course and gave myself over to the lure.

To the tether that pulled and pulled.

I quickly wound into the racks and displays, keeping myself concealed as I went. I followed the far wall before I ducked into an aisle stocked with dishes and kitchen utensils; then I cut across the store, following the wails of the child and the bleakness that seeped out like wisps of poison curling through the air.

She was up ahead, turning right down an aisle.

I followed her, tracking, keeping far enough behind that she wouldn't feel me. So I wouldn't incite more fear when she was already riddled with it.

So close to breaking.

She took another turn, this time into the baby aisle. She stopped at the diapers, pulled out a pack, wavered, then put it back.

The whole time, the voices howled, and the baby screamed.

"Do you hear his misery? You did this to him. Only you can give him the mercy he deserves."

Agony radiated from her as she wound back around until she was in front of the dressing rooms. She unbuckled her son, brought him to her chest, and whispered, "Please."

There was no attendant, and she disappeared into the rooms. I followed her. Energy crashed, and my limbs twitched with the intensity that coiled in my being.

She was on the floor when I turned the corner, her back to the wall and tears streaming down her face as she rocked and rocked the child.

Her eyes widened when they met mine.

"He wasn't meant to be here." She mumbled the confession. Her grief. Her torment.

I dropped to my knees in front of her and took her face in my hands.

Cold streaked through my veins, the air ripped from my lungs, while the connection burned.

A fire curled up my arms.

So hot I might as well have been consumed by flames.

A chill raced down my spine, and flickers of darkness encroached at the edges of my sight.

A barren plane. Vapors and mist. Shadows rose and lifted and swirled through the wiry elms. The night thick, the sky low. Evil prowled across the lifeless ground.

Thunder cracked, a whip of wickedness, the force of it strong enough that it nearly tossed me back. I had to fight to hold on to her. To keep the connection as a dark shadow raged and tore and thrashed.

I held firmer, and a rush of images and emotions battered against my mind.

The pills. The paranoia. The voices that had haunted her since she was just a little child.

Hidden under her covers.

Shaking.

Shaking.

No joy. No peace.

End it now.

End it now.

There'd been a flicker of joy. Her hand on her belly as she'd looked at the positive test.

Maybe she had something to live for.

But the child had cried and cried.

"You knew better than to bring him here. You should have killed yourself before you got into this situation. How could you be so selfish to think a child would change anything? You're a fool, because he is cursed, too."

Poison dripped from the slithering voice.

"If you love him, you'll end it now. What's waiting for him is so much better. You'll see. You'll see."

Gasping against her pain, I tightened my hands on her face.

Her eyes blew wide open as I tried to push my mind into hers.

I leaned up high on my knees to get closer, squeezing my eyes closed so I could see.

And it was there. A shadow that thrashed and writhed, forever trapped in her mind. An aged Kruen of great strength. Its face contorted by the evil that made its shape. Its mouth gaping, a blackened hole of nothingness as it howled.

It hissed when it saw me, and a fiery tendril lashed out. It struck me in the chest.

At the contact, agony splintered through my body, but it was different from when asleep because I was already awake. And I held on, focusing with everything I possessed.

An orb of light swelled.

Glowing from the depths of me.

From a place that shouldn't exist.

I pushed it out, through my middle, where the energy raced down my arms and to my hands.

Propelling it, urging it toward the Kruen that lashed against the chains.

The bindings that surrounded it.

It screamed and screamed, as loud as the infant who wailed.

But I didn't let go.

I poured everything I had into destroying the beast.

An electric current rushed.

A bolt of lightning that lashed.

I felt it streak from my hands, and it struck the Kruen in its abdomen. It wailed in torment, the demon thrashing on the lifeless ground.

And in a flash of glowing darkness, it disintegrated into dust.

Gasps raked from the woman as the voice was silenced, and I knew the only thing she felt in its place was a hollow ache. She slumped back, still clinging to her son, who now only whimpered.

The two shackled by their shared spirit that the Kruen had tormented.

They are freed. They are freed.

Dizziness blurred my mind, the pain so great I couldn't see. Wheezing around it, I tried to stand. To climb onto my feet. But I had no strength left. Everything I possessed had been given to them.

They were worth it. They were worth it.

I stumbled backward, and somewhere in the back of my head, I heard a scream as I crumpled to the ground.

Chapter Twenty-Nine

PAX

I tossed the bags into the trunk of the car, all while I warred with the need to turn around and march back inside. I fought for the respect that Aria deserved, but I was also unable to shake the cold dread that chugged through my veins.

My spirit screamed, the call inside that bonded me to Aria refusing to let go.

It didn't just shout.

It gripped me by the motherfucking throat.

Something was wrong.

I could sense it, the way the energy had become cloudy and dark.

Scanning the lot, my attention returned to the door, praying to find Aria walking out of it. But another moment passed, then two, and there was nothing I could do but give in to the bands I could feel stretching between us.

Fierce and unrelenting.

Beckoning me forward and urging me into action.

At my approach, the door slid open, and I stepped into the chaotic energy that whipped and whirred. I started toward the restrooms, though the crackling against my flesh persuaded me to change course and drove me deeper into the store.

Mayhem suddenly broke out, and shouts sliced through the air as random people began to scramble toward the disturbance that I felt all the way to my spirit.

My heart jumped into my throat as terror pummeled through me, and I started to run, racing through the racks and following the commotion.

A crowd was gathered at the front of the dressing rooms, and I pushed through the people who were trying to get a peek at what was going down.

"Hey." A middle-aged man scowled as I jostled past.

"My wife is in there," I growled, knowing it was what would get me through, even though everyone parted once they shifted enough to look at me anyway.

But the only thing I could focus on was the girl who was crumpled in a ball on the floor just inside one of the dressing rooms.

"Aria," I wheezed. I hurried the rest of the way to her and knelt at her side.

A woman was across from her, sitting on the floor with her back pressed to the wall, her face covered in a sheen of sweat, her arms shaking as she desperately held on to an infant who whimpered in her hold.

Awareness spun.

Sickness and fear and pride collided when I realized what Aria had done.

"Aria." Slipping an arm under her back to support her, I brushed back a lock of hair matted to her forehead. My spirit cracked when I saw blood had begun to saturate the front of her shirt.

What the hell?

"Someone call an ambulance!" an attendant shouted.

"No, she's fine," I grunted. I prowled around my head to find a suitable excuse. "She just gets low blood sugar, and I need to get her something to eat."

I scooped her into my arms, hoping no one would notice the pooling red on her chest. She hadn't put her sweatshirt back on since she'd tried on the jacket, and the only thing that covered the trauma was the thin fabric of her tee.

"She's fine," I grated when someone tried to push up to check on her.

I prayed to God it was true, because this was something we hadn't dealt with before. Something unfamiliar. Something I didn't understand.

Our lives were already an impossibility.

But Aria?

She was beyond it all.

Rising high above.

Hope and light.

Her breaths were harsh and shallow, and her body was limp, even though I could feel her shaking at her core.

My gaze landed on the woman on the floor, who stared up at us.

Shocked.

Disoriented.

Confused.

A tear streaked down her cheek, and I could feel her confused gratitude soak the atmosphere.

In acknowledgment, I gave her a jut of my chin before I began to weave back through the people who were vying for a closer look.

No doubt, most of them had gathered for the entertainment. Morbid curiosity. I knocked my elbow into some chick who had grabbed her phone to record, making it topple to the floor, tossing out a quick "Sorry." Acting as if it were an accident.

We were fucked if someone posted about this.

If someone stopped us and started asking questions.

If someone looked too closely.

I couldn't take the chance that someone would recognize her.

I had to get her out of there.

Most of the crowd had broken up since it had turned out to be a simple medical emergency that wasn't worthy of anyone's time, and I strode through the store as quickly as I could, somehow managing to get out without anyone else stopping us, though there were plenty of heads turning our way, me carrying her out drawing more attention than I wanted.

Relief hit me when most seemed to go back to their day, though that relief didn't last long, since Aria slumped into the front seat of my car when I carefully set her inside.

She moaned, and I brushed the hair back from her face, my voice clogged with dread. "It's okay. It's okay. I'm right here. Just rest."

I was in the front seat and flying from the lot a second later, searching for a motel with exterior access at the light we came to, another dump where we might be able to go in unnoticed.

It took fifteen minutes to get there since it was on the outskirts of town, and I pulled into the covered area at the lobby. I hated leaving her for even a second, but I didn't have much of a choice.

Leaving the car running, I clicked the locks as I ran inside. I drummed my fingers on the counter as I waited for someone to help me, agitation lighting me through. I kept glancing back through the windows, making sure no one got close to my car with Aria in it, not when she was at her most vulnerable.

An old man with a stained white beard and a bald head finally came shuffling out from a back office, shooting me one of those speculative glances I was accustomed to. Distrust roiled from him, though I was sure he saw plenty of seedy fucks rolling through here.

That was confirmed when I doled out the cost of the room and he didn't ask questions when I tossed in an extra hundred.

Cash always bought you what you needed, people going tight-lipped when you paid them to do so.

Two minutes later, I was pulling into the spot reserved for Room 117.

Aria whimpered when I picked her up from the seat, so drained that she couldn't get her arms around my neck.

A shattered breath left me as I curled her into mine.

I maneuvered her around so I could unlock the door and support her at the same time, and I managed to get the traditional key into the lock before I opened the door to the dingy room on the other side.

Heavy drapes covered the window, the room laden with a dusky gloom.

It only had one king bed, and I pulled back the covers and laid her in the middle.

Exhaustion rolled from her throat, though my name was woven in it: "Pax."

"I know, Aria, I know."

Except I didn't. I didn't fucking know how to handle this. Who she was. The power she wielded. The danger it put her in. I hated even more the way it wiped her out when she used it.

The way it stole a piece of her.

But right then, I was more worried about the wound that now soaked her shirt. I only noticed then that there was a hole in the fabric from where it'd been scorched.

I pulled the neck back enough to expose the gnarled wound seeping underneath, the skin flayed open and charred at the edges the way it always was when we sustained a burn in Faydor.

I exhaled a shaky breath.

What the fuck? How was this even possible?

"I need to take this off," I muttered, giving the smallest tug to the tee.

Aria managed to nod, and she gasped against the pain of the fabric peeling away from the burn as I slowly drew it up and over her head.

I ignored the fact that she writhed on the bed, wearing nothing but her jeans and a plain white bra, and instead focused on the marred flesh that sat right in the middle of her chest.

My teeth ground with rage, and I murmured, "I'll be right back."

After jogging out of the room and to my car, I grabbed our things, then ran back inside. I tossed the bag of medical supplies to the floor beside the bed before I went into the bathroom and wet a washcloth at the sink.

On my knees beside her, I gently pressed the cloth to her wound, wiping up the clotted blood the best I could.

Then I poured hydrogen peroxide onto gauze, hesitating, because fuck, I hated the thought of causing her even an ounce of pain. But I knew I had to clean it.

"This is going to hurt." I issued it through clenched teeth.

"I know," she rasped.

It didn't matter that she was prepared. Her face contorted in agony when I pressed it to the seared flesh.

Unfortunately, it was the only thing that killed the poison—at least, that's what Timothy had told me right before I'd stepped into Faydor for the first time, when he'd put one hand on my shoulder and warned me that I was never going to be the same.

I'd never been told a greater truth.

The wound bubbled as I carefully dabbed the gauze to her skin.

Sickness billowed in my gut, nausea coiling at being the one to make her suffer more than she already was.

The pain was excruciating enough to jolt her from the stupor.

From the exhaustion that had sucked her under.

Pale, disoriented eyes flew open. Her gaze was riddled with torment and an apology.

"They needed me." She barely managed to gasp it.

I set my palm on the side of her face, my thumb tracing the hollow beneath her eye before my lips were pressing to her forehead, to her temple. And I was murmuring it again, my mouth to her skin, "I know, baby. I know."

Because she had no reason to apologize. She would do whatever it took to fulfill her duty. Just like I would do anything to fulfill mine to her.

Chapter Thirty

ARIA

Night had fallen an hour ago. I'd slept for most of the afternoon, finding sanctuary in Tearsith, resting in the thick grasses, held in the cool breeze that whispered over my skin, my mind lulled by the babbling brook that sang to the meadow.

Pax sat on the very end of the bed now, keeping several feet between us, watching me carefully where I was propped on a pillow against the headboard. I knew he'd done it the entire time that I'd slept. Even within the boundaries of Tearsith, I'd sworn I could feel his eyes on me as he kept guard.

"Are you sure you can't eat any more?" His voice was a rumble as he gestured to the fast-food container that sat on the nightstand.

"No, if I ate another bite I would burst."

He'd called in tacos for delivery, and they were the best thing I'd eaten in days, even though I'd only managed to get down two of the three.

"You need to keep up your strength."

"I am, I promise." Except I had little of it then.

Strength.

My limbs felt as if they were steel poles, immoveable and heavy, and the fatigue made me sluggish and slow, even though I felt a million times better than I had when I'd fallen asleep shortly after Pax had tended to my wound, then covered me in a fresh T-shirt.

His care had been stark.

His tenderness at odds with the ferocity that vibrated beneath his skin.

And his understanding . . . It was there, though I knew it was underscored with his own fear of the choices I had made, as if he wished he could protect me from who I was but knew it would be absolutely wrong to try to stop me.

It made it really difficult when I didn't understand any of this, either. The burn on my chest plagued me.

How I could have sustained it.

What it meant.

Pax pushed from the bed and came over to gather the container and my napkin. Gray, tumultuous eyes flicked toward me every few seconds, like he was worried I might disappear.

"You don't have to take care of me like this," I told him.

I shivered when his fingertips were suddenly on my face and running down my jaw. "Yes, I do."

Our connection shimmered. Brighter than ever, though it glowed with a current of dark.

Of a need that whispered of our desolation.

We were up against the impossible.

Hunted.

Forbidden.

My spirit stirred against it.

In a revolt that shouted that was what was really impossible.

Not loving this man.

How could I not? Not when he'd been everything to me for my entire life.

"Thank you."

His head barely shook, his voice shards as he tossed everything into a plastic sack. "I would do anything for you, Aria. And I need you to know that you don't need to lie to me the way you did. I'll support you no matter what. I understand your need to protect those around you, so please do it with me at your side."

My nod was shaky. "Okay."

He turned, his hewn, sinewy body moving through the small space. He tossed the used paper bag inside the small trash bin; then he edged over to the window and checked outside again.

I couldn't look away as he moved through the confined walls within the room.

He wore a tight black tee that stretched across his shoulders and back, the muscles defined and rippling. The tattoos seemed to come alive over his scarred flesh, visions of darkness that crawled and slithered with each movement he made.

My throat went dry.

He seemed to waver before he finally turned back to me. Hesitation brimmed in the savage lines of his face. Uncertainty of where we were supposed to go from there.

"Will you lie with me?" I whispered into the tension that strained between us.

"Aria . . ."

It was a warning.

Pain.

Need.

This confusion of who we were meant to be.

"Please."

Reluctance radiated from him before he blew out a sigh of submission. My stare was locked on him as he slowly edged around the opposite side of the bed. He was still in his jeans, though his feet were bare when he climbed onto the mattress.

It dipped beneath his weight, and his spirit thrashed in the night. I could feel it—like it was mine.

Flailing.

Pleading.

Desperate.

And I wondered if perhaps we shared a piece of each other the way that mother and son had earlier today. Their spirits bonded for eternity.

Or maybe what Pax and I shared was entirely different.

Because my stomach tightened in an anticipation I'd never felt.

Chills skated across my skin as he carefully scooted closer. It felt as if there wasn't enough oxygen yet I could finally breathe.

I shifted on my pillow so that I was lying on my side, and those eyes were on me as he rolled to his, too. Facing me, he wound his arms around my waist and pulled me against him.

A wave of energy slammed into us.

A riptide that kicked our feet out from under us.

No foundation but for the one we found in the other.

Shakily, I exhaled, and Pax pulled me even closer.

Close enough that my head rested on his biceps, and I could hear the thunderous pounding of his heart even though there were still at least six inches of space separating us. His breaths were shallow, as if he were terrified of inhaling too deeply, though it was my name on his lips when he whispered, "Aria."

A muted glow from the bathroom filtered into the room and played like temptation over his face.

The man was half-shadow.

Half-light.

A darkness existed in him, so much deeper than I'd expected when I'd imagined him for all those years, but somehow, it still felt expected.

As if I'd known this piece of him all along.

With trembling fingers, I reached out and ran them along a scar hidden beneath a serpent on the left side of his neck. "Tell me about your family. I want to know you."

Pax flinched. "I don't think I need to bore you with those details, Aria."

No question, boring me wasn't his concern.

I saw the demons lap in his eyes, the icy gray swirling with hurt and hate.

"If you knew the amount of time I spent wondering what you were doing in the day, Pax, where you were, who you were with, if you were happy—then you'd know there is zero chance of me getting bored."

The pad of his thumb ran the length of my jaw.

Tentatively.

Tenderly.

Affection softened his gaze. "I spent every second thinking of you, too. Worried about you. Wondering if your family took care of you. If they loved you. If you were safe."

"Were you?" I hedged it on a whisper. "Were you safe and loved?"

With the few things he'd admitted, I knew well enough that he was not. Never before had I wanted to be the one who was there to provide everything he'd lacked more than right then.

His laugh was hollow. "No, Aria, I wasn't safe and loved."

Sorrow billowed. His and mine.

He wavered for a moment before his tongue stroked out to wet his dried lips. "From the beginning, my father thought I was a freak. Of course, I can't remember, when I was really young, what he might have thought the first time he looked at me, but I can only imagine it was disgust."

Grief fisted my heart, and I set my hand on his cheek. My thumb brushed along the defined angle as I stared at him, waiting for him to continue.

His voice hitched in pain. "I had four brothers, two older and two younger, and my father never let me forget that I was different from them. He did his best to beat it out of me, to whip his freak son into shape. My mother was too busy with the others to give a shit."

Horror lanced through my being, and tears stung my eyes. "That breaks my heart."

His shoulder shrugged beneath my cheek, like it didn't matter. Like it didn't make me sick. Like the same protectiveness Pax watched me with didn't well inside me for him. "For a lot of years, the blows were enough to make me think there was something wrong with me. The older I grew, the more I thought I had to be fucking deranged. Crazy. Every time I looked in the mirror, I felt the same disgust my father felt when he looked at me."

His voice lowered to a wisp. "But in the end, even if I was crazy? Insane? None of that mattered if it meant I got to see you night after night."

"I hate them for you." It was true. I'd never felt that emotion as strongly as I did right then.

Pax cracked a smirk. "Probably about as much as I hate your parents for you."

My head shook.

But mine weren't cruel.

My father might have made mistakes, but I knew he made them out of fear. Out of his love and hope for me.

Not because he was repulsed.

Pax's fingers fluttered through my hair. "I finally skipped out when I was fifteen. Left home and hitchhiked across the country. No destination in mind other than getting away, because I couldn't take living under their roof for a second longer."

Hesitation darkened his features, and his voice grew thin, threaded with a warning. "I might have escaped them, but it'd already changed me. It carved out something ugly inside me, and it left a hole that opened me up to the depraved."

His words were gravel, and I knew he was leading me back to the confession he'd made at the store earlier today.

A frown furrowed my brow, and my attention jumped all over his face like I might be uncovering every one of his secrets. "What exactly did you mean earlier? When you told me about the money? You . . . look for people doing wrong during the day?"

Pax exhaled a rush of heated air, and he fiddled with a lock of my hair. "I just figured if I was chosen for this life? To fight in Faydor? Why wouldn't I be fighting the same evils during the day?"

Uncertainty barreled through me, and I was sure he read it in my expression. "So you look for evil?"

"Believe me, Aria, I don't have to look that hard. It's all around us."

"How do you know?"

His fierce brow pinched, and those eyes watched me through the shadows that danced in the room. "I don't think it's quite like what you experience . . . the voices you hear. The desperation. The hopelessness. And I sure as hell can't see a Kruen when I touch someone. But I can *feel* it . . . the pure wickedness. I can sense it when someone has fully given themselves over. I know when there's no good left."

A tremor rocked through my body, and I could feel the grim foreboding that radiated from his being.

"And when there's no good left in them . . . you . . . kill them?" I tripped over the question, and my mind pitched back to the man who'd attacked us in our last motel.

A man who was dead because Pax had been protecting us.

But I knew, by the dimming in his eyes, that what he typically did was different.

"Yes." The single word was a jagged stone. There was regret in his voice, though it lacked any true remorse. Silence curled around us like the serpent that slithered up his neck as I tried to orient myself to his confession. To the reality of who he was when he walked through the day.

"Are you scared of me?" His question whipped through the tension. Was I?

I reached up and smoothed out the harsh, defiant dent that furrowed his brow. "Am I afraid, Pax? Yes. I'm afraid of what you do. Of the position you put yourself in. Of the risks you take. But am I afraid of you? No. We both defend this world in the way we've been called to do."

"You think the blood on my hands is a calling?" The spite that ripped from his mouth wasn't directed at me but rather at himself.

"When you do it, is it to stop them from hurting someone else?"

His jaw clenched. "Always, Aria, always. Because the only thing these monsters have in mind is destroying. Ruining. I just see to it that I ruin them first."

I gathered the hand of the fingers that had been playing through my hair, and I brought his palm to the ravaging on my chest. Right over the spot where I'd been struck. "Then yes, I think it's a calling."

Pax drew me closer. The heat of his hand blazed into my flesh, his voice gruff when he murmured, "Because you're so good you can't see anything else."

"You're wrong, Pax. I see you. You're the only person I've ever really known. I might not have known all the details, but I know your heart. And I know your soul."

"Aria." My name murmured from between his lips, and his hand wound in my hair. A shiver streaked down my spine as he plastered me against the powerful lines of his lean, packed body, his arms ruthless and steady.

Heat flamed where we were connected, and my stomach tightened into a fist, a throb that pleaded between us like our own, desperate song.

He groaned as he pulled me even closer. Every inch of his body was sealed against mine, hard and raging, keening as our spirits begged.

He stared at me. Stared at me in torment and need, and I whispered, "Please."

A pained sound left him before he snapped, and his mouth was on mine.

I gasped at the connection. At the flash of light that burst behind my eyes.

Pleasure rushed, so close to overwhelming I couldn't see, and I was washed in a swell of lightheadedness.

The kiss was slow and powerful. His soft, red lips moving over mine. He tasted of dreams and possibility. Of need and desperation.

I whimpered and fisted my hand in the fabric of his shirt and begged again, "Please. I need you."

A groan reverberated deep in his chest, and he rolled me onto my back as he shifted to lie on top of me. He kept his weight on his elbows, though he pressed himself against me where he was wedged between my thighs.

His body was a flame that incinerated.

With the way my body burned, I knew there'd be nothing left of me but ash.

"Aria," he whispered at my lips before he deepened the kiss and stroked his tongue into the well of my mouth. I kissed him back, just as desperately, our tongues twining and twisting.

Tiny bolts of bliss streaked through my veins.

I clawed at his back, my nails eager and raking as he barely began to move, rubbing himself against my center.

I swore lightning struck in the middle of me.

A crackle of energy that pulsed.

"Oh God," I begged, wanting more. Wanting it all. "Pax, please. Take me."

Need vibrated through him, and he pulled me so close against him I was sure that we could become one, though he groaned and broke the kiss.

He dropped his forehead to mine, and heavy pants ripped from his chest.

"Fuck," he cursed. "Fuck."

He started to scramble away, but I grabbed for him, my arms looped around his neck as I murmured, "Stay. Just stay."

Every muscle in his body was coiled in restraint. In shame. A sigh toppled from him as he shifted to bring us both to our sides, face-to-face and breath-to-breath.

My entire being was still shimmering, a fluttery need burning in my belly.

"I'm so sorry," he rumbled.

My head barely shook as I reached out and touched his cheek. "I'm not. You're the only person I've ever wanted to kiss me. I've imagined it so many times, but this? This is something I will carry with me for my entire life."

He exhaled and wrapped me up again, pulling me close. So close that I could feel every jagged beat of his heart.

He pressed his lips to my forehead and urged, "Go to sleep, Aria, and tomorrow we'll forget I was the bastard who touched you like this."

The night pressed in around us, and the exhaustion sucked me under, the safety of his hold lulling me toward the respite I could no longer resist.

With Pax's aura holding me fast, I drifted and floated.

Then lights flashed before I flew.

Chapter Thirty-One

ARIA

Tearsith

Aria appeared at the edge of the meadow. Peace had followed her, as if the way she'd fallen asleep had carried her here on a cloud of serenity. She inhaled, drawing the sweet floral scent of the vingas into her lungs, and she opened herself to fill her senses full of Tearsith.

The gentlest breeze whispered with the perfect temperature, and she inclined her ear to the babbling of the stream and the murmur of her Laven family, who had already gathered at their great teacher's feet.

Her spirit jolted, already sensing the presence of her Nol a second before he flashed in at her side. It was the brightest light that shivered through the air and ricocheted through her body.

Energy.

Electricity.

A magnetism not held by the rules and bounds of the mortal world, but something else entirely.

Something all their own.

She thought the entire fabrication of her being might have been altered by the kiss.

Aria saw Dani jump to her feet the second they appeared. Anxiety radiated from her aura as she hurried their way, concern in her gaze as she approached.

It felt disorienting to know it had only been the night before when they'd all begun hunting the single Ghorl in the recesses of Faydor before she and Pax had been jolted awake by the intruder.

Dani immediately reached for Aria, her tiny hand on Aria's arm. A frown pulled through Dani's expression, and she cocked her head, her face so pale and thin with the shock of cropped-blond hair surrounding it that there was no chance those in the day couldn't sense that she was otherworldly.

"What happened last night? I was so worried about you." Her eyes jumped between Aria and Pax. "For both of you."

Timothy was suddenly there, too, taking them in. Dread clear in his gaze.

It was Pax who sighed, scrubbing an unblemished hand over his face, one that Aria now knew appeared so different in the day. He warily glanced between Dani and Timothy. "A man was sent for her. I woke to find him in our room."

"Fuck," Timothy spat beneath his breath. Worry lined his face as he stepped closer. "What happened?"

"I took care of it." Pax lifted his chin, and Aria was sure there was no mistaking what that meant.

Dani choked a quiet sound of horror, and she hung on tighter to Aria, as if her touch could act as a shield and stop anyone else from getting to her. "Are you okay?"

Aria attempted to tamp down the emotion. It was both fear and joy that she felt, this gift a blessing and her biggest curse.

Likely her demise.

But it was what she'd been given.

"I am for now."

She wouldn't keep the truth from her friend. The truth that neither she nor Pax knew how long they could stay out ahead of. How far they could run.

Pax hovered beside her. A quivering, violent fortress.

A shield.

Both here and awake.

"Did anyone else find anything while you hunted?" Pax asked, his attention flitting between Timothy and Dani.

Bleakness filled Dani's features. "No, none of our family heard it last night."

Disappointment blew through Pax.

Timothy visibly warred; then his voice came out as grit when he spoke. "Let me come to you while awake. Maybe I can help."

Surprise and gratitude filled Aria's heart. Apparently, with his concern for her, he was also willing to take the chance of coming together.

"You know I can't ask that of you," she whispered.

"You're our family," he argued, his demeanor urgent as he angled his head.

An offering.

Supplication.

"I can't stand aside and know someone is coming for you."

Alarm pushed Pax forward a step. "Don't do something foolish, Timothy. You know you can't put yourself on the line like that."

Disbelief puffed from Timothy's nose. "Don't do something foolish? Like you going for Aria? Like you *taking care* of some monster in the day? *You are our family.*"

Aria reached out, shaking as she took his hand. "You *are* my family. In my heart and my spirit." She reached for Dani's hand with her other. "And I love you both. But you know this isn't something you can get involved in during the day. You have your lives, the people who rely on you. And we don't know if all four of us together would make it even worse. If it would be even easier for the Ghorl to find us. They need you here, to fight in Faydor," Aria added. "It's what's important. You know that."

"*You're* important." Dani pleaded it.

Aria shook her head. She couldn't imagine asking them to step into the danger that surrounded her. Dragging them into it the way she had Pax.

Pax's spirit thrashed, a vibration that buzzed between them, and she knew there had been no option for him. Pax couldn't have physically stayed away.

Dani went to say more, only the atmosphere shivered, as if the ground rolled as their Laven family parted and Ellis and Josephine slowly made their way across the meadow.

"If there is anything more we can do . . . please . . . just say it," Timothy muttered under his breath.

"What we need to do is end that Ghorl," Pax grated.

"Has there been danger?" Ellis's voice was filled with caution, though Aria was certain of the awareness in his eyes. The weathered edges of the old man's face deep and knowing, a chasm carved of alarm and misgivings.

"A man broke into our motel room. I saw him in Faydor, through the Ghorl's mind. I was awakened before Aria and I were able to bind it," Pax explained.

"Oh my God. What happened?" Ellis asked.

"I ended him," Pax spat, venom on his tongue.

Surprise gripped Ellis in a fist of dismay, his pale, pale skin blanching to white. His nod was grim. "It was the only thing you could do. The energy will be greater with the two of you together. Everywhere you go, they will know you are there. They will be drawn to you."

Pax's head shook. "No. I don't believe this is about us. It is about her. It wants her."

"But why does it want her?" Dani asked, her voice hollow, needing answers to the questions they'd all asked themselves a million times that remained undiscovered.

"Because of this unfound power," Pax said, completely sure. "It's a threat to them."

Timothy ran a hand down his face. "How did she develop it? Never once have we been told of it."

Uncertainty cut through Ellis's expression. "As I told Pax, I'd only heard of it happening once, many years ago, before our time. There is only one obscure mention of it in the great book, though it is a reference to a Laven with a greater gift, so I have to assume it is a most rare treasure."

Treasure.

A blessing and a curse.

"There have to be more teachings on it," Timothy mused. "Answers that can help. Why would Valeen leave her vulnerable like this without anything to go on?"

"We have not all the answers, my children. We are given what is important—and that is the truth that Kreed birthed Kruen to destroy humanity, and we have been charged as humanity's guard. Aria has developed the extraordinary ability to wield this power in both places, and I believe Ghorls were bred as a direct counter to that power. The only thing we can do is continue to hunt this Ghorl," Ellis said. "Fight it. Pray we can put it to its end, and when we do, this critical danger Aria is in will be resolved."

Stepping forward, Ellis gathered Aria's trembling form into his arms, hugged her as a father would as he whispered, "Fight with everything you have. You are strong. Gifted. I saw it from the beginning, and I see it even stronger now. I never understood it, and I still don't, but the one thing I do know is, it floods from you on a current of power."

Aria lifted her chin to him. A promise that she would. She would give it all.

Then Ellis turned, his voice lifted, the words carried on the breeze. "It is time, my family, to descend on Faydor. Together we fight for Aria. For our sister. Bind the Kruens you come across, but listen, search, seek. If you hear or see anything pertaining to Aria, make it your priority."

A rumble of agreement rippled through the crowd. Mournful yet determined eyes washed over her, and they came to her, two by two, their fingertips brushing across the backs of her hands and the sides of her shoulders as they passed and headed across the meadow toward the dark energy that pulsed before they flashed through the threshold.

She and Pax slowly trailed behind.

With each step, she could feel chains that yanked at her spirit grow in intensity. The horrors that howled. It grew louder with each step they took, so loud that it screamed in her ears.

"We find it. We end it." Pax squeezed her hand in a firm grip. She nodded; then they took the last step forward.

Blistering cold streaked over her flesh, and she clung to Pax's hand as they fell through the consuming darkness. The vast desolation that slayed. Horrors screamed louder.

Aria and Pax slammed to the barren floor, making impact with Faydor.

They didn't hesitate, rushing headlong into the voices.

Struck by the instinct to fight. To hunt down the wicked and end them at their source. Ignoring that it was excruciating. Pain licked across her flesh as the voices howled.

Lightning cracked across the darkened sky, so close above that Aria felt the electricity quicken and the hairs rise across her flesh. They ran beneath it, over the barren plane toward the evils that intoned.

They ran through the abyss, through the disorienting maze of depravation, in the direction of where they'd tracked the Ghorl the night before. Their ears keen, their hearts manic.

Nothing.

Nothing.

They ran farther and deeper than they ever had before, twisting through the gnarled desolation and into the nothingness that went on to eternity. Darkness somehow both crackled and glowed as they raced.

Aria suddenly fumbled to a stop, unsure of what it was that had halted her. Pax threw a glance at her from over his shoulder, urging her forward. "This way, Aria."

She blinked, confused.

"What is it?" he asked.

Her head shook, uncertainty pulling through her consciousness as she searched for what she'd felt. A disorder amid the depravity. Something bigger than she'd ever felt.

A gravity that tugged at every organ inside her body.

Turning to her left, she stretched out a palm as if she were reaching for it.

The air shifted where she dragged her fingertips through the vapor. It felt as if she could step through the rippling air and disappear into the haze.

So similar to the way it felt when descending into Faydor from Tearsith. An energy calling to her.

"Aria?" Pax moved to try to peer at her face.

Confusion clutched her in a vise.

Then she froze when she heard it.

It was the faintest intonation in the distance. On the opposite side of where she'd been turned. It was a Ghorl's thoughts, echoing from far away. The one demanding her demise.

It was farther away than they could ever travel in a night.

The intonation was vague.

So obscure she wondered if she were making it up.

"It's her fault that Aria escaped. She's weak. Pathetic. Punish her."

Her father's face flashed through Aria's mind, one moment before the back of his hand struck her mother's face.

The image was smoke. Mist. Gone in an instant.

A shiver rolled down her spine.

A second later, Pax had her by both shoulders. "Aria? What is it? What's going on? You're scaring me."

"Did you hear it?"

Uncertainty slashed across his fierce brow. "Did I hear what?" Blinking, she shook her head as if she could clear the image. Pax hadn't heard it. She had to be making it up. Hearing things that weren't there.

So she whispered, "Nothing."

He hesitated, then urged, "We need to push on."

She swallowed hard, nodded, and took his hand. She only glanced behind once before she raced with Pax into the depths of the night.

Chapter Thirty-Two

PAX

The barest traces of light flooded in from the crack in the heavy drapes that covered the window, nudging me from sleep. It was always fucking disorienting, going from asleep to awake. From the battle of Faydor to the quiet calm of a room. From the howls of the depraved to the lapping shadows that played in a deceiving peace along the walls.

Heart still beating a manic pace when I woke up alone in bed.

Unless I'd been burned and awakened writhing in pain and fighting the screams of anguish that I held bottled in my chest.

There were things I'd learned to survive in this twisted reality. Things that helped me fade into the background. Things that allowed me to skate along the fringes of society without drawing too much attention to myself.

Rule number one had always been to never be so stupid as to fall asleep beside anyone.

Ever.

If I slept with some girl? I always made sure I was long gone before night fell.

Not that there was really a chance of that, since those interludes were always detached. Someone I met in passing. Someone I found in the seedy places I slipped into as I hunted the sickest, most warped of humanity. Someone who'd been morbidly compelled by the darkness they could feel vibrating around me rather than repulsed by it. Someone who was also looking for a physical connection without anything else.

I'd allowed myself that simple pleasure.

The physical.

And it was never anything more than that.

A release from the violence that streaked through my veins. A distraction from the constant torment that battered my heart and mind.

I never made attachments and had always known that I would travel this life alone. The freak loner, the way I'd always been.

Now my eyes blinked open to the dimness that covered the motel room and landed on the face of the one person in this world who had ever left a mark on me. On the one who was scored so deeply inside me that I didn't know if it was possible to exist without her.

Written on my soul and inscribed in my being.

Aria was still asleep, and her eyes twitched frenetically beneath her lids as she continued through Faydor, the only place I was ever supposed to know her.

Except she was wrapped in my arms, and her body was pressed to mine, our legs and spirits tangled the exact same way we'd been when we'd drifted to sleep last night.

That kiss still burned on my lips and played on a loop through my mind. I would never get over the way it'd felt to experience her like that, the way my heart had sped and my spirit had leaped. The way every inch of my body had come alive. And for those fleeting moments, my soul had howled that she and I were meant for more.

Touching her that way couldn't be wrong.

Then she'd begged me to take it further, and I'd come slamming into a brick wall of reality. I couldn't have her that way.

Yet still, I couldn't let her go, hadn't been able to all night, and I drew her closer right then.

Heat flamed where we were connected, and my stomach was balled in a fist of need.

My insides quaked as I thought of the hunt last night. How we'd failed at picking up a trace of the deviant. Funny how that tragedy had lent a speck of peace for us right then since no one had come for her during that time.

What left me really fucking unsettled, though, was whatever had gone down in Aria's mind right before I'd awakened. The way she'd seemed to get locked into some kind of trap. Unable to move or process. No doubt, all this bullshit pressure was getting to her. The strain was too great for any one person to suffer.

I felt the shift in her. When the rigidness of her muscles eased and she became light in my arms. As if she floated through the nothingness, through time and space and eternity, one moment before the palest gray eyes fluttered open to me.

They were already aware, no shock at finding me lying beside her, like she'd already known I was waiting for her as she fell. Ready to catch her even though she'd been in my arms all along.

Her tender gaze traveled my face.

Gently tracing.

Softly memorizing.

Shivers raced like tendrils of fire when she reached up and ran her fingertips through the stubble on my jaw, and my heart thundered harder.

The air was thin.

Shaky and turbid.

My voice was gravel when I spoke, grinding through the tension that strained between us. "I'm sorry we didn't find it last night. But we will. I promise you, we will."

"There is nothing for you to apologize for, Pax." She hesitated like she was going to say more.

"What is it?"

Her head barely shook. "Nothing. I'm just thankful to be right here. Right now."

My hand went to her head, fingers weaving in the locks of her long, black hair, caressing down until I was holding her by the back of the neck. "I just want to take care of you. Protect you."

"You are. You are right here. Exactly where I need you." The words were wisps, and the fingers she had on my face traipsed lower until she had them curled in my shirt. She drew me closer as she pressed her chest against mine. Desperate to erase the space. To fill the void that ached between us.

"I need you." She whispered it like a prayer.

A plea that I felt like a punch to the gut.

"Aria." It was restraint. A promise. A warning.

I knew I needed to unravel myself from where we were tied. Push her away and stop this recklessness before it spiraled out of control.

Before I did something I knew we would both regret.

But in that second, I could barely breathe. Could barely think. Everything was skewed by the greed that ran rampant.

It howled in my ears. Clouded my mind. Laid siege to my senses.

I was consumed with what it would be like to peel her from her clothes. Touch her. Sink into her.

Like she'd witnessed every salacious thought blaze through my mind, Aria whimpered a tiny needy sound, and her plump, swollen lips parted.

She arched. The peaks of her small tits were hard and pressing at my chest.

Electricity crackled and snapped, a bolt of lightning that shocked through the room.

Thunder came from a place that shouldn't exist, and I swore I felt the ground tremble.

My palm spread wide as I let it rove down her shoulder and skim her side, and my fingers dug into her hip, somehow both pushing her away and drawing her closer. "You're everything, Aria. I don't think you know the way you changed everything the first time I saw you. Standing there in the doorway of your room in the facility . . . when I looked at you?"

My fingers burrowed deeper as the words scraped like shards from my mouth. "It wasn't like being reborn. It was realizing why I was born in the first place."

"You were the truth inside me when I never knew what was real. My hope. The hollow place inside that only you could fill," she whispered.

Shifting, she dragged her leg over the top of mine, and those eyes flared as she purposefully rubbed herself over my cock, which had hardened to stone.

She gasped at the contact.

A thousand flames leaped.

Fuck me.

She'd barely brushed against me, but I thought I might pass out from the feel of her.

Sparks of pleasure shot up my spine, and lust rolled through my insides like liquid steel.

"And kissing you last night?" I said. "It'll probably go down as the single most perfect moment of my life."

Her teeth raked over her bottom lip like she could taste it. Like it was going to be the most perfect moment in her life, too.

Still, I was forcing out, "But we can't do this, Aria." The words were coarse. Gravel that scattered between us. "I crossed a line last night I never should have crossed."

The promise I'd made to Ellis echoed through my mind.

"Protect her while awake. Stand at her side until we see this through. We will find it and destroy it here. But you must leave her then. Once this is finished. And you must never give in to what I see in your eyes."

Aria peeled herself back.

It felt like I was being cut in two.

Both hurt and understanding were etched into every line on her face as she looked at me for one second before she rolled away, and the bed creaked as she sat up on the side, facing away from me.

I flopped onto my back, and I turned my focus to the ceiling like it might be able to staunch this ache. Soothe the way it felt like my chest might cave.

Or maybe . . . maybe if I looked hard enough, I might find a cure for who we were and who we were supposed to be.

When Aria's words broke into the tense silence, they were so low, so quiet. "I was meant for you, Pax. We might have been told it's wrong, but I know all the way to my soul that it's not. How could you ever be wrong?"

Energy swirled around us, that connection that followed us into the deep. Into the darkness, and now into the light.

It crashed as it crested.

Wave after wave.

"I don't know how many days I have left, but I do know that I don't want to spend them in regret." Her words were so quiet that they barely broke the air.

I was on my knees behind her before I had given myself permission to make the move. I wound one arm around her left side and across her chest as that hand went to the right side of her jaw.

I had her boxed against me, but it was Aria who had me caged.

My mouth dropped to her ear. "Don't speak in days, Aria. Not when I will give it all so you have a life. A real life. A future. Peace. Love. A family, if you want it. Whatever makes you happy. Whatever brings you joy. It's the only thing I want for you."

She shifted enough to look back at me from over her shoulder. Gray eyes glimmered, a sea of glittering silver in the slice of sunlight that cut through the slit in the drapes. "I already have love, Pax. It's bold and bright and never-ending. It's always lived inside me, hidden in my dreams. It's *you*, where you'll be forever written inside me."

Then she unwound herself from my arms, and through the shadows, I watched as she walked into the bathroom and locked the door behind her.

It felt like she was trying to put a barrier between me and her confession.

There was no chance of that.

It whispered on the connection that bound.

Rode on the tether that tied.

One so fierce, I was sure it was going to follow me into death.

Chapter Thirty-Three

ARIA

Hot water pounded against my skin, close to scalding, where I stood beneath the spray with my face tilted toward the steamy fall. I was hoping it might erase the need that blistered through my body. Burn it away. Eradicate the ache that consumed—body and soul.

I wanted to know his touch so badly that I felt it as a hollow cavern carved out in the middle of me. An empty space that throbbed and moaned and begged. A match to the pulse of my spirit.

Because I wanted him everywhere, pressing in and taking over. Beneath my fingers and gliding through my veins.

But I also understood. Understood his reservations and why he held on to the fear.

But that didn't mean I didn't know with every beat of my heart that what I felt for Pax couldn't be wrong. How could it when not loving him was an impossibility? There was no piece of me that could ever accept that he could turn against me.

Blowing out a sigh, I used the shampoo that Pax had placed in the shower with the rest of the things we'd picked up at the store.

I let the coconut-and-pineapple scent invade as I envisioned the foolish fantasy I'd allowed myself yesterday when we were walking the aisles of the store.

Pax and I on some deserted beach, our toes in the sand, with cool water lapping up the shore. A breeze wisping against our faces. Our fingers twined where we rested together.

It would be a place only meant for us. Where nobody knew us. Where nobody could find us. Where our dreams didn't carry us away, but instead, we slept soundly in the safety of each other's arms.

My daydreams were ones of simplicity.

But I didn't get that—simplicity or safety or sanctuary.

An intonation of my father's voice flashed through my mind, distant and faraway, dust that gathered on the horizon before it blew away.

It's her fault Aria escaped.

My chest squeezed with terror. A dread that clamored through my senses. Talons that sank into my spirit in a gutting awareness.

Because of me, my mother might not have any of those things, either.

Safety or sanctuary.

She was in danger.

I could feel it. I could feel it penetrating all the way to my soul.

I hadn't been able to bring myself to confess it to Pax this morning, unsure of how to handle it or process what it meant—or more, what I would have to do.

I couldn't just turn my back on them and pretend as if I didn't know.

My spirit sagged, burdened with so much. With the hazards that came from every direction.

I hissed when I pried off the bandage Pax had placed over the fresh wound in the middle of my chest yesterday.

It was a wound that shouldn't be possible.

A scar that I was sure would go deeper than any other had before.

A new question that marked me in doubt.

How had I sustained it? How was it feasible?

The memory of the woman and her child sparked in the spiral of my thoughts.

They were worth it. They were worth it.

I carefully cleaned the wound, dabbing the cloth against the oozing flesh. The blood that I wiped came away in black, charred clumps.

I rinsed, then stepped out and wrapped myself in a towel.

I eased out of the bathroom, almost wary to meet Pax's fierce gaze after what had happened between us earlier. But I wouldn't regret it. I would never regret confessing my love for him when it was my truth. I didn't think that I had it wrong when I said it was his, too.

His attention was hesitant from where he stood across the room, digging through his duffel bag, and he roughed a hand over his face the way he did when he was agitated. Then he dropped it like a brick to his side before he suddenly strode across the floor.

Heat shocked through me when he gripped me by both sides of my face, his hold so intense that it burst through me in a shock wave of light.

"Don't you dare ever think you're not everything, Aria. I need you to know that. I need you to know that every fucking thing I do, I'm doing it for you."

My eyes flitted over his expression. Tension was drawn deep in the lines of his face. I had the overwhelming urge to pick up a charcoal pencil and draw him like that. To trace his shadows. To capture his demons.

I stroked my thumb over the lines carved in his harsh brow. "I know, Pax. I know."

His throat bobbed when he swallowed; then he stepped back, tearing himself away. "We should get moving. Get you something to eat."

I nodded. "Okay. Let me get dressed really quick."

His own nod was clipped, and he slunk around me and moved into the bathroom, locking it behind him.

There was no missing the sharp exhale he released, the creak of the door as he leaned against it. No defying the energy that pulled and lapped, the need that wept like its own entity.

I moved across the room and picked up the duffel bag Pax had bought for me in Pennsylvania. Looking at it almost made me smile. That morning felt like a lifetime ago, when only mere days had passed. My time was speeding away.

The only regret I had was that Pax was in the bathroom, trying to rein himself in rather than being tangled in me.

I dressed in a pair of jeans and a sweater, dried my hair, and brushed my teeth, then packed the rest of my things.

A moment later, Pax emerged, and he moved to the sink, ran his fingers under water before he drove them through his hair, before he began to brush his teeth.

I watched him through the mirror as he did.

Awareness moved between us.

Thick and sticky.

Pax finished getting ready and packed his things, then grabbed our bags. "There's a fast-food place across the street. Is that okay?"

"Yeah, that works."

He cracked open the door.

I swore I felt an ice-slick of depravity blow in with the frigid breeze as Pax peered out.

When he was satisfied it was clear, I followed him out onto the walkway that ran the length of the upstairs of the motel, retracing the footsteps where he'd carried me in yesterday when I'd been too weak to stand.

The sky was clear, the same as it had been yesterday, but there was something forbiddingly cold that curled through the air.

I trailed Pax down the stairs.

His muscles bunched and flexed beneath the white T-shirt he wore, as if he were immune to the icy blast that whipped over my skin.

He tossed our things into the back of his car before he set his hand on the small of my back and began to guide me toward the restaurant.

"Are you good?" he asked. No doubt, he was picking up on the anxiety that had taken siege the second we'd stepped out.

"Yeah, I'm fine."

Except nothing felt fine.

Everything suddenly felt off.

A new dread kept spearing through my mind.

I couldn't get the image of my father's hand cracking across my mother's face out of my head. It'd been so distant and vague in Faydor last night that I'd had to believe it wasn't real. But I couldn't shake it. Couldn't maintain that belief. Not when a sense of foreboding rushed me like a rogue wave.

My attention flitted everywhere, over my surroundings, then at Pax, not sure what to do with my attention or where to place this feeling.

The sense that something was building.

Something dark and ugly that I wasn't going to be able to escape.

He shifted to take my hand, and there was no stopping the shiver that rolled down my spine at the contact.

His near-white hair thrashed in the winter breeze, the man a gale force that blew through the atmosphere. Skin so pale beneath the shimmering rays of the sun.

That steely gaze cut right and left as we hurried to the burger place that was connected to the same lot as the motel. A big sign hung in the window advertising that they were open early for breakfast.

This area had a different vibe than the other places we'd stayed.

Busier, and the parking lot was nearly full, which I guessed should be expected since we were staying on the edge of the city rather than in a small uncharted town like we'd done every time before.

I kept my face downturned the best I could, trying to keep it concealed, praying no one would recognize me.

A man who was climbing into his pickup truck paused when he saw me and Pax approaching. I felt the weight of it burning into the side of my head as he just . . . stared as we walked toward the door.

Pax twitched, and the exposed tattoos on his neck writhed over the scars they covered, as if he felt the force of it, too, and he tightened his hold on my hand. "Stay close to me."

"I will."

He swung open the glass door, and we stepped inside the restaurant. Three people were in line in front of us, and another two were loitering off to the side, waiting for their orders to be called. About half the tables were taken by customers.

It felt like every eye in the place swiveled in our direction.

Pax stepped closer to me. "I don't like this," he mumbled.

"It's fine," I returned beneath my breath. "I think we're both on edge."

"I'm not sure there's any other way to be right now."

I squeezed his hand. "It's going to be okay."

It wasn't, but I couldn't help reassuring him.

We got in line. The couple in front of us inched forward, trying to keep as much distance between us and themselves as they could. Unease rippled through their bodies as they cast a glance back.

I could taste their fear as they looked at Pax, at the dangerous, violent beauty that he radiated.

Or maybe what they feared was the chaos that whipped from my being.

When it was our turn to order, we shuffled forward. A young girl worked the register. Sixteen or seventeen. Her smile was kind.

I blinked, and when I opened my eyes, I swore that I was looking at my sister.

Smiling.

Laughing.

Our father's hand fisted in her hair and yanked hard. Pain and fear bottled her whimper. "Daddy, no."

A shocked gasp raked up my throat, and when I blinked again, the same young girl I didn't know stood behind the counter. "Welcome to Jay's Burgers. What can I get you today?"

My head spun and my knees felt weak.

I was seeing things. The worry was pushing me into paranoia. That was it. That was what it had to be.

"I'll have a number three with an orange juice," Pax told her, though he peeked over at me in concern when he felt the disturbance that echoed from my spirit.

"Small, medium, or large?" she asked.

"Large, thank you."

She turned her attention to me. Warm brown eyes blinked back, and her face was my sister's again.

Her lips moved but no sound came out.

Help us.

Dizziness rushed, and I had to hold on to the counter to keep from reaching for her, to keep from clambering over it to get to her.

I bit down on my tongue to keep Brianna's name from sliding from it.

"Um, did you want something?" The girl angled her head, a perplexity furrowed deep into her brow as she waited for me to answer, her face her own again. I attempted to clear my throat when it became apparent that I'd been staring.

"I'll have the same thing." I croaked it, barely able to form the words.

"Aria?" Pax's voice was razor thin. Low and harsh and urgent.

I swallowed around the bile in my throat. "I'm just . . . I need to wash my hands."

I took off toward the restroom.

"Aria." Panic wheezed through my name when he called out behind me. I didn't slow. I rushed down the side hall and into the restroom. I went to the sink, turned on the faucet, and splashed cold water on my face, trying to breathe through the tumult that I couldn't shake.

And I thought maybe I had finally snapped. Lost the sanity my parents had never thought I possessed. I wished it were true. I wished it were that easy.

But I knew.

I knew.

I smacked at the handle of the paper-towel dispenser, then ripped a piece free, my breaths ragged as I pressed it to my face and prayed it would blot out the images that racked my mind.

Behind me, the door swung open, and I whirled, expecting it to be Pax. I figured he wouldn't let me out of his sight.

I could see that he was out in the hall, peering in at me from behind the woman who came in instead, holding the hand of a little girl with blue eyes. I could feel the war of reservations and resolve spiraling through him, and I knew he was half a second from barging in to find out what was wrong.

"I've got to go pee really bad, Mommy," the little girl said.

"I know, sweetheart."

The woman led her to the first stall, and the child turned and grinned up at her mother. "I'm a big girl, so I get to do it all by myself."

Her mother let go of an affectionate laugh. I could feel the love that radiated from her. The solid devotion. "Okay, but let's get you a seat cover first."

She helped the little girl get situated, then stepped out and shut the stall door.

She smiled in my direction, though I thought it had to have been the first time that she'd actually looked at me, because she flinched when she met my eyes. Eyes I should have kept hidden, but I wasn't thinking straight right then.

She fought to keep the kindness on her face as she searched the distress on mine. "Are you okay?" she chanced. Her tone reeked of caution.

I swallowed around the ball of barbed wire in my throat, tamping down some of the desperation but allowing a small amount to remain.

"I think I lost my phone, and I was supposed to call my mom and let her know when I finished breakfast and was heading to school. I'm going to get grounded again."

I wrung my hands together, and the tear that streaked down my cheek was real.

Desperate.

A plea.

Her laugh was soft. "Oh, I remember those days . . . And we can't have your mom being worried about you. I know how I'm going to feel when Cassidy is your age."

She dug into her back pocket and pulled out her phone. "You can use mine if it will help."

"Really?"

"Sure, it's no problem."

"Thank you so much."

I tried to keep the anxiety at bay as I all but snatched it from her hand, and I rushed into the farthest stall and shut and locked the door behind me. There were only the three of them in there, but at least it was some kind of barrier.

I could barely control the shaking in my hands when I dialed my mother's number, and there was no stopping my heart from bashing against my ribs as it rang and rang. Four times before she finally answered.

"Hello?" Her voice was cautious. Suspicious and hopeful.

"Mom." I tried to keep the sob out of it, but I couldn't.

"Oh my God, Aria." It was a wheeze. Torment. Relief. "Are you okay? Please tell me that you're okay."

"I'm calling to ask you the same thing."

The sudden silence was sharp. Acid dumped into my ears. Howls of warning. An omen.

"What do you mean?" It was the smallest whisper from her.

"Are you safe?" I whispered back.

"Is that her?" My father's voice might have been muted in the background, but I could still tell that it sounded different from normal. A new cruelty woven into the fabric.

"Mom, I want you to get Brianna, Mitch, and Keaton and go stay with Grandma for a while," I rushed, praying she would hear the urgency in my voice.

"Aria," she begged, trying to turn it back on me, "tell me where you are."

"Please, Mom. Just . . . trust me. Trust me for once."

"Cal," she suddenly cried out through a clattering and a bang, and I knew he'd yanked the phone from her hand.

His voice was cold when it traveled the line. "What lies are you spreading now, Aria?"

Sickness boiled, and vomit climbed my throat. "Dad . . . you have to fight the voices. Whatever ruthless, horrible thoughts and urges strike you, you have to fight them. It's not Mom's fault. It's not Brianna's fault. You know that. Deep down, you know that."

"No, it's yours."

"Dad, please."

"You should get home now, Aria." His tone was detached.

Vacant.

As if it no longer belonged to him.

"Dad," I pleaded one more time before the line went dead.

I shoved my fist to my mouth to staunch the cry that threatened to tear free. Horror barreled through my senses as hot tears streaked down my cheeks.

My family.

Oh God, my family.

Sniffling, I swiped the moisture from my face with my sleeve and tried to gather myself. Tried to make sense of what was happening.

The far toilet flushed, and the stall door banged open.

"All done."

Light footsteps padded, and water ran in the sink.

Their voices were soft as the woman helped the little girl wash her hands.

A second later, there was a light tapping at my stall. "Are you okay in there?"

Wiping more tears, I sucked down the emotion the best that I could. "Uh, yeah, sorry, my mom's just really mad that I lost another phone."

I unlatched the stall and stepped out.

Sympathy pulled through the woman's expression, and the little girl swayed at her side as she held her mother's hand.

"These silly things cost an arm and a leg, don't they?" the woman said.

My nod was choppy as I handed her the phone. "Yeah. Thank you for letting me use yours."

"No problem at all. I'm happy to help. Hopefully, you can get yours replaced soon."

I forced a brittle smile, and the woman led her little girl to the door. When she opened it, she called, "Good luck."

The little girl shifted to look back at me.

My heart seized because it wasn't the blue eyes that stared back.

They were the palest gray eyes.

Wide and curious.

No longer the same face as the little girl who'd been standing beside her mother a moment ago.

It was the same child who'd peered at me through the car-door window at the rest stop.

Good luck, the little girl mouthed.

I blinked, and she'd morphed again.

Right before the door swung shut behind them.

Chapter Thirty-Four

PAX

Aria's spirit crushed me in a fucking fist as I stood outside the bathroom in the hallway, doing my best not to lose my goddamn mind as I waited. I would have stormed right in there if I hadn't known there was a mother and her little girl inside.

But fuck me.

How the hell was I supposed to stand out here when I knew Aria was distraught? I had felt the shift the second we'd stepped out of the motel room fifteen minutes ago. The way the air had gusted with a current of cold.

It was different from the effects of the temperature, though.

It'd been like touching down on Faydor.

It had seemed as if there had been a sudden break. A snipping of the thread of sanctuary we'd managed to find ourselves cocooned in last night, even though every fiber had been frayed, the fabric we were forming so fucking tattered that there was no chance it wasn't going to fall apart.

Pacing the hall, I listened to the sound of a flushing toilet, then the running of water, and I yanked at my hair to try to tamp down some of the anxiety that lit through me; then I was heaving out a flurry of hot air when the door finally swung open.

"Good luck," the woman called as she pushed through, leading the little girl out by the hand.

There was no focusing much on either of them. Not when Aria stood in the middle of the bathroom, all the blood drained from her head and her skin so fucking white there was no chance she could remain standing.

It was like she'd just been exposed to the most horrific scene, which was insane, considering the grisly shit we witnessed every night.

The door drifted shut as the woman and child passed, and the second they rounded the end of the hall, I pushed back open the door, feet eating up the space before I had Aria in my arms.

She was shaking.

Fuck, she was shaking so hard.

Terror gripped me by the heart, by the throat, by this desperation. "What's wrong?"

I angled back, taking her cheek in my hand, bending down to peer into the roiling depths of her eyes. "What happened?"

I was trying to make contact.

To snap her out of whatever had her twisted.

"I . . ."

She couldn't even form words.

I startled when the door swung open, and an older lady fumbled to a stop in the doorway. I was pretty sure she was wavering between running to the front for help or pummeling me to death with her giant purse.

"Are you okay?" she asked Aria.

Aria managed to nod, and she finally gathered herself enough to speak. "I just wasn't feeling well, so he came in to help me."

The woman frowned like she was questioning the validity of it, and I didn't hesitate to loop an arm around Aria's waist so I could haul her the hell out of there. By the time we got up front, they were calling our number, and I snatched our bags and drinks, because there was no chance that Aria was going to be able to sit at a table and act like everything was fine.

She kept her head down as I ushered her outside, and we hurried across the lot to where the car was parked. I helped her in, then rounded to my side and slipped into the driver's seat. I kept glancing at her as she tugged at the end of her sweater like she might be in physical pain.

I reached out and spread my hand over the tight fist she had hers in, hoping I could assuage whatever the fuck was going down, calm her, give her peace, all while losing faith that I had the capacity.

"What's going on, Aria?" My words were jagged.

"I . . ." She swiveled her attention to look over at me. Agony bled through her expression. "My family."

She choked on it, and there was so much torment in it that I nearly came apart right there.

My brow furrowed as I lost myself to her grief. "I know, Aria. I know you're worried about them, but we already talked about this."

Her head shook. "You don't understand."

I was going to respond that I understood perfectly before she was hugging her arms over her chest and a sob was erupting from her throat. "I . . . I thought I heard a voice last night when we were in Faydor. I thought I heard the Ghorl whispering to my father. But it was so far away from where we were that I couldn't be certain. But I swear, Pax, I swear I saw him hit my mother."

I shifted in the seat so I could fully face her, my hand on her leg as I tried to calm her, though I doubted there was much of a chance of that. Not when she was caught in a turmoil so great it didn't fully belong to her.

This pain was bigger than the both of us.

Gasping over a cry, she fumbled through the explanation. "But I felt safe with you this morning. When I woke up in your arms. It felt like it was exactly where I was supposed to be. Even if it was only for that moment, it felt perfect, Pax."

My hand curled on her thigh, and my chest was squeezing tight as my lungs compressed.

And still, I didn't say anything. I just waited for her to explain. To give me this since the only thing I wanted to do was hold everything for her. Be her buoy, her raft, her safe place when I was sure she was getting sucked into the depths of despair. An ocean of desperation swallowing her whole.

"And then, when we were ordering . . ." She hiccupped, then tightened her arms like she was doing her best to hold herself together. "The cashier. I kept seeing my sister's face in hers, and I swore she was asking for help."

Ice slicked down my spine, and a cold dread seeped out to saturate every cell in my body.

"I went into the restroom to try to gather myself because, obviously, I had to finally be losing it, right? I mean, I had to really be seeing things. Hallucinating. Then this woman came in . . ."

Aria looked at me then, her chin quivering as she lifted it. "I asked if I could use her phone."

Alarm banged through my insides, and my fingers dug deeper into her leg, holding on, too.

Trembles rolled through her as she swallowed, and she looked at me point-blank when she admitted, "I called them, Pax, because I *knew*. I knew I wasn't hallucinating. I knew I wasn't losing my grip on reality. I knew that it was real."

She inhaled a shaky breath. The cut on the edge of her lip tweaked down at the side. "My mother answered. She was distraught, begging me to tell her where I was, while I begged her to go to my grandmother's with my sister and brothers. I tried to warn her. I tried to warn her. A second later, my father ripped the phone from her."

The same way as that bastard had done when she'd called them the first morning.

Disquiet gusted.

I'd always hated her father, my gut warning me he'd be a part of her demise.

"I could hear it, Pax . . . I could hear it in his voice. I think he's fully succumbed. I think my mom and my siblings are in danger. I have to go back."

In a flash, both my hands were cupping her face. Fear ate me alive. "You can't, Aria. If this is true? If it has gotten to him? Then it did it as a way to get to you. It's a trap."

Tears streaked hot down her unforgettable face, the beauty of her devastating. The one who was written in my dreams and carved in my soul.

"It doesn't matter. I can't turn my back on them."

"And I can't risk you." My words quaked in emphasis. "There has to be another way. Some way to stop this. I can't just take you back there and lay you at that monster's feet."

"I love them."

"I know you do. I know you do." My gut knotted in fear, and I leaned in closer to her until our air was getting mixed and she was the only thing I was breathing. "But I have to protect you. And if you're hearing them . . . in the day like this?"

How was any of this possible? The binding while awake was difficult enough to process. But at least she was right there, next to the person. I could almost wrap my head around it.

But this?

Aria was so much more than anything I could imagine.

Her power greater than anything any of us had ever known.

"We need to find out why this is happening to you." So much shit had happened the last two days that we hadn't been able to research more. Maria Lewis's name beat through my mind. I was reticent to trust, but at this point, I couldn't shun any chance of figuring out more.

I shifted and took both her hands she still had fisted in her sweater, prying them away. I pulled them up close to my chest. "We have to find out how these hands can reach out and bind the darkness."

My lips found their way to her temple. "How this mind can see, can hear, can feel the things that it shouldn't. You are special, Aria. So fucking special. And they want to snuff that out, and I can't let them."

I inhaled, filling my aching lungs with the scent of pineapple and coconut, wishing with all of me for that fantasy of the two of us on a secluded beach, so far removed that it would be impossible for anyone to get to her.

Not in the day and not in the night.

"How?" she begged. "How, when I can feel they're running out of time?"

"Not sure, but I think we start with Maria Lewis."

My forehead was against hers, the two of us rocking.

"Somehow we'll find answers." I pried myself back, holding the side of her face and brushing my thumb over her cheek.

In my periphery, I took note of a man walking by the front of my car, though he had his hands in his pockets as he casually strolled by.

In an instant, I was hit with the disturbance that radiated from Aria.

"What's wrong?" It shot from my mouth.

Her attention was fixated on the man who'd passed.

He was a plain-looking guy. Wearing a button-up and slacks. Blond. Maybe in his mid to late thirties.

He didn't seem to be paying us much mind as he strolled around the corner of another building and disappeared.

Confusion bound her, and something unsettled toiled in her spirit.

"Did you feel something about that guy?" I demanded.

Uncertainty pinched her brow. "No. But I swear . . . I swear I've seen him before."

Agitation crawled through my chest.

"Where?"

She blinked through her memories. "The first morning. At the diner. He was sitting at the bar next to the old man. I didn't feel anything strange from him then, either."

Dread seeped through my insides. "Are you sure it's the same guy?"

Air puffed from her nose as she gave a harsh shake of her head. "No. I'm not sure of anything. I think I might be paranoid. Seeing things that aren't there. Maybe all this is catching up to me. It's all so much."

"And I don't think we should discredit a single thing you feel," I told her as I put my car in reverse and whipped out of the parking spot and out onto the road.

I searched for someplace secluded we could go, and five minutes later, we pulled into the lot of a park. Figured it'd be quiet at this time of day, which it was. I whipped into a spot, left the car idling, then handed the phone to Aria.

"You ready for this?"

Aria gave me a tight nod. "Yeah."

Chapter Thirty-Five

ARIA

My hands were trembling as I dug the piece of scrap paper out from my pocket. "Where do we start?" I whispered.

"Search the name she has in caps?" he suggested.

I typed *Charles Lewis* into the Google search bar on Pax's phone. The hope I was feeling sank when it populated with more than three hundred million results. How would we ever sift the information out?

Thoughts spun through my mind, and I narrowed the search, typing in *Charles and Maria Lewis, Pittsburgh, Pennsylvania.*

The results were much more manageable, and I started to scroll down the page, looking for anything that stood out.

I wasn't sure what it was, but my spirit rattled in awareness when I crossed an article that read, **Charles Lewis, Local Artist, Found Dead at 38.**

It was an article from more than twenty-five years ago.

I glanced at Pax, who vibrated at my side, his body shifting so he could also see the screen.

He gave me a look that said he was interested, too, so I clicked on the news article.

Charles Lewis, a local painter known for his sweeping, scenic murals found throughout the city, was found dead in his home Saturday morning. Authorities arrived at the scene after a frantic 911 call from his wife, who found him unresponsive after he'd suffered a gunshot wound. There was evidence of a break-in, and authorities are currently searching for any clues regarding the incident.

There was a picture beside it of the backside of a Black man as he stood on a ladder, painting a mural onto the wall of a building. He swept a scene of color and beauty. But the beauty . . . it was Tearsith.

"Oh my God," I whispered.

Pax exhaled a heavy breath. "Laven."

My nod was frantic, and I hurried to type in another search. *Charles Lewis, mural artist, Pittsburgh, Pennsylvania.*

It populated with a Wikipedia entry at the top.

Charles Lewis was an American painter.

Born: April 23, 1960, in Pendleton, South Carolina

Died: September 2, 1998, in Pittsburgh, Pennsylvania

Known for: Painting

Spouse: Maria Watkins

Parents: Carl Lewis and Isabel Lewis

Charles Lewis was an artist in Pittsburgh, Pennsylvania. He gained the interest of Pittsburgh locals when murals began to spring up around the city, though the artist remained elusive. Lewis remained unknown for nearly a decade until his identity was discovered while he painted a mural in an alley behind Omni William Penn Hotel. While Charles Lewis declined to take credit for the previous murals, sixteen of them were attributed to his distinct styling of lush landscapes that touched on fantastical elements. After the discovery of his identity, he was commissioned to paint three murals at Pittsburgh Children's Center.

Lewis's works were cut short when he was found dead of a gunshot wound at thirty-eight. His death was ruled foul play, though his killers were never brought to justice.

"Fuck, Aria," Pax breathed, and I could feel the way his heart ravaged.

I knew exactly what he was thinking.

Exactly what he was adding up, just like me.

Three Laven. Three artists who couldn't keep Tearsith from bleeding from their fingers. Two dubious deaths . . .

"He was married to Maria," I muttered as I tried to swallow around the lump in my throat. I looked at Pax, and he gave me a knowing nod.

The two of us in tune.

Barely able to breathe, I dialed the number Maria had left us and put it on speakerphone.

A crack ran down the middle of my heart, thinking of her loss, terrified but unable to stop my mind from spinning through a thousand assumptions.

I would be next.

It rang three times, and my eyes dropped closed in disappointment; then they flew back open when she answered, her voice wary, "Hello?"

"Maria?" I rasped.

Caution filled her tone. "Yes?"

My throat was raw. "My name is Aria. I was in the library a couple days ago."

Silence pounded through the line before there was shuffling around, then the sound of a door clicking shut. "You were with another?"

"Yes," I confirmed.

"Laven," she whispered.

My heart seized. I couldn't believe I was talking with someone who knew what we were. "I researched your husband. I'm so sorry."

Sorrow infiltrated her voice. "He was my ultimate gift and my greatest loss."

"You knew what he was?"

She scoffed a soft sound. "We grew up together. Went to the same school. Knew my whole life he was different. That there was something special about him. He was the shiest, brightest person I'd ever met. He did his best to stay away from me, trying to hide what he was, but I was drawn to him. And soon, there were no secrets between us."

She hesitated before she continued, "At first, I was terrified to believe him, but I think I'd always known there was a piece of him that wasn't a part of this place. There was too much of him to be contained by this simple world. Plus, I saw the scars. Held him when he woke up with them."

My chest clutched, heavy with emotion. Pax placed his hand on my thigh. Warmth streaked through my body.

"He was an artist," I murmured.

"A brilliant artist. He'd told me he felt compelled to paint. As if he couldn't keep the images from the places he went while he was asleep contained."

I guess it'd been the same for me. Why I'd been unable to heed the warnings I'd been given to never speak of it. How I'd shared with my parents, as if the beauty of our sanctuary had to find its way out through me. How I could never keep it from my drawings.

"He was killed?" I hated that I phrased it as a question when I already knew the answer. But I didn't know a better way to broach the topic.

Hatred and horror surged through the line, and her voice thinned to dismay. "It was hunting him."

"What was hunting him?" I almost begged it.

"He called it a Ghorl. Stronger than the ones he fought in the night. It wanted him dead."

Terror fisted in my stomach, and I could feel the apprehension roll through Pax.

There'd been more of them.

"Why?" I asked, scared to give it voice but needing her to give me the confirmation.

"Because he was different from the others. He could do the same work while awake that he could do while asleep, not that I could ever pretend to understand what that really meant. I just knew it made him significant. Special, the way I'd always known he was."

Oxygen wheezed in and out of my lungs.

"A Valient," she murmured in awe.

Surprise froze me for a beat before I whispered, "A Valient?"

Her voice dropped. "One with great power gifted by Valeen."

Gasping, I sat forward. "How do you know this?"

"That new power manifested in him a couple months after he turned thirty-eight. It was just . . . there one day. An urge he had to reach out and help people. But as soon as he did, horrible things began to happen. Mugged outside his shop. A drunk driver hitting him in a crosswalk. Attacked at every turn. And he could hear it . . . feel that the Ghorl was after him. He sought the knowledge of Valeen, was on his knees both awake and while asleep, seeking an answer. It was whispered upon his soul that he was a Valient—the greatest of Laven and the only ones who possessed the power to extinguish a Ghorl."

She paused, and I could feel the rush of her pain, her words choked. "He was killed before he was able to destroy the Ghorl. I was devastated, but I also couldn't sit idle in it. Over the years, I've researched everything I possibly could. Read books and articles and letters. There was little to be found, but I believe I discovered mention of several others."

The name of Abigail Watkins spun through my mind.

I didn't have time to respond before Maria continued, "Each of them were artists. And each met a questionable demise. You must ensure you don't succumb to the same. Because that's what you are, isn't it? A Valient? I felt some of the same in you as I felt in him."

A knot grew tight in my throat, and I warred with the truth. "Yes. My power appeared about a week ago. A Ghorl is already hunting me."

Pax twitched, and I could see the aggression roil beneath the ink on his skin as he leaned toward me, his left hand keeping him steady on the steering wheel and the other gripping the headrest of my seat tight.

I could almost see her reticent nod. "I'm so sorry to hear that. But Valeen gave him hope that he could defeat this, and Charles believed his purpose was possibly even greater than he understood. He didn't have the time to discover it, but you . . . I pray that you do. That you find the strength to end this."

It felt like I had razors in my throat as I swallowed, and I nodded as if she could see. "I'll fight with everything I have."

"I'd offer my assistance, but I doubt I am of much use in this."

"You've been more than helpful. You've answered many of my questions."

She'd been a bolster, an encouragement, but she'd also left me fraught with more questions and fears.

"Well, at least it seems you have someone with you who might also be of help. I wish you both safety. Take care, Aria the Laven. If you ever have need of me again, do not hesitate to call."

With that, the line went dead, and in an instant, I was in Pax's arms. The man holding me so tight he was the only thing I could breathe, his heartbeats one with mine.

"I'm so scared, Pax. All the other Laven who were like me were—"

"Don't say it." The words raked at the top of my head before he leaned back, set a palm on the side of my face, and his voice went soft. "Don't say it. Because the same fate will not befall you."

Chapter Thirty-Six

ARIA

After we left the park, we headed west with no real destination in mind. The scenery blurred as we traveled, nothing but dashed rows of crops in the rambling fields and a terrain that had turned barren with sparsely dotted trees.

Tiny towns passed by in a blip.

I barely noticed anything at all since I'd been lost to turmoil and determination and a looming sense of doom.

I could feel it. Rising all around. As if each end of the Earth had gathered to see through my demise while the good was fighting to keep me here.

My mind had been tossed into a brand-new chaos that defied the logic we had found.

Fear slithered in with it, and the heaviness sitting on my chest was so close to suffocating that I felt it with every jagged inhale.

The visions of my family.

My mother's desperation and the vacancy in my father's voice.

My love for them called me back. Urged me to return. I had to find a way to protect them and also to destroy this Ghorl. Protect myself. Fight it the way I'd promised.

All while the information we'd gleaned from Maria Lewis confounded it all.

There had been more like me, and each time, they'd been hunted. I did my best to remain hopeful beneath the weight of it, but it was difficult to cling to that when all the evidence ripped it away.

Night had fallen, and our headlights cut across the gravel lot in front of the tiny motel Pax pulled into. We were somewhere in Texas, and we'd stopped to eat about two hours before, thankfully, for once, without incident.

Here, the area was desolate, the town barely more than a sporadic gathering of houses, a gas station, and a small convenience store across the road from the motel. The motel itself was two stories, with exterior doors facing out to the road. There were five units on each level, and only three cars were parked in the lot.

The office was a small jut-out on the far end, and an old vacancy light flashed, though the first two letters had burned out.

Pax stopped in front of it.

Tension bound. So thick we inhaled it as if it were poison that coated our lungs. There was something in the air here. Pax blew out through the heavy strain. "Maybe we should keep moving."

"No. You're exhausted. We should rest, and we need to get back to Tearsith to see if anyone found anything last night."

He wavered before he nodded. "Yeah. You're right." Then he glanced around, peering into the nothingness that surrounded us to ensure it was clear.

When he was satisfied, he murmured, "I'll be right back."

"Okay."

He hopped out, leaving the car running and locking the doors behind him the way he always did before he strode to the glass lobby door and swung it open. It was bright inside, and his hair struck like white flashes of lightning as he moved to the counter.

Vicious and powerful.

God, he was beautiful. Beautiful in that dark, dangerous way that twisted my stomach in greed. Greed that made me want to push further into the boundaries that he believed were his duty to set.

He was in and out in less than ten minutes, and I watched as he strode back out the door.

White hair whipping in the wind, and that fierce, vicious face marred in his glory.

I wondered how anyone could look at him and see anything less than brutal perfection.

He slipped into the car and whipped a U-turn in the dirt lot and drove the short distance to park next to another car close to the stairway.

Immediately, he climbed out and went to the trunk to grab our things.

I followed, shuffling up to his side.

He glanced at me. "I don't hear and feel anything off."

I forced a grin, trying to find any lightness in the middle of a raging storm. "Now you're *hearing* things?"

The harsh, stony angles of his face curled into the semblance of a smirk. "What, you think you're the only one around here with extra powers, Princess?"

My stomach quivered. God, I loved when he was like this. When it almost felt like we might have a chance at normalcy. Love and a life.

"Powers? You're talking like I possess some kind of magic," I told him.

Pax reached out and brushed his calloused fingers along my jaw. Shivers flashed. "I think everything about you is magic, Aria. I think you radiate it."

My teeth clamped down on my bottom lip, and my stupid heart leaped.

A guttural noise rumbled in Pax's chest, and he used his thumb to free my lip, his steely gaze flicking between my mouth and my eyes. "Like I said, magic, the way you hypnotize me."

We got stuck there for a moment before he exhaled and grabbed our bags from the trunk. He shut it and clicked the locks.

"Upstairs. Room 2B," he muttered, and he ushered me up in front of him. His presence enclosed me from behind, his breaths salient in the cold air that clung to the night.

Unlocking the door, he flipped on the light. We paused in the doorway to take it in.

It was the dreariest, most run-down of all the rooms we'd stayed in, the walls covered in wood paneling and the carpet worn and coming up at the edges.

An old TV sat atop a battered dresser on the wall closest to us, and one small bed was pushed longways against the far wall to the left to allow room to get through to the bathroom at the back.

"Sorry, Princess, but apparently this is the best the motel has to offer," Pax grunted as he shut and dead-bolted the lock behind us, a hint of amusement gliding from his words. "Lap of fuckin' luxury."

"As long as it's warm, I don't care."

"Not sure you're even going to get that," he mumbled as he moved to the thermostat and cranked up the heat. "It's cold as fuck in here."

I sensed the true chill as he mentioned it, and dread slithered, and I got another sense that there was something different in the air.

I swallowed it down. "It will be fine once we get under the blankets."

Pax's fingers brushed my arm over the sleeve of my sweater. "It will be. I promise you."

There was far more meaning to it than us speaking of the temperature.

"Do you need to use the restroom?" he asked when he stepped back and dumped our bags onto the floor.

"No, I'm fine right now."

"Okay. I'm going to get cleaned up then."

"I'll be right here."

"You'd better be." Another smirk.

My stomach fluttered, that need I couldn't tamp down fighting for a way to fly out.

His aura covered me as he angled by and went into the bathroom.

Blowing out the strain, I grabbed my bag and tossed it onto the bed so I could pull out a pair of leggings and a long-sleeved tee to sleep in. I changed quickly while Pax was in the bathroom, and once he finished, we changed places.

I used the restroom, washed my face, and brushed my teeth, feeling antsy and probably a little too eager when I stepped out.

He'd already flicked off the lamp, and only the smallest strains of light filtered in through the thin drapes that hung over the windows. The blips grew brighter with each flash of the vacancy sign.

Pax had made a makeshift pallet on the floor next to the bed, one composed of only a sheet and a pillow. He climbed down to lie on top of it.

"You don't have to sleep on the floor." It came out as a whisper from where I hovered at the edge of the room.

Lying on his back, he stared up at the ceiling, his words cut into fragments when he forced out, "I think it's best if I do."

Tension bound the dense air—the memory of our kiss. The way his weight had felt so perfect against me. I could feel the power that urged us back to the same space.

"You'll get cold."

Even in the dimness, I could see him pinch his eyes closed. "Please, Aria. It's been a long day, and I'm already close to breaking."

Vulnerability spilled from him. His truth. His struggle.

I hesitated. At war with everything I needed. At war with what was to come. At war with who we were supposed to be.

Finally giving in, I shuffled on bare feet to the small bed, stepping around him before I climbed onto the bumpy mattress and slid under the covers. I pulled them up to my chin.

"I can't believe we ran into someone who knew what I was. Someone who was married to another Valient," I said into the lapping night.

Silence pressed down. "Don't think it was coincidence. I think she was meant to find us. To give you answers. To give you hope."

He rolled onto his side, lifted his arm, and curled his palm over the side of my face. His thumb stroked so lightly as he affirmed, "You are magnificent, Aria, and this world can't do without you."

I wanted to stay just like that forever. With his hand on my face and his thumb caressing soothingly across my cheek.

But sleep called to me.

An unfound promise of peace.

Darkness enveloped and minutes passed, and Pax's arm fell back to the ground as he twitched and shifted on the floor below me. Tension bound his muscles. An edge of violence firing through his nerves.

I waded there with him, in his anxiety, which thrashed through his insides before his breaths finally shifted.

They turned short and light as he fell away into a different existence.

I closed my eyes to follow him there, to meet him in Tearsith, to follow the call into Faydor.

I drifted. Floated and hovered on the cusp. Where the lights flickered and my spirit danced.

Only at the thud outside the door, my eyes flew back open.

Darkness swam through the room, and a vat of shadows played across the walls and crawled the ceiling. I sat up and angled my ear to listen.

I heard nothing, but I could feel it.

A whisper. A prodding. A call to my soul.

My heart panged erratically, and I shifted so I could peer down at Pax where he remained asleep. His jaw was clenched, and his hands were fisted in a fit of restless slumber.

I swallowed hard as I slipped out from under the covers. Careful not to disturb him, I stood and quietly padded to the window and pulled back the drape.

Night echoed back, the stillness only disturbed by the whipping of the wind that tossed through the sparse, leafless trees.

Only my gaze moved, drawn to the top of the stairs just to my left.

To the little girl clinging to the railing, with the palest gray eyes staring back.

Chapter Thirty-Seven

ARIA

Aria peered back into the room where Pax lay in a fitful sleep. Her heart climbed to her throat, each beat so heavy that it clotted out the flow of air as she struggled to inhale. Time moved as if it both raced and had been set to slow.

Every molecule of her being trembled as she returned her attention out the window.

The little girl with eyes so pale they were nearly white remained, staring back at Aria as if she possessed a tether that ran directly to Aria's soul.

A beacon.

The child was wearing only a pink-and-white nightgown—no shoes on her feet, and her blond hair whipped in the frozen wind that disturbed the slumbering night.

Never taking her eyes from Aria, she took a step down the staircase with one hand clinging to the railing.

She then took another and another as she began to descend into the nothingness below.

Panic surged through Aria, a blistering heat that burned through her veins. She didn't know why, but she had to get to the little girl. Reach her. Stop . . . something.

Frantic, she looked back to where Pax slept.

The urge to call out to him was almost painful, though she found she couldn't make any words form on her tongue. The knot in her throat blocked all sound. The words lodged, dead in her chest.

She turned back to the window. The little girl was nearly to the bottom. Dust blew through on a gust of wind, stirring the air into a darkened cloud. The road was barren, though at any time a car or truck could come barreling through.

Aria's breaths were short and broken as she hurried to undo the lock. Metal grated harshly, and when she finally had the lock disengaged, she stepped out.

The cement was frigid beneath her bare feet.

And the child . . . The child peered back at her from over her shoulder. That tether pulled taut. A lure that Aria couldn't resist.

She had to get to her.

Help her.

Get her back to her room, where she would be safe.

Only the little girl edged deeper into the wisping, dust-laden shadows that covered the lot. The vacancy sign flashed through it in serrated, bent strikes of white.

Aria felt it gather and cover.

A shroud of depravity. An intonation of evil.

It shivered over her flesh, and she sprang into motion and hastened down the stairs, clinging to the railing as if it were a lifeline since she could hardly make out her surroundings.

"Hello?" she shouted. "Hello? Where are you? Please. Come back!"

Another gust of wind whipped through, and the air thickened as a mist of clouds rolled in.

Disorienting.

She scoured through them, desperate to find which direction the child had gone. Her heart thundered, a pounding that throbbed in her throat and reverberated in her spirit.

Aria stepped off the bottom step and onto the packed dirt below.

Cold lashed her face, her flesh, her hair thrashing and scorching her cheeks as she searched through the blinding shadows that enclosed.

She stumbled forward, fumbling through the confusion.

She caught a movement in the distance, just off to the left, in front of her.

"Hey!" she shouted. "Please! Come back!" The sound echoed, and the tinkling of laughter rippled back.

Soft and delicate.

The little girl's.

Aria began to jog in that direction, ignoring the bits of gravel that dug into the soles of her feet as she followed the faint laughter. It was coming from the direction of where the road had to be, just up ahead, even though she couldn't see more than a foot in front of her.

Dread filled her to overflowing.

A powerful urge to help her.

"Please, come back!" she called again, lurching along behind the child, who always seemed to remain the same distance ahead no matter how quickly Aria moved. Her feet scraped over the bitter ground as she fumbled and rushed through the disorder.

The child kept running.

Giggling.

Laughing as she peered back at Aria with the palest eyes, though Aria was coaxed toward them like they were a lighthouse that beckoned in the darkness.

She hurried that way as the child neared the road. Headlights cut through the vapor at the same moment the little girl darted onto it.

Aria screamed.

Screamed as the blare of a horn shattered through the night.

She gasped, clutching her chest as the truck didn't slow but blew right through. Tears poured down her cheeks as it passed, then disappeared into the misty fog.

Rushing forward, she frantically searched through the thick vapor.

She nearly fell to her knees when the tinkling laughter rolled, and she caught sight of the child standing on the other side of the road. She faced Aria as she swayed back and forth before she turned and darted into the field of high, dead grasses on the other side.

Relief pounded through Aria, though that frenzy still battered through her body as the child disappeared. Aria inhaled a shaky breath and raced across the road, following the path where the child had gone. She wove through the maze of tall grasses, winding and turning and fighting her way through the labyrinth, following the tether that had a direct connection to her spirit.

Giggles billowed as the wind thrashed. Blades of grass as sharp as razors whipped across Aria's face and hands. She ignored the sting and hurried toward the call she couldn't resist.

She came to a stop when she suddenly stumbled into a clearing. A clearing where the clouds swirled over a blackened pond.

The little girl glanced back just as she dipped one toe into the water, then fully stepped in with the other.

"No!" Aria shouted. She lurched forward in an attempt to grab her, but the water was deep, and the child immediately sank beneath the surface.

Aria didn't hesitate. She dove in.

Frigid ice chilled her to the bone, and she struggled, lashing one direction and then the other to try to discern where the child had gone.

Daggers of glittering light speared through the waters, illuminating the depths, and Aria's pulse stopped when she saw the child was on her back, her arms and legs limp as she sank, her blond hair billowing around her angelic face as she drifted deeper into the abyss.

Aria broke the surface and took a gulping breath of air before she dove back under and swam with everything she had toward the girl, who continued to sink.

Deeper and deeper.

The pit bottomless.

Fathomless.

Frantic, Aria propelled herself, and she stretched out to grab the child's wrist. She nearly wept in relief when she wrapped her hand around the fragile arm.

Only the second she did, the child's eyes flashed open.

And those eyes . . . The palest gray eyes had turned a blinding white. Shafts of light that cut through the disorienting water, and her lips twisted in a demented grin before they opened wide, and a storm of shadows rushed from her mouth.

The child's features began to morph.

Her face flashed between the child's and a man's.

The same man Aria had seen earlier outside the fast-food restaurant. The one she'd seen days before at the diner.

It was him.

It was him.

But she could no longer focus on the blipping facade.

Because she was surrounded by the shadows.

A hundred.

A thousand.

Wisps that curled and twisted and took new shape, transforming into screaming, horrific faces.

The faces of Faydor.

Kruen whirled and whirled, a blur that spun around her as they dragged her deeper into the depths of the chasm.

Aria fought, thrashing and flailing as she tried to break away, to get loose of the tendrils that wrapped around her limbs.

She fought.

She fought.

Yanking and kicking and trying to get free. She struggled against the burning in her lungs that begged her to breathe.

She couldn't.

She couldn't succumb. She couldn't give in.

She thrashed more, but there was no give.

No break.

No relief.

That pain in her chest became overwhelming, and it hurt so much—agonizing—the feeling that she was suffocating, as if a thousand-pound boulder sat on her chest.

And there was nothing Aria could do.

She opened her mouth in search of the oxygen that wasn't there.

And she inhaled the frigid water into her lungs.

Chapter Thirty-Eight

PAX

I jolted awake, pulled from sleep—by what, I wasn't sure, though my soul hammered in unrest.

Something wasn't right.

I'd waited in Tearsith for her, my hands continually curling into fists as my spirit had roiled with this sticky, unsettled feeling that had taken me hostage. It had swelled and grown, and by the time our family had completely descended into Faydor, it'd become a frenzy that beat through my veins.

Whatever it was, it'd shocked me upright from where I was on the floor of the shitty motel.

The room was dark, save for the wedge of light coming from the bathroom where I'd left the door open an inch and the bare flashes that lit up behind the drapes in the window.

The floor was hard beneath me.

Aria was on the bed.

Asleep.

Which wasn't fucking right, since she hadn't been in Tearsith.

Only she wasn't still. She was flailing. Her arms and feet frantic as her body jerked and twitched. The mattress squeaked with her frenetic movements, and her breaths were nothing but these gurgled, strangled sounds.

Panic jumped straight into my bloodstream, and I was on my knees on the bed just as her name ripped from my tongue. "Aria."

She thrashed, and my hands shot out to grab her by the shoulders. Confusion bound me the second I touched her.

She was soaking wet.

What the fuck?

Teeth gritted, I shook her. "Aria. Wake up."

She writhed, arms swinging, and her inhale was filled with the rattle of pain.

Horror kicked in, fear a thunder that raced through my manic heart, and I rushed to climb over her. I straddled her at the waist, my weight on my knees as I shook her harder. "Aria, you have to wake up! Listen to me. Follow my voice. Open your eyes."

Desperation poured out with the words.

Only the gurgling in her throat increased, and her body tremored in these spasms that made me terrified she was losing her life. Dread clutched me in a fist, and I shook her even harder, lifting her up and slamming her down onto the mattress when she still didn't open her eyes.

"Please, please open your eyes. I won't let you leave me. I fucking won't."

They couldn't have her.

I wouldn't let them.

The thought of it cut through me, flaying me open wide, deeper and more brutal than any wound a Kruen had ever inflicted.

This world needed her. I needed her. Fuck, I needed her.

"Aria, please, baby, please."

Frantic and shaking, I splayed my palm over her chest, fingers stretching wide, the single word haggard. "Please."

Then I pressed down.

Hard.

Her body bowed beneath me as I compressed her chest.

I did it again.

And again.

Desperate. Pleading.

"Please, Aria. Please."

Her head rocked back, and her chest stretched for the ceiling before she suddenly bolted upright.

Her pale eyes were wide with terror as water gushed from her mouth.

And she was wheezing. Deep, jagged breaths clamored from her lungs as she tried to draw the oxygen she'd been missing into the wells of them, anguished and full of fear as a sob erupted from her throat.

At the sound of it, relief pummeled me so hard I could have sworn that my ribs cracked.

I pulled her shivering frame against me, my arms shaking like a bitch as I wrapped her in them.

And Aria . . . Aria cried against my chest. Deep, guttural moans that bled from her spirit.

"Pax," she sobbed.

I kept one arm looped around her waist as my free hand wound in the dripping tendrils of midnight locks, which were drenched and stuck to her face. I pressed my lips to her crown, my voice the roughest scrape as I murmured, "It's okay. It's okay. You're safe. I've got you."

She cried harder at my words, and her fingers curled into the fabric of my tee as she clung to me, like I could be a buoy.

Her safe place.

It was the only fucking thing in this world that I wanted to be.

"Pax." She wheezed it, my name a riddle in the middle of her horror and shock and disbelief. She rose up on her knees and pressed her freezing body against mine.

"I know. I know."

Except I didn't fucking know. I had no clue how any of this was possible.

A ferocity beat chaos into my blood, my devotion and fear so intense that it pounded through my bloodstream.

So loud I could hear it booming in my ears.

So hard I could feel it booming in my spirit.

But it was Aria who had always boomed in my soul.

"Tell me what happened." Getting the question out was close to impossible.

She gave a harsh shake of her head, and she pushed her face up into my neck, her fingers digging into my shoulders to draw me closer, her breaths panting against my flesh. "I don't want to talk about it. Right now, I need you. I need you."

Her plea filled my senses.

Sweet and intoxicating.

"You have me, Aria. You have me, just like I have you. I won't let you go. I won't let them have you. I won't let them hurt you."

Our connection screamed. A howl that echoed through the room.

We began to rock where we were, both on our knees on the bed, taken on a wave, set out to sea. Her lips rolled up my throat and over my jaw until she was panting at my mouth.

Her eyes were open wide.

Eyes that scored on me like the haunting of a dream.

Our bodies quaked and writhed, and her nose brushed mine, and she whispered, "I will never believe that loving you this way is wrong."

At her words, the last threads of my restraint snapped, and there was nothing I could do but take her mouth in a kiss.

A fucking fire erupted at the contact, and Aria opened on a gasp. Her nails sank into my skin, and our tongues tangled in a fit of greed that I wasn't sure could ever be sated.

Desperation billowed between us. Tendrils and flames that wound and claimed.

"Aria," I murmured against her lips, never breaking the kiss, which had turned frantic.

"I need you" rushed out of her in return, and she was clawing at my tee. I edged away so she could pull it over my head.

My hands slipped under her shirt, and I splayed my palms across the silken flesh of her back. I was singed by the cold that clashed with the heat.

"Please." She fisted my hair as she pushed herself closer.

And there were no boundaries left between us.

No veiled rules that could stand in the way.

No walls left to climb.

Because she was right. This was the way we were supposed to be. I was created for her, and she was created for me.

Our connection was bigger, more profound, than we'd been led to believe. There was no stopping the feeling that swept through like a windstorm, the impact of this touch that glided through our veins.

I dragged her soaked shirt up, and we broke apart long enough that I could pull it over her head and toss it to the floor.

A sharp breath punched from her lungs before she threw herself back at me. She pressed her bare chest flush against mine. Her nipples were pebbled and hard, and fuck, I thought I might die just from the feel of her like that alone.

I groaned, and her name left me on a prayer. "Aria. You're every dream I've ever had. Every vision in the day. Every hope that I've dared to have. All of me, it's yours."

Chills rolled through her, and she curled her arms around my neck while I threaded my fingers in the drenched locks of her hair, my other arm looped around her waist as I kept her close.

She kept kissing me and kissing me, just as fiercely as I kissed her back.

Sweet hands explored. Riding over my shoulders and down my sides. Nails raked my chest, sending pleasure shooting through my body, and every inch of me was trembling when she reached far enough between us to slip them under the waist of my sweats.

I hissed, and my stomach tightened. "Is this what you want?"

"You, Pax. I want you. All of you, like you promised me. I don't know how long I have. How long I can run. But I do know that if I get to have one wish, it would be to experience this with you."

There was only a faint voice at the back of my mind warning me that this was wrong. A voice warning that I was crossing a line that was only going to bring more destruction.

The rest of me knew there wasn't a chance on this godforsaken Earth that I would deny her this.

So I carefully scooped her up and slipped off the bed. Laying her on the thin sheet on the floor, I stared down at the girl who stared up at me.

She searched me, like she might find the answer to this life written in the scars that marred my flesh. Find it hidden in the lines that dented deep in my brow.

I searched her, too.

Gaze tracing.

Exploring.

The sharp angles of her face were so striking. Unforgettable. This woman who was carved into every recess of my being. I got the sense right then that my heart had been woven with the fabric of hers.

I brushed my fingers through her hair and let my thumb stroke her cheek. "Are you sure?"

She reached up and set a trembling hand on my cheek. Right then, her pale eyes were the warmest thing I'd ever seen. "I've never been so sure of anything in my life."

Inhaling a shaky breath, I leaned back on my knees and hooked my fingers in the band of her leggings. Slowly, I peeled them down, revealing her inch by inch.

I edged back enough so I could wind them from her ankles, leaving her completely bare and exposed.

A needy sigh pilfered from between her lips.

I took her in through the dim, hazy light. Her body was littered in scars, and I leaned in and started to brush my lips over each one.

Her legs.

Her thighs.

Her right hip.

I kissed up her abdomen where the bulk of them were engraved, the battle scars of the life we lived. Our fate. Our hope. Our demise.

She writhed and gasped with each gentle brush of my lips, and those fingers wound in my hair as I went.

As I adored her.

Worshipped her.

In it, I prayed she knew what I meant. This woman who made me recognize my true purpose in this twisted, messed-up life.

The one who'd become my reason.

I let my nose wander her collarbone, inhaling her scent.

Coconut and goodness and this power that I couldn't come close to comprehending.

Then I dragged it up the delicate column of her neck before I planted both hands on either side of her head.

I gazed down at her in the wisping, murmuring night.

She never took those eyes off my face as she reached between us and started to push my sweats over my hips, and I shifted so I could unwind the rest of the way out of them, kicking them free of my feet.

Sparks licked across our naked flesh, and the energy that dragged us through two realities crackled in the space between.

I dropped to an elbow, careful not to crush her but wholly covering her with my body, wishing it to be a shield. Her protection. Her pleasure. Her everything.

Cupping her cheek, I murmured my one single truth: "I love you."

Then I pushed deep inside her.

And Aria?

I swore she fucking glowed.

Chapter Thirty-Nine

ARIA

My mouth opened on a shocked rasp, and my head rocked back as the Earth cracked wide open beneath me.

Light burst behind my eyes, so bright I felt it streak through my veins. So bright it was blinding.

Though in spite of it, I could still make out every aspect of Pax.

The glorious edges of his severe, exquisite face. His slashed, brutal brow. The clench of his rugged, rough jaw. More than anything, it was the love that stoked the white flames in his eyes.

It felt like the moment was held.

A beat of infinity where I was lost somewhere between pain and pleasure.

This feeling of being split apart and pieced back together.

Crushed and made whole.

It was a staggering, beautiful devastation.

Pax choked out a delirious sound of restraint as he clung tight to me, covering me like a shroud.

Like solace.

Like peace.

Part of me wondered if I was still dreaming. Locked in a realm that shouldn't exist. Or maybe I'd drowned and I'd awakened to my own perfect eternity.

"Are you okay?" His words were shards that sent ripples murmuring through the dense, mesmerizing air.

My nails scratched down his back, the tips of my fingers trailing over his pitted, gnarled flesh.

Coarse breaths raked from my lungs as I adjusted to the stunning feel of him. A long moment passed before I was able to speak. "I told you when I first saw you that I came alive that day. But I think there was still a piece of me that was missing. A piece carved out in the middle of me that longed to be filled. And that piece doesn't ache anymore."

He gathered my hand and splayed it across his heart, which was ravaging at his chest, his eyes pinching tight before they opened to me. "You're right, Aria. It doesn't ache anymore. Not in me, either. You are my beginning. My conclusion. My completion."

I swallowed around the rawness in my throat. "It is right. We're right. Show me exactly what that means."

Pax had me gathered tight against him as he slowly began to move. He watched me as he did, our gazes fettered as he loved me in a way I'd never believed I would ever get to experience.

He showed me what it meant to be touched.

Adored.

He moved slowly but wasn't exactly gentle. I wasn't surprised, since nothing about Pax was. It was like a dam that had been built too high had burst under the pressure. A flood of greed that washed through him and took us both under.

I moved with him, lifting my hips, desperate for him.

Heat shocked between us, skating across my frozen flesh like his touch could chase away the fear that saturated every cell of my being, and he dipped down and took my mouth like his kiss could calm the storm that rioted in my spirit. Mitigate the deep-seated reality that I couldn't escape the danger I was in. This danger so much greater—so much more powerful—than I could fathom.

For a little while, he erased it.

Healed it.

Promised it would be okay.

A fire roared in the place that I had held for him. It burned up my insides and seared like signets being branded into my flesh.

Flames that lapped and licked and grew higher with each second that he gave himself to me, torching the horror that I felt.

Just for this moment.

Just for this time.

This time that was meant for us.

Because the terror had no place to stand right then.

Not when it was him and me.

Lights flashed behind my eyes.

Dizzying.

Euphoric.

Pax started to move faster, his chest pressed to mine and his arms curled around me. My fingers were in his hair, dragging through his white locks, which seemed to glow in the strikes that came from the sign outside the window.

Flashes of brightness that lit him up.

"Aria," he muttered against my lips. The rugged reverberation spiraled through my senses. It sounded of a claim.

A connection that went so much deeper than the physical.

I started to jut.

Passion taking over.

A feral instinct that raged and whipped the oxygen into a disorder.

It tasted of the oxygen I'd been lacking. Oxygen I'd found in him.

Pleasure curled deep inside while the love I'd forever kept for him like a sordid secret gripped my heart in a fist.

"You found me," I whispered into the rapture of his kiss.

It was he who'd saved me again. He who'd heard the shout of my soul. He who possessed.

Pax edged back, his expression hard and fierce. His palm came to my cheek, and he brushed the pad of his thumb over the hollow of my eye. "I will always find you, Aria. I promise, I will always find you."

Then he pushed up onto his hand. It changed the angle as he drove deeper, and he let his other hand slide down over my breasts, then my belly.

Need ricocheted through me when he drifted lower between my thighs and began to rub his fingertips over the sensitive spot that had me gasping.

In an instant, my blood heated and my stomach twisted in a way it'd never done before.

Desire throbbed and pulsed.

Sparks of bliss.

I pitched and bowed, silently begging him to quicken as I chased after the sensation that grew like a storm at the edges of my being.

Flares that flickered at the edges of my sight.

I whimpered while Pax let go of a sound so deep in his chest that I felt the rumble of it all the way to my toes.

My pulse raced wild.

In sync with his.

A stampede.

Out of control.

"Don't fight it, Aria. Sink into it. Let go. I promise that I have you. Just like you have me. You've always fucking had me."

My heart squeezed. Squeezed with the amount of love that I had for him. With what he'd always meant. With what he'd come to be.

My sanctuary. My sanity. This moment of peace in the middle of a war that I didn't think we could win.

I wondered if he could feel it.

The gravity.

Because he started to rock. The snap of his hips hard as he wound me to a place I'd never been.

"So perfect, Aria. So gorgeous. So good." He ground out the words.

His fingers rubbed harder, stroking in time with our bodies.

A frenzy churned in the middle of it, and our connection strained so violently that I feared I might rend apart.

His breaths were harsh, and his chest expanded with each one. I inhaled them like I could draw his spirit into mine, and my nails sank deep into his shoulders to keep myself from floating away as everything intensified. As everything became too much and too little.

I wanted more.

I wanted forever.

"You have me," he said like he'd heard my thoughts.

Pleasure built, gathering from the farthest recesses of my body.

Coiling and binding.

Rising and lifting.

Heightening to a boiling point.

The whole time, Pax watched me, never looking away as he brought me to a place that I knew could only exist with him.

Because when I split apart, it was so much more than a mere sensation that I'd never experienced before.

It was truth and light.

It was rapture.

Pure ecstasy that stretched out to touch every corner.

Heart and body and mind.

It was death.

Because there was a part of me that would never be the same.

It was an ending.

It was a beginning.

It was life.

Energy erupted as my body blazed.

An inferno of white, disorienting light.

My mind spiraled through time and realms. Thoughts flashing to when Pax and I had been young. When I didn't understand our design but still knew he would be the most important person in my life.

And it had never changed, who he was, even though it felt like everything had right then.

Walls were toppled as new obstacles were built.

His rigid jaw was clenched as he worked over me, the man so ferociously gorgeous as he thrust and rocked and consumed.

Every sinewy muscle in his body was stretched taut, coiling and flexing beneath the feverish drag of my fingers.

Then he dropped his chest to mine, clinging to me as he drove into me so deep, and he stilled as a roar ripped from his throat.

Those tense muscles bowed as his body tremored, and a shock wave of bliss rolled through us both, rushing high to take us over and pull us under.

My body arched as his name chanted as a whisper from my lips again and again.

"Pax, Pax, Pax."

It was prayer.

My claim.

He swallowed it with his mouth, shooting me high once again with the gluttony of his kiss.

I could taste it.

His love for me.

"Fuck, Aria. Fuck."

Our bodies twitched and jerked and spasmed with tiny aftershocks, and he held me through them until they had completely faded.

Eventually, the bright glare that had blinded my eyes ebbed, and the inferno that had blazed dimmed to embers as his kiss slowed and became languid.

Soft, featherlight whispers.

I relished the feel of him as he exhaled in the deepest satisfaction, then sagged against me.

His beautiful body a blanket that covered mine, our hearts thudding hard against the other.

For a little while, we lay there listening to the impact of it. To the way the thunder of our hearts was the loudest thing in the room. The way they beat in sync, a thrum, thrum, thrum that hummed of completion yet still sped up in relief.

His forehead dropped to mine, and when he spoke, his words were hoarse. "A long time ago, I gave up on the idea of there being any beauty in this life. Gave up on the idea that I would ever experience any of it. I was wrong. So fucking wrong. Because there's you, Aria. There's you. And there could never be anything more beautiful than that."

Chapter Forty

PAX

I eased back onto my knees, taking Aria with me, and I scooped her trembling frame into my arms as I pushed to standing. It seemed crazy that she could feel so fucking light in my hold.

Delicate.

Fragile.

A distinct contrast with the way she oozed an implacable vibration of strength. It climbed into the dense, thick air like the whispering of wind that spoke of a great, haunting power.

I curled her tight against my chest as I carried her to the bathroom. Her slight shape was slotted against my body like we were notches of the same mold that fit perfectly together.

My mind raced and my spirit spun with what we'd done. With the boundary we'd crossed and the decree we'd defied.

The mandate we'd shaken.

It might have been our greatest rule, but I couldn't find a place inside myself that could regret it. I got the sense that maybe we'd been here all along and had only been giving in to what was already done.

Valeen was wrong. I knew it in my soul. There was no chance Aria and I weren't meant for this. No chance she wasn't supposed to be mine and I wasn't supposed to be hers.

And I might have been standing right then, but I was on my knees.

An offering.

She had those arms looped around my neck, holding on to me like I was some kind of savior.

I'd give it all to be.

Her savior.

The one who would see her purpose through. Stand behind her while she rose.

My insides twisted with the fear of whatever had happened that had led to this. To the girl drenched and choking in her sleep.

Anxiety clambered through my insides as I angled into the tub and turned the water on full force, still holding her in my arms like they might be strong enough to protect her.

But how the hell could we stop this wickedness when we had no idea it was coming at us from every direction?

Her breaths were shallow, and she panted as I held her there while the water heated, her body still twitching from the aftershocks of her pleasure.

I would never be able to wipe the memory of it from my mind.

The way she'd glowed when I'd filled her.

A luminescence radiating from her skin, her spirit a whispering flare that speared into me.

Like every cell in her being was trying to find a way to join with mine.

No question it had, and neither of us was going to be the same.

Once steam had begun to fill the enclosed space, I stepped into the tub with her.

Chills rolled through her the second the heated spray hit our flesh. The cold that had seeped down to her bones had thawed, the ice melted by the connection we shared and the warmth that fell over us in sheets and rivulets that skimmed down our bodies.

I eased her head back under the steamy fall, saturating her hair with the heated water while she looked up at me with those fathomless gray eyes.

Bottomless.

Eternal.

Right then, they toiled like a dark sea tormented by a violent, unending storm. But right in the middle was an island.

Her pupils firm with a fierce, stark love.

With hope.

With belief.

Unfound and undying.

My heart hammered in spasms of volatility. I brushed my fingers through her long, black locks, chasing away the lingering cold steeped in the strands. My voice was brittle when I finally forced myself to speak. "Can you tell me what happened?"

Blinking, she shook her head in doubt, and when she spoke, her voice was rough from the trauma she'd sustained. "I thought I'd almost fallen asleep, but then something woke me up. I was here, in the room, and you were sleeping on the floor, but when I looked out the window to figure out what the sound was . . ."

Droplets of water trailed down her face, gathering with the tears that got loose from the darkened pools of her eyes. "The little girl was there."

A bolt of terror rocked through me, and my molars ground.

There'd been something about the little girl that hadn't sat right.

It'd felt like an omen.

A harbinger.

"She was outside, alone in the cold. Barefoot and only wearing a thin nightgown."

Distress pinched Aria's brow. "It was like I could feel her out there, calling to me, and I knew I had to help her. But there was also something about it that warned everything was wrong. Instinct kicking in that what I thought was happening wasn't. I tried to call out to you, but I couldn't make the words form. It was like . . . I could make no sound. Had no control over my actions. The only thing I was capable of was unlocking the door and following her out."

A tremor rolled through me, and my arms tightened around her.

I didn't respond; I just waited, letting her sift through the debris.

Aria inhaled a shaky breath. "She darted across the lot. I shouted for her to stop, but she just looked back and laughed before she turned and ran farther away. I knew the road was out there, so I followed. There was a heavy fog, and I could barely see. It was so disorienting. Like everything I'd remembered from when we'd pulled in had ceased to exist—the motel disappearing behind me, and rather than there being a gas station on the other side of the road, there were fields. The only things remaining were the road and the little girl."

I couldn't breathe as she continued to explain. "Right before I got to her, she ran across the road. A truck blazed through, and I thought she'd been hit."

Her nails sank into my skin as her explanation hitched. Then the words started tumbling like a landslide from her mouth. "Only, once it blew by, she was on the other side, and she was laughing and laughing. I followed her, Pax. I followed her into the maze of high grasses on the other side, even though I *knew* something was off. I could feel it. But it was like I was shackled by a panic that wouldn't let me go, and I kept chasing her. Pleading with her to stop. She kept going until the field opened to a pond, and when she stepped into it, she immediately sank."

Fuck.

Fuck. Fuck. Fuck.

A ball of razors rolled down the length of my throat, and I pulled her closer and clung tighter. Desperate to get her close enough that I could protect her from every threat. From every monster. From every evil that hunted her, night and day.

Aria felt the torment of it, too. The hopelessness that roared inside me. How could I truly protect her when I had no idea what we were up against? How, when whatever the fuck this was echoed with a power unlike any of which we'd ever been told?

"I didn't think, Pax—or maybe I did know it in my gut and I just didn't have the choice—but I jumped in after her. I saw her sinking toward the bottom, so I swam after her. Only, when I finally got hold of her, her face shifted."

Aria's expression pinched in turmoil. "It was the man . . . The man from earlier today . . . The same man I'd thought I'd seen the first night after you rescued me from the facility. It was him. And it was her."

Her pulse flew as fast as the words that poured from her tongue. "Their faces were flashing between the two of them, and when she opened her mouth, shadows began to flood from it. Wisps that curled and spun before they grew to take shape. Kruen."

Ice slicked down my spine.

"They wound around me. They bound me the same as if I were bound in chains and kept me under. I tried to fight them. I tried so hard, but I couldn't break free."

Tears blurred those mesmerizing eyes. "I would have drowned if you hadn't awakened me. If you hadn't heard me."

I shifted so I could pull her flush against me. My hand went to the back of her head and my fingers wound in the strands. My other arm looped around her waist as I crushed her in my hold. "I will always hear you, Aria. Feel you."

"I think I'm running out of time, Pax."

"No, Aria. No." My voice croaked over the rejection.

She blinked up at me. "If they can get to me this way? Keep me from passing into Tearsith and instead drag me someplace else entirely? How can I anticipate an attack when they're coming for me from every direction? Awake? Sleeping? And in the in-between?"

I edged back to put a foot between us, and both my hands flew out to frame her face as the water pounded into her back. I dipped down to make sure she was looking at the truth of what I said. "I won't sleep. I won't drink or eat or rest until I've ensured that you're safe. Not until we end that Ghorl."

Curling her hands around my wrists, she peered up at me. Trusting me. Loving me. All while a storm battered in the middle of us, raging against our shores.

Reverence filled her voice. "I want you to know, whatever happens or however this turns out, that tonight, with you? It was the best thing that's ever happened to me."

I inhaled a shaky sound and crushed her against me, her cheek pressed to the ravaging of my heart.

Her fingertips dusted up and down my chest, over the designs that howled and the scars that wept. She peeked up at me. "Is it always like that?"

My lips pressed to the top of her head as I released a weighted sigh. "No, Aria. Not even close. There's nothing that could compare to you. It was . . ."

How the hell did I put that into words?

"Otherworldly." I figured it was the best I could do.

Her nails scratched a little deeper as she looked up at me. The softest smile teased the edges of those red lips, which were swollen from my kiss. "Magic?"

I tossed her a weak grin. "Something like that, considering the way my princess has me enchanted."

Pink lit on her wet cheeks, and she clamped down on her bottom lip. For one second, the two of us gave ourselves over to the type of easiness that could never be ours.

Just simply flirting with someone who made our hearts go boom.

Then she sobered, and she brushed her lips over the organ that would always beat for her, no matter how many days it was given. "I think it was just us, Pax."

I swayed her in my arms, the water pounding over us, my murmur barely breathing, "Yeah, it was just us."

Lightly, she dragged her fingertips down my side and to my hip. I nearly lost myself all over again as she kept touching me.

"Do you regret it?" she asked.

The way my spirit reacted to the question was visceral. A rush of incredulity gushed from my nose. I'd been so sure all this time that I should. Shame striking me at the idea of having her this way. Worry that I was only going to make things worse. Put her in more danger.

It didn't take much to discern the only regret I could ever find would be in hurting her in some way.

"Do you?" I asked instead of answering.

"No, I could never regret you."

"Then no. Not even a little bit. You are the only good thing that's ever happened to me. I fucking love you. I didn't even know what that meant until I saw you in that room. I had no idea that every second of my life was adding up to bring me to that very spot. And I promise that every second I have left? Each of them belong to you."

"I dreamed of it . . . of you loving me that way. Back in my room when I felt so alone."

I hugged her to me. "You're not alone anymore, Aria. And as long as I'm still breathing, you're never going to be."

We washed each other then, letting our hands drift and explore.

It felt like with each caress, the stigma of what we'd believed was washed away, giving way to a new understanding.

Our understanding.

We were in this thing together, in every fucking way we could possibly be.

When the water began to cool, I shut off the faucet and scooped her up again, and I grabbed the two thin white towels from the rack and wrapped them around us as best as I could. Then I carried her back out to the dull glow in the dingy room.

"I'm capable of walking, you know." She whispered the affected, soggy words as she peered up at me.

I pressed my lips to her temple. "I know, but I don't want to let you go."

So, rather than doing that, I climbed down onto the floor with her, laid her out on the white sheet, and grabbed the blanket that had slipped off the bed when she'd been trapped. It was only damp on one edge, so I tossed it out, unfurling it so it coasted down to cover us.

Then I took her in my arms again.

Our naked bodies plastered together.

No barriers left.

"You should try to sleep," I murmured where my lips were pressed to her forehead. "I'll be awake, watching over you."

Aria barely shook her head, and she took my hand and wove our fingers together. She pressed our hands tight between us. "Come with me, Pax. If you hold me like this? I'll be with you wherever you are. I can feel it."

Anxiety had that ball of razors taking a tumble down my throat again. "I'm terrified of losing you there."

"You won't," she promised, and she lifted our hands and kissed across my knuckles. "You won't. Just hold on to me."

Somehow, I managed to pull her even closer, and I dipped down and kissed her, my fingers threaded in her hair and my spirit tangled in her soul.

I inhaled her, took her into my lungs.

Coconut and the girl.

And I whispered, "I won't. You are what my heart knows."

Chapter
Forty-One

ARIA

Tearsith

She and Pax ran through the bowels of Faydor, their feet pounding across the lifeless desolation. Cruelties moaned and wept, and they slowed only to slay the Kruen they passed, quick and succinct as they tracked.

Their ears were tuned. Listening for the one who would seek to extinguish the life force that beat frantically through her veins.

Pax had begged her to stay in Tearsith after what had happened, but her heart understood its call, and she knew they had no time to waste.

Refusing, she had stepped through the threshold and fallen into the depths.

They might try to pretend, but she was no princess, and she couldn't afford to be pampered.

Now they raced into the abyss.

Deeper and deeper.

Winding through the craggy plane, dodging the wiry elms and enormous boulders as they cut down as many Kruen as they could.

Voices echoing from her right slowed her.

Familiar voices that called their names. "Aria! Pax!"

"Timothy and Dani," Pax rushed, glancing back at Aria in surprise. It was rare to find another during the hunt with the way they spread out, their speed so much faster than anything they could match during the day, covering miles and miles of decay-rotted eternity.

Aria ran in their direction with Pax's hand held firmly in hers. Only they skidded to a stop when they came to where Timothy panted and Dani wept. Torment blazed in Timothy's pale, pale eyes. "I'm so sorry, Aria. We found it again, but we couldn't bind it. It's so strong. Stronger than anything we've ever encountered before. I'm afraid it might be greater than our abilities."

She heard what he said without him fully issuing the words.

It couldn't be stopped.

It couldn't be smashed.

Despair wound through her consciousness, making her knees sag with the weight of what he was saying. But more so, it was the gutting sympathy that coated Dani's gaze that made the ground tremble beneath Aria's feet.

It felt as if she were standing in a war zone beneath the barrage of a thousand bombs that fell from the sky.

Tumultuous waves slammed into her again and again.

"What are you not saying?" she demanded.

Dani glanced at Timothy once before she spoke. "It had shifted gears tonight and was seeking to prey on your family."

Horror spiraled through Aria. Hopelessness taking seed, though she wasn't surprised. She'd known from the visions it was using her father.

Dani gulped, her delicate throat thick as she wavered before she continued with the confession. "We saw what it has planned. Your father . . ."

She trailed off like she couldn't bring herself to say it.

Aria reached out and snatched her hand, the cruciality whipping from her tongue. "Tell me."

A tear streaked down Dani's cheek, and she sniffled around what she believed could not be stopped. "Your brothers. Your sister. Your mom. It will be a massacre."

It was the blow that dropped Aria to her knees.

A guttural wail broke from her chest. "No!"

No.

She would stop it.

She had to.

She had to.

Pax knelt in front of her, taking her by the face. "Aria, it's okay. It's okay."

Only they both knew that was a lie.

It wasn't okay.

And she wondered if it was the grief that carried her, what catapulted her from one realm to the next.

Because the next second, she woke up gasping on her back, gazing toward the ceiling of the dank motel room with one of Pax's arms belted across her chest.

Chapter Forty-Two

PAX

I awoke to her in a frenzy, jumping to her feet and charging to her duffel bag, which was packed and zipped where I'd left it at the door in case we had to flee in the middle of the night.

She knelt, and the sound of the zipper ripping open bolted through my body and shot me upright to her frantically digging through her things.

"Aria," I called, voice hoarse with the aftermath of everything that'd gone down tonight.

It didn't even come close to breaking into her alarm. Wasn't even close to touching the chaos that swirled like a tornado around her body, a force of its own that hammered against the thin walls.

Shaking out of control, she tossed a shirt over her head.

I was on my feet and across the space in a second, flat. Leaning over her from behind, I curled my arms around her shoulders, trying to drag her back from the tumult. "What are you doing?"

Without looking at me, Aria gave a turbulent shake of her head, the words cracking on her tongue. "I have to go back. Don't try to stop me."

I could feel her turmoil race through me, my blood poisoned by her grief and my spirit bound by her sorrow.

I experienced it as if it were my own, and I knew after what we'd done earlier, I'd be tied to her in an entirely different way, because this girl now beat through me like she'd become the blood in my veins.

Every thud of my heart was a resonance from her chest.

Every breath of my lungs fed from the oxygen she emitted.

My bleeding spirit sank to the pit of my stomach, and I fell to my knees behind her. I tightened my arms around her as I brought her back to my chest.

Holding her so fucking close there would never be any prying us apart.

I put my mouth to her ear. "Then we go together, and we end this thing."

Chapter Forty-Three

PAX

We drove straight through, and we made the trip in just under twenty-four hours.

Exhaustion had set in hours ago, but it was the antsy kind. The kind where reality was skewed and you fought to keep your eyes open, but you knew even if you did let them drift closed, your heart would be pounding so goddamn hard there wasn't a chance you'd be able to sleep because of the drumming in your ears.

Aria had slept on and off, fitfully, her body twitching in tumult and not allowing her to fully rest. We'd made our plan during the trip, and decided it was best that I didn't sleep at all since I basically was going to need to go to sleep on command.

Now both Aria and I were wide awake as we took the exit off the freeway that would lead to the neighborhood where she'd grown up.

She itched in the seat beside me, sitting forward, clutching at the dash as she peered out the windshield, like sitting that way might get her there a second faster.

I reached over and wove my fingers through her hair, rubbing my fingertips into her nape like I might be able to soothe the riot inside her, which was probably faulty planning, considering the way I was vibrating like a beast released from its cage into an arena.

Ready for the fight even when it knew it was about to get slaughtered.

I didn't like it.

This fucking plan.

Aria was the one who had insisted on it, told me it was the only way and there was nothing I could do to sway her from it. Truth was, she was the only one who was capable of seeing this through, *if* seeing it through was even possible. She was the one with the strength.

But knowing that didn't do shit to calm the piece inside me that wanted to wrap her in fucking bubble wrap.

I could barely stomach the idea of her putting herself in harm's way like this. But I knew her loyalties. Knew what she would give, just the same as I would do for her.

"Left," she rushed, gulping around her anxiety, and I slowed and made a left off the main street and into an older family neighborhood.

It was just after one in the morning, and darkness shrouded the modest houses that lined each side of the road. Not a soul was out at this time.

Everything was still.

Too still.

Bated.

Held.

A thin dusting of snow covered the long-dead front lawns, and the trees were barren in the winter cold. Their branches were so gnarled and twisted it was like looking at a distorted mirror of Faydor.

"Take a right at the next road," Aria rasped as she pointed at the approaching street. My stomach was in knots as I followed her directions.

Our headlights speared across the vacancy, illuminating the obliteration that was to come.

I had to fight with all the willpower I possessed against the instinct to whip the car around, fly from here, and carry Aria away someplace safe.

But it'd become clear it didn't matter where we went. The one who wanted to ruin Aria would only meet us there.

I could feel the weight of Aria's swallow ricochet through the dense, crackling air, and she inhaled a shaky breath as she whispered, "It's the second house on the right."

Slowly, I eased to a stop at the curb in front of it, my limbs shaking like rattling chains as I took it in.

It was two stories. Brown and plain and innocuous. The only light glowed from a sconce hung on the wall beside the front door.

But I could still feel the evil radiating from the walls.

The depravity that oozed and wept.

Aria did, too, and she flinched as a shock wave of dread rolled down her spine as she peered out the passenger-side window.

"Are you sure you want to do this?" My words scraped like barbs that impaled her back.

Aria's response was haggard. "I have to protect them. They didn't ask for this."

"You didn't ask for it, either."

She glanced back at me. Tears blurred her pale-gray eyes. But they would always be the warmest things I'd ever seen.

"But it's who I am, isn't it? And if there is any way I might have the power inside me to stop this? To protect them? Then I have to try."

Fear pulled taut between us, apprehension billowing on our connection at what we were about to do.

I reached for her at the same time she reached for me. My hands tangled in her hair and hers fisted in my shirt as I captured her mouth in an anguished kiss. Intensity lit, a viable, palpable thing, the protectiveness—the possession I felt—tangible in the connection.

She poured everything I gave her right back into me.

A promise.

Our truth.

Our love.

I didn't want to end it. Didn't want to let go.

But I finally slowed and dropped my forehead to hers, gasping through the devotion that I had for her. My palm was splayed over the side of her head when I begged, "Please be careful."

She nodded against me. "I will. This is going to work. It has to."

A light flicked on somewhere on the first floor of the house, jarring us back from our cocoon, and we both knew he was awake inside. A trap had been set that had led Aria back to this place.

To the place I'd hated for as long as I could remember.

To the people whom I'd always worried would be her demise.

Turning back to me, she set her hand on my cheek, her thumb caressing a soothing path over the scar cut down the right side of my face. "I love you, Pax. Forever. For eternity. What happens here doesn't change that."

Inhaling a steeling breath, she cracked open her door. She paused for one apprehensive second before she fully tossed it open. Then she strode across the frozen thatch and angled up the walkway to the door, the long length of her black hair trailing behind her.

For a beat, she looked back, meeting my gaze through the window.

That stunning, unforgettable face was locked in determination.

She gave a tight nod.

A go.

And I reclined my seat at the same moment she walked through her childhood door.

Chapter Forty-Four

ARIA

Attempting to not make a sound, I pushed down on the door latch. It clicked, and the metal gave without any resistance. I felt it like an extended hand from the sinister.

A foul invitation.

I swallowed around the knot in my throat as I carefully stepped inside and quietly shut the door behind me, trying to keep myself concealed.

Darkness reigned like an oil slick, heavier than it should be when a light glowed from the kitchen off to my right. I crept forward, my footsteps muted as I slunk through the shadows of the room toward the disturbance I could feel emanating from that side of the house.

Where normally the house was filled with laughter and the commotion of the day-to-day, now it was silent.

So silent I could choke on it.

My chest arched against the suffocating weight, and my mind whisked to Pax in his car outside, parked on the street, my spirit reaching out to discern where he was.

Drifting.

I didn't know how I could feel it, but I could. I could sense him as he floated.

The man was caught between sleep and awake, hovering in that shimmery plane of nothingness. I swore that I felt the moment he slammed into Tearsith one second later.

He was asleep, which meant he would immediately descend.

A shiver rolled the length of my body as I forced myself to move forward, through the swaths of gloom that crawled across the floor. The only sound was the faintest swish of the soles of my shoes as I moved across the carpet.

Still, everything screamed. The walls and the ceilings and the toxic air.

The disturbance flailed the closer I got to the opening to the kitchen, and the barest sound breached the atmosphere.

A whine.

A moan.

A plea.

Chills lifted the hairs on the back of my neck before they spread out and rushed, skimming just beneath the surface of my skin, and my pulse that had already been thready sped in frantic beats.

Erratic and out of control.

From where I was hidden at the side, I quickly stole a glance through the threshold and into the kitchen. It was lit by a single dull light above the dining table. Stillness echoed back, no sign of anyone around.

Inching through the opening, I kept my breaths as shallow as possible.

I flinched when my shoes made a squeak against the gray plank tiles, and I completely held the air in my lungs as I tiptoed deeper into the kitchen, moving between the island and the dining table that sat beneath the window.

My gaze swept from side to side, searching for any trace of my family.

Alarm scattered through my senses, and a whimper crawled my throat when I broached the far side of the island and my attention moved to the left.

My mother was there, sitting on the floor with her back tucked into the corner of the kitchen cabinets. Her hands and feet were bound, and a piece of duct tape covered her mouth.

Even though I'd known my father was being led by the Ghorl, I was pummeled with aggrieved disbelief that he could do this to her. After all the years of loving each other? How? How could it come to this?

Horror blew her eyes wide open when she saw me, and she thrashed like she was the one who thought she needed to save me.

She released an agonized wail against the barrier of the tape and fought to break her bindings.

Panic zapped through my nerves, and I started to rush for her, to beg her to stay quiet so I could get her out of there, only I froze when I felt the movement from behind.

In a flash, the temperature dropped by fifty degrees.

It was like standing in Faydor. In the freezing cold that sank all the way to the bone.

Sickness roiling in the pit of my stomach, I eased around, too terrified to breathe as I faced my father.

He was sitting on the floor on the opposite wall where he'd been hidden by the table. His feet were planted so casually on the floor, his demeanor one of careless nonaggression, though he spun the tip of a hunting knife against his knee.

He had on the same brown khakis he'd always worn, but his mind was so far gone that he didn't seem to notice that blood saturated the material from where the knife had punctured his flesh.

And his eyes . . . they were as cold as the room.

He cocked his head to the side, slowly, though there was no missing the fact it was full of menace. He *tsk*ed. "You've been such a naughty girl, Aria—running away like that and making your mother worry about you."

A sob slammed against the tape on my mother's mouth, and she jerked her arms, trying to loosen the rope that bound her wrists.

It was so difficult to speak, but somehow, I found my voice. "Dad, you have to listen to me . . . The voices in your head are lying to you. You don't have to hurt anyone. You don't. You have to resist it. Find the love that you have for Mom. Your love for Brianna and Mitch and Keaton. Remember how you promised to always protect them. *Remember.*"

I begged it, praying to reach him, to touch on the place inside him that remained unblemished. Where his goodness was unmarred. I couldn't believe that he'd fully succumbed. Couldn't believe that there was nothing worth saving in this man who'd raised us.

Cared for us.

The memory of his deep laughter rolled through the back of my mind. His infectious energy as he'd wrestled with the boys and made them howl. His cheers for Brianna at her dance competitions. The way he'd run his hand down the back of my head when he dropped me off at school and promised that he loved me.

Only now his laughter was cruel, and he slowly pushed to standing, a phantom that rose in the night. The knife was slack at his side as he took a single step toward me. "Oh, but you're the reason for it, don't you know? It's your fault I have to make sure your sickness doesn't run through the rest of them. We can't have those types of delusions tainting the world. Your filth. I'm simply cleansing this place of you."

His voice twisted on the last phrase, becoming high-pitched, not his own.

At his vicious words, pain speared me to the core, and I held on to the counter behind me, telling myself he wasn't the one who was issuing the vile insults. I stalled, silently chanting prayers that Pax, Timothy, and Dani would find the Ghorl.

Prayed that their feet would carry them to where I needed them to go. Prayed that there was a chance we could pull this off.

Prayed, above all else, that I could get my mom and siblings out of this. Since she was here, I had to believe the kids were, too.

He took another step forward, and I began to ease back in an attempt to lure him from the kitchen. The farther away from my mother, the better.

He clucked his tongue and his brown eyes boiled black, his voice so twisted it wasn't recognizable. "There's no need to run, Aria. I'll find you."

He took another step, and I grabbed a chair and swung it around to create a barrier between us. I held on to the back, leaning in his direction, trying to reach him without getting too close. "Look at me, Dad. Look at me. Remember me. You love me. You have love inside you. This is not you. The voices are not your own. You can't let them control you."

Hissing, he sliced the knife through the air. I jolted back on a gasp. The tip of it had missed my throat by a mere inch. He roared when he realized he hadn't made contact, and he grabbed the chair and threw it out of his path.

Wood clattered against the tile as it toppled over. He stepped around it, and I kept backing away, trying to anticipate his moves, what he would do next.

But I knew there was nothing inside him that was rational. He'd lost touch. Had lost logic. Had lost soul.

Still, I tried. "Do you remember when Brianna was born? Do you remember holding her in the chair in the living room, her chest against yours as you patted her back? She used to wind her fist in your hair and tug it as she cooed. You swore she was saying she loved you. She was. She was telling you she loved you, and she's always loved you as much as you love her. You love her. You love her. Just like you love the rest of them."

I kept hoping to knock him out of the trance, to make him come to without it having to come to more than that, but I was losing that hope.

The hollowness in his eyes promised I wasn't doing anything but agitating him more.

I took another step backward, inching toward the living room.

He slashed the knife toward me again.

I cried out in surprise when it nicked my left shoulder.

Manically, he grinned. "We'll give you some scars now. Real ones."

Oh God. I choked over the sob that threatened to wrench its way out, but I forced myself to focus. To remember my purpose of coming here. I needed to get him away. Alone.

Torment ripped from my mother, though it was garbled by the tape.

I took another step backward, but he didn't follow. Her cries had stopped him, though I sensed no sympathy in his vacillation. There was only hate. Vicious, cruel hate as he changed course and slowly walked around the island in her direction.

Grabbing a fistful of her hair, he forced her onto her feet and put the knife to her throat. She yelped, and I saw what swelled and over-flowed in her eyes.

She was begging me to run. To save myself.

Tears blurred my own, and I wanted to run across the kitchen and throw myself between them, but I knew better than to make any sudden moves.

I carefully inched forward, and I did my best to keep the tremors from my voice when I forced out, "It's me you want. Let her go. She has nothing to do with this. I came back because you want me. Because *he wants me.*" My voice dipped in emphasis on the last words.

My father's nostrils flared, and for a second, he contemplated it before he sneered. "You've always been a little liar, Aria. I won't let you get away with it this time. Come here to me."

I stalled, hesitating, my attention trained on them both.

When I hadn't moved, he shook my mother hard. Her cry was muffled when just the tip of the knife pierced her throat.

"Come here," he hissed.

Gulping down the terror, I inched around the island, moving closer to him. My hands itched to reach out and touch.

To heal.

To bind.

But more predominant was the repulsion that quickened in my veins. The warning that it might be too late for him.

Still, there was something there. Something that made me believe there might be a chance.

Even if there was the tiniest flicker, I would fight for him.

"Let her go, and I'm yours." The words were crushed gravel from my tongue.

Black eyes gleamed, and the sickness that oozed from him crawled along my flesh.

Sticky and wet.

I took one more step, and I lifted my hands in surrender. "Free her. Let her go. And I'm yours."

He wavered, torn between getting to me and the truth that saving my family was the only reason I had returned. The bare logic he possessed at odds with his thirst for death.

I nearly wept when he gave in and ripped the tape from my mother's mouth.

She gasped in shock, inhaling desperate breaths as she coughed.

He didn't slow, taking the knife and cutting through the rope in one swipe, first at her feet and then her wrists.

"Aria," she wheezed. "Oh my God, Aria."

She tottered forward like she was going to come for me, and he shoved her hard. "Run, you stupid bitch."

My mother's eyes were wild. Darting between the two of us.

Torn.

Terrified.

"Run! Get the kids and get out. Run to the neighbors and call the police!" I shouted. "Hurry! You have to get them out!"

Her brow pinched and her head slowly shook, as if she was going to refuse, but I shouted once more, "Go! You have to get them out of here before it's too late!"

There was one strained beat of resistance before she finally relented and snapped into action, which I knew she was only doing because of my brothers and sister, and she fumbled around the island and out into the living room.

It was enough to distract my father for one fleeting second.

It was the only opportunity I had, and I took it.

I grabbed a pan that had been left on the island and whipped it around. It whooshed through the air and smashed into his wrist in a flurry of pain and desperation.

He lost hold of the knife, and it clattered to the floor.

A roar barreled out of him, a sonic boom of fury. Rage spiraled through the disorder that instantly struck in the room.

A match and hate and gasoline.

It combusted in dark, wicked flames.

He came for me at the same second I flew for him. My hands were outstretched in a bid to take him by the face. If I could just touch him. Reach him. See into his mind so I could free him from his chains.

My hands landed on his cheeks for the briefest flash. They were seared at the contact, and agony streaked up my arms.

I choked on the pain, and I struggled to hold tighter, to push through the darkness in his mind that clouded everything.

Only a blow came out of nowhere as my father drove a fist straight into my stomach.

It rocked me back, and I could barely remain on my feet as the air was knocked from my lungs. I bent in two, gasping, battling to stay oriented.

He dove for me, and he sent me flailing into a chair at the table. A shock of pain ricocheted up my back as I struck the wood. He threw another blow that landed at the side of my face, and it sent me toppling the rest of the way onto the tabletop.

He leaned over me, trying to pin me down, and I struggled to get to him, reaching for his face. I finally got my palms against the bristle of his cheeks.

Lightning struck and thunder rolled, and visions of darkness crawled through my mind. It was there.

The Ghorl.

The one we'd hunted.

Desolation whipped around it.

"Kill her. She's the one responsible for ruining your life. She's poison. Your wife will never forgive you. It's over. It's over. End her now. Then end them all."

A cry hitched at the base of my throat at the wicked intonations, and I hung on, pressing harder against my dad's jaw, trying to possess the light. To stretch it out. To bind the evil that zapped like the lick of an exposed electric wire.

A violent shout screeched from my father, and he ripped himself back as his hands flew to his face.

Heat blistered my palms, and invisible flames burned up my arms. I wondered if his cheeks felt the same as he roared and stumbled and floundered in an enraged circle.

And I knew there was nothing I could do to stop him, to stop this, when he finally regained his composure.

It was too late. Too late.

Because he stared at me in nothing but stark, unmitigated hate. Death brimmed in his eyes.

A torrent of fear rushed through my veins, dousing my spirit.

I'd wanted to be strong, and I searched around inside myself for the piece that had promised to fight. But I thought maybe Timothy had been right and the beast was bigger than all of us.

Beyond our power.

But it was me it wanted, so I forced myself up off that table as he started to stalk back in my direction, and I ran out of the kitchen.

"If you want me, then come and get me."

I sprinted through the living room, my feet pounding across the carpet toward the door. I had to lure him out. Make him follow. It was their only chance.

I could feel him behind me. Harsh breaths panted from his mouth, his determination steel.

I had to make it out ahead of him.

A scream tore up my throat when a hand pushed me hard at the upper back. It sent me reeling forward, and my arms pinwheeled as I tried to remain upright, but there was no subduing the forward momentum.

I lost footing and flew, and I slammed against the floor.

My elbows took the brunt of it, and a new pain splintered up my singed, fiery arms.

He flipped me over and straddled me.

I wailed, bucking up and trying to get free, wheezing, "No, no, let me go."

It all felt so similar to that day when they'd taken me to the facility.

When my lot had been cast.

When my fate had been decided.

I'd known then that everything would change. Had known somewhere deep inside that I would meet my end.

And I knew right then that I had.

Now the wholly unrecognizable face of my father glared down, distorted by pure hate. "You ruined everything. It was you. You!" he snarled.

I fought, thrashing my arms and kicking my feet. I whipped my head from side to side when he wrapped his hands around my throat.

He squeezed.

Squeezed so hard it closed off my windpipe, the oxygen locked in my lungs. Nothing could get in or out.

Terror bulged my eyes, and I struggled to get a breath, to war, to do anything to change what I already knew was coming for me.

He squeezed and squeezed, and panic lacerated my thoughts.

My mother. My brothers and sister.

No.

I couldn't let him do this.

I had to stop him.

I had to fight.

Consciousness began to ebb, flickers of light and flashes of darkness as the world began to fade.

I could feel the life in my veins bleeding out.

Horror slammed me when my mother was suddenly there, yanking at his back and screaming, "Get off her. Get off her! That's our daughter. Please, oh my God, please. Aria, oh my God, Aria!"

He tried to shove her off with his shoulder without letting go of my throat.

"Wait your turn, bitch. I'm going to take care of you next."

Sickness churned, and that urge that had first found me in that facility roiled, building from deep within, beyond the tide of succumbing. It was a wave that gathered strength and rose to take power.

The impulse to touch him overwhelming.

Somehow, I managed to find the strength to jerk my arms free from where he had them trapped beneath his legs, the man too lost to the need for my execution to notice the shift.

He kept squeezing my throat as I reached up and gripped his face with my hands.

The same familiar cold streaked through my failing veins, my hands afire, an inferno burning me alive.

But I could see.

I could see the Ghorl.

"End her now. Don't let go. It's her fault. She's the one who destroyed this family, not you. She's poison."

Tightening my hold, I tried to wrap my mind around it, to contain it, to push out the light from within and *bind* it.

I fought with all of me to separate the black spirit from his.

But it was so powerful. So strong. Still, I projected the light. The Ghorl wailed when a tendril whipped out and struck it in the side.

My father's hands loosened for the bare flash of a second, and I inhaled a shattered breath, sucking oxygen into my aching lungs.

I hung on with everything I had.

Something different passed through his eyes as my mother continued to beg him to stop, confusion glittering through his gaze.

"Cal, why are you doing this? Please, stop. Listen to me. Oh God, please stop."

The Ghorl regrouped, massive and enraged.

"Kill her now. Do it. It's already too late. There's no turning back."

My father's hold tightened again, and I fought harder, with all the strength I possessed, pulling from the deepest place inside me.

In a place that shouldn't exist.

The Ghorl shrieked as a glance of energy hit it against its middle, and a piece of it fell away, burned to ash.

For one second, it lurched back, but then it was right back on me, the venom in its voice filling the room.

"I will destroy you. I will destroy you all. None of you will survive."

I nearly lost hold with the force of it, with the horror that it was speaking directly to me.

I fought just as desperately as it did, my father's hands its weapons as he squeezed so tight that I thought he was going to crush my throat.

And the lights began to flicker again, the oxygen growing too thin, my body succumbing to my human limitations. My heels dug into the carpet as I tried to buck up to knock him off.

Blackness gathered at the edges of my sight, and still I tried.

The Ghorl suddenly roared, rearing back as streaks of light hit it from all sides.

Shock rounded my father's eyes, confusion bounding, his mind stuck in two places.

His hands trembled, his decision wavering.

It was enough—enough for me to press further into his mind, and I gripped his face as tightly as I could as I peered at the Ghorl who was being attacked on all sides.

Pax.

Pax was there.

He was flanked by Timothy and Dani, and Ellis and Josephine were on either side of them.

Relief slammed into me.

They found him.

They found him.

Each stood glowing, rippling with power, vibrating with the light that streaked from their beings.

"Fight, Aria, fight."

And I could feel Pax's words through time and space. Through realms and eternities.

"Fight."

And I did. I fought. I stretched out the light.

Wisps and tendrils of electric current struck it like arrows.

It flailed and screamed and writhed, whirling around as it tried to retaliate.

Fragments of fire lashed out, but each missed my Laven family.

We all gathered every dreg of strength we possessed and harnessed it.

Pouring out our authority.

Searching for the good.

Fighting the evil.

"End it, Aria. You're the one who possesses the true strength. You're the only one who can do it."

Pax's belief filled my mind.

I gathered the last crumbs of strength I had left, and I projected the rays of obliterating light.

And in a flash of glowing darkness, the Ghorl was crushed.

Nothing but dust.

Chapter Forty-Five

ARIA

Ragged juts of air wheezed in and out of my lungs as my father's hands went slack, and my back arched from the floor as if to get me closer to the sweet reprieve.

Exhaustion pinned me to the spot while my father fumbled backward onto his butt, and he used the heels of his shoes to backpedal across the carpet as if he was suddenly spurred to put a mile of distance between us.

Horrified in his confusion.

Bewildered in his disbelief.

His back hit the wall, his eyes wide, his expression gutted.

While my mother was at my side on her knees, her hands trembling so hard they rattled as she gathered me up against her chest and began to rock me. "Aria. Oh my God. Oh, my sweet girl. You're okay. You're okay."

Sobs ripped from her, each pouring out, more desperate than the last. "Aria," she whimpered.

She tried to scoot me back, away from my father, who was pinned to the far wall, her voice edged in hysteria. "I need you to stand up. We have to get out of here. I took your brothers and your sister to your grandmother's like you told me to. They're safe. I'll make sure you're safe, too."

My chest squeezed. She'd listened to me, at least partially. She'd taken the kids but hadn't stayed there herself. And when my father had told her to run, she hadn't. She'd stayed. *She'd stayed.*

"Please, get up," she begged, her hand frantic on my face as she wept. "Tell me you're okay. We have to get out of here."

A wave of dizziness spun my head, and I fought for coherency when the depletion threatened to drag me under. But it was different this time. There was a force that continued to run through my veins, a shivering high that stroked through me with relief.

"He won't hurt you now." Each of the words snagged as they scraped up my raw, sore throat.

A sound of torment echoed from the other side of the room. An agonized regret that wrenched through my father's soul. I doubted he could comprehend the full extent of what he'd done, of what he'd nearly surrendered to, the vessel he'd become, but I was sure he still had access to the memories of the psychosis he would likely think he'd been under.

My mother's face blanched in a coil of misery, a pasty, mournful white, full of misunderstanding and misconceptions. She frantically brushed back the matted locks of hair stuck to my sweat-drenched face. "You came back. You came back. And he—"

She choked on the last, unable to give voice to my father's actions.

"How could he?" She cried out her sorrow.

I took her hand and tightly wrapped mine around it. "He didn't know. It's not his fault. His mind wasn't his own."

Sobs continued to tear from my father, and his face was pressed in his hands as he rocked. "Aria, oh God, I don't . . . I'm so sorry. I'm sorry. I don't understand. I wouldn't . . ."

He choked off the last because I think it was clear that he would have if the Ghorl hadn't been stopped.

I couldn't respond, my focus on my mother.

Confusion and doubt twisted her expression, and I knew she was worried that my father might have suffered the same delusions she'd believed that I had, only his had turned violent.

I wondered if she could ever truly hear me.

See me.

Believe me.

I started to whisper my truth, but a scream tore from her when the front door suddenly burst open. She gathered me tighter against her, her arms shields as her attention flew up to the person who raged through the open door.

Pax.

His white hair struck in the bare light, his marred face slashed in ferocity, his pale, pale eyes flaming with white fire.

My mother went weak, and a strangled sob hitched in her throat.

Shock and fear and disbelief convulsed in her being.

Pax's attention volleyed between us and my father, who was speared to the wall by terror.

His rugged jaw clenched, and I could feel the war go down in the middle, part of him wanting to rush across the room and put a final stake in my father for what he'd done. For what he'd nearly caused. Forever believing him the catalyst that would be my end.

But it was his love, his devotion, that brought him to me, though his movements were slowed as he approached.

"Aria."

My name was affliction.

Devotion.

Relief.

He dropped to his knees at my side, and a cry erupted from where it'd been locked somewhere in my consciousness, so big and loud it banged through the room and ricocheted from the walls.

"Pax."

In an instant, he had me pried out of my mother's hold and pulled me against him.

Terrified, my mother scrambled away, her mouth held in shock as her mind reeled at the sight of the one person whose name I'd been forbidden to speak.

"Pax." I cried it again, and I knew I'd sing it forever. "Pax."

Sure, secure arms held me close against him as he exhaled the near tragedy, his voice so low as he murmured at the top of my head, "You did it. You did it. You ended it. You're safe."

He inhaled on that, breathing me in, drawing me deep into the well of his spirit. "You're safe."

I curled my arms around his middle, hanging on as I wept.

As I wept for the little girl who'd spent her childhood terrified of being seen. As I wept for the traumas that had been inflicted because of it. As I wept for my mother, who'd only done it out her ceaseless love. As I wept for what we'd endured over the last week.

And most of all, I wept because we were free.

Pax shifted so he was sitting on the ground, and he pulled me onto his lap, my side tucked into his chest as he kissed along my crown, my temple, my brow. "You're safe."

"It's over," I finally wheezed.

I felt him nod against me. "It's over. You did it. You ended it."

My fist curled into his shirt. "We did it."

"What's happening? Oh my God, what's happening? Am I going crazy?" My mother yanked at her hair from where she rocked, sitting upright on the floor. Tears marred her red, chapped cheeks.

I hated that she continued to question the truth that was set right out in front of her, though there was still a piece of myself that understood her disbelief.

Even I, having access to all the things I'd seen and experienced, had questioned my own sanity.

But maybe now she could finally see.

Sniffling, I unwound myself from Pax's arms, even though I could feel his resistance in my doing so, and I pushed to my feet. My legs wobbled, but I could stand. I moved to my mother, and I stretched out my hand. She clung to me as I helped her up. A deep line cut between her brows as she warily watched Pax from over my shoulder, as she glanced back at me, silently begging for answers.

"It was never a lie, Mom. Who I am. The scars that I hold and how I got them. And I know it's difficult to understand, that you never believed it possible, that you thought I was unstable. I don't blame you, because it's beyond the unfathomable. Who we are."

I looked back at Pax then, lost to the steadfast devotion that blazed in his eyes. Then I turned back to my mother. "Everything I ever told you was true, all except for the lies I'd been forced to tell to try to hide who I really am. But I won't hide who I am anymore."

She waffled with the inconceivable, her mind and heart torn, and her gaze traveled to Pax, whom I could feel was standing behind us, the man in the middle of the room, a power all his own.

I knew what he looked like to other people, but I knew right then that the only thing that really mattered was the way he looked to me.

"He's real. It's . . . real." Blankets of moisture poured down her face as she shook her head, as if her logic urged her to refute it while her spirit swam with the realization.

"It is. And the reality of it put you all in danger."

My attention swept to my father, who was silently sobbing against the far wall, rocking and rocking as he looked at us.

"I don't . . ." My mother's expression pinched. "I don't understand."

I squeezed her hand. "The ones we fight were after me, and they used Dad as a way to get to me."

Tears of disbelief poured from my father's eyes as he continued to sob.

"Pax knew I was in trouble, and he came for me. He got me out of the facility to protect me. But I knew you were all in trouble, so I came back."

I simplified it times a thousand since I knew she couldn't fathom all that we were and all that had happened in the last week.

"Because of me? Because of my disbelief, this is what happened?"

Sorrow clutched my chest. "No, they would have come for me anyway."

Guilt crushed her features. "I still don't—"

"It's okay. You're not supposed to understand. I think you need some time to let this settle. Why don't you let us take you to Grandma's, and tomorrow, we'll meet for coffee and you can ask me anything you want."

Obviously, I couldn't leave her here. Not after what my father had done. I didn't believe he was a threat to her any longer, but I couldn't imagine her having to stay in this house with him. And I had no idea what the future would look like for them.

My mother stumbled forward and threw her arms around me. "I've always loved you. More than anything. It's why I . . . I'm so sorry. I'm so sorry."

I hugged her tight to me, wrapped her in my arms, which should have been weak after the energy I'd just expended but somehow vibrated with power.

"I forgive you."

My smile was sad when I finally pulled away. I took two steps back just as Pax took two forward, and he threaded his fingers through mine the way he'd always done in Faydor, though now, it felt like a promise that he would always do it here.

Panic blanketed my mother's features. "And where will you be?"

"With Pax. Because he's where I belong."

My mother didn't pack anything. She simply took my hand and allowed me to lead her out the door while my father continued to quietly weep.

I'd touched his forehead, murmured, "I forgive you," before we'd left, unsure if I would ever speak with him again.

If I could ever trust him again.

But I also knew how powerful the Ghorl had been, and maybe there were no humans who could have resisted that type of influence.

The only thing I knew was that I was filled with hope as we pulled up outside my grandmother's house in the earliest hours of the morning. I stepped out of the passenger-side seat and lifted it so my mother could climb out. She wrung her fingers, unsure, her gaze slanting between me and Pax, who sat in the driver's seat. "I don't—"

I reached out and squeezed her hand, and I promised, "Tomorrow."

Her nod was shaky. "Tomorrow."

Without saying anything else, she hurried up the walkway to the front door of the single-story condo, and she dipped down to grab the key that was hidden under the same rock where it had always been. She unlocked the door; then she paused to look back at me with a soft, adoring smile on her face.

I lifted my hand in a goodbye, and she lifted her chin before she walked inside.

Chapter Forty-Six

PAX

I reached over and ran my knuckles down the defined line of Aria's jaw where she sat facing me in the passenger seat, her expression both sorrowful and serene.

I'd expected her to be completely spent after the ordeal, to be wasted the way she'd been when I'd found her in a heap on the floor of Target, but it was different. Life beat through her veins.

"I can't believe it's over," she murmured into the darkness, which covered the car like a shroud. Lights flickered over her gorgeous face as we passed beneath the streetlamps that tossed a dingy glow through the thick fog of Albany.

"I was so fuckin' scared, seeing you through that Ghorl's mind," I admitted. "I wanted to jump right through it so I could get to you and rip his hands from your throat."

"I was scared, too, but it feels so different now." Her voice was hushed, like she was issuing a secret.

I glanced from the windshield to her, and I stroked my thumb over the tiny scar at the edge of her mouth. "You don't have to be afraid anymore. Don't have to run anymore."

Uncertainty held her, and I peeked over to where she was staring across at me.

"Are you sure you don't want to stay with your mom?" It caused me physical pain to ask it.

I kept glancing between her and the road, and her pale, pale eyes were wide in the flashes of light. "You don't want me to go with you?"

Rejection twisted my stomach. The promise I'd made Ellis at the beginning of all this flashed through my mind—the one where I'd said that after we ended the monster, I would leave her behind.

That fucking nagging worry at the back of my mind. The *what if* that questioned if what we'd been told might be true. That I'd *turn* on her.

My head shook sharply.

No. Not a fucking chance. And even if she asked me to, I didn't think I'd be able to do it. "The only place I want you is with me," I admitted, the words rough.

"Because that's where we belong."

"That's right. You belong right here, with me." I reached down and squeezed her upper thigh.

The air shifted, tightening with greed. With the hunger we'd tried to suppress.

Guess we shouldn't have been surprised that there'd been no chance of that.

"Where should we go after this?" Aria asked, her voice just short of a tease. She curled her hand over mine, which was still attached to her thigh.

"Taking my princess to that island sounds like a pretty good plan right about now."

Slush fell from the drizzling sky, and my wipers swished over the frozen moisture.

"I think I'd like that," she said as she turned her gaze out the window, her demeanor going wistful.

"Yeah?"

"Yeah. Though anywhere I go with you would be perfect," she murmured, turning her sweet attention back to me.

"Thinking a hotel room tonight, and not one of those shitty ones we've been staying at. I want to lay you out right." There was no keeping the need out of my tone—not that I was trying.

A flush lit her cheeks, and I could feel the heat glide through her veins.

I loved that we could be like this. That I could flirt with my girl and show her what it was like to really be treated right without the worry trailing our every step. Loved that maybe, for a little while, we could let go and relax.

"What about what happened at the facility? Are you not afraid of getting caught?" She whispered it like she was afraid that if she said it too loud, I might.

Thing was, I had committed so many crimes in my life that I hardly considered them anymore. That one was close to inconsequential compared with the rest.

"We'll face it if it comes to that. We should probably settle somewhere away from Albany, though."

"We aren't going to stay on that island forever?" The teasing reemerged. "What, am I only a part-time princess?"

I moved my hand to squeeze the inside of her thigh. A squeal of laughter rolled out of her. God, I loved the sound of it.

Her joy.

Her freedom.

Exactly what I'd hoped to give to her but had never believed could truly make happen.

"Nah, baby, you're my forever princess."

That blush deepened, though it was affected, and affection dragged a pretty flush over the surface of her milky skin. "I'll take that."

I sobered, too. "I'll give you everything I can, Aria."

I pulled into a hotel about ten minutes away from where we'd dropped her mother off at her grandmother's. It wasn't quite a five star, but it was a place where we could get cozy and rest. I parked, grabbed our things, and for once, I didn't ask Aria to wait for me to get us a room. We strolled in together like it was what we were meant to do.

The guy working registration didn't blink when I pulled out a wad of cash.

We rode the elevator to the fifth floor, and I slung my arm over Aria's shoulders, and she leaned into my side as we walked down the long hall with doors on each side. I touched the card to the sensor and let us into the room.

Aria moved in ahead of me, and she spun in the middle of the living area, where there was a couch against the wall and a round table beneath the window. Something seductive played over the edges of her features. "Oh, you really are trying to spoil me."

"That's the plan, though it doesn't have a thing to do with this room."

Her teeth scraped that lush bottom lip, and she moved to the door that led to the bedroom at the back. She peeked back at me. "Are you sure about that? Because I was hoping it might involve this big, comfy bed."

A smirk climbed to my mouth as I let the door swing shut behind us, and I clicked the lock and stalked across the room toward my girl, who was shifting anxiously on her feet.

And I wanted to play, to keep it light when we'd been through so much bullshit, but the second my hands slanted across her cheeks to frame her face, I couldn't speak.

I didn't think there were really any words for *this*.

This connection that blazed.

The flames that warmed and the embers that licked.

She exhaled a soft sound, too, like she was just as moved.

"You amaze me, Aria. Fucking knock the wind out of me with who you are. And I know I'm the luckiest man alive that I get to be here to witness it."

Her eyes narrowed and creased at the edges. "I don't think I'm the only special one here, Pax. There's something . . . between us. Something we can't see."

I gathered one of her hands between both of mine and pulled it tight to the thunder at my chest. "But we can feel it."

She blinked with the slightest nod, a soft affirmation. "Yes. We can feel it."

"I've always felt you." I murmured it.

A confession.

An oath.

She hiked up on her toes and threaded her fingers through my hair, and she brushed a whisper-light kiss across my lips. "Always."

And that was all it took for us to snap, and I dove in to take her mouth.

This kiss?

It was fevered but slow. Fierce yet languid.

Demanding brushes of lips and delirious nips of teeth. Her blunt nails scraped down the back of my neck when my tongue played against hers in a slow slide of need. Desire rolled up her throat, and she kissed me back so intensely that I was struck with a rush of lightheadedness.

Her lips enchanting.

So damned sweet.

I backed her into the room. We only broke apart long enough for me to peel her sweater over her head and for her to rid me of my shirt.

Cool air skimmed across our bare flesh, and chills lifted on her skin. I chased them with my mouth. Kissing down over her jaw, the delicate column of her throat.

She whimpered when I delved over the swell of her left breast, then licked over the fabric of her bra, my hands eager as they wrapped around her to flick the clasp.

I groaned when I edged back so I could draw it down her arms, my stomach in knots of lust and fists of devotion.

The light from the attached bathroom was enough to illuminate her in silhouette, and my fingertips dragged down her stomach, over the scarred, marred flesh.

She did the same, her hands exploring, the woman leaving trails of fire over my jagged, uneven skin.

The marks of who we were felt profound in the night.

Every touch was filled with reverence.

Every caress filled with praise.

I kissed her and kissed her, my hands bunching up in her hair, gliding over her shoulders, skimming her back, before I cupped her small breasts in the palms of my hands.

On a moan, Aria pushed harder into my touch, and I brushed my thumbs over the hard peaks of her nipples.

"Pax."

"I know, Aria. I know what you need."

She slipped her hand down to the waist of my jeans and flicked the button, and the sound of the zipper ripping open filled the heat of the room.

I edged back an inch. "On the bed, Princess."

Another blush, the girl standing there bare from the waist up, black hair raining around her shoulders and cascading down to brush over her breasts.

Aria scooted onto the high mattress, her hands planted behind her to keep herself upright as she watched me lean down to unlace my boots, then shuck out of my jeans.

I straightened, standing before her completely bare.

A full-body offering.

"You're so beautiful." Her words cracked in the dense, dense air.

"No, Aria, it's you that's beauty. It's you who's the light."

I was just the lucky motherfucker who got to bask in it.

I knelt in front of her, between her knees, and I looked up at her as I popped the button of her jeans and loosed the zipper, and a breathy sigh left her as I began to peel them down her legs, taking her underwear with them.

I crawled up over her then, hovering above her and gazing down at the ferocity that she was, at the gut-wrenching power that rippled across her flesh.

She scooted farther up onto the bed, and I rolled us so she was on top.

"I need to see you," I murmured.

This exquisite woman straddled me, her hands planted on my chest.

My hands cinched down around her waist, and she eased back to take me.

A tremor rocked through us when she sank down.

An earthquake.

A flashfire.

And again, Aria glowed, lit up in striking lights that speared me to the core. To the center of who I was. From my beginning to my end.

"Pax," she whimpered as she began to move.

"You feel so good. So perfect." The words were grunts.

She was my perfection. My ecstasy. My completion.

Aria rolled over me, taking me again and again. Pleasure licked up my spine, and my head spun with dizziness.

With the rapture she created.

She arched and pitched and rocked, and I curled my hands around her narrow waist, holding on, chasing down the pleasure that was meant for only us.

"Touch me," she demanded, and I slipped my hand down her hip and rolled my thumb over her clit.

I swore lightning struck in the room, and she bucked, taking me harder, deeper, wholly.

Bliss sparked at the edges of my being. In every corner. It sped inward to gather in a pinpoint to become one giant molecule of pleasure.

"I need to feel you come around me," I urged, and I jolted upright so I could kiss her.

So I could swallow the sounds of her pleasure that erupted from her tongue as an orgasm rent through her body.

Her throbbing around me cut me in two, and that molecule exploded. My climax hit me so fast and hard that I couldn't see. Couldn't think. Couldn't process anything but the feel of this woman around me.

With me.

In me.

And we were there, on a plane that belonged to only us. Aria and I elevated. Removed. Floating on a sheet of pure white.

And there was no darkness.

No regret.

No fear.

There was only stark, gutting relief.

Her nails sank deep into my back as we rode it out. As we rolled and writhed and coasted through ecstasy.

Finally, Aria slumped against me, exhausted and sated, her chest heaving against mine as those sweet arms clung to my neck.

I brushed back the locks of hair stuck to her cheeks and edged back so I could look at her stunning face. I had one hand bunched in her hair, and the other was on her cheek. "I will always find you."

She dragged her fingertips over my lips, her soul eternally etched onto mine, and she whispered back, "Forever."

Chapter Forty-Seven

ARIA

I curled up against Pax beneath the plush covers, soaked in his warmth and swamped in his spirit. His breaths were long, and his gaze was unhurried as he continually gentled his fingers through my hair.

Our bodies were pressed together, our hearts in sync, our minds in time.

And he murmured, "Sleep."

Aria took his hand where they stood at the boundary of Faydor.

Darkness wept, whispered, and called.

Pax squeezed her hand tight as he cast her a glance. One that promised they were in this together.

Forever he would fight by her side.

But it felt different that night—as if spirit and mind had been opened and a piece of her had been freed.

So they descended, fell through the crash of wicked voices, through the depraved and the iniquitous, an eternity that landed them in the searing cold.

The bare glow at the edge of Faydor was the only light to guide their way as they tracked over the hard, frozen ground. Their breaths were salient as they panted around the frigid air that filled their lungs.

Blood crashed through her veins as she searched through the perpetual night.

Their footsteps pounded in her ears as she and Pax ran headlong through the heavy vapor that snaked over the lifeless ground and curled around the wiry, leafless elms.

Lightning cracked across the low-hung canopy, a crackle of sin and perversion.

Hisses of iniquity filled their ears, the whispers of the Kruen casting their evils into any willing mind.

They slaughtered each as they passed. Fighting for the good. For the protection of those who had no idea of the battle that was fought for them each second of the night and every moment of the day.

They ran deeper, and their strength felt unmatched, brighter than it'd ever been.

The dread, the fear, the weakness that had once held her no longer existed. She didn't know what the future would bring. If another Ghorl would manifest. Find her and hunt her. But she understood now that she did possess the strength. Understood this didn't have to be a death sentence.

She knew her purpose, and she would seek that purpose with Pax at her side.

Fighting during the day for those who needed her most. Using this gift to its fullest and in every way, as she was sure she'd barely tapped into its power. While asleep, she would hunt with her Laven family. Remain steadfast in the call to extinguish as many Kruen as they could as they fought through the night.

Only she slowed when she felt the frisson charge through the ice-slicked air. It was a current that ran through her like the blade of a knife.

It stopped her in her tracks.

Pax shouted, "Do not falter, Aria, we have it," his attention on binding the Kruen that thrashed in the distance ahead of him.

But Aria could not heed his voice.

She could only heed the hook she felt impaled in her chest.

She reached out, touching the disturbance in front of her.

A void that rippled like black water in the atmosphere.

A gateway.

Not unlike the one that drew them from Tearsith to Faydor.

Though this one was stronger, radiating a power she'd never felt before.

Confusion bound her, but she was compelled, unable to stop herself from moving forward.

She gasped as she was sucked through the darkness, wholly unprepared when she was suddenly tossed into a world on the other side.

Fear blanketed her spirit as she tried to figure out where she was. Where she had been taken. Her surroundings completely foreign.

It was quiet there.

Small and enclosed.

Too still.

Even colder than Faydor, though a bright orb of light hung at the horizon.

A shape was in the distance.

A man standing, facing away with his hands clasped behind his back.

A blond man.

Her stomach plummeted when he slowly turned around.

His smile was both placating and malicious as he stared across at her as if she were nothing more than an artifact to be studied.

It was the man from the diner. The one outside the fast-food restaurant. The same one who'd shared the little girl's face in the frigid waters of the pond.

He grinned.

"I've ended your kind for twenty generations. Did you really think I'd stop with you? No, Aria. You must die like the rest."

About the Author

A.L. Jackson is the *New York Times* and *USA Today* bestselling author of *Give Me a Reason* and numerous series, including Regret, Closer to You, Bleeding Stars, Fight for Me, Confessions of the Heart, Falling Stars, Redemption Hills, and Time River. She writes emotional, sexy, and heart-filled contemporary romances about boys who usually like to be a little bit bad. If she's not writing, you can find her hanging out by the pool with her family, sipping cocktails with her friends, or, of course, with her nose buried in a book. For more information, visit www.aljacksonauthor.com.